THE
PURCHASE

THE
PURCHASE

LINDA
SPALDING

EMBLEM

McClelland & Stewart

Cloth edition published 2012
Emblem edition published 2013

Library and Archives Canada Cataloguing in Publication

Spalding, Linda
      The purchase / Linda Spalding.

ISBN 978-0-7710-7936-8

      I. Title.

PS8587.P215P87 2013   C813'.54   C2012-908296-1

Typeset in Sabon
Printed and bound in the United States of America

McClelland & Stewart,
a division of Random House of Canada Limited
One Toronto Street, Suite 300
Toronto, Ontario
M5C 2V6
www.mcclelland.com

2   3   4   5   17   16   15   14   13

In memory of my brother Skip, son of Jacob,
who was son of Boyd, who was son of Martin,
who was son of John, who was son of Daniel Dickinson.

THE
PURCHASE

PART 1

D aniel looked over at the daughter who sat where a wife should sit. Cold sun with a hint of snow. The new wife rode behind him like a stranger while the younger children huddled together, coughing and clenching their teeth. The wind shook them and the wagon wounded the road with its weight and the river gullied along to one side in its heartless way. It moved east and north while Daniel and all he had in the world went steadily the other way, praying for fair game and tree limbs to stack up for shelter. "We should make camp while it's light," said the daughter, who was thirteen years old and holding the reins. But Daniel wasn't listening. He heard a wheel grating and the river gullying. He heard his father – the memory of that lost, admonishing voice – but he did not hear his daughter, who admonished in much the same way.

Some time later the child pulled the two horses to a halt, saying again that they must make camp while the sky held its light. The new wife arranged dishes on the seat of the wagon, and the child, whose name was Mary, pulled salted meat out of a trunk at the back. It was their fifth day on the road and such habits were developing. By morning there would be snow on the ground, the fire would die, and the children would have to move on without warm food or drink. They would take up their places in the burdened wagon while Daniel's fine Pennsylvania mares shied and balked and turned in their tracks. A man travelling on horseback might cover a hundred miles in three days, but with a wagon full of crying or coughing children, the mountainous roads of Virginia were a sorrow made of mud and felled trees and devilish still-growing pines.

The children, being young and centred on their own thoughts, were only dimly aware of the hazards of the road and of the great forest hovering. They hardly noticed the mountains, which were first gentle and then fierce, because all of it came upon them as gradually as shapes in an unhappy dream. The mountains only interrupted a place between land and sky. The forest got thicker and darker on every side. They had, within a few weeks, watched their mother die, given up home and belongings, landscape and habits, school and friends. They had watched people become cold to them, shut and lock doors to deny them entrance. How were they to understand? There were other wagons leaving Pennsylvania and going south and west, but none were so laden with woe as the one that carried the five children and the widower and his new bride.

Daniel spoke of the trees and told his children which were the yellow pine and which the white oak. He pointed to a deer standing still as vegetation in the bushes, but he made no effort to hunt or to fish for the beings that swam in the streams. As a Quaker, he did not own a gun and would depend on his store of food until he could raise his own crops. It was November, an ill-advised time for travel, but in spite of rain and cold winds and sore throats, he looked down at the rushing river and told himself that he had no choice. The Elders had cast him out. He had been disowned and now he was rudderless, homeless, alone on a crowded road. He did not count the new wife or the children as companions. They were plants uprooted before they had formed into shape or type. They were adrift on this high road

4

above a river that divided them from everything they had come to expect. "When I inherit we will have a good piece of land," his dear Rebecca had said whenever he'd chafed at his dependence on her family. She had always said it and he had eventually decided there was no shame in having a wealthy wife. He had spent twelve years working for the tobacco firm owned by his father-in-law, but then Rebecca had sickened after her fifth childbirth. All so sudden, it had been, and everyone bewildered while Daniel stared into the flame of his wife's bedside candle, trying to understand. Neglecting his work and forgetting to eat or wash, he gave over the details of the children's daily care to a fifteen-year-old girl he had brought in from the almshouse, an orphan. Her name was Ruth Boyd.

Mother Grube fussed in the kitchen while Rebecca lay in her four-poster bed holding her husband's sleeve. The entire Grube family kept arriving and departing without announcement, but when Rebecca died, on the twenty-first day after Joseph's birth, they seemed to evaporate. The sisters were married, with large families of their own, and the parents were elderly. Alone in his study, while neighbours brought food to the kitchen door, Daniel wept and prayed and waited to learn what was required of him.

"Thee shall cause scandal by keeping the servant girl in thy house," his father admonished. "Thee must find a proper mother for thy orphans."

"Ruth Boyd is also an orphan," Daniel had replied. It was a listless argument nevertheless. He had taken her from the almshouse on a bond of indenture and did not feel he could return her. He said simply, "I cannot take her back there." He thought of the way she had run out to his wagon wearing a torn plaid dress and boots so old they were split at the sides. Her cape was unmended, her felt hat unclean.

"And when thee is written out of the meeting for keeping an unmarried girl?" his father had asked. "Then where will thee go?"

"I will go to Virginia." It was a muttering, a threat. "Land of tolerance."

"Land of slavery." Daniel's father had a mason's heavy hands. "And does thee know what James Madison has done there?"

"Yes, Father. But it is only a very mild law which holds . . ."

"Which holds the constitution in contempt," the old man spluttered, "although the Virginians are intent on breeding presidents and, in fear of justified reprisal by the Federalists, are building a militia." Daniel's father had taken his hat off and was fanning his face. "Next they will decide to leave the Union altogether."

"There is religious freedom . . ." In Brandywine, the Elders sat in judgment, measuring each person's response to the voice of God within. Discipline. The sense of the Meeting.

"And no paid labour to be had," his father had stated gloomily.

"I shall labour for myself." This was said with a hint of sinful pride. "Thee once quoted John Woolman to me that if the leadings of the spirit were attended to, more people would be engaged in the sweet employment of husbandry." Daniel had gone out to his horse then, remounted, and tried to imagine himself as different from the quiet, internalized person he had always been. He would make himself worthy of farm work, although he had so far never lifted a hand in such labour. He would find rolling land and a fast-running creek. He would drive his children through the Blue Ridge Mountains and by the time they found a homeplace none of them would look back. They had already crossed the Potomac at Evan Watkins's ferry. They had pushed on into Virginia, the old Commonwealth. The children would see this as adventure instead of exile.

When they passed the first plantation, Mary pulled hard at the reins. "There will surely be someone here to suckle poor baby," she said, thinking of Luveen, who had raised her mother and then all of them but who would not come with them to Virginia, where she could be mistaken for a slave. *There's a betta world a'comin* . . . It was something Luveen used to sing.

But Daniel would not see his child nourished by slavery. He turned and lifted the baby from his cradle and put him into the stepmother's empty arms.

They spent a cold night in a roadside field with the children huddled in the wagon and Daniel on the hard ground underneath. He heard nine-year-old Isaac ask his brother if he was afraid of going where Indians might take his scalp. He heard Mary singing Luveen's lullaby. He heard Ruth Boyd lift the baby from his cradle in order to feed him milk from the cow that had come along on this journey as unwillingly as the rest, and he turned on his side and covered his ears and thought about Joseph fleeing out of Egypt with a young, chaste wife. For twelve years he had made himself valuable by poring over deeds and other documents and he surely knew enough about land and its value to find the right location for a new home where he could bring his family back to respectability. These were his thoughts as he lay on the ground under an ill-equipped wagon, listening to his children complain.

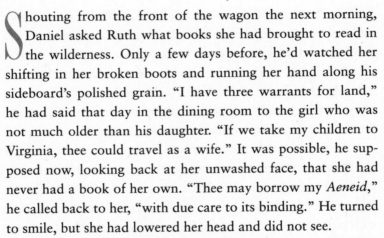

Shouting from the front of the wagon the next morning, Daniel asked Ruth what books she had brought to read in the wilderness. Only a few days before, he'd watched her shifting in her broken boots and running her hand along his sideboard's polished grain. "I have three warrants for land," he had said that day in the dining room to the girl who was not much older than his daughter. "If we take my children to Virginia, thee could travel as a wife." It was possible, he supposed now, looking back at her unwashed face, that she had never had a book of her own. "Thee may borrow my *Aeneid*," he called back to her, "with due care to its binding." He turned to smile, but she had lowered her head and did not see.

But I am reading it just now, Mary wanted to say. That book was the one thing she shared now with her father. It was theirs. She stayed silent.

They were entering that earthly system of hills and gaps called the Shenandoah Valley, said to be ablaze with rhododendron and carpeted with blue grass in the summer but just now covered with early frost and air bitter to the hands and face. Daniel thought for a moment of his house, his table, his chair and his bed, the radiant life he had lost. "I have decided this day that we will give up our 'thees' and 'thous,'" he announced, speaking only to Mary, who sat tense at his side, "so that we do not set ourselves too much apart from our new neighbours."

"I have given up enough," Mary replied, throwing a meaningful glance over her shoulder now at Ruth Boyd, who had come to them as a servant and stolen their name, causing them to lose home and friends. Ruth Boyd! She'd seen her fingering linens hand-cut and embroidered by Grandmother Grube. She'd seen her fingering the silver ladling spoon. She said sternly, "Jeptha, who was a judge in Israel, did thee and thou his daughter, and she did thee and thou her father the judge." She had left her grandparents. She had left her school. She had left her mother in the ground of Brandywine. And Luveen, never to be seen again, never to listen to troubles or joke or sing about a better world. She had been shunned by the children she'd always known. Except for Taylor Corbett, they had turned their backs on her and refused to speak. Because her father had married Ruth Boyd. A Methodist. She thought of the things her father had sold, things she had known so dearly and touched so often, even the camphor trunk with its tropical smell. She had lost everything but her brothers and the babies, one of them thankfully female, but now that she thought of it, maybe the two of them were not fairly blessed. "Thee and me," she said, pulling Jemima, who was almost two years old, up to the front of the wagon to sit on her lap, "are we heading into a bitter world?" She liked to mix up the two words: *bitter* and *better*. She did it now on purpose, but as a baby, first learning to talk, she had been teased by her parents for saying after scoldings, "I be bitter now." She thought of her father making up his mind to move all of them away from home and family and friends. Would a mother make such a demand? And now he wanted to give up their way of speech. "What of that?" she asked, pointing at his big Quaker hat. "Is thee going to throw it away?"

"The People called Quakers will not put off their Hats, nor bow, nor give flattering Titles to People." Daniel could quote the old Catechism as well as Mary. "You," he said, turning to try out the new word on Ruth Boyd. It was a simple word, but it stung his lips. "I asked, what books did *you* bring?"

Ruth bowed her head and said nothing. She sat on the floor of the wagon and her muscles ached and she longed to stretch but she could not run alongside the wagon like the other children. She was married now. All day the road had been muddy and rutted or icy and slick, and even when the children stayed under the canvas, crammed together for warmth, she sat behind the riding board in the wind. She slept with the children on the bed tick Mary put down in the wagon while Daniel lay on the ground underneath, but she was apart from the others all the same. "My mother stirs just this way," Mary would say when they prepared a meal. Or "My mother picks those dark kernels out and throws them away." Mary would not speak of her mother as a person who had passed on to Heaven, which Ruth knew to be fact. She would not seem to realize that Rebecca Grube Dickinson was no more part of this earthly life and that Ruth had taken her place as Daniel's wife. In a family, everyone thought alike and ate alike and prayed alike. She had never been part of a family, but she could imagine the narrowness of belief it must require. In this one they were Quakers, so-called, who did not have a preacher and dressed in an old-fashioned way, the men in long coats and short breeches and wide-brimmed beaver hats, the women in gowns without pattern, without colour, without lace. And if any person's thinking or praying got a little different, the different person could not send his children to the school or visit with a neighbour in the street. No one would employ him or give him trade. "Is it myself here in your house that makes trouble?" she had asked one day in Brandywine when she'd stood across from her employer. She'd wanted to say, I am nothing but what God made me, but his thin face had darkened and his eyebrows had come together and she would not defend herself. She could not read, but she could think and see! She had stood by the sideboard, running her hand along the ribbony grain while her employer had stared at her uncombed hair and soiled dress. He was sitting at the table and had one boot braced against his knee. This was the way he liked to sit and now he put his hand on his heart and laid out his plan, as if speaking to himself and never to her. "I shall travel and settle where land is nearly free." She had listened and felt the smooth wood and looked at his face and then looked away. She had felt sorry for the widower. Then the clock in the dining room had started to chime and he'd said softly, "Thee could travel as a wife." How could she ignore the defeat in his voice? But she could count enough to tell the hour and she counted while outside in the street a donkey was braying and upstairs Luveen was rocking a baby whose mother was cold in the grave. One . . . two . . . three . . . four . . . The clock had not finished its chiming when Ruth said, Yes.

What had he told his children? He'd said that this road had been there since the Creation. Indians and herds of buffalo had used it. The boys sometimes listened. The newborn cried. Benjamin and Isaac got out of the wagon and ran alongside as the ancient trail pulled them up through a gap or across a creek. Fording, they climbed back in and held on and shrieked, sometimes getting soaked by icy water. On the road, they listened to Mary's stories about a flying horse named Pegasus. Borne through space, what would the road below look like? How small would the wagons and travellers be? Pegasus was white, and he had great feathery wings.

In Harrisonburg they stopped for a night in the company of several Mennonite families who were going to make a settlement there. Mary said Tick's milk should be shared and the strangers were glad of it. "Papa, please," said the tired children. "Let us stay here."

But Daniel shook his head, wanting no part of another pious sect. He watched his boys run with the other children as clouds began to gather and the wives covered their cook fires with their capes. He watched the men unhitching their horses and putting them to grass. He untied Tick from the back of the wagon and let her wander at will and watched as his family melted in with the others so easily. Men he had known for years had turned away from him in Brandywine. The Elders had so quickly condemned him that the door to the Meeting House had been locked when he arrived to pray. I will go into the wilderness, he had told his father, and labour for myself. His mother had said something about locusts and honey.

"Papa, there is a boy standing there all bare to the skin." Mary pulled at her father's sleeve.

Daniel studied the naked child, who stood on the far side of a creek that ran through the stopping place. The Mennonite men had gathered in a cluster of concern near their wives.

"He must be cold," Mary whispered.

"Will he scalp us?" asked Benjamin.

Daniel climbed into the wagon and came out with a quilt. Mary bit her lip hard to stop herself from crying out that it was her mother's best. She felt a twist in her heart that was both pleasure and pain. A moment later, her father was sloshing across the creek in his boots and putting the quilt around the boy's thin shoulders while everyone stood still and watched. "Bring him to me," Mary whispered, wanting the boy, but Daniel returned alone and spoke quietly to the waiting Mennonite men. "He says Shawnee are coming. He says it is dangerous for us here. He is Cherokee."

"Wants to be rid of us," said one.

"Listen not to savages."

Mulberry and Miss Patch had not yet been unhitched and now Daniel sent Isaac for Tick and turned back to the road. Soon snow began to fall while he sat straight with the reins in his hands and, for a few minutes, felt the light in himself again.

Two days later they came to Looney Ferry, which would take them across the James River. "Here," said the children again because at this point of land, where the Allegheny and the Blue Ridge mountains touched, the ferryman had built a mill and there would soon be a town. "Here, Papa, please." But Daniel told the ferryman to load up the wagon and brace its wheels. He brought Tick and the horses aboard himself and held their leads in his hands. When they had disembarked, he studied his map, putting his finger on Wallens Creek. It had been forty days since they'd left Brandywine under a cloud that seemed to follow them, and now they crossed the James and turned north, fighting to keep the wagon steady on the narrow track. Days later, when they came to the great Powell River, the horses skirted a ridge that was narrow and icy and laid their ears back. Snow pelted the wagon and Daniel spoke to Miss Patch in the voice he reserved for her. "Now then, good lady," he said, "we have a trial ahead." He had taught this chestnut mare to pull a buggy without long lines by tapping her on her right or left shoulder with a willow stick. He had taught her to whinny in reply to his questions, and now she looked down at the rushing water with flattened ears and rolling eyes while Mulberry, whose darker coat matched her disposition, stood at the edge of the river tossing her head and pawing at the ground.

"We should stop right here," said Mary firmly. "In the morning we will find a better crossing. Think of poor Tick!"

Daniel had set his teeth. "We will cross here and now."

"The bank is too steep, Papa, and the river is wide here and just look at the terrible current." In a smaller voice she said, "It is much too fast."

Daniel folded the map and tucked it under his hat and, because he was unsure of himself, cracked the willow stick and started the horses down the slope at a slant, pulling back on the reins as he urged them forward with his voice. The water was tumbling past with such a roar that both horses balked at the edge, locking their legs as the weight of the wagon pushed them fast into the current, where they ran against branches and fallen trees. Tick had disappeared briefly and resurfaced, paddling her four legs as if she would climb into the wagon and sit with them there. Mulberry began to roll and kick, causing the wagon to tip and Benjamin and Jemima screamed. The baby wailed and Ruth reached to pull him out of the cradle while Mary grabbed at the reins Daniel held. "Lord, have mercy, dear Jesus!"

"Quiet, Ruth Boyd!"

If one of the horses foundered, all of them would be swept downstream over whatever rapids lay ahead. The children were sobbing. The wagon bucked and bounced, cold water streaming in over its sides. Tick choked and bellowed, swimming hard.

"Quiet!" Daniel yelled at the elements.

Ruth clutched the howling baby to her breast. If they were going to die, she would hold on to something. The mares crashed against branches, legs swirling as the wagon plowed into the hitch and the tailgate fell open and all of them heard a heavy splash as the trunk with their store of food slid out. Corn flour and white, bacon, dried beans. The mares pawed at the water, eyes rolling, chests heaving, and the sealed trunk floated for a moment, then sank. Daniel was shouting at all of them, at no one. Mary was holding hard to the reins, bracing herself with her feet, more afraid than she had ever been. This, too, was all because of Ruth Boyd – exile, danger, and foolishness. But four-year-old Benjamin flung himself at Ruth and buried his head in her lap. It was the only triumph of her journey since none of the children had touched her even once since she had first come to their Brandywine house. Now little Benjamin held on to her for dear life, and she put an arm around him and took him into her heart with a love that would never change. Lord

Jesus, have mercy, she said again, but only to herself, and some minutes later the horses were crawling out of the river, heaving the wagon up its short bank, and Ruth saw that Daniel's hands covered his face. Tick had not drowned, but she stood apart from them sullenly as they climbed out of the wagon shivering, cold, and wet to the skin. Ruth asked Benjamin to collect some dry branches for a fire, patting him with a confidence she had not felt before so that he ran off bravely, and some minutes later they all stood by a warming fire, small as it was.

Then there was Wallens Creek to be crossed the following day, and it was not so terrible as the river but it made a rushing noise in its shallow parts that worried the horses after their last experience. On the other side, they came to a flat length of ground surrounded by hills and stopped to rest where there was only low brush and emptiness and a few birds holding forth. The boys were longing to be loose and ran off into the field while Mary sat with her father and Ruth stayed in the back under the canvas with the baby.

"Is it you are looking for some place?" A shape had appeared out of cooling mist. Words from an apparition.

Daniel started. "I seek a place indeed, yes."

A wood grouse fluttered in the underbrush. "I got a piece to go," said the apparition, who was wrapped in oilcloth as if rain might descend upon them.

Mary groaned. "No, Papa. Not here," but Ruth moved cautiously up to Daniel's side. They had come to the end of Virginia, and she pushed her hair back and pinched her cheeks. A few miles beyond, the Cumberland Gap divided the world into halves, the far side belonging to Napoleon or King George or to Philip of Spain. But here were mountains and hills and trees dark and bare. The horses were pawing for grass under a thin layer of snow. Daniel got out of the wagon and the two men walked back and forth, talking in voices not to be heard by Mary or Ruth.

That night the family camped under two huge sycamores with brittle, clattering branches, Mary saying this was no place for children to be raised with no houses, no school, no store, and the boys saying they were afraid of wolves and bears while Ruth held little Benjamin and Joseph lay in his cradle. One of the sycamores was almost empty in its middle so that a fort could be imagined within it by the boys and all of them used it for hide and seek, chasing through the dark. In the morning, the field around them was studded with small icy flowers, as if they had sprouted under the snow as invitations to stay and Daniel said it was a sight to behold. Later, having studied the six acres offered by the apparition in oilcloth, Daniel offered him a warrant worth one hundred dollars. He had not much else to give. He'd sold the furniture and china and flatware. He'd been sorry to do so, but he'd exchanged those goods for two hundred dollars and three warrants of the type given to veterans by the government. Veterans of the War of Independence had thereby bought this Quaker pacifist his six acres – the first land he had ever owned – but he could smile at the fact of it and scuff up the dirt that was dampened by melting snow and even bring Mary a small yellow flower. He rolled up the sleeves of his shirt, which had not been washed since he'd left Brandywine, and set to work building a lean-to, using logs he cut with his axe. The logs did not fit together but they could be chinked. It was cold in the hills of southwestern Virginia, but there were plentiful trees and Daniel worked up a sweat so that by Christmas Day, the family could sit in the lean-to for a cold hour of silent prayer after which Mary served up a pot full of beans she'd been given by the apparition's wife. They were German settlers who also provided a side of venison, a bag of cornmeal, and fodder for the two horses and weary Tick. The fire burned feebly on a piece of ground that was cleared of snow, sheltered by the wagon's oiled canvas, while Daniel reminded his children to be thankful and the children thought of their mother, sharing one homesick mind. The younger ones thought of her as a ghostly presence while Mary knew her as an absence, a hole in her life. More and more, the person she missed was Luveen, who had been like a tree they were allowed to hold and climb. When their father told the children that the Lord had brought them to a place of tolerance, each of them heard the words differently, some with bitterness, some with sadness, some with anticipation of coming events. There was variation in character among the children, but there was not one among them who refused this Christmas feast.

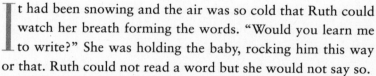

It had been snowing and the air was so cold that Ruth could watch her breath forming the words. "Would you learn me to write?" She was holding the baby, rocking him this way or that. Ruth could not read a word but she would not say so.

Mary put down her quill and slapped at the baby's damp coverlet. "Feel this now, Ruth Boyd. It's shameful, our baby so wet. And I cannot 'learn' thee. And I have no time to teach thee when I must see that poor baby is dry and then be a mother to the rest." Mary tilted her head. "And who would thee write to, Ruth Boyd?" Leaning her back against the rough headboard her father had made from logs, she bent her knees so that Ruth's view of her paper was blocked. She poked her quill into the small pot of ink that rested on a ledge.

To Taylor Corbett What Adventur we are haveing among Red Indians and bears. A naked boy took my mama's best-made quilt for his need was greater than ours but we have come to a wild land here where no school waits for us and no store has food for us and we will have to build a house made of trees. I guess I shall ask a travllor to carry this letter with sincer best wishes from
  Mary Amelia Dickinson January 1799

"There now, Ruth Boyd," she said, blowing on the wet words to show her resolve. "Best move those snooping eyes and look after baby."

Ruth grabbed Joseph and tied him tightly to her front, then walked out into the snow, slamming the worthless door behind her angrily. "The Lord don't give a thousand warnins," she shouted, kicking furiously at the ground and feeling the shame of tears because she wanted so very much to read and who was there to teach her but this girl? She kicked at the snow with her still-split boots and what she saw underneath was dark, loamy soil. "So it was never open yet," she said out loud, ignoring the baby tied to her front as a sweet smell rose up from the wet earth and clouded her in the first happiness she had known for months. Dirt. This was the skill she had kept to herself – this knack she had learned where the orphans, always hungry, had to grow what they ate and enough to feed Matron as well. Ruth had made of herself in those years a studier of soil and a collector of seeds. She had tried the raising of five different types of corn and knew well her preference for which to give pigs and which to save for seed and which to send to the cook to grind and bake. She had seen Matron make use of everything in sight – old husks of grain for mattresses, hog hair to fertilize – there was no end of usefulness for anything on this round ball of water and ground the Lord had made. Squalling baby or not, Ruth had saved the ashes from every cooking fire since they arrived, and now, as she dug at the soil with the heel of a shoe, she promised to scatter some in for good measure, as a way to put something in before she took away. She had no way of reading the labels on the seeds Daniel had packed, but she knew them well enough: wax beans, string beans, lima beans, cabbage, turnips, yams and taters, beets, pumpkins, and squash. Soon. Soon. The snow would melt away. The corn she was bound to sort but she found no shell peas to plant, no onions or carrots or cucumbers. What kind of kitchen could do without? And radishes! She liked them cooked.

That night, when Joseph was twitching and wailing in his cradle and the other children were wrestling themselves to sleep, Ruth thought of those seeds. She thought of the ashes she had saved and the clatter she would make with the cooking pot, even though Mary had laughed at her wrongful idea of a cake for Daniel's birthday. "I would fix him johnnycake," she had told Mary, "if I had an egg."

Mary had laughed. "To think my pap would celebrate his thirty-sixth birthday as if *he* is poor as thee! My mama made real risen cakes, Ruth Boyd. Just believe."

Lying stiff in the crowded bed, Ruth remembered her angry reply. "We must be poor in the same way," she had answered, "your papa and me, for I am his wife." But she did not know how to bake a cake, and the next morning it was Mary who told her that Daniel had left for an auction, that it was a long way he had to go, and that he would not return for at least another day.

The road was narrow, full of climbs and turns and so over-laden with heavy wet trees that Daniel's wool coat was soon damp. He had thought of leaving Mulberry behind, for her right front leg seemed to bother her a little more each day since the long wagon-pulling trip. He had no one to mention such worries to now. Unlike his daughter, he no longer had a friend to whom he could write, since he had kept a girl in his house after the death of his wife and, worse, had quickly married her, and she a Methodist. Everyone had turned against him and if Daniel had need to converse now, he spoke to his mares in slow, thought-ful sentences. "I bring you only to speed our journey," he told Mulberry. "But I will make it easy for you, as will Miss Patch." At midday, he stopped to eat his bread and speak his further con-cerns to Miss Patch, who, like his dear wife Rebecca, listened but never judged. This mare might glance at him or twitch an ear, as if aware of the self-interest in his debate, but unlike Mulberry, who had no real breeding, Miss Patch was a fine chestnut out of a famous sire and thoroughly compassionate. She had consoled Daniel on many occasions, and now she moved at a pace to keep the man as well as the doleful Mulberry placid.

For a while Daniel hoped, as he drove the mares south and east, that someone might stand up on the roadside and offer himself for hire. Then he gave up that thought and began to imagine a runaway slave dashing through the trees and begging him for refuge. This thought excited him a little and he allowed his mind to play over details of such an encounter. He had asked his German neighbour, Jonas Frederick, who preferred to be known as Frederick Jones, about the availability of hired help. That good neighbour had a son named Wiley who was old enough to work but was much needed at his own homeplace. The neighbour had then looked at Daniel in a friendly way and told him to speak to Jester Fox, who lived on the north side of Sawmill Creek. "Have you not seen his house? It was built by black hands skilled enough."

Daniel had said, "I am abolitionist."

His neighbour had shrugged and Daniel had gone then to see Jester Fox in order to put the question of paid labour to him.

"You be takin on trouble," Jester Fox had said when Daniel found him. "But the only choice in this here county is to buy yoursef a nigra, rare though they be."

Daniel had said he would do no such thing.

"Well, I speak God's verity," Jester Fox had said. "When it comes to house raisin and not ta mention if you desire ta farm in these parts, you got no realistic choice less your sons grow into workers overnight."

Astride Miss Patch, Daniel had gazed up at the frame house inhabited by Jester Fox and his family. Every human being was part of the divine; enslavement was abomination, nothing less. Daniel wondered how he could love such a neighbour and looked at him unsteadily, as if the very looking implied complicity. His neighbour was red-haired and red-bearded and his freckled face was featureless – eyes, nose, and mouth all sunk into pale flesh.

"Nothing I'd like better'n ta help out by offering a nig for hire," the neighbour had said. "'Cept here is what I come up agint. We got our clearin brush and trees, and the wood ta split and cartin manure and sowin now it's comin spring. Hear me out now, sir, rather than turn your face away. In buyin, you gone ta give to a nigra a life better'n whar he come out of and most likely whar he is." The red beard, shovel-shaped, bristled, slightly wet. The teeth were small and separate. "They be happier in our care," the neighbour said, adding that there was to be a slave auction down by the Tennessee Line and that Daniel would do best to go on down there and pick up the tools he might also need in order to farm. "I see you got no local expertise, so I aim to set you up fair and square. The whole of a farm down at the line is to be sold off so as to put a widow lady's financials to the right. You'd be doin your Christian duty to her alongside your own."

Daniel had lost cornmeal and sugar and wheat flour and bacon in crossing the rushing river, along with the salted meat and beans. He needed, as well as food, a good many tools for building. His cow was tethered to the side of the lean-to, since he had not yet built a fence. To begin his house, he needed a pole axe. To split shingles and shim, he'd need a shingle knife. For tilling, he would soon need a plow. *To press deep behind a groaning ox*, he told himself, since Virgil kept his spirits up, although his Pennsylvania mares would have to do for now.

On his way to the auction, he was travelling alone, as he did not wish the children to take part in any such occasion, although, in the event that he came upon a runaway, how good it would be for them to witness Christian charity. The thought bore into his mind as he drove, that by purchasing a slave a man became part of an injury wrought not just on another human being but on the entire society. This he explained to the horses, speaking in gentle tones through the long hours of the journey, imagining that his dear Rebecca could also hear his words and must agree with him as usual. It was only at such times, rare now, when he was alone, that he allowed himself to dwell on his departed wife. Privacy was required for this grief and now he indulged in it, seeing himself as a younger man standing at the foot of the winding staircase in Rebecca's father's house, forcing his eyes away from her rustling gown, which was steely and cool and made a noise like dry grasses against whatever it was that was underneath. Gracefully she came down the stairs as he closed his eyes and let himself drift, following Rebecca into her father's parlour with a pounding heart while his mares pulled him along the narrow road to an event that was going to change several lives. He remembered the lift of Rebecca's chin as she turned her back to pour him a cup of cold coffee. He had not known whether to stand or sit. His father was a Lancaster mason, a cutter of millstones. Daniel had been sent to find new customers among the Brandywine Friends, and knowing that, as he sipped the cold coffee, he thought he knew something else. He'd been sent to find a wife.

There were eight wagons and two buggies gathered at the roadside when Daniel dropped the reins. He felt dismal, knowing the amount of money he had brought and the variety of things he needed. He must choose carefully and wait for his price. He must guard his purchases. There were thieves on the border. Outlaws. Indians. There might be thieves here among the purchasers. A chunk of land was up for sale, along with house and furnishings and tools. Word had it that the young owner had died, leaving his wife and children in debt. Briefly, Daniel imagined himself the holder of such an empire. Then he remembered the humiliating sale of his own household goods and felt sorrow for the widow. He saw a wooden stage in the centre of the farmyard and ten or twelve men standing near it. Pulling at his coat sleeves, he took his first steps toward them. "Tennessee trader's in a mighty hurry," he heard someone say and looked up to see a man leaning on the fence, one boot on its bottom rail. "Could be good on us. Or not, dependin." Daniel fed himself into the crowd, hoping that tools and equipment would be auctioned first, but there was a stir near the farmhouse where a group of slaves stood facing a wall.

The auctioneer wore a black hat and a jacket so shiny it might have been greased. His boots were oiled and the gloves he would wave during his display of wares were a bright shade of yellow.

"Gentlemen of Virginia," he intoned in a voice that commanded all friendly and curious chatter to stop, "we are right close to our border here at the finest farm I've had the fortune to put up on offer. We are right here next to Tennessee, where chattel carry scars and bitterness such that it ruins them for work among honest men, but here in Virginia," he went on without drawing a breath, "we sell only well-tended, healthy Virginia-born flesh. That is our law up here now. No more importation, do you see? Parents or grandparents may have made the harrowing journey from Africa. They may have made landfall in the tidewaters of Virginia or Charleston or the Caribe. More'n likely they got brought into New England is my suspicion, where we all know the most profit in black flesh is made. Here now, today . . . Come on up here close, gentlemen, and see for yourself some fine Virginia-raised merchandise." The auctioneer threw his arms out and a stirring and moaning overtook the slaves.

Daniel remembered the song old Luveen used to sing. *There's a betta world a'comin. Will you go along with me? Oh go along with me!* Once he'd thought of it, he found he could not banish the tune from his mind even as six faces peered out from the pen where they had been placed along with several cows and four sheep. He understood, in that instant, why Luveen had refused to come to Virginia although she had been with his children since they were born and with his wife from her birth to her death. Luveen had been a servant, decently paid and entirely free. This was something very different, something he had not quite imagined even when he listened to the exhortations of Quaker abolitionists. His mouth felt dry. He retreated to his wagon and stood by it, dismayed. *Will you go . . . along . . . with me . . .* Still watching, in spite of himself, he saw a woman pulled up onto the stage. He saw the auctioneer open her dress, where there was an infant latched to her breast. Daniel was not a man who had looked on bare arms or shoulders. He had never seen his own dear Rebecca's entire self, but the dress opened like a wound and he stared now at a woman's flesh.

The auctioneer declared that the girl was full of good seed and rich milk. "Jus you look here at this baby fat and male and worth an extra fifty dolla. Ima start the bid at a hunnert for this breeder."

A bareheaded man standing close to Daniel spat a long stream of tobacco juice into the grass, knocking the dusty hat he held against his knee at the same time. "Ain't so young by the look of her titties," he shouted.

"Shut it up!" yelled another man amid other and worse complaints. The crowd was eager. They did not want to tarry or amuse themselves. Someone bid and then someone else and the girl was pulled off the stage while a man held her arm in his bunched-up fist.

Daniel watched a young man of sixteen or seventeen years get sold to the slave trader for two hundred and twenty dollars after he had been made to describe his talents. "Which the Lord says we must not waste," the auctioneer reminded him, shaking a plump gloved finger. Having spoken, the young man was thereafter silent, never taking his eyes off the yellow gloves, never opening his mouth or closing his eyes for a minute.

Next a pale boy was brought up and two or three people roared out that he should not be on the block. "This lad's Irish!" someone yelled.

"Here now, gentlemen!" shouted the auctioneer. "Settle your wigs and hear the facts. This lad is the property of the householder like all the rest. How much am I offered for this pretty houseboy?" the auctioneer curtsied flirtatiously. The men gathered below the stage could see the boy's dark mother come up close and reach up to him. Daniel felt his throat close again but a sound came out of it. He bent his head and moved forward.

The man who'd earlier spat turned to look at him. "Why don we let him go loose, is that it?" He smoothed his hair back with two fingers and put the dusty hat on his head. "But he don have true feelins like us, bein mixed with black. So let us get on with what we come here to do."

Daniel sat through the auctioning of the boy's mother, then, and he hated the men as they yelled up their bids but he told himself they would now get to the useful tools when a boy the size of Isaac climbed up on the stage without prodding. He was surely older than nine but no more than thirteen and he got up on the stage as if daring the men below to challenge his right to stand above them. From that height he stood looking down at the pink and white faces below as if he hoped to lock eyes with the one person in the crowd who dared to take charge of his fate – although if his fate can be charged to anything, thought Daniel, it can only be to God as He speaks through each one of us. It occurred to him then to pray for the boy but he did not know where to begin. Instead, he went on trying to organize his understanding of God's plan and he felt his right arm go up as if pulled by a string.

There was sudden laughter. "Hey! Mister Quaker? Ain't you wanta listen to the details before you bid?" someone hooted, and the laughter got louder and the right arm would not come down.

The auctioneer started the bidding at four hundred dollars. "And lookee over there to where I got my first offer! Somebody goin to raise it?" He joined the surrounding laughter, bobbing his head and showing teeth in his smile.

"No, no," Daniel stuttered, trying to shake his head and yanking at his right sleeve with his left hand. "I haven't got it," he said, pulling the arm down forcefully as if it belonged to someone else.

The auctioneer in his shiny jacket, buttoned vest, and black hat had a face blazoned by sun or alcohol and he aimed it at Daniel, as if to inspect a man whose credit was in jeopardy. His hands in their yellow gloves made flourishes in front of his stomach. He walked to the edge of the stage and leaned out.

"Says he ain't gotit!" the spitter of tobacco juice shouted.

"Got a fine pair of mares over yonder," yelled another.

"Made the bid, dint he?"

"I saw it."

The gangly boy stood on the stage without moving. He was watching his brother being put into coffles by the slave trader and, with another slave, marched away.

"His hand went up, it shore did!"

"For twice moren that nigger's worth," someone sneered while Daniel thought of his infant son, though he had no reason to connect the baby to this awful event. There was a pull on the back of his long Quaker coat. Then two men had hold of his arms and were guiding him off to one side of the crowd where there was a table and chair set under a tree. In order to make himself understood, Daniel enunciated carefully. "I have made an *error*." More slowly, "A mistake. I must forfeit the bid." Each word was a piece of gravel in his mouth because what kind of mistake is a hand raised up by the Lord, which it must have been?

"What cash you brung?" said one of the men, who chewed thoughtfully at a stick he held between his teeth and whose right eye was unfocused, as if it were coated with dust.

The second man said simply, "How much?"

Like most Quaker men, Daniel wore no beard and this, along with his outdated clothing, may have increased the antipathy of the men now gathering around him uttering threats. "I have some amount just over two hundred dollars," he admitted quietly. "A little over, which I was told would buy me a plow and farming tools for my new homeplace. Which is all I have come for today. And which represents my entire life savings." A Quaker must never entail debt.

"Might have done so too," said a man who seemed to bear a grudge, for he nudged at Daniel with a stick.

"Except that you are in for two times what you brung," said another, holding up two fingers and rubbing them together.

A Quaker does not swear or take an oath. Daniel licked his lips. He had been driven from the refuge of his people, but his moral nature was unchanged. He looked at the two businessmen and swallowed the last saliva in his mouth. His dry lips parted. "I give you my word," he said, biting back shame. "I will raise what I owe." His mind was swinging. Where could he find such a sum?

"Ain't no use ta me." The auctioneer had arrived at the table. "I'll take a mare," he said hard and clear.

There was general assent. Yes, that's it, then. Yes. Yes.

Daniel took a step closer to his wagon. It sat on the other side of the fence but he seemed to be shaking, legs and hips, as he forced his knees to bend, his legs to lift his feet. The two businessmen moved along beside him, focusing on a wagon that was as worthless to them as it was valuable to Daniel, and then gazing at the horses. "That chestnut is nice enough," one said.

Daniel was partly glad because Mulberry was slightly lame and it would not do to send her off with a careless man. Moving to his more beloved mare, he touched her muzzle and breathed into it and promised her that he would redeem her, that she would not be taken from him for more than a few days. "Even if I have to sell my land," he told her. He said to the auctioneer, "I give her only as mortgage on my debt."

The auctioneer winked at the listeners, who were waiting for drama. "Fine. Fine. And with the lame mare you can get yourself home at least," he added with a note of benevolence. "The road to my place is marked out by old Eagle Rock when you come ta redeem."

Daniel touched his right arm, which had betrayed him. He ran the criminal hand along his favourite mare's warm flank. He put his head against her neck and again whispered his promise into her listening ear. By four o'clock that same afternoon, he was moving along the road behind Mulberry, who had been separated from Miss Patch as abruptly as the wiry boy in the back of the wagon had been separated from his brother and from everything else in his former life.

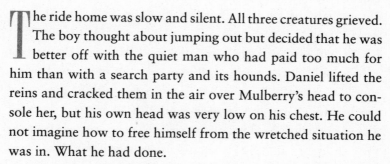

The ride home was slow and silent. All three creatures grieved. The boy thought about jumping out but decided that he was better off with the quiet man who had paid too much for him than with a search party and its hounds. Daniel lifted the reins and cracked them in the air over Mulberry's head to console her, but his own head was very low on his chest. He could not imagine how to free himself from the wretched situation he was in. What he had done.

"I have five children living in a lean-to," he said into space. "I need to put up a house and get a crop in, which means plowing up a field that was never broken yet. And I have no tools. Which is what I came for. And no plow."

Behind him, the boy said nothing.

Was it possible to ascribe blame? An arm had no mind; it was only part of a man. A man was only a small part of God. And had he not been led?

"Can you build?" Daniel shouted over the noise of hooves and the sound of blowing, starting rain that came as cold, almost as ice.

"I ken not," came the boy's voice, sullen and forbidding, as if Daniel had taken the last friend that voice had ever loved in this world, which is just what Daniel had done by not bidding for his brother, who must be in a coffle on his way to Tennessee.

"You have planted." Daniel made it a fact.

The long silence that followed seemed to go on until the sun dropped down behind trees and made its reflected shine on the wet black road. "I brung up pigs," the boy said at last.

Daniel regretted the afternoon with such intensity that he decided it was his father's warning that had doomed him to shame: *A place of slavery . . . a place where no paid labour is to be had . . .* If I had been innocent of such warnings, thought Daniel, my hand could not have been raised even by the Lord. He thought of Christ telling his disciples that one of them would deny Him . . . before the cock crows. He thought that Christ had created Peter's downfall and that it might be best if he should never see his children again. It might be that he should drive on and on with the lame horse and the purchased boy and his shame and apprehension. What hope was there for a world in which earthly and heavenly parents created the holes their children fell into? He should never have come to the auction, where it was certain that his right hand would be raised up in protest or diligence, who knew which?

Had he raised it himself? No, he had not. It was beyond his imagination, this notion of the vile purchase he had made. A human being! A child! And yet, he was now the owner of a boy who could not be given freedom until Miss Patch had been redeemed. Without the boy, how would he ever make enough profit to bring his horse back? He had not a cent in the world. He had no tools and no way to build. Somehow he and this stranger must find, between them, a way to raise two hundred dollars by making with their four hands something valuable and worthy. And it must be quick! They must do it fast. Tobacco, he said to himself, is too slow. And so is wheat. But everything would be slow now, since it was taking twice as long to get back home without a second horse and the dark was falling hard with fresh, cold rain and he had purchased a growing boy for the trade of two hundred dollars and that much needed horse, which was, in and of itself, a sickening thing.

Certainly, this boy was not what he had bargained for, not that he had bargained in the first or even the second place. No, this boy was not what he needed and he at last began to pray. As usual, the prayer was without words, was even mentally silent. Then words sprang up of themselves: *Thee did not choose me, but I chose thee that thee should go and bear fruit.*

When she'd first shown Daniel into that long-ago parlour, his dear wife Rebecca had pointed him to a straight-backed chair, then gone quickly to a silver urn, poured cold coffee into a cup, and offered it without apology. "Luveen?" she'd called out. "Go tell my father he has a visitor from Lancaster. Someone *selling* something." There was such disdain in her voice. Daniel had simply sat. Several minutes had simply passed. A piece of cake was brought into the room by the tall black woman who had met Daniel at the door and he had almost stood, unused as he was to the company of servants. The dog had lifted a paw, and behind her servant's back Rebecca had surely winked. In the wagon, with its one horse and its sullen slave, Daniel remembered the wink and wondered what Rebecca would think of him now, parking his crippled horse under the rain-drenched trees with a tired wagon and its unwelcome cargo. He climbed down. There was a loaf of bread and Daniel split it and took his fill from the water flask, then handed it to the boy. "What is your name?"

Silence.

"Don't you have a name?"

"Onesimus."

Daniel tried to remember the story of Paul saving Philemon's slave, Onesimus. The man is now a Christian, Paul had written to the runaway slave's owner. So I send him back and hope that you receive him as a brother. Daniel hoped he was more Paul than Philemon. He said, "I shall call you Simus. I have my jacket that will do as my bed. Please take the blanket." He climbed back into the wagon.

The boy was holding the flask without putting it to his lips. He took the blanket that was handed down to him. His brother must by now be on his way to some demon place fastened to a coffle and driven to a shed to be branded. Onesimus looked at the ground. He would not take the water but gave the flask back up to Daniel. Any slave known to put his mouth on the rim of a white man's cup would catch the whip. What man, white or black, didn't know that?

Daniel thought he heard the moon rise up through the trees as if it were knocking against the branches. He thought he heard Miss Patch, her tender whinny, far away. What was he doing here in the darkness alone with a boy who meant nothing to him, a boy he had inadvertently purchased? He wanted to run back up the road on his own two feet and take back what belonged to him. But he would have to find two hundred dollars first and then he would have to find that accursed auctioneer. In his pocket, he had a receipt for his mare and on the receipt was the auctioneer's name. Now the jacket was stretched over him and he was stretched out in the bed of his wagon as if he had fallen into it. Under the wagon, the boy was a shadow, doubling him. *Thee did not choose me, but I chose thee.* Daniel wondered what such a boy would dream. He thought that if his arm had been lifted by the inner voice that sometimes guided him, he might perhaps be doing God's will.

They left the stopping place long before dawn, with Mulberry finding her way by feel or scent. The moon sank at last and the sun began its rise and the two went on in the wagon without anything more to eat although the lame horse had replenished herself. When they came to the road that led to his homeplace, Daniel turned. "It is a few miles more. Will you not sit up here with me?"

The boy leaned against the side of the wagon, resting his head on its edge and rubbing his eyes. Mulberry went on pulling the wagon over the road, which was steep now and hard to climb.

M ary was watching sparrows. They would soon make a nest and lay pretty eggs. *"Yea, the sparrow hath found a house,"* she said to them, although she couldn't remember the rest. Then she spoke other words. *"I watch and am as a sparrow alone upon the house top.* Psalm 102:7," she told the sparrows. "The other is Psalms something or other." The sparrow's house would have fledglings and in time the fledglings would flutter from branch to branch. A short time ago, she had watched baby Joseph learning to crawl, lurching and pocketing into the bed tick or onto a quilt spread out on the dirt floor. Now she watched the birds and thought how necessary it was to have parents, both male and female. While the father kept guard, the mother taught the babies what they needed to know just as her own mama would have taught baby Joseph the ways of this provoking world, with all its habits and contradictions. I watch and am as a sparrow while Papa is married to someone who does not belong with us, someone who had no mother to teach her, someone with no proper upbringing. She put her head down and smelled the new grass. She watched the sparrows. *Even the sparrow finds a home, and the swallow a nest for herself.* That was it. Her eyes felt small and she closed them and fell asleep.

So it was Ruth, pacing the floor of the lean-to with baby Joseph, who heard the wagon round the bend and ran out to the road to take in Daniel's situation at a glance. She noticed the absence of Miss Patch and the presence of a boy resting his head on the side of the wagon as if he didn't care to look around.

"Here is our help," Daniel called out.

Ruth looked at Daniel's wet, mud-spattered coat and brushed her hand on it as he stood, allowing her hand to be on him.

"Get down now," Daniel said to the boy in the mixture of irritation and shame that would mark his communication with this purchased human being.

Ruth plucked at the coat again. Even as his employee, she had avoided the problem of naming him, since Quakers used no Mister or Missus but called each other by both Christian and family name. In the beginning, then, she could not say, "Mister Dickinson, do you desire coffee?" And now it was impossible to call him simply Daniel when the other children referred to him as Papa or Pap. Instead, she sought to move his mind from its dark concerns by adopting his antiquated verbal usage. "Come see what I done for *thee*," she said, turning quickly, like the girl she really was, to run across the matted grass and mud, swishing her skirt as she went.

Glad to be quit of the wagon and the sight of Mulberry's heaving flanks, Daniel came along and as he followed Ruth, he was followed in turn by the boy, who had climbed out of the wagon and wiggled away from the younger children's stares.

Mary was dreaming of a dog and an owl. The dog catches the owl and carries it in his mouth. The owl has a broken wing. She opened her eyes and got to her feet, brushing her dress with nervous hands. "Who is that, Papa?"

Daniel shook his head. "Call him Simus and leave him be, Mary Amelia. He is in the hands of God." Daniel could not understand his own irritation. He looked from Mary to Ruth, who was pointing at a hoed-up place marked by ten broken sticks poked into the ground. She said, "Here is my garden all planted next to where we should put the house."

Daniel lashed out, "I gave thee no seeds! I made no decision about the house. And this ground is too wet for planting! Any seeds planted here will rot before they sprout!" He wanted to shake his child bride. "How could thee take such advantage?" He put his face close to hers. "I plan a Virginia kitchen separate from my house that will not be here but under the sycamore trees as anyone with any sense could –" He stopped himself, noticing the watching eyes of the purchased boy, and shuddered. Ruth held herself straight, but the day had darkened for her and she would have unhoed the sacred ground of her own first garden if Mary had not been watching.

"How many seeds did thee waste?" Daniel asked, forgetting himself again.

The boy stood back, but he listened. And that night, Ruth lay in the bed full of Daniel's children and decided that if the Lord had saved her with this marriage, she was still not altogether in the right with Him. Not after what Mary had seen and the boy had heard. Ruth had her pride and she would not forget the injury it had suffered. If there was a tax of shame to be paid on safety, she had paid in full. Outside, the seeds she had put in the ground were enlarging and complicating their vegetal lives. God made us pure and simple and we make ourselves complicated. This was Ruth's thought. Now she, too, would divide herself – stem and leaf. Outer face and inner heart. Never would she let these Dickinsons see her weakness again. She would start by taking a more comfortable position on this crowded bed, and she reached for Benjamin and pushed her face into his curls and smelled the sour sweet of his scalp. This child had become her solace – the one bit of love she could take for herself. Jemima was restless, a light sleeper, a drooler. Awake, she stuck close to

Mary. Isaac was aloof, and the baby lay in the cradle whimpering or asleep. In the almshouse, when they came in very young, they never survived. Maybe Joseph was like that, like a lamb with no will. She'd been five when she got to that place of foundlings. Five will survive, Matron always said, and so she had.

Outside, not far from the newly planted seeds, Daniel and Onesimus were awake most of the night. Daniel now had the entire responsibility for this stranger's life. It had been given unto him. Unless, he thought in the moon-dappled darkness, he had raised his arm up for his own benefit. "Thee would harken always to thy inner voice," his father had often said to him. "But can thee be sure it does not simply echo thy secret wish?" Perhaps there was no accident in his purchase of Onesimus, no right hand of God but only self-interest. He was lying in the wagon again, comfortable enough on some of the family bedding, but he got out of the wagon and stood beside it in his woollen stockings. Having never owned anything in his life, he had paid for these good six acres of trees and water and dirt, but he had also bought a boy who was lying awake in a rolled-up blanket. He could not see a face, but the blanket was human enough, showing the shape of arms and back, head and legs. Daniel walked around and around the boy-shaped blanket. He brought back the farewell argument with his father in which he had stated his plan to labour for himself. "I fear," his father had sighed, "thee will be tempted to the vile practice so cherished in the southern states." And Daniel, desiring to point out the error in his father's predictions, had expressed his abhorrence of human bondage. "And what of Ruth Boyd?" His father had asked, scowling. "Did thee not make a contract to keep her indentured?"

Daniel had retorted that Ruth Boyd might soon be in a different state of commitment to him.

"So thee would marry the girl to free her, is that it?"

"May I not offer refuge?" Daniel had said it brightly.

"There is a long list of people to be saved and half of them are female."

Nevertheless, Daniel had made his announcement at First Day Meeting in Brandywine among Rebecca's relatives and friends. "I shall marry Ruth Boyd," he had said, speaking in the midst of a silence that might otherwise have lasted through the morning. His father-in-law had opened his eyes. His mother-in-law, on the other side of the Meeting House, had sobbed audibly. One of the Elders had cleared his throat. Then there was a hush so protracted that a bee could be heard outside in the dying flowers. A dog on a distant street had barked.

Daniel looked down at the rolled-up form on the ground and thought of the girl on the bed inside his lean-to. He remembered the conviction he had felt that First Day morning when both his inner and outer voices had been sudden and clear. He had been sure of himself for that narrow crack in time, sure for an hour or a little more that he had been directed by his inner light, his own connection to God. Now he stepped over the bare feet that protruded from the blanket, adjusted his shoulders, which were sore from pulling the reins, and tried hard to find that conviction again, but the lamp he had always felt like a beacon in his breast was as unlit as the sky overhead.

"What is that a book of?"

Daniel was perched on the tongue of the wagon, drinking a mug of black coffee and licking his finger as he turned each page of a manual. He closed it so that Ruth could see the cover and said tiredly, "It explains the ways to survive the wilderness by following the principles of science."

"Don't the Red Indians survive in this wilderness?" Ruth leaned over to see if there were pictures.

"Savages survive but not efficiently." Then he thought it only fair to add, "About Indians, it says, for example, that the women take sticks and off they go to poke the ground to raise up the weeds. The weeds, after a day or two, dry out and they burn them for ashes. Then with the little sticks, they make holes and they put in a few grains of corn and cover them up with the ashes. It's luck if they do not starve since they never invented even a plow." Daniel picked up the manual, hoping to discourage further conversation.

"*We* have no plow," Ruth pointed out.

Daniel said, "Today I shall lay down lines for the house." He snapped the manual shut and handed Ruth his empty mug.

That afternoon, he and the boy, Onesimus, began to work together, Daniel reading directions from the manual and the boy using the few tools Daniel had brought with him from

Pennsylvania. It was the neighbour, Frederick Jones, who furnished the iron body level so that walls and sills would stand straight. He loaned out his finishing saw and told Daniel that the Virginia kitchen could wait. "Best to cook in the fireplace," he advised, "to also warm house."

Daniel had in his possession a heavy adz, a broad axe, and a good wood mallet of five pounds weight. "Buy you a moulding plane," Frederick advised. "I have none as my boy Wiley left it to ruin in rain." He made a sound from his German past.

"My efforts must go instead to earning two hundred dollars and not to spend anything," Daniel replied. "For the return of my mare."

Frederick Jones studied the back of his hands. "A good horse for an ungrown boy was not good trade."

In the forest, the ungrown boy was cutting and hauling logs, bedevilled by his fear of snakes and surrounded by the strangling limbs of water oaks and cypress trees. Off and on there was a light fall of snow or rain to increase his misery, but by midweek there were three straight trees cut down and stripped of their bark. Each of them had been pushed and shoved and heaved. There was only Mulberry to do the hauling afterward and she was still slightly lame. The boy kept saying one word over and over. "Mule," he said, "mule," while the lame horse pulled and dragged, slipping and stumbling on the lumpy, soggy ground as the boy also slipped and stumbled and coaxed and threatened and kept an eye on the vines that hung out of the trees. He had seen a man killed by a snake. Viper, it was. Work of the dickens. He thought of the faraway farm, where he had been in charge of pigs. He thought of the way his brother had been sent out to the fields and put to picking and lugging and hauling and how certain words had escaped like sweat and covered him in the sorrow of whips. He must not make the same mistake, he decided, as he drove Mulberry through the swamp and his eyes darted up at the swirling branches.

At the clearing, wrapped in his Quaker coat, Daniel thought about a foundation for his house. They would not have time to build a solid one of stone. If Miss Patch were here, such a thing might be possible, he said to himself. They could pull heaps of flat stones from the creekbed and pile them up in no time while Mulberry hauled up logs. But the scientific decision at this point was to put the floor up on rock legs with a crawl space underneath. He would anchor the house to a sturdy chimney, which would also require stones, but they could look for those when the walls were finished and he had redeemed Miss Patch.

He did not wonder how he would come by the two hundred dollars he needed because the Lord would somehow provide. The creek would provide its stones, his neighbour would provide his aid, and the Lord would surely reward his own efforts to do what he had it in his heart to do. There were fine, round boulders up near the rapids, but that was beyond his property line. For now, he would collect flat pieces of limestone that could be piled under the sills of his house like legs. For now, he would muster the boy he had bought for just such a purpose, although he must not have known it at the time. When Simus appeared, driving Mulberry and the first log, Daniel asked him to set to work with the axe. "Hew off the top of the log and cut notches in the underside every arm's width. If you would, please."

No one had spoken to the boy in that tone even once in his life and he looked at Daniel suspiciously. He had helped put up the tiny cabin he and his brother had lived in on the farm, although he would not admit to it. He had put up the cabin and he had watched other men doing the same. His mother had lived there such a short time that he was reminded of his sorrow with every cut of the axe. On the flattened topside of the first log, he cut notches to accommodate the long narrow sleepers that would stretch across the width of the house, remembering the day he and his brother had tried to do the same thing with small, dull knives. His mother had been singing; he remembered that too. As he worked, a mat of chips grew around him so that the children came running over to play. Even Mary skipped through the wood chips, taking Jemima's hands to swing her around in the air. Isaac threw the chips over his head and watched them cascade down while Benjamin laughed at the sunlight flashing off flakes he called daystars.

The purchased boy watched the others play. He stood with his mouth turned at the corners and his eyes glued on the children and thought of his brother, who had sometimes raced him to the pond where they looked for frogs and caught fish. His brother had taught him to build a snare. Lying quiet on the ground, they had waited for rabbit and grouse. His brother had taught him patience, but now his stomach was reacting to his fear of snakes or to the change in his diet and he left the children and went off by himself. His stomach ached and each log must be brought up from that timber lot where there could be anything alive in the trees and on the wet ground. He was cold. His shoes had no ties and came off in the mud. Time after time, he went to the horse, where she was standing, and took up her reins. We is the same, he would have said to her, if he had thought to speak, but the boy did not voice his thoughts. Instead he made noises, clucked, whimpered, hummed a single note, and felt a grieving sadness whenever he watched the innocent children play.

While the children scattered wood chips, Daniel paced the perimeter of his future house, counting off facts. Walls not of oak – it takes too long to cure – but of poplar or chestnut. Floor of oak cut at the old of the moon. In summer the bark comes off of itself – but now we must hack it. Cure the joists up off the ground until they are bone hard and joint them to the sleepers, the number of which depends on the length of the building. Cut them six inches shorter than the width of the house. Hew them off on each of four sides. Like the slave, he was driven by fear. He needed a house but spring was nearly upon them and he should soon be planting. What, he wondered, had he done with his life? His childhood had been spent in the Quaker community of Lancaster, where his father had been a mason. Daniel had wanted to work at a desk. The chance to sit in a chair all day had seemed cultivated. So he had learned nothing of tools, nothing of farming, nothing of creating out of nothing. What he had learned was the business of writing bills of sale and deeds.

Mary put Jemima down and went to Simus. She had seen him watching her. She had felt ashamed. "How do you do that?"

"Nothin only ta make this axe chop down." Simus wiped his wet face with his hand.

Mary saw his predicament. If the work looked too easy, he would be given more of it. But he had taken that risk for her.

Dear Grandmother Grube

There is no school here it is a pitie we cannot learn History or Latin. How shall I ever grow useful now I wonder. I will teach my brothers but I would rather come ther and live with thee if I may althogh the weather improves it is still cold. Our shelter is fragile but we still must Trust in the Lord,

> *Mary Amelia Grube Dickinson*
> *Fifth February 1799*

On February 10, the six acres were finally surveyed. The day was cold, but Daniel woke up feverish and built up the fire, deciding to make enough coffee for the surveyors. There was a thick fog on the ground and he went behind the lean-to to check on the boy, who was still asleep. The boy had the habit of wrapping himself in the blanket he'd been given and then burying himself in a pile of leaves. That morning the pile was covered with a light dusting of snow. Daniel threw the coffee Mary had ground the night before into a pot of water and let it boil. Then he took a mug full of the drink and went out to walk his land, although the light snow had crusted and the fog lay heavy and he could hardly see his way through the mist. Taking careful steps, the walk took over an hour, by which time the coffee in his mug was in his belly and the sun had brought its rosy light. His land was going to be surveyed and his house was going to be built and he who had never slept in the open until four months ago would again have a proper roof.

He followed the creek, picking his way around fallen logs that were hidden in the snow and descending the slope to the rapids, which lay several poles past his boundary. From there, he looked back, as a prince would survey a kingdom. Without moving an inch, Daniel could count black walnut, hickory, sugar maple, poplar, chestnut, and oak. He knew them even without the advertisement of leaves. There were sycamores at the house site. There were those mysterious cypresses down past the timber lot. There were mayapples and mulberries and there was marsh that would turn to meadow in the spring. He thought of the seeds he had brought and was sick at the waste, but for this hour of walking and drinking warm coffee, he felt the swell of a landowner's pride. Never before had this small piece of land had any meaning at all, but he would imbue it with purpose. *Surveyed six acres on Feb 10 by virtue of entry made Dec. 4, 1798*, the Lee County Deed Book read later that day. *Land warrant 684 dated Sept 6th.* Daniel remembered the purchase of that warrant from a veteran in Brandywine. The Elders would not have approved, nor would Rebecca, but he had bought it from the veteran who had received it as a war payment and he had laid it in the camphor trunk he'd made as a wedding gift for his Quaker wife. Laying up treasure, an affront to the Lord.

That morning, having walked the perimeter of his land with the two surveyors – Hiram Craig and Benjamin Sharpe – he went to talk to Frederick Jones, who had come to this country with the name Jonas Frederick. Why had he twisted his name in such a fashion? It had been reported to him by Hiram Craig, who said that the German was a benefactor who had single-handedly created the town.

Daniel found the settler's wife at her hearth, making potato soup. It was her specialty, she told him, but when Daniel slanted himself through the door without removing his hat, she looked at him in the way of a woman who is surprised by a neighbour's lack of courtesy. Should he explain that a Quaker does not remove his hat because all persons are equal and a show of such shallow respect creates a society of hierarchy? He stood in the doorway, framed by it. He was out of his depth in this kitchen, unfamiliar with the ways of farm wives. In his Quaker way, he would have addressed her by her given and family names, but he did not know her given name and she would find it impertinent of him to ask.

"I was surveyed today," he said.

"Mister Jones is out to his barn," said the wife in her accent.

Daniel put his hand over his heart meaningfully. He nodded.

"You are to building a house," she said.

"Aye. But I am not a young man anymore to be doing such a thing."

"We are such a pioneer," said the missus. "Even in the capital there is a new house being now built."

"Yes, for the president." Daniel laughed agreeably. The farm wife was making an effort. He said, "I see a plenitude of fine, large stones by your rapids." *Your* rapids. Daniel was mastering the English, just as she was.

"You have some interest in rock?" The farm wife stirred her soup. She said her husband, who owned one hundred and thirty acres, had given away half of them to the township. "It will be named for him," she said. "Jonesville." Her mouth spread wide in a smile, showing places without teeth.

Daniel stood with the door still framing him.

"Did you meet Wiley, who is the son?" She looked at her walls and chairs and dishes as if they had all been created for this single offspring, and to deprive him of the boulders at the rapids would be to rob him of his inheritance.

Daniel felt the rebuke. "I have not had that pleasure." On the ground behind him, he heard scuffling steps.

"Ha!" Frederick Jones was surprised to find Daniel in his kitchen but he put out his hand. Then he asked a question in order to make his neighbour feel welcome. Did Mister Dickinson know about sprung legs on a young mare?

Daniel said his own mare was lame and that his wife had been treating the leg with rags soaked in lamp oil. "I will admit that Mulberry is still lame," he said, shrugging affably. "And that my wife has never owned a horse nor ridden one to my knowledge."

"Lamp oil," said Frederick Jones.

Daniel said that he had it in mind to build a chimney. "There are stones of good size in heaps around the rapids," he said, eyeing the farmer's wife.

"Needed for a mill. What my son is to build. He has already sixteen years." He looked at his wife.

Daniel mentioned his second warrant, in exchange for which he might have the bit of land and some much needed cash in which event he would build a grist mill. "There are stones enough for both," he told his neighbour, adding that he would build the mill once the house was roofed, and he would hire young Wiley to operate it, which would be to everyone's advantage.

Jones said, "Warrant means only paper. So pay me up fifty dollars. And then build a mill." He was glad to have a neighbour settle and glad to have his son relieved of constructing a mill he had not the aptitude to build. The deed was drawn up in town before Daniel could change his mind.

Indenture: Feb 10 1799 Frederick Jones to Daniel dickinson for $50 to be paid out for the lot lying on both sides of Saw Mill Creek (a part of the tract whereon said Jones now lives) also a lain one rood wide for use by Jester Fox beginning at a stake in a road by head of Jones's spring thense 65 feet and 22 poles crossing the creek to a white oak.

By the end of the month, the shape of the future was marked out on the snowy ground: a dwelling of twelve by fifteen feet that could be extended, amplified, increased at some later date. Every morning Simus took lame Mulberry down to the timber lot for another log to fit against the log below it. In the afternoons he hauled stones from the rapids Daniel had bought. Daniel's stones. Daniel's water. Daniel's house. The nights were cold but the snow melted in the afternoons so that the low parts of the timber lot were soggy and the boy had to struggle through mush and mud.

One morning, he went earlier than usual to the timber lot, hoping that the ground would still be hard. He chose one of his felled trees and hitched it by use of long hemp lines to the horse. This animal he never called by name, any more than he called any person by name, but he kept up a steady stream of wordless sound, which calmed her. The hitching was slow and the way back to the house site was through the marsh. Mule. Mule, he thought to himself and shook his head, just then losing his footing as the horse tugged and the great log she was dragging knocked him off his feet and rolled over his leg. It took a split second, nothing even to count.

For a while in the cold marsh mud he felt only surprise. Winded, he turned his head and looked at his leg and saw something growing out of it. What came from his mouth then were sounds so piercing that the horse heaved forward and he let go of her lines.

Daniel was looking at his manual. The boy had not arrived with his log so he also took a moment to look up at the sky his shingled roof would soon interrupt. The clouds were galloping along as if they had somewhere to go. Below them a hawk was circling. There was no sign of the boy. Daniel thought of Miss Patch, who would speed up the work when he got her from the auctioneer except that he had not earned the two hundred dollars and he owed fifty more to his neighbour for the acre of stones at the rapids. House building would have to continue at this slow pace and Miss Patch would have to suffer a little longer with the auctioneer.

While Daniel considered this, Mary was bent over the outside fire, stirring and wiping her apron across her face. Simus had snared a rabbit the day before and he'd skinned it and cut it up for her to cook in the iron pot, promising to show her how to skin any animal she could catch. He was going to show her how to make a snare because he didn't mind that she was a girl. If her father would allow it, she would learn these skills down in the timber lot, which was where Simus was always working – watching, darting, and finding things to eat even under a thin covering of snow or ice. She put the long-handled spoon down and went back in the bushes to relieve herself because her father hadn't built a latrine. Her father said there were more important things to build but she knew what her mother would have said. Mary pulled up her skirt and squatted down and closed her eyes. She pictured her mother in her camisole dress with the silk collar that matched her cap. She listened to the sound of her

water hitting cold ground and making steam. When she smelled
the mix of urine and snow and dirt, she put her nose to her wrist
and tried to remember the smell of Luveen. Something between
spicy and sweet it was and hadn't they had a perfect bond, the
two of them? Hadn't they understood each other even without speaking words? When her papa was away all day at his
work and her mama was reading or sewing or resting, she and
Luveen had performed like a perfect team, taking care of the lit-
tler children with never a sour word. Or so it seemed now. Mary
chose to forget the small infractions she had sometimes made
against Luveen's rules and the sullen acts of rebellion. What she
remembered was the perfection of her former life and the arrival of Ruth Boyd, who had ruined it, wiggling herself into the
family from the very first and making her mother die of sorrow.
Standing up and adjusting the skirt she was outgrowing, Mary
thought, if only I had saved my mama, Ruth Boyd would be
back at the almshouse where she belongs and I would still be
in Brandywine with Taylor Corbett and Caroline Corbett and
Stella George and my other classmates. I would still be with
Luveen, who let me bake pastries. When Mary turned and
saw Mulberry gnawing on the frozen grass, hitched to a round
log from the timber lot, she stood staring for a minute, then
screamed, "Papa!" and hiked up her skirt and ran to the place
where Daniel was measuring the sky. "Mulberry's in her hitch
without Simus." It came out in a rush.

It was another half-hour before they found the boy shivering with shock, unable to drag himself even an inch because of
his terror at the sight of the bone sticking out of his leg. What
he was doing was throwing curses at a circling bird, come as
malign spirit, flapping and gloating.

"Poor Simus," cried Mary, letting herself down in the mud to
hold his head in her lap while Daniel stood gaping.

"Run quick to Jester Fox," Daniel said because on foot, by crossing the frozen creek, she would get there sooner than if she went out to the road and ran to find Frederick Jones. "Hurry, child! Just cross the creek where the ice is thick and you'll see a frame house." White stars or flecks of bones were swimming in Daniel's eyes and he lowered his head and took deep breaths while Mary squeezed the boy's hand and told him to be brave and then ran off, skirting the boggy ground as Simus and the horse should have done. "Please, God, let Jester Fox be home. Please save Simus and I will be nice to Ruth Boyd." Mary ran through trees, and when she got to the creek she skated across without falling. She was saving Simus. Saving Simus, who was pleasant to her even though her papa had made him a slave. "Please fetch us a rabbit for dinner," she'd tell him and he would go loping off although she had never seen him take an order from Ruth Boyd. A few days ago, he had made her an embroidery hoop and he said he would show her how to dye coloured threads. "Please, God, don't let his leg come off." She made up an incantation as she ran: "Save Simus save Simus save Simus." She felt bolder than she had ever felt.

Jester Fox was in his field with two workers. When he heard Mary yelling and saw her streaking across the stubbled stalks, he met her halfway, his face as red as his hair and covered in sweat that continued on into his curly beard and down his thick neck.

"I am Mary Amelia Dickinson and there is a bone coming out of Simus!" Mary gasped, taking firm hold of the neighbour man's jacket. Her face, too, was running with sweat but also with tears now that she heard what she was saying. In a minute, even her braids were salty and soaked.

Jester Fox nodded. "You run on up the house and get my girl, Bett. She can heal a stone."

Mary ran. She passed an outbuilding, not quite a barn. There were chickens in a coop, one cow, and two pigs. There was a lamb behind a fence and there was a redheaded boy carrying a pail.

From a distance, Jester Fox yelled, "Tell Bett to take her healin bag!"

When Mary reached the house with its two glass windows, she knocked on the door and waited on the porch. It had a steamy feel to it, she thought, until she felt that it was her skin that was steaming, and her breath. "I am Mary Amelia Dickinson," she blurted when the door was opened. "Will you come with me because there's bone sticking out of a leg at our place?"

Bett was darker by a shade than Onesimus, who was dark as night. Her wide-set eyes assessed Mary in an instant and she turned into the kitchen and came back with a large cloth bag, her dress covered by an apron, her hair by a handkerchief. Mary was pumping her knees, practically jumping up and down with impatience, and she reached for Bett's hand. It was a mile and a half they had to run and they stayed close together, their feet striking the wet earth in similar black boots, left right left in the same rhythm. Saving Simus saving Simus.

The two running girls ran on into the field and beyond it through prickly bushes that snapped at their arms and legs. They did not stop to speak to Bett's master or the field work-ers, who were also slaves. Their feet pounded at the ground. They slid across the creek and ran on through the mud that was stickier now than it had been and sucked at their boots but they pulled them up and out and kept on running, running. Mary was panting but she did not hear Bett take in or let out breath. Her legs ached. Her shoes were too tight. One braid had come loose. She did not stop until Bett was crouched over Simus with a curled-down look on her face.

Both Daniel and the wounded boy looked at her in surprise. "But where is Jester Fox?" asked Daniel.

"Papa, this is Bett and she can heal a stone."

The boy did not move, but the cries he now made sounded animal strange.

Bett looked hard at the leg. She moved her hands just above it, then took a broken shoe off his foot and rolled him gently onto his side. By the time he finished screaming, she had cleaned the bone splinters out of the gash, tucked the bone inside its torn covering of skin, closed the opening using careful fingers, and asked for clean water from the creek. With that she began to make a clay paste out of the mud they were sitting in. She sent Mary for two pieces of wood that were thin and straight and commenced to humming in order to calm her patient.

Daniel had pulled himself up on his wobbly feet. He had been on his knees, quite unnoticed in the crisis of setting the leg, and he had watched Bett's skill with astonishment. While he stood over Simus, Mary carefully moved the boy's head onto a pillow of leaves and ran all the way back to the house site before Daniel could blink. She took up a thin piece of oak that had been hewn and set aside for pegs all the while feeling she was breathing a stranger's breath, watching what happened around her through a stranger's eyes.

In the clearing, Bett drew a flat bandage from her bag. It had been cut into tails on both sides and these she lapped across the front of the leg. Next, the clay paste and finally, when Mary came back, the splints. These were tied with straps while Mary held the boy's head in her lap again and brushed her fingers across his closed eyelids.

Daniel's plan was to get the boy up to the house site, where he could be kept dry and fed, but Bett said firmly that it mustn't be that way. "His leg must just set now, sir, for a number of days without jostling. Best put up a shelter," she instructed while she rummaged in her bag and then brought out a tin full of powder and a bottle that gave off a smell when she loosened its cork. She mixed powder and liquid in a tiny tin cup from her bag and told Simus to swallow it. "All up."

Daniel went back to the house site while Mary marched through the timber lot looking for pieces of wood. All around were the sounds of the forest, for the sun was angled and the trees were hospitable to living things. They were alive now with almost returning spring, and the boy who was going to help build a house for them was lying in the timber lot and she had found him and saved him and her heart was light.

D aniel looked at his hands as if anything they touched would break. He knew a moment of self-pity but swallowed it back. Since Rebecca had gone . . . had died . . . had disappeared into her grave . . . nothing, ever . . . He was sorry to be thinking of the two hundred and fifty dollars he needed and the house to be built instead of the injured boy and his pain. He was sorry to be thinking of his unsheltered children who would lack a house as well as a mother here in Virginia when there was a boy lying on icy cold ground down in the timber lot with a shattered leg. He was sorry he had come to Virginia, although what choice did he have? The Elders had drawn the new map of his ruined life when an unschooled Methodist girl had offered the only help in sight. "What do we do now?" she asked him as he sat with his head in his hands, but it was that part of afternoon when birds and animals and men have nothing to say.

"Read to me from the manual," Ruth told him, tucking a piece of hair behind her ear and picking up the axe. "Tell me how to start."

"You cannot build a house, Ruth Boyd."

"You will have the good of four hands and one head."

"You don't credit yourself with a brain?"

"I didn't name whose head, did I?" Ruth looked at the bare ground where their boots – two large and two small – were moored side by side. Her stockings were torn inside her boots and there was skin visible, but she tucked her feet back and watched a beetle crawl up the pile of thin rocks that held the house frame. She thought what a long way it was for the beetle and yet to her it was nothing. She thought then that there was no one single truth, even in size. Daniel handed her the book. She said, "You read while I cut notches."

"Only to cut off your hand."

"Or my nose to spite my face." Ruth laughed a little and even nudged him gently.

Daniel began with the words that described the hewing of notches. He said she could try to do that while he went to check on the boy. Ruth did not like the boy and would not venture close to him. Ruth picked up the axe, which was not very big, and Daniel went to the clearing, where he found Mary and Simus squeezed inside a shelter of sticks. "Mary Amelia, what business has thee . . . have *you* . . . down here? Take yourself up to the house this minute!"

"We have no house," said Mary. "Not anymore."

Daniel kicked at the flimsy shelter and the boy covered his head with an arm while the sticks came tumbling down on him and Mary scrambled out of the way. "I gathered all of that," she said crossly.

Daniel thought for just a moment. "And who do you suppose is looking after your little brothers and your sister? Where is Jemima just now, and that rascal Benjamin? It is your job to keep track of them all. The boys are to keep the fire and you must watch them to be sure they manage. They are not . . . country lads . . . after all." He was watching Mary and, out of the side of one eye, seeing the boy on the ground surrounded by sticks. This was no place for his Mary to be loitering. He turned to look straight at Simus, who was staring up at him, frightened. "Isaac is to gather the wood . . ." Daniel muttered, feeling sorry he had frightened the boy and a little ashamed of himself. "Benjamin, the kindling . . ." his words trailed off.

Mary got up, brushed twigs and sticks off her dress, and began walking away without a glance back. Always, he left her in charge of the others, and she continually failed to satisfy him. Now she would not let him see that she felt the sting of his words. She would not remind him of the way she had run to the Fox place to save a boy who was lying alone on the dirt with a leg snapped off. In order to show that she would never hurry – not for little children who were healthy and fine when here was a boy who had nearly died – her walk was slow and indignant, almost a trudge. Nobody to look after poor Simus and his brother lost forever to a Tennessee slave trader while he was stuck in the frightening woods like bait and where was Ruth Boyd? Wasn't she hired to look after the little ones? Wasn't she the reason they had come to this nasty place where boys were made into slaves?

"Father," she said that evening when the younger children were in bed with Ruth and she and her father were sitting close to the outside fire. Father. It was the name she rarely used, preferring Papa, which was affectionate. "Who made Simus a slave?" She was mending her hem with white thread and the stitches were crooked because of the lack of light and she kept her voice low although she was once again furious.

"The institution is as old as time, Mary Amelia," her father answered sadly.

"Old as time? That isn't scientific."

"Child, slavery was known to the ancient Hebrews and is spoken of in the Bible. In Rome, there were house slaves and farm slaves. Virgil writes of them living in Mantua."

"Simus is not Roman, though. And we are abolitioners."

"Simus is safe here with us, I can promise you." Daniel stared at his daughter, who was sitting cross-legged on the ground by the fire. "Although a Quaker does not make a vow," he admitted with a sly smile. "Does he?" Over them an array of stars shone so brightly that the embers on the ground hardly counted for light as Mary pushed the needle in and out of her torn hem. Daniel stretched his legs. "I doubt that Simus knows the name of his ancestral home and he will surely never see it again so we must take care of him."

Mary said, "That's what I was trying to do," but she said it under her breath. She thought of her lessons at school in Pennsylvania. *Who inhabit Western Africa?* Answer: *Numerous Negro Tribes in a barbarous condition.* She said, "But who brought him here?"

Daniel remembered suddenly that the slaves in Virgil's province had been interred in rich tombs. He said, "I did. And before me, it was someone who sails to Africa to trade goods for men. As you learned in school last year. About the Indians and how they couldn't do useful things for the colonists, remember? So then Africans were brought to Virginia to raise things like tobacco and rice. We cannot farm without labour. And we must farm to survive."

"Although we never did before."

Daniel took off his hat and scratched his neck. He ran his hand over his chin and decided it was time for another shave. He was getting careless. And his daughter was showing quick intelligence. "Ah, Mary . . ." The boys were young enough that they didn't wonder at things or question him. They were sorry Simus had hurt his leg. They mentioned him now and then, but they did not go into the timber lot, which was dreary and dark.

"Thee should give up thy Quaker hat," said Mary, "if thee is no longer an abolishoner."

"Abolishonist. And I will give up my hat when I can afford a better."

"Like violinist. Like gardenist. When you can afford a better hat, you will buy back Miss Patch, who you traded for Simus." Mary bit off the thread and inserted the needle in her apron at the shoulder, where she could be sure to find it. She wished she could say goodnight to her new friend, who would be frightened down there in the timber lot lying on his back with his leg wrapped in straps and clay so that he couldn't move. He had such a fear of snakes. He said he dreamed of vipers that wore masks. Mary said she would tell him the story of Aeneas so that he would feel brave, although her father wouldn't let her take the book outside for it was delicate. She would read a chapter every morning and then retell it while Simus lay in the shelter Daniel had built by hauling a bundle of house logs down to him in the wagon cover and arranging them back and forth using nails, which she had not had when she built the first shelter. Nor had she had the canvas to use as a roof, weighed down with rocks. And she was only trying to be kind or what her father would call compassionate when he remembered what mattered in this world.

At the door of the lean-to, Mary turned and looked at him. She watched him take back the fire and stretch out in its warmth, but even as she watched, she was thinking of Simus, whose shelter sat so crookedly in the distance, a dark shape in the dark.

Dear Taylor Corbett, Sincer thanks for the letter carried here by a person with a wagon loded full to the sky but I think ours looked as strange as that and the letter now I keep under my pillow to warm me at night. Can it be my school is performing Shakespear while here I only teach my pupil to read. He fell and broke his hole leg. It was terrible to watch his awful suffring. I wish I could come back to Brandywine, if I could. Please bid my Christian love to Caroline, although she does not write a word of love to

Mary Dickinson April 25, 1799

When Mary told Simus about the wooden horse and the ships that sailed away from Troy to find a new home, he said, "Like I," and she wondered if he had sailed from Africa to Virginia. She told him about Hector and Achilles. "Everyone loved Hector," she said. "He was more brave than any man."

Simus disagreed. "You say to me that Aeneas carry his father on his back to leave Troy and make a new home. That is more brave."

That night, while the children sat around the rough puncheon table Daniel had built, Mary told them that Simus thought the Trojan horse had wings. "But that one is Pegasus," Benjamin said and even Jemima laughed, although she didn't know what it was that they found funny. She loved the story of the flying horse. Daniel levelled a stern gaze at Mary. "Why mock the boy?" he asked. "Is it for this that you provide him with stories?"

Mary studied her plate. The boys were giggling again but it was in nervousness.

The scene worried Daniel during much of the night along with the thought that he had brought his children into a sense of superiority through the purchase of an unlettered boy. "You surely want your freedom," he said to Simus the next day. "And I wish to offer it. But you must help me earn two hundred dollars first or how will I get my horse again? I cannot make such a sum alone. Do you see?" It seemed that the Lord would only help those who could find devious ways to help themselves. "For the present, you will mend your broken bone and merely cut pegs. But when the leg is healed, you will go out to work for others in the evenings. That way we will earn cash . . . have an income . . . and . . ." Daniel would have the money required to redeem Miss Patch and it would be possible to free the slave boy. Pleased with this idea, arms folded across his chest, he waited for the boy to react.

But Simus said nothing. Knowing Daniel had paid too much for him and knowing that half the amount paid would be beyond his ability to earn in the span of his life. What was there to say? "Full day pay two bits," he finally replied.

"Well then, Simus, when our corn comes in, you will pull the fodder and sell it. There are plenty of people with animals to feed. We have only the one cow."

"Lessen you git some pigs. You gon need meat come the cole nex yer." The lying-down boy braced himself on his elbows and looked at Daniel, who was crouched at the entrance of his log pile shelter.

"How would I feed pigs when I barely feed my children?" Daniel got lower in the crouch and peered around the canvas door that Simus said a bear could go through or a snake. Suck my blood and bite my head, he said. Now he screwed up his face. "Hog fatten hissef up on acorn and hickry. He root in dis wood. Don you know it?"

"That does not bring back my horse."

"Pigs can be sole when fat."

"You could look after them? Even while the leg heals?" Daniel began to imagine the boy out in the world, working his way along from one job to another. Simus would be free and he would be the cause of it. Slavery need not be a lifelong sentence.

The boy said, "I kin do with Isaac hep. And make pegs mentime. And sell off meat come fall. Sell off meat to free Onesimus." He grinned.

Daniel had not much insight into the raising and killing of animals, but he thought he had an asset in Simus, after all. He went off in the wagon that afternoon, taking Isaac and Benjamin because it was good, at such times, to be surrounded by enthusiasm and a blessing not to have to meditate in solitude while branches and shadows converged on his mind. At the trading post owned by Silas Murray, he was told of a farmer who had piglets. It would be a long ride.

Virgil had written of horses and dogs and bees and cows but he'd said nothing of pigs. He'd also said nothing of daughters, and this was another subject on which Daniel needed advice. Lately, Mary had seemed distracted. Perhaps it was her age. Perhaps she was missing her schoolmates. Perhaps it was time to put her to serious work teaching Isaac, who needed schooling. Even Benjamin was ready for an alphabet. While he considered this, Daniel allowed the two boys to sit next to him on the riding board, although it was somewhat dangerous. Children had been known to fall off. But Isaac and Benjamin were soon bouncing and shouting and helping him hold the reins as Mulberry picked up her pace. Her ears flicked and twitched at the boys' laughter and at the trees singing on both sides. Trees do sing, Daniel thought, being full of birds at the first signs of spring.

At sundown, they came to a cabin that stood alone with no fields discernible. Daniel saw girded trees but no clearing.

"It be the Indian technique," said the owner of the cabin, whose grey hair hung limp on his shoulders and whose face, under a coonskin cap, looked like something known to the elements. "And the dangdest thing," he went on. "For as the girdled tree takes its time to die, it sure do loose its leaves so plantin can be done right underneath without the bother of cuttin limbs and choppin trunks and pullin out stumps. It saves a heap a human labour." Taking Daniel and the boys around to the back of his cabin, he aimed his forefinger at a pen with a sow and ten piglets. "They be ready for any leavins you create," he said, slapping Daniel on the back and patting Isaac's thin shoulder. "Yep, they eat up our sins, for sure. Pig be man's best friend as I make it out. Not dog. Unless you like to eat dog." He gave a hearty laugh and poked at the sow with his boot.

Isaac saw that the poke was friendly and he grinned. He had taken a liking to this wild man and his unwild pigs who ate up sin.

"Watch out! They savour flesh." The old man laughed again.

All the coins Daniel had brought were borrowed from Ruth and he intended to pay them back even before he paid his other debts. "Ruth," he had said, neglecting, for once, to use her full name, "when you were in my employ, there was some payment. Is there any of it left?"

Ruth had gone to the homespun pouch in which she carried everything she owned. In it there was a comb, a needle, a dish with a picture of a ship, eight hairpins, and a linen envelope. Her eyes had been bright as she opened the envelope. It held coins in the amount of five precious dollars. It was more than Daniel had expected, but he took all of it.

Now the two men made a business of quibbling. The old man was no crook, but he took Daniel for a man with no understanding of pig value. Daniel knew that Quakers were sometimes defrauded of their money since they were unable to swear to the fact of theft in court. A Quaker cannot take an oath. Nevertheless, while the boys put hands into the pen and stroked soft, pink, shivery bellies and backs, he paid out the whole of Ruth's saved-up money, rubbing each coin as he brought it out of the linen envelope and thinking of Rebecca, who would be shaking her head if she could see him in this circumstance. At night he heartily missed the feel of her under the quilts. Those long legs sheathed in cotton. Sleeping in the wagon alone, he wrestled with the thought of it, trying to understand how the source of such comfort could be rotting in a grave, trying not to picture it. For twelve years he had come home to her every day with a sense of accomplishment. Their expenses were few, a bit of rent money on the house and their supplies, and she was always pleased by his efforts. There was no need to save. In a Quaker community, prices were fair; tradesmen were honourable; children were taught to trust everyone. But without community, nothing was easy to understand. Now, when Isaac and Ben climbed back into the wagon, they had four piglets loose between them. The wagon began to move and the old man called out, "I hear tell Mister Shoffert's land is going up for sale."

Daniel showed no interest. The Shoffert land abutted his own near the boundary he shared with Jester Fox. Driving away, he took another look at the old man's trees. Most of them had been stripped to the bone by the width of a fist. "Look, boys," he said to his sons, pointing at the girding, "and see that this man is growing his food without clearing so much as a garden plot. Now I ask, what nourishment can he expect?"

A piglet is a shivering, rooting, ornery thing and heartbreaking to its beholder. When four of them were carried down to Simus in the timber lot, his face broke into the first smile Mary had seen there. She had spent the afternoon telling him a story. "There was a father who loved his two children," she had begun it, "although both of them were boys." With that, she had wanted Simus to laugh because sons are a bother and brothers are worse. Then she remembered his brother lost to the Tennessee slave trader and felt sorry and said that the father in the story loved his sons and gave both of them coins and one of them was very good but the other ran away and spent every cent.

"Jes like Onesimus in de Bible run. And Mister Aeneus for his place."

I shall be a schoolteacher, Mary thought, because she was proud of her pupil's quick response. She was glad to have an effect on him, to brighten his view of the world. It was surely compassion, what she was showing, and she was enjoying every bit of it. I will go back to Pennsylvania as soon as I can, where people appreciate an education, she said to herself while Simus sat with his injured leg propped up on a log, his face full of concentration. He was whittling a knot of oak that kept his hands occupied. Inside an hour, he had made the knot into a head with a fine-featured face. He had carved onto the head curls that moved with the grain of the wood, and when Mary stopped her story to admire it, he said, "It be yourn if yun sew it a body, Miss Mary."

Mary did not like dolls. She, who had a new baby brother and toddling sister, thought dolls were lifeless things. Who would dress up a piece of wood when there was a real baby crying to be carried and a little sister in the hammock waiting to be pushed? "This girl is of the oak race," she said. "Carve her out some hands and feet so she can feel and walk."

Simus rubbed the nose and eyes and chin of the doll's head with his thumb. "Oak race," he repeated, and he learned about the father's love for his two sons although one of them was prodigal and wondered about his lost brother. Then the four piglets arrived, carried down by Daniel and Isaac and Benjamin, and the smile unfolded itself. It was easy enough to build an enclosure for little pigs, Simus said, for they had only a few inches of legs to climb up and out with. What worried him was fortification against bears and wolves and snakes. He decided to keep the pigs with him at night. "For ta grow fatn make us fat too."

In this fashion, spring began to announce itself. Geese and ducks returned from farther south, filling the sky with noise. Robins pecked at the ground, bushes and trees dressed themselves in bright colours, wild flowers sprang out of the fields, and the smell of the land was inviting. The sparrows, as Mary had predicted, built little nests and laid pretty eggs, though the robin eggs were best. Ruth gathered dandelion greens. Jemima carried the oak doll around by hanging on to a leg. Joseph began to crawl more evenly on the warming ground, and Daniel bought, with his two remaining warrants, a hundred and seven acres of Michael Shoffert's rolling land. "Most of it I will sell," he told the family. "Jester Fox will be keen, as the Shoffert land surrounds him on two sides."

"And another side is us," Ruth said with some satisfaction.

"With Frederick Jones on the fourth, Jester Fox is surrounded," Daniel agreed, then added, "I must make him a fair price."

On a hot day in May he walked the perimeter of the new land, touching the rough trunks of elms and sugar maples. Then he examined the lands' interior, where there was a small, deep pond and a locust tree so tall and dark and thorny it rose above the others like an ominous sovereign. Its furrowed, scaly bark had untold history stored in its pores, but its branches bore fragrant flowers now, in the spring. St. John's Bread, the tree was called because the saint had survived on locust pods and honey in the wilderness, and Daniel remembered that locust pods had also fed the prodigal son in his servitude, and they had been fed to pigs in Virgil's time. Historic tree! He would reach up, pluck a few flowering stems, and carry them home to the cabin as proof of his purchase. With his arms extended, he wondered if the old tree had stood there before human beings ever came to this meadow, if it had stood over the migrating herds he'd described to the children on their long journey across Virginia. In the autumn, the pods would be musical instruments played to the other trees and the thought of such a rattling symphony made Daniel laugh and the sound of his laugh blew out against the surrounding silence.

The Shoffert place had no access by road. And it will be the devil to clear, Daniel thought irreverently, but Shoffert had bought this land to sell and Daniel had obliged him with his last two warrants. Shoffert would use Daniel's warrants to buy another piece of land to sell and each sale would make a profit, which was the way of the new frontier. He touched the rough trunk of the tree. Perhaps the pleasure he felt derived from his solitude, he thought, turning his horse along a rise that was furred with pines. Even as a child, he had been always crowded, always admonished. He remembered a table, a line of heads, hands kept firmly in lap, tongues behind hard, clenched teeth. He remembered eyes turned down. He so seldom thought of his sisters or brothers or childhood friends. Friends. Every breath. Friends. Right-thinking, dutiful. Not like Daniel, whose livelihood now depended on the milking of cows and the raising of pigs, which, though not ruminating, are said to be a link between the herbivorous and carnivorous animals. He laughed again. The omnivorous pig was apparently capable of converting almost anything into nutriment, according to his manual. And although in the Mosaic Law the pig is condemned as unclean, there was apparently no domestic animal so profitable. Daniel's sows might bear two litters in a year, the breeding seasons being April and October. He leaned forward to pat Mulberry's damp neck and decided to butcher the boar in late September and to breed the sows to a different male, and it was good to think of the profit to be made in flesh, profit that would help bring back his chestnut mare, also made of flesh.

"That floor floats on the air," Ruth said one afternoon, pointing at a drawing in the manual. Now Daniel saw that book reading was not simply a matter of letters made into words. It was a whole way of looking at symbols and understanding them as such. He sighed and put down the post he was holding. Six months had passed since he had purchased Lot #3 in Jonesville, and yet, against the time needed for Ruth to grow into adulthood, this long winter and spring would be as nothing. He rubbed his finger across the words as if to erase them. "Who is watching after my children?"

Ruth thrust out her lower lip, turned fast, and walked away. There was no need for such investigation on Daniel's part. Baby spent his afternoons in a hammock she had strung up between trees. If insects bothered him, she wrapped a piece of cheese-cloth around the hammock and hoped for a breeze. Sometimes Jemima liked to rock him, although Benjamin had to be kept from rocking him too hard. Which sometimes she overlooked because Benjamin was her favourite and she had a lenient way with him. He was the only one of the children ever to come to her. During "the crossing," as she thought of it, he had leapt into her lap and since then he had clung to her, even nuzzling up against her in the bed at night and staying by her every morning. But at noon, he and Isaac went down to the timber lot with Mary, delivering dinner to the boy who lay on his back with his broken leg up on a log. And what a waste of a horse the trade for that boy had been.

Ruth did not know that Mary told the boys to follow the pigs into the woods the minute they got to the timber lot. She did not know that Mary then forgot her brothers entirely and only applied her vigorous program of instruction to Simus, who listened so ardently. Mary's instruction consisted of introducing Simus to one new word each day and then stringing the words together into something resembling sentences, although she found that he did best with nouns – things he could touch and feel. *Stone, pig, boy, acorn, tree.* With the help of drawings, these were words he quickly learned to read. Verbs, adjectives, and adverbs were much harder, since she had no way to make a picture of bigness or highness or slowness. Whenever she tried, he grew impatient and even laughed at her. Well, his hands were not idle during his learning process anyway. Listening all the while, he used a drawknife to make octagonal house pegs because Daniel insisted on this odd shape. "No doubt dbook tellm so," Simus scoffed, but he came to see that Daniel and the book were right: an octagonal peg held the joists fast. Simus fashioned pegs and Daniel and Ruth applied them to the hewn beams and then to the logs, and by early summer the house had four right-angled sides.

"Mary is with the boy again," Ruth once complained to Daniel because the friendship chafed at her like scratchy cloth. "Teachin him to read when he should be harder workin."

Daniel wondered if he allowed Mary to go on teaching Simus precisely because it proved his tolerance. Ruth might well go to Prayer Meeting every day of the week but she would never come up to his fineness of feeling with regard to Simus. And it would not hurt the boy to learn to read simple lists and perhaps even make his signature since he would one day be free. Isaac would provide inspiration, for he was a clever student. In fact, Daniel was bound to prove Ruth's narrow opinion wrong by allowing Mary to go where he would prefer she didn't go, although this pride in his own emancipated view would have been harshly addressed by the Quaker Elders if he had not been disowned from their fellowship.

Once or twice Daniel walked down to the timber lot after dark, when everyone else was clammed together in the bed, and on those occasions he heard Simus talking to himself in a whispered voice. Perhaps he was memorizing the alphabet or saying his prayers. Or talking to spirits only such as he could see? Daniel did not believe the listening he did was unworthy. He believed that he was the boy's protector, although Simus seemed oddly content now sticking to the timber lot with the piglets who were fast growing into pigs. The boys, Simus said, were not yet strong enough, not yet even growed enough to manage those pushing, snorting animals. They were growing alongside them but not so fast, Simus said, when Daniel announced that the bone was surely healed enough now to bear his weight with the aid of a crutch and that they must begin work on shingles for the house roof. It was then that Simus admitted that he had not been entirely truthful when he said he had never done any house building. He had helped his mother build their cabin in the quarters, he said. He was ashamed of his efforts, however, and knew every inch of his failing. "Yesar. My mam never knowed a night without rain or stick fallin to her head." Simus concluded that his master must be regretting the day he had bought so useless a slave.

Daniel said kindly, "You will follow my directions, Simus. And in the evenings you will please me and plant out my corn."

"Miss Root dun plantit out," Simus replied.

"No, Simus, of course she did not as she would first have to borrow a plow."

"She plantit wid a pokey stick down da hollow where she strippin trees."

Turning fast, Daniel ran out of the timber lot toward the hollow. "Ruth Boyd!" It was too much to bear, the utter and futile waste of his family's provision after his lecture about the loss of garden seeds. "Ruth Boyd!" After months with his family, logic was as foreign to her as Latin. Daniel stopped, put his hands on his thighs, and leaned over to breathe. She is a child still, he reminded himself. But. Then. She is older than Mary by two years. Would Mary take such thoughtless advantage? He commenced to running again, thinking that even fodder would be lost to his cow and pigs. Everything he had hoped for. Because he had married Ruth Boyd. Because his father had been correct. *Thee must find a proper mother for thy orphans.* And the Elders, who had refused to speak to him and turned away from him in the street, who had even barred the door to the Meeting House when he came there on First Day – they also were right. And when they refused to open the school door to his children, lest there be contagion due to the Methodist in their midst, they were right again! Ruth Boyd was a contagion, a spoiler of things. Still running, still panting, he tried to discern which sin it was that he had committed in marrying her. Neither greed nor sloth nor envy . . . but he had not wanted to accept advice. Like the prodigal, he had ridden away from his parents' home without looking back. Marrying Ruth had been an act of pride, and life provided no opportunity to take back his mistake. His children would go hungry. His animals would starve. As he reached the hollow, which bordered the creek downstream, he saw his child bride bent over a line of green sprouts. Daniel pulled to a halt, took a deep breath, and shouted, "Ruth Boyd! What are you doing there?"

When Ruth looked up, she was smiling.

Dear Grandmother Dickinson,
We name the bean sprouts which are like friends because
we have no others and we eat them or dry them to plant
for next year because we are farmers now. My papa is
a farmer. And with no teacher, no school, no friends or
Mother I wish I could live with my grandparents where
I could be helpful and of use and provide cheer from
*   Mary Dickinson June 1799*

Isaac and Benjamin followed the pigs while Mary sat with Simus, telling him about Aeneas or David and Goliath or anyone she could think of who might interest him. She drew pictures on her little slate and wrote words above them. *Hero. Horse. Ship.* Then she put the slate away and lay on the ground next to him and told him about the beautiful city of Carthage where Dido long ago lived as a queen. She told him that Aeneas loved Dido and was altogether happy with her but that he sailed away in his ship.

"How he can do it?"

"Aeneas must find a place for his people to be free. They do not want Dido for a queen."

When Simus did not find this explanation satisfying, Mary told him the story of Joseph and his many-coloured coat, explaining that Joseph was also a slave. She told him about the sin of envy while Simus used the drawknife to make good roof pegs.

In July, Daniel rode to the Jones place. It was hot and he urged Mulberry to trot so that he could feel some wind on his face. He approached his neighbour without removing his hat or signalling a greeting, and Frederick Jones stopped hoeing and turned to take in Daniel's straight shoulders and the long fingers that twitched and jerked over his chest as if he were counting. "I have gathered enough stones now," said Daniel abruptly, "for the chimney that is to be added to my house." Then he remembered himself. "Good morning," he added. "I am growing unused to civility."

Jones chuckled. "A chimney is no addition but necessity," he said kindly, reaching out to pat Daniel's long leg. The German settler's brow was red from the sun, and he took off his neck scarf and put it over his head, giving himself the look of an old woman when he bobbed his head. "And how be those rooting pigs?"

Daniel shrugged. "They are fine, Frederick Jones, but the angle of the flue . . . on the chimney, you see. I cannot leave it to chance." He looked at the chimney on the Jones house. "Did you and your son build that? It looks to be very fine. Does it draw well?"

Jones clutched his hoe and stirred it a little in the soil. "No, sir. No . . . We did not build such a fine chimney piece. My boy is only good as a hunter of game. And pretty girls. The new world, it spoils him for other working. It is Mister Fox over just to the north is the stone man. Irish as he is, and built my chimney making no smoke to come in the house. He would do for you the same if you was to pay him by a pig. You got a roof on yet?"

Daniel said he was ready to make shingles. Did Frederick Jones own a shingle knife? And Frederick went off to find it while Daniel sat on his horse thinking his thoughts. When Frederick Jones handed the shingle knife over, he told Daniel again to speak to Jester Fox. "A piglet in the autumn will sure to make the deal."

That evening Daniel told Ruth that he was going to sell the cow. "I have to think of the roof now," he said. "For shingles, we must have nails."

Ruth said, "Your children need milk more'n shingles."

Daniel said, "They need a roof over their heads."

"There are men without wives who would buy butter if we had a churn," said Ruth, staring him down, hands on her narrow hips and lips thrust out. "Also wives who are too lazy to churn."

Daniel hitched Mulberry to the wagon and drove into town, where Silas Murray's trading post operated out of the front portion of his house. When he returned to his family, he growled at Ruth. "A churn is beyond our means. I have nothing to trade for it but the cow."

That Saturday, Ruth built a fire and boiled water in the cooking pot. Until now, she and Mary had seen to their own washing, going down to the cold creek furtively with a bit of soap to scrub clothes while they scrubbed themselves. Ruth had never asked Daniel if she could wash for him, but now she told him to bring his shirts and trousers. Mary had good reason to keep her laundry to herself, for some of it was spotted with blood. Was she dying the way her mother died? She was afraid to ask. But fifteen-year-old Ruth would not have had an opinion. Her body was immature and her mind was uninformed. She brought her small pile of clothing outside – all but the linsey dress she was wearing and the bloomers under it. The pile consisted of two brown aprons with plain bodices, a pair of bloomers, a shift, a pair of stockings, and one overskirt. She had already collected the children's things.

Daniel was lying under the wagon out of the sun and he watched Ruth wipe her face with one of the boy's filthy shirts. Then he rolled away from the wagon and stood up stiffly, reaching into the bed of the wagon and handing Ruth three cambric shirts and his collars. He handed her a pair of woollen breeches and his extra stockings. Ruth said, "S'posed to be a pastor come Sundee."

Daniel now offered a misunderstanding: "We shall take the wagon then," is what he said. He did not say that he would merely drop Ruth at the door of the cabin where the pastor was going to preach. He did not say that what he knew about preaching did not accord with any spiritual example, that the more he heard of such sermonizing, the more Quaker he felt. He did not say that a pastor was a priest and to be avoided.

The next morning he changed into his clean clothes so as to drive Ruth to the Sharpes' cabin, where the sermonizing would take place. He kept a small piece of silvered glass in the wagon, well away from Mary, who might be tempted to look on herself with interest. The mirror had belonged to Rebecca and now he used it to shave and to trim and comb his hair, asking Mary to see that his collar was put straight. Then he stood forth in his clean clothes, having brushed his hat.

Ruth came out of the lean-to with something sure in her stride as she got herself into the wagon without his aid, tying the ribbons of her straw hat under her chin. She had washed her long hair along with the family clothes and it was pulled into a tight knot through the use of several pins. Daniel clucked at Mulberry as they set out, meaning it as a sign to Ruth that he had noticed her efforts. They were alone together for the first time since the hour he had driven her home from the Methodist Church in Brandywine. No wonder they were aware of themselves, of their newly clean clothes and unfamiliarity. "It is a nice hat," he said.

Ruth looked out at the landscape she had not really seen, having been bound to the lean-to for several months. All winter she had been pasted, glued, cemented to Daniel's six acres. Now they were going out.

Daniel remembered travelling to the Meeting House for First Day worship with his family, all of them snug in the carriage, with Miss Patch snorting proudly as they passed other carriages, carts, and buggies. Men would nod and women barely smile. Children were less inhibited, waving and calling out. What contentment used to fill him at such times. He glanced down at the child he had married. For mercy, if nothing else.

Ruth smiled up at him. Nice hat, he'd said. Well then, if he had forgotten that this was the hat she'd been married in, why so he had and what of it, for at that time hadn't he been full of earned grief? She listened to the wheels against the chalky road. A ping of gravel, a shush of sand. Then, in the unbuilt town, Mulberry was pulled to a halt and Ruth stood up in the swaying wagon bracing her legs.

"Wait," Daniel commanded lightly. "Until I hand thee down."

Sitting back quickly, Ruth made as if to smoothe her hair, although it was well tucked under her hat. No one had taught her etiquette. Orphans grew up to be kitchen maids or seamstresses or field hands. When Daniel got out and put his hand up for hers, the confidence she'd felt during the long ride disappeared. At that moment, coming down over the wheel, she was bare of everything. Who, after all, was Ruth? What beliefs did she own? What talents or thoughts? She remembered the landscape of her earliest childhood, but not the faces, not the voices, not the events. Sometimes she tightened every muscle of her mind and tried to bring some part of that formative infancy back, but aside from the smell of apple trees in spring, and the feel of clay between her toes, and the strange song of the almshouse mockingbirds, there was nothing on which to build a history. Sometimes in the dark of night, she thought she remembered being tied to a tree so as not to run.

"Take my arm," commanded Daniel, and he saw that she was not looking a minute older.

"This must be Mister Dickinson with his daughter," the pastor exclaimed, reaching out for Daniel's hand. The pastor was small and pink and nicely rumpled. He was a man who rode the circuit of his parish to preach in a different house or cabin every Sunday. He dropped Daniel's hand and reached for Ruth's and shook hers up and down as if she were a child, which she was, and a daughter, which she was not. Daniel let the pastor's mistake stand uncorrected and began to back away, but the pastor grabbed hold of his sleeve and pulled him into the cabin where anyone who cared to pray – anyone but an Episcopalian – was welcome Sunday mornings. Daniel saw that Ruth should have brought a chair, except that they didn't own one. He began to perspire. He looked toward the door and shuffled his feet, longing to escape. Unless he left the confines of this one-room cabin, he would be held hostage to scriptural dictates. He looked around nervously, saw that the altar was merely a box laid with a plain white cloth, and began to relax very slightly. The plainness was welcome to him who had been raised in the precinct of a bare Meeting House and who had only during his marriage to Rebecca become accustomed to worship in a place of polished maple beams and a floor of waxed oak. He stood next to Ruth without uncovering his head as the five or six people who were sitting in the cabin stood up bareheaded and began to sing.

The hat drew glances, but it stayed.

After the hymn, the pastor pointed to the narrow door, which was open to the summer breeze. "Here is the door to salvation," he said with a lilt in his voice, "although each one of you has been found guilty and sentenced to death . . ." He leaned forward and moved his eyes from face to face. "Guilty," he said again. "But I tell you now, God may withhold this penalty if you enter here." The pastor next proclaimed himself a direct descendant of John the Baptist, and Daniel raised his sight to the window where the glass was thick and various and the natural world wavered. He thought of the warm silence of the Lancaster Quaker meeting. He remembered his father dozing in a corner, exhausted after a busy week. He remembered his brother kicking him repetitively in his shins, as if keeping beat to some secret music. He closed his eyes then and bowed his head, and when he clasped his blistered hands together, Ruth believed he must be praying. She had not attended the Friends Meeting House in Brandywine and had no idea how strange this public exhortation was to the man who had married her. "Not so long ago our brothers and sons and fathers were slain in battle," the pastor reminded his listeners, "so that we can be free! And do we use that sacred freedom to serve one another, as Galatians has directed us to do? No, we do not, brothers and sisters. No, we do not." He paused to wipe his brow, as if the facts he had stated were warming him past comfort. Pastor Dougherty was a small man with childlike hands that he waved as he spoke. His delicacy provided some fascination to his listeners, who were often spellbound by the waving of his hands and the rocking of his frame. Even so, his eyes blazed with religious passion. "We forget that Satan hopes to bring defeat and disgrace upon us. And we forget with zealousnous. Oh yes indeed, temptation is our daily bread, and as Jeremiah says, 'The heart is deceitful above all things and beyond cure.' But if you would struggle against Satan, I tell you now to take him captive. Make him your slave. Sin is no longer your master, for you no longer live under the requirements of the law. Instead, you live under the freedom of God's grace. Yea, brothers and sisters, you have escaped like a bird out of the fowler's snare . . ." The pastor held his arms up and spread them wide and for an instant Daniel thought of rushing into them. He had heard the line intoned here and there since childhood, but hearing it here, among these strangers, he felt slightly faint. "Do you not know," the pastor went on, "that Satan is the fowler and that you are the slaves of whom you obey, whether of sin that leads to death or of obedience that leads to righteousness? Have you deserved this great land that is opened for us by the blood of our fathers and brothers?" The pastor's arms fell and he looked again at each of them as Ruth looked at Daniel, whose shoulders were stiffly drawn up. Just then she was thinking that he had come all this way to a Methodist Prayer Meeting and that this, in itself, was remarkable. She was pleased. With Daniel. With herself. They had come out together. She touched the brim of her hat, to see that it was straight.

Outside, the pastor shook Daniel's hand again, and Ruth slipped away so that Daniel could explain that she was no child but a legal wife. She drifted over to the pastor's missus and spoke to her, and when Daniel next saw her she was waiting quietly at the wagon, hands clasped at her waist. "We can stop at the pastor's for a butter churn," she said with a pleased intake of breath.

"Now then, what have you done, Ruth Boyd?"

The Doughertys lived in a frame house four miles east. From it, the pastor covered a circuit of some fifty miles in the course of a month. He and his wife had given up their cow. "I haven't the time these days," Missus Dougherty had explained to Ruth, "and would be glad to buy butter." At the kitchen door, she invited the Dickinsons in, but they stood in a kind of supplication until she pointed to a shed where she stored the unused churn. "I could take five pounds on a weekly basis," she said proudly. "I so often send Mister Dougherty out on his travels with bread for the people who house him on his circuit and of course I like to bake for the church women."

Daniel went to the shed, which was a jumble of broken tools, barrows, the churn, and a milking stool. He put his head out and asked if they might . . . and held up the stool while Missus Dougherty nodded vigorously.

"We have only the one cow," Daniel reminded Ruth as they rode home with the churn rolling noisily in the wagon bed. "Although Tick is a fine Alderney, to be sure."

"A *fine* Alderney, to be *sure*," Ruth sniffed because even at the pastor's house Daniel had not seen fit to clarify her position. Miss Dickinson, she had been called, and again Daniel had not bothered to correct that mistaken impression.

At home Mary had been making a meal of pancakes. She had tried to make burnt sugar syrup and had succeeded well enough that the boys thought the churn must be something to celebrate. The family sat around the outdoor fire on this Sunday afternoon and ate pancakes and felt the sun bright and warm on their faces. Daniel leaned back on his elbows and stretched out his legs. He was growing accustomed to life on the ground, but he thought of Rebecca's way of sitting so very straight on a chair and that led him to a memory of her graceful, sliding walk and the way she had handed him his china plate and silver fork the day they met. Then he remembered that it was Luveen who had brought the plate and wondered why had he changed the truth of it. He must be careful about his memories and keep them pure. He must remember the lurch of pleasure he had felt in his breast, sitting across from Rebecca on her painted chair, and the way his gaze had travelled up her arm from wrist to shoulder and then to blue-eyed face. Their eyes had met and she had winked and all of it had happened in the space of the longest minute of his life. Whether cake or lace had been served, it had been done with a sly, teasing manner that had made him lonely for her before he had left her presence. For weeks after that, he had been in an agony that he had no name for, calling to mind her voice and gestures and a certain weather that seemed to encircle her. He believed that he had courted her diligently, and finally won her hand, having no idea that she had set her cap for him from the start or that her father had never been averse to the union. Daniel, younger than Rebecca by three years, was a second cousin to John Dickinson, who had signed the constitution and helped compose the first amendment. John Dickinson was now president of Pennsylvania and a worthy relation in any case. In terms of the family business, Daniel could be moulded. He would raise the children as living parts of God. But look at them, Daniel thought, sitting around a fire like Red Indians. He thought that if Rebecca were among them, she would be mortified by their sudden lack of station. Eating from their hands. Chewing with mouths open. And they had forgotten to pray. He looked at Ruth in her straw hat. All the way home, she hadn't spoken to him. Now she was sitting on a log with her legs stuck out in front of her laughing at something Benjamin was saying. He tried to imagine his beautiful wife – his *other* wife – in such a place as this. Sitting on a log . . . Then he saw the purple ribbon on Ruth's straw hat blow across her laughing face and felt a pang of surprising desire.

M ade of cedar staves and bound with smooth brass hoops, the churn was Ruth's first true possession and she carried it down to the creek and scrubbed it with sand, studying the lid with its hole in the centre and the smooth, round dash with its crossed wood staves. She filled the churn with water, seized the dash, and jolted it up and down, imagining all the gold that was to come. Gold to be turned into nails. Gold for Miss Patch. And a plow. The afternoon was warm and Ruth unbuttoned her dress and patted the creek water on her face and neck. The water was pleasure. The solitude was luxury. Looking around, she pulled the dress over her head, unbuttoned her boots, and took off her woollen stockings. Now, wearing only a shift and bloomers, she left the churn behind on the bank and stepped into the water, which was cold even in summer.

Never having been in a body of water larger than a tub, Ruth moved cautiously, feeling the chill move up her legs and numb them strangely. Under her bare feet the rocks of a thousand years rolled and she slipped and yelped as she lost her footing and went in up to her neck. The water was not very deep and she began to trust it slightly, feet still on the ground and moving upstream. Taking tiny steps, heart racing, feet clinging, she let the water push her back a little, then grabbed at the sand and stones with her toes and moved ahead slowly, hearing the rapids in the distance, pushing and gliding farther and farther from known safety.

A picture came to her for no reason. The poorhouse. Matron. Such a tall woman she had seemed to Ruth, with furrowed brow and pointing fingers. Yet Ruth had admired her. She bore herself from one place to another with such authority, making everyone around her seem small by contrast. Ruth would never be such a woman, as she had no height, no bravery. She put her mouth in the rushing water to drink and pretended she was a bird. Birds made ferocious melody. She listened, heard a mockingbird, and drank again. What song was he singing? Clouds flitted. Leaves trembled. The water was solid, hard as a wall. She moved along carefully, pushing against the current. It might have sent her shooting back to the beginning of everything except that she clung to the bed of the creek with her toes, amphibious. Holding time, holding place. I will never see Matron again, she thought. There was a pool under the rapids but she could not move against the rush of water to enter it. The rapids were becoming more and more decisive. Using her arms and feet, she tried to push, inch by inch, as if the destination mattered, cresting an underwater mound of rock where the water was speaking its multitudinous language. *Speak out*, she heard as she closed her eyes. The voice was whispery but clear in its meaning. She let her feet and legs float up to the surface outstretched. She lay back and opened her eyes, floating backward, staring at overhanging cottonwoods that doubled and tripled themselves on the water's surface. One bent branch held a shivering shape that made the leaves dance and Ruth studied that shape with a jangle of nerves almost ecstatic.

Speak out.

"There was someone in a tree talkin at me from above," she reported to Daniel when she had floated back to her skirt and shoes and bodice and cap and apron and dressed by the water's edge on the marshy bank. "Talkin and I never said a thing." She'd found Daniel in the company of Simus, looking at the four growing-up pigs.

"You were dazed by the cold of the water."

"It was saying for me to speak out, but why? What did it mean?"

Daniel stared at the pigs.

"It was a sweet voice, very natural but strange."

Simus sucked in his breath, hung his head, and said, "I prays." Or perhaps he said, "I praise."

Ruth said, "I was on the watertop and I don't know how to swim and I was held up." She saw that the boy was attentive to that, his look showing a new regard for her that allowed her to think, as she set out across the meadow, which had earlier been a bog and which was now covered in wild flowers, yellow and white and pink, that she had been visited by some unearthly form of grace. And it must have been for a reason, she thought. It must have been a message, she said to herself as she took up the churn without feeling its weight. Then she stopped in her tracks, listening to the boy's hobbling gait behind her. The sun was lowering in the sky and she dropped the churn and walked ahead while he stopped, picked up the churn, and followed her with his limp.

"We're to have nails," she said over her shoulder. "You get to makin shingles with Mister Jones's knife now." A slave was lower than an orphan, and this one limped behind her and when she got to the half-built house he put the churn down and waited while she sent Isaac to the box in the wagon to find the borrowed shingle knife. "Tonight you sleep out here longside your pa," she said to Isaac. "I need more space in the bed." She found the milking pail and went to Tick as she did every day at this time. She saw again in her mind the vision in the tree, dancing, jittery, and sat down on the milking stool with the thought of it in her head. She had been to church with her husband, met the pastor's wife, acquired a stool and a churn, and been visited by a presence that had spoken a message in words. *Speak out.* She laid her river-washed face against the cow's flank while her hands pulled at the teats and the teats released warm, yellow milk. The world was rearranged, dusted, and shined.

Standing against the wall of the lean-to, Simus said, "I to put all cream in the holy water before butter makin."

Ruth stared at him and saw that he was right, although she did not like his watching or his interference. She did not like his skin, which was night-coloured and unsavoury. She had never known a black man of any kind. She had known Luveen for a time, but that was different. She saw that this slave boy was drawn to participate in something that was hers alone, yet she acknowledged his reverence. Without his tears in the timber lot, she might not have understood the importance of the angel's words. Angel, it must have been. Finished with the cow she got up, pointed to the pail, then walked away while into a pitcher Simus poured enough milk for supper, then covered the pail with a cloth and took it away to cool. Tomorrow he would skim the milk and put the cream in the old Pennsylvania crock. The crock would be set between river rocks to make holy the cream inside.

Ruth was ready with five pounds of butter by the end of the week and there was still milk for the family. Would Daniel drive her to the pastor's? Daniel hitched Mulberry to the wagon and found an errand to do in town. "I was visited by an angel the other day," Ruth told the pastor's wife.

Missus Dougherty raised an eyebrow.

"At our creek, ma'am. And this here butter got cooled in the waters right under her wings. She was high up a tree, just restin for a bit." Ruth was surprisingly composed at this moment. Her unruly hair was shoved under a cap, and while her apron was somewhat stained, her face was without a single doubt.

Missus Dougherty put a finger in the butter and then in her mouth. "Well, it's tasty, I'll say that. But do not go boasting to the pastor of your angel, Miss Dickinson. It will get him riled up."

Ruth said, "*Missus* Dickinson, ma'am."

Missus Dougherty glanced at Ruth's waistline.

"I be married from a church and unspoiled to this day," Ruth assured her.

Missus Dougherty was to have a social gathering the next day, and there it was heralded that the young *Missus* Dickinson had been visited by a spirit of some kind on Sunday afternoon at Sawmill Creek where she lived married but as chaste as God had made her. "Untouched!" crowed the pastor's wife. "If you can imagine, and her husband must be passing strange." Bringing forth the biscuits she had made for the occasion, Missus Dougherty went on to say, "The preserves are mine, dear friends, but the butter was fanned by an angel's wings. A talking angel, apparently."

"Since when?" Missus Jones wanted to know. "I know that creek pretty good, I should think, and no such being has yet spoke to me."

Each of the five ladies who had gathered in the modest parlour put a pat of the butter on a biscuit. Each of them took a bite. "It is," Missus Sharpe then offered, "unlike other butters. Isn't it?"

"It's heavenly," said Missus Craig decisively and added, "Must be a Jersey cow. It was my husband who surveyed that land. And the creek." She nodded solemnly.

Missus Dougherty said, "We'll call it Heavenly Butter."

"Is that sacrilegious?"

"It's an adjective, Missus Craig."

"Healing and Heavenly. That might be better."

"She could start a going business."

Missus Jones fanned herself impatiently.

Missus Fox stood up. "Well, I'll say it right out. This is plain Dickinson mischief, is all it is. First, he bought the land from Mister Jones to squeeze us out and now Mister Dickinson and his little wife bought out Mister Shoffert and have us surrounded on all sides. Next he took our water access that you sold to him!" She directed a glare at Missus Jones. "And now this, about spirits! Ghosts in our water. As if any Christian could believe such heathen hokum meant only to scare us off our place altogether."

Missus Sharpe said with an edge in her voice, "An angel would not scare a Christian."

Missus Jones said, "You have the accessing to water, Missus Fox, and why should they want to scare a good neighbour away, if it is a good neighbour?"

Missus Dougherty began to fear that her party was dissolving in acrimony. She shook a finger at the gathered ladies to show her disappointment, but Missus Fox would not be stopped. "So as to get our land, which is smack in the middle of what they got from your husband and that Mister Shoffert, who has got no wife."

Missus Jones, the good German immigrant, looked at Missus Fox without a blink. She picked up her coffee, which was weaker in body than she liked, and took a good swallow of it to calm herself. What she knew of her Quaker neighbours was too little to make any meaning of their designs, but she had sometimes considered their plight with sympathy and now she put her cup in its saucer with a little clatter.

"They are stealing my house girl too!" said Missus Fox to prove her point.

Missus Dougherty said firmly, "Surely not. Missus Dickinson is raising up five orphans. She needs all the help we can provide."

"She has such an uncomplicated temperament," said Missus Sharpe cheerily. "I find it hard to imagine she has motives."

"And it's such nice butter," said Missus Craig.

"Made in a churn that was mine until last Sunday," Missus Dougherty noted, with a hint of warning to the doubters. "And I'm set to help her make a business of it. That was an inspired idea you had, Missus Craig."

Later that day, the pastor's wife took her buggy out to the Dickinson place, where the sight of three children playing listlessly in the hot shade confirmed the sympathy she had felt for the stepmother. The girl had taken on this horde while denying herself her husband's embrace. *Unspoiled*, she had said of herself. Chaste. And there she was on the very milking stool that had stood in the Dougherty shed unused for more than a year. Mister Dickinson was sawing a board and a darkie was shaving shingles by the unfinished house. A lump of infant lay in a hammock under a tree and a lass with dirty hair, stringy and uncombed, was chopping at the carcass of a rabbit that lay on a board across her knees. None of this was immediately surprising to Missus Dougherty, but she saw that there was no proper house and noticed that the family was entirely bereft of adults except for the young father, since even the darkie was merely a tall, limping boy.

She had come in a buggy and was still sitting in it when Daniel put down his saw and approached. An odd fellow, she thought, to marry a girl so young, who can hardly be useful to him. Missus Dougherty allowed Daniel to help her out of the buggy, saying that she wished only a few scant words with his wife. Holding her skirt up in one hand, she said, "I mistook her for a child, Mister Dickinson, but I was wrong in that."

Daniel brought her over to Ruth and left them together, and Missus Dougherty told Ruth that she was making up a stack of waxed papers for the sale of Ruth's butter and that she was lettering these papers with the words HEALING & HEAVENLY.

Ruth was surprised. She then said she thought she had seen the angel again, but when she blinked her eyes for a second, it flew away.

"But what does she look like?" asked Missus Dougherty, putting fingertips to her throat.

"Oh, I can't say." Ruth took her hands off the cow's teats and put them in her lap. Closing her eyes and raising her face, she made her voice whispery. "Speak out . . . You feel a longing . . ." She opened her eyes and looked at the pastor's wife, who touched Ruth first on her shoulder, then on the thick, dark hair that covered her neck. Ruth's teeth were crossed over each other in front, but the effect was not unpleasant to Missus Dougherty's way of thinking. "This one cow can make a scant amount of butter," she said, "but when cream is brought from other parts and churned and chilled in your creek, it can be sold back to the customer who brought it. Don't you see, dear, that your creek and the butter it chills are blessed?"

Dear Taylor Corbett Our new house is small thogh ma-
tereal wealth is not to be savoured is it as we savour
learning. I am teaching Isaac and Benjamin geography
and sums even thogh they are like animals in the forest
always climbing into trees. Believe me that a visitor
from Brandywine would be most wellcome to sampel
our activities, such as exploring and hunting although
Papa never allows a gun so I use a snare to catch our
supper such as the cottontail and then with a rock I kill
it quickly. I am learning too. From my pupil. My brother
Benjamin put a MOUSE under my pillow just where I
keep thy letters but it is my dutie to love Benjamin even
if I love Joseph best. We are starting a dairy business.
    Sincerly Mary Dickinson September 12, 1799

That first Virginia summer, the days had been fused together as one long series of hours brought by the early rising sun and ended by the song of cicadas. The ground had at first refused to welcome its new tenants and then spread itself with corn wherever Ruth planted it. Lashed to the stalks, vines grew beans and squash, and by mid-September a small patch of wheat was ready to be cut with a scythe. Birds sang out on low and high branches, deciding whether to stay or move farther south. Trees crowded close around the log house protectively. The sycamores rustled above it, their trunks fat with age while in the surrounding forest the trees put on a thickness of leaves that moistened the air and made a canopy so dense that no sun came through to warm the ground. In that deep shade, Simus taught Mary to recognize mushrooms, huckleberries, and fox grapes as well as sheep sorrel and poke. For a while it felt eternal, the safety Mary found under the sheltering canopy, and the other children ran freely in the woods looking for wild onions and leeks and these mixed well with the rabbits Simus brought down with snares and killed with a sharp blow between long, soft ears. Every afternoon Mary brought out the slate on which she had written words with a moistened fingertip. *Pig. Rabbit. Achilles. Pegasus*, and, of course, *Onesimus*, for he was the hero of a story she was helping him create. It was the story of a boy who would one day be free, reading and writing, also walking wherever he wished. The first Onesimus had found a kind person to educate him and now the second Onesimus would be the same.

Simus had usually done a bit of hunting by the time Mary arrived and in his turn he taught her how to snare and pluck a woodcock and catch catfish and trout. Out of sight of her father, she unbuttoned her boots, took off her stockings, and stood in the clear water of the creek, using her bare hands or a piece of net. The fish were creaturely and they brushed against her ankles and caught the light as she lifted them up in the net Simus had fashioned and the water ran off the mesh and the fish twisted inside it and she was happy for the first time since her mother had died, listening to Simus as she had never listened to anyone else. Under the falls there was a deep pool with hidden, circling bass and Simus showed her how to fish for them with a bamboo pole and a small frog as bait. He told her to wade in up to her waist and spin the hook and line and play the fish if he bit. And sometimes she would return to the house with this treasured catch and Ruth would fry it in a pan over the fire while Simus lay in his crooked hut thinking of the words he had learned and the stories she had told him that day as reward for his interest. "The first Onesimus belonged to a slave owner named Philemon until finally he ran away. But one day he went out walking in the open and he met Paul the evangelist, who made him a Christian by teaching him. Paul wrote a letter to Philemon the slave owner, who was very angry that his slave had escaped. In his letter, Paul said, Dear Philemon, I send Onesimus back to you, but not as a slave. I send him back as my *brother*, sincerely Paul. At the very bottom of the letter he wrote, If he owes you anything, please just charge that debt to me."

Simus loved these words. He had heard them spoken by his mama and he never tired of them. Sometimes he'd say, "What it mean, you think?" so that Mary would say that Onesimus was such a good man that the apostle Paul had made him a brother.

"But Paul a white man?"

"Nevermind about that."

"Why Onesimus go back to Philemon then?"

"Because he belonged . . ." Mary stumbled over this.

Dear Taylor Corbett, Summer is waning in Virginia. One year ago my dear mama died and I am thinking of her with my sad heart and of others in Brandywine who are, i hope, well enough to write soon to
Mary Amelia Dickinson in Jonesville, Virginia
September 21, 1799

Mary felt older and wiser, as if she had read the entire *Aeneid* in Latin, although that was an impossibility since there was no one to teach her. When she told Simus the story of Aeneas, she invented a family in Dido's city of Carthage with a son named Onesimus and a daughter named Mary. Simus listened closely. His long eyelashes fluttered as he watched Mary's hands clutch her dusty slate. She was a girl who knew precious things, but until he met her, she had never run on the grass on her own bare feet. She had never climbed a tree or jumped off a rock, but now she had such pleasures and now he could read what her licked finger wrote on the slate. He'd say to Isaac and Benjamin that they should go and watch after the pigs.

Only one trouble with that.

Like Simus, Isaac was afraid of the timber lot, where a bear could appear or a wolf. He liked better to be with Simus, who sometimes carved out a bow for him and made good sharp arrows. Simus would tell him to go on now and look after the pigs, and when Benjamin ran back to the house to help Mama Ruth, Isaac would have to go off alone into the trees and underbrush. When Simus told him to watch for a boar that might be tempted by the sows, Isaac was surprised. What about Hiram, he wanted to know, who had fattened on acorns and hickory nuts and chestnuts and pawpaws and persimmons and might like to be a father? Simus had begun to feed Hiram a small allowance of corn, justifying this to Ruth by explaining that the meat would be fatter and the renderings would make better shortening. They must not be in too great a hurry to butcher, however. "He a brother and not to mix," he explained to Isaac, thinking of the story Mary had told him of the prodigal son, although it did not apply. He wondered if a sister could be prodigal. Could a girl run away? He knew nothing of his mother's life, of her beginnings or couplings. He knew nothing of women or girls but what he had learned by watching Mary, although now and then Bett came to see him secretly and they lay together and spoke their stories, but he knew girls to be as different from boys as his kind were from white people or as horses were from pigs. He knew also that a brother and sister, whether pig or horse or human, should never mate.

Ruth noted the growing worth of the pigs and gave Simus his way. Her garden was flourishing but when her second crop of corn was almost full-headed, a week of rain caused the kernels to mildew and she picked three bushels before the heads were ripe and begrudged what was given to Hiram. The coins she was earning with her butter were needed for building supplies, but she bought six chickens and watched them grow while she churned. Jemima built towns for the chickens and Benjamin kicked at the towns and made them collapse, but in Ruth's eyes no one loved Benjamin enough or understood his needs and she always told Jemima not to tempt her brother with those improvised towns and to go play by herself. "Build your house not on sand but on rock," she would say, wondering about her own log house.

Daniel had cut down two saplings and driven them into holes in one wall about two feet from the floor to create a bed. Supporting the saplings with posts, he had laced them with pieces of hemp rope back and forth, side to side, and at last the family moved out of the lean-to and into the unfinished house. It was unfinished because it lacked a chimney and fireplace, but the new sapling bed was occupied at night by Ruth and Jemima and Mary, while Daniel and Isaac and Benjamin slept in the loft and Joseph lay in the cradle because he could still not crawl out. Often enough, Benjamin climbed down the narrow ladder to sleep nuzzled by his stepmother and Jemima was pushed aside. It seemed that neither Benjamin nor Jemima missed their mother or even remembered her. What they missed was something comforting they couldn't imagine or specify.

In the new bed, Mary whispered the prayers she had been taught by her Quaker mother and Ruth muttered the prayers she'd been taught at the Methodist almshouse. Mary prayed for Simus. Sometimes she prayed for her mother or to her mother, she didn't know which. Ruth prayed for Tick, who continued to give rich milk although she had not been bred in a year. She thanked the Lord for the new bed, which was the only piece of furniture Daniel had built other than the table. At mealtimes, the children sat on the floor with bowls in their laps. They needed a window frame and glass, a door and a latch. Two bowls had been broken and should be replaced but it was no good talking to the Lord about that. It was no good talking to Daniel either, since his mind was full of stones and the plan and description of the chimney still to be built. He had not sold any of the Shoffert land because buyers were using old warrants handed out by the government and only cash would redeem Miss Patch. He had tied a notice to a roadside tree, *For Sale Good Acres, D. Dickinson*, believing Jester Fox would see it and be tempted. Daniel needed that neighbour's help now in the building of a good drawing chimney.

Sand or rock. How did the log house sit?

There were people in the new town of Jonesville who desired to put a bare hand or foot in Ruth's holy creek. Missus Craig brought her mother in a cart and splashed the old woman's arthritic legs. Missus Dougherty sent a visitor who had complained of headaches and Ruth led him down through the timber lot to a spot under the cottonwoods where she told him to keep his eyes shut tight. "Don't look up at her," Ruth said, "or she might never come back." News began to travel on the Wilderness Road, and once in a while an emigrant would stop at the log house and ask about the healing water. Simus therefore hollowed out a log and dragged it up to the roadside and filled it with a wooden dipper and a pail full of creek water. He put a small handmade basket for coins near the log with a sign that was to read, *Holy Water*, except that the *W* was upside down and looked like an *M* so the sign read, *Holy Mater* and Daniel flung the pail across the road, saying it was Popish.

There were visitors who asked for a packet of butter, but most of Ruth's supply was taken to Missus Dougherty in the wagon, which Ruth drove by herself now since Daniel had given her lessons with horse and lines. Her trips took place just after dawn, when the light was soft and the butter could be kept cool and damp and when the cream brought by her customers to Missus Dougherty would not sour on the long return trip.

One morning Ruth stopped at Mister Murray's trading post on her way home. It seemed very bold to get down from the wagon, leaving six jugs of cream covered by a wet cloth and shade. It seemed bold to enter the post by herself, but she had a dollar tucked into her waistband that she'd collected from Missus Dougherty along with a new idea. "I want a dozen jars," she announced too loudly, unaccustomed as she was to making any kind of purchase. And Mister Murray stepped out of his dark room at the back of the store, moving a curtain aside to make his entrance. It was a moment of triumph for Ruth, who would put up vegetables for the winter at Missus Dougherty's suggestion. "Twelve," she said, to be precise.

Mister Murray scanned his customer's small frame, one eye glinting behind a monocle. He said he would bring the jars out to her wagon in a carton. The cost of the jars, he said, was fourteen cents.

Ruth did not want to show him the cash hidden inside her waistband, so she turned away, pretending to be interested in his window display when her eyes fell on what looked like a large doll in the window wearing a soft blue dress. Each blue sleeve bore two stripes of velvet and the skirt had three velvet stripes above its hem. Ruth looked at the doll, which was painted and unrealistic. Who would play with such a thing? Then she smiled, realizing that this doll was only there to wear the dress, which must be for sale. How would it be to wear such a dress with its full skirt and velvet stripes? Would she look like a married woman? Would such a dress erase the pity from Missus Dougherty's eyes? She stretched out an arm impulsively, although the doll was well out of reach.

"Not for sale, miss," the storekeeper said. "That frock is put there only to exemplify the use of the fabric I purvey."

Imagining the weight of that fabric swirling around her legs, Ruth angled her face toward the storekeeper and allowed as how she had not much time to look but might she examine this article of clothing made not to be worn but to be instructive.

"Yes, but it would not do for me to sell the dress, miss, lest how would the customers find inspiration for the cloth they purchase?" Mister Murray crossed the small open area of the store and put both hands on the garment his wife had so artfully fashioned. He was remembering that this was the girl who made the butter his wife bought from the pastor's wife. "Mustn't to wrinkle it up," he said with a smile that was kind enough as he lifted the large wooden doll down from the ledge. Then, more kindly, "Your sales in butter go well enough these days, do they?"

Ruth said the Lord had provided the cow and the creek and the churn and she was thankful. She did not mention the angel, since she still had not followed her instructions, not knowing what words she was meant to speak out. Perhaps she had failed in her part of the bargain and the butter was no longer graced, but that would be a disappointment to her customers. What she did say was that there was none of them could sew a stitch in her house, and if Mister Murray would perhaps let her buy this dress that was already fading in his window . . . if he would do that then, even though the dress be sun-bleached, he would have a person to be walking around in it to show at church and two pounds of butter to keep or sell. "I'd display it better'n a doll ever could," Ruth said. "And cover up the sun mark with a handkerchief."

"Sun-bleached?"

Ruth pointed. "It don credit the fabric," she said.

He thought she was, after all, a young lady who was forthright and brave and that good Missus Dougherty had taken her on as a cause, saying she was selected by the Lord to take charge of a passel of motherless orphans. Perhaps then, adorning her in a dress from his window would be somewhat of a Christian act and Missus Murray could make up another window dress within the week. "I guess one-half a Virginia dollar could make it yours," he agreed.

Ruth asked him to wrap the dress, gave him her money, and left the store in a rush, forgetting the jars and driving off in a clatter of wheels and hooves. She had never bought anything for herself. Not a dress. Not a cape. Not even the black straw hat or the felt cap she wore every day. She had been given those things as second-hand goods and if in truth she had been trained to sew and mend, there was no time now for honesty about such things. She would have a Sunday dress to look like a married wife.

The package safely stowed, she slapped Mulberry with the reins and let her trot when they got to the edge of what passed for a town – Mister Murray's store, two log houses, and a forge just built. There was the land for a courthouse given by Mister Jones, a good man and provider of tools. Ruth made her way home with the cream to be churned and the dress to be worn and rounded the last bend standing up in the wagon with the long lines of the hitch in her hands. Then she saw Daniel and sat down fast. She had spent money that could have been put to the return of his horse or to buying more nails, or even to window glass. Ruth pulled to a halt and grabbed the package and threw it into a tall patch of weeds as the wagon rolled on past. Some of those weeds had been earlier mashed by wheels, but most of them stood up straight for a hiding place and Daniel was even then coming to help her carry the jars of cream.

"What is that?" He was pointing.

Ruth's mind jumped around.

"There, over in the weeds?" He walked back in the path of the wagon and bent over the paper package.

"It's a secret," Ruth said hastily, turning her voice to a whisper and climbing down. She averted her face, which was flushed. Her eyes had been bright in the wagon, but they faded and she brushed at the air. "Isaac said to me that Mary has just turned fourteen. I thought a dress could be a present from her papa."

That evening, while Ruth was churning the new cream in the cool air, Mary slid out of the house in the velvet-trimmed dress. "Look here, Ruth Boyd, and see what my papa bought me."

"You seem to be steppin on its hem."

Mary swirled around, throwing a moon shadow across Ruth's churn. "I can just tie it up with a sash." She looked down at herself. "It's odd that Papa bought it, though, since indigo is made by slaves and Friends are not allowed it." She held the skirt in both hands and examined it. "Maybe Papa doesn't mind that now. . . ." Her voice trailed off.

Ruth moved the paddle. "Better wait til you're growed to wear it."

"I *said* I can just wear a sash and tie it up." Mary looked at Ruth coldly. "There's a way to make butter come fast, but I guess you don't know it."

"My butter comes just fine."

Mary began swirling. She got the skirt of the blue dress in a spin so that her bloomers were showing. "Come, butter, come!" She clicked her heels. "Peter's waiting at the gate. For a butter cake." She dipped, lifted her arms up over her head. "Come, butter, come."

Ruth said, "Oh, I do feel it thicken, my Lord, yes."

Mary came closer, surprised to hear the Lord's name taken in vain.

"My Lord!" said Ruth again. "It's comin so fast now it's a plain miracle." She jerked her arms up and down. "Try it for yourself." She let go of the paddle and sat back, glad to straighten her shoulders and rest her arms while Mary grabbed the paddle and thrust it up and down.

"I did not even feel it before," Mary said sharply, "so how am I to know?"

Ruth said, "Well, this butter business is growing so busy I might need a partner to share the profit if I could find someone qualified. Do you know a thing more about butter than for a rhyme?" She looked at the dress and pulled her eyes away, for the sight hurt her strangely.

"I am too occupied with everything a *mother* should be doing, Ruth Boyd."

"Down in the timber lot all day."

"Why not have Simus for your partner? You only need someone to churn for you and wrap butter in bits of waxed paper. It's nothing."

"And he's surely underworked, lying on his back with his feet up while a girl who should know better carries his food to him."

"Maybe you don't like him because he reminds you of being our servant, Ruth Boyd. But if he had a paying job, he could buy his freedom."

"It is the definement of a slave to work with no pay. And why should I care to lose him now that he can get up and walk and do for us as he should?" A whippoorwill called out the end of day from the ancient, unstoppable forest. They were far from other people, other families. It was that first summer of sewn-together days.

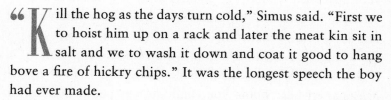

"Kill the hog as the days turn cold," Simus said. "First we to hoist him up on a rack and later the meat kin sit in salt and we to wash it down and coat it good to hang bove a fire of hickry chips." It was the longest speech the boy had ever made.

So. They would hang the meat, salt it, and render the lard. They would pray for a cold winter to keep the meat from spoiling. It would make for a celebration of their first year in Virginia, but they must make a place for butchering where a hog could be hung high enough to be gutted. Explaining this, Simus pointed out that the pigs had been the best investment the Dickinsons could have made. "Costn no teng," he said. "And grub fer free."

Daniel did not like to say what he had paid for the pigs, but he was bound to admit he knew nothing of butchering or salting or smoking.

Simus said, "Leavm ta me for I kin do all an make soap an tallow for the missus."

As if the gods had no hand in this, the four pigs continued to snort and scramble in the woods, bumping and chasing and squealing with pointed ears upright. Their mottled skins were camouflage. They came back to the hut each night replenished, and Simus found comfort in their snorts and firm bellies but Daniel now ordered the children to stay away from the pigs and out of the timber lot, wanting no sentiment when it came to butchering.

"But, Papa," Isaac argued, "Hiram and Martha and Corry and Bathsheba are my friends. They will be sad if I don't come down to visit as I always do and it is bad for pigs to be sad. What if they forget to eat?"

Hiram. Corry. Daniel asked who had named the pigs. He was up early putting shingles on the roof of his house. "Isaac, you must wean yourself of connection to the animals, as they are all to be eaten one of these days. That is their purpose. In a few days, your Hiram will be butchered so that we may survive the winter. You must not consider the animals over yourself. It is God's plan for us to have dominion and not to live among the beasts as friends. Would you climb up here and help me with the roofing?"

Isaac thought of Hiram's round snout and the pink lining of his ears. He thought of the long face and pocketed eyes, which blinked at him. He tried not to cry, but the pain in his chest was more than he could bear without tears and he let them roll out of his eyes and down his cheeks. For the first time, his father had invited him to participate in a thing he had desperately wanted all summer – to be part of the house building. Now, if he climbed up to feel the new roof under his boots, to look down the chimney hole, to look out beyond the lot and the road, he would be agreeing to the murder of his friend. His father had laid a trap for him and scaling the wall of the house would mean that he could never complain. Then he wondered, How much would it help Hiram if he turned away from his father now? And if he couldn't help Hiram, was an act of defiance worth the loss of that rooftime vantage?

———

In the meadow, Simus was building a hog hoist, stopping occasionally to gaze at his hut, for within it there had been a visitor the night before. "My life was once safe," Bett had told him when he asked about her past. "In the first house, I played with my mistress's children and never thought about it twice. My grandmother schooled me to read and write and heal the sick."

Simus had asked if their people were the same.

"I cannot tell," she answered quietly. "My grandmother came from a land she called Guinea, where she was kidnapped." Then, while she checked the wound on his leg and the strength of the bone she had knit back together, she told him of the place she lived now and the trouble she knew there. Only a little time they'd spent like that for soon enough she had taken her short-cut back, moving fast out of fear. Otherwise, as she said, there would be no breakfast on the stove making its goodness felt, no clothes being pulled out of the cupboard for the children to wear, no Bible set out for Mister Fox to read out loud to his family. She told him this too: that the two girls were under her direction, along with the cleaning of the house, the laundering and cooking, the mending and spinning. And when there was sickness in the quarters, she was sent out to the fields to make the workers well, for her grandmother had died a little time ago. Gone all night! Not come back! That's what they would say if she stayed and what would then happen was not to be imagined, she had said, although he knew enough about such things. She had to get back, but Simus could gaze at the hut where he lived in wonderment that it had been ever so briefly shared.

Mary went on with her teaching, and Isaac tended the pigs, and Benjamin and Jemima, still too young to wander, stayed close to Ruth, who had the care of sickly Joseph and the garden and the chickens and Tick, the good cow, as well as the fast-growing butter business. Sometimes she took herself down to a certain place on the bank of the creek to wait for encouragement, but the shivering angel never came.

One bright afternoon in October, Jester Fox rode up to the Dickinson house in a roll of red dust. Daniel had put up a second notice at the trading post and he listened to the hoof beats on his road, hoping it was his north-side neighbour come at last.

Acreage for sale. Inquire D. Dickinson Wilderness Road

As Daniel stood forth, Jester Fox arrived with angry shouts. "Come down here, you land-grabbin-sonofaweasel!" The horse foamed and snorted.

Daniel had turned sheet white and was already wringing his hands. He had been piling up stones, intending to speak to this neighbour about his chimney as well as the Shoffert land. It was imperative, now that autumn had come, to finish the house and create a source of heat.

"Your nigger bigged my house girl!" Fox bellowed. He grabbed his hat, crushed it in his hands, and began beating it against his leg while the gelding pawed at the ground and pranced, pulled at the mouth by hard-held reins.

"Surely not," Daniel croaked. "Onesimus lives close by, with an injured limb, which would never carry him as far as your place." He wanted to say, Nor would he do such a thing, but he found that he wasn't sure of that. His hands now dangled at his sides. His heart was fast. His small sons were hiding under the porch near his feet. He must stop shaking and find some authority within, although he had no idea where to look for it.

Fox shouted, "Tha *limb* must be mended good enough to climb on a girl and fornicate her!" and went on hitting his leg with the crumpled hat and biting his red moustache.

Daniel watched his neighbour with a growing fear. This was a situation beyond his experience or reckoning.

"I require twenty dollas here and now to recompense."

"Recompense?" Daniel found his voice. "I say it is not possible for Onesimus to walk so far as to your place, but if it is true that he did so, has he not *enriched* you by one, providing you with yet another unfortunate piece of living property?" Daniel hoped the listening children had not taken his meaning, but he could not calm his sense of outrage. Under the porch, the two little boys must be gazing out in terror at the horse, which had reared up now and was pawing at the air close to their hiding place. Astride the horse, Jester Fox had become half-man half-beast, but when the hooves hit the ground and the man jumped off, Isaac crawled out from under the porch and ran to him with doubled-up fists. "Don't touch my papa!" he cried. "Or I will kill thee!"

Daniel looked at his child in stunned horror. He had raised his children devotedly as pacifists and now one of them had uttered words of mortal aggression. He stepped off his porch and strode over to Isaac, grabbing his shoulder, telling him to apologize instantly.

Isaac shook his head.

Jester Fox sneered. "Brave little man you got there, but I want my twenty dollas and your nig to beat alongside of mine."

Daniel, who believed there were times in his life when his pacifism was encouraged by weakness, advanced a step toward his neighbour, aware that his sons were watching, that he must master his fear and stop his trembling. "Neither one nor the other," he said, but the voice that came out of him was now puny to his own ears.

Jester Fox spat out a spiral of tobacco juice. "You think I'm bat blind to your policies? I seen you take Shoffert's land so's to keep me small. I seen you buy up my water rights to drive me off. And now it's my girl servin' as your strumpet!" The red hair on his head stood out stiff as wire and his face was splotched under the skin. "Which of you goes first on her, I wonder, you or the nig?"

Daniel felt rage come in a flood. "If the girl is what you say, you cannot blame Onesimus!" It was wicked to win his argument at the cost of the girl's honour, but it was what the loosened rage demanded. He heard the word *tarnation* escape his lips and clamped them shut.

Jester Fox thrust out his arm and struck his hat across Daniel's face.

Seeing nothing, feeling nothing, Daniel stepped back. It was the first chance he'd had in his life to turn the other cheek but that did not occur to him. His mind was blank. Then his heart resumed its loud beating. He had not considered Jester Fox to be a danger, but now he saw the edge of violence in himself and it was terrifying.

"I coulda bought up this place," Fox snarled.

"But you did not," Daniel threw back. "Nor will you set foot on this land again or rue the day!" It was not fear he felt now but untempered, untrammelled fury, which is the arsenal of the devil, he told himself, and I have entered his range.

"I catch her over here, I'll hang your nig's festerin cock up a tree," Jester Fox stuttered, and he went back to his horse and took hold of the reins and pulled himself into the saddle almost gracefully, looking around just long enough to take in the unfinished state of the house, which was entered by climbing two bare wooden planks. He saw that an empty window sat on one side of the door braced by its sash. And there was no chimney, only a pile of stones on the ground varied in size and shape. "I'll be waitin for the twenty dollas and the nigger to be brought," he growled. "But I'll not wait for more'n a day."

Mary, Ruth, and Jemima had heard every word of this awful encounter while standing inside, behind the door, and they had felt variously about Daniel's response to their neighbour's threats. Jemima believed her father to be brave. Mary was glad of his lack of violence and surprised by his rage. But Ruth was ashamed, for she had expected Daniel to leap on Jester Fox and prove his strength. Instead, she had seen only cowardice.

That night, when the moon was high enough, Daniel left the cabin, believing everyone to be asleep. Listening to leaves crunch under his boots and feeling a thorn come through the sole of one of them, he stopped to pull it out and found himself on his knees in the crackle of all the living and dying life around him. He was not a man to put words to his prayers, but he gave his whole weight to the ground and felt it push back. He let the muscles of his calves relax, slid the tops of his boots around on the elements – soil and pokeweed and grass and leaf. He put his wandering thought to the two slaves and considered their form, which was human, and their needs, which matched his own in so many ways, believing they, too, must contain a spark of the divine. This thought brought him comfort and many minutes passed before he stood up in his boots again and saw that the dark had come on fast, as if answering some need he had not expressed. Now he could move stealthily, feeling his way through the trees, limb by limb and trunk by trunk, for he knew the feel of each of these parts of the path. He had given Simus a lamp, but there was no light inside the little hut and no sound, so the boy must be well asleep. Simus had been recently feeding the pigs an allowance of corn, justifying this by explaining the benefits. "Soon tha hog to be dress and salted down," he'd said. "He to be smoke afta the brine form up and I build a smoke house for him." The boy was excited about his venture and this was all very well, even admirable, but Simus must atone for the advantage taken of an unknowing girl and the cost to Daniel's standing in the newly made community. Double shame it was, and reprimand must be meted out or Simus would not comprehend the serious nature of his wanton conduct. Or was *conduct* the appropriate word? As he crept through the underbrush surrounding the meagre hut he had built over the boy, Daniel wondered if the two young slaves even understood the act that had created yet another unfortunate soul to be enslaved by a man without heart or decency, a man to be loathed although the gospels taught otherwise. How could he love his neighbour? How could he turn the other cheek? *Conduct.* He turned his tongue around the word. It was likely the boy and girl had coupled out of lonely instinct, like wild animals, for that is what they were, lacking all education and refinement, lacking even self-respect. Without learning and understanding, how is conduct possible since it requires intention?

Under the canvas door, the opening was fenced halfway up so that the pigs, full grown now, could not escape. It is the chain of life, Daniel thought tiredly, one kept by another by another and by another. He had the fleeting impression that he, too, was a slave to something, but in a moment that impression was lost in his surprise at finding the hut empty except for the softly grunting and snorting pigs.

What if the boy had word of the girl's situation and had gone to her on his limping leg? Daniel pulled the canvas back over the hut's opening and rushed back to the house, which he did not enter. Instead, he saddled Mulberry quickly and took to the road, which was bare and moonlit.

Unaccustomed to night rides, the horse thudded heavily through the dark, flaring her nostrils and heaving her chest. The full moon was in a fit of fast swimming across the sky, moving among the scuttling clouds as if it were buoyant. In its bright light, Daniel made out a hobbling shape on the road ahead and pulling up next to it saw that he had caught up with Simus. "What are you doing out with that shingle knife?" he demanded.

Simus had the knife in his left hand and a walking stick held like a cane in his right. The knife reflected moonlight and starlight on its angled blade. Old men, too feeble to swing an axe, were given this tool to split kindling. It was used to split barrel hoops and lath flats and willow poles and none of these employments explained the boy's walking out with it on the road at night. Simus said nothing.

"On your way to the Fox place, is it? To cause yet more trouble? Do you want to endanger that girl further?" Daniel got down from the horse and stood facing the boy, clenching his teeth and wanting to grab Simus as he had grabbed Isaac earlier in the day. "Listen now!" He reached out, holding his eyes on the boy's starched face. "Give over that knife."

Simus stepped back, reckoning his chances at anything but death now, anything but death including flight. He raised the knife.

Daniel made himself louder. "Listen hard and believe. I will act on the girl's behalf." He paused and drew breath and thought that Simus could not know what he meant however hard he listened. He took the boy by an elbow so that the walking stick dangled from his hand. "Hear me now. Hear me now . . . Jester Fox is raging. Go home. Go back. This is an order I give."

The boy pulled his arm away and with the lifted blade struck his right hand so suddenly that for a long moment, the blade hung in the flesh, wavering. Pierced through the meat between thumb and forefinger, the hand was nailed to the walking stick. "He always takin her," Simus said, looking down at the hand. In sorrow, in defeat, he turned his face left and right. The walking stick fell with a hollow clank and Daniel watched the boy's blood dripping onto the road, watched it illumined by the moonlight as it made a dark pool at their feet. He did not for an instant believe what the boy had said about Jester Fox, but the smell of blood and the thought of such unworthy lust sickened him. He remembered then that Fox had accused him of the selfsame crime, but it was too much to think about or examine. "You've given yourself a terrible wound," he muttered, swallowing the bile that had risen in his throat. But why? Why? Would a dog or a wild animal do such a thing? There seemed to be nothing with which to stanch the flow of blood, for it did not occur to Daniel to remove his own shirt.

The hand, lowered now, was gushing dangerously and Simus did not make a sound, although he still held the bloodied shingle knife.

"An injury to thyself pains the Lord," Daniel whispered. He had forgotten the quiet intensity of his prayer in the timber lot. "Take Mulberry home," he said. "I will walk on to the Fox place to see how things stand with the girl."

———

It was a week after the purchase of the blue dress that this incident on the road occurred, although the second thing did not follow the first in any logical sequence. Certainly there was no cause, no effect. First the dress had been bought and given away, the butter had been churned to a chant, and then Jester Fox had arrived, struck Daniel with his folded hat, and Daniel had left the house late at night. Must events be related? The moon, full and stately, was still swimming through the clouds as Daniel trudged along the road. He kept his hands behind him as if they were chained and his head down, as if every stone on the road must be studied as a potential piece of chimney. Simus was turned toward home and surely Jester Fox would . . . what? Daniel's thoughts moved like the moon, in and out of possibilities. He thought of the girl's face the only time he had seen it. She was not much older than Mary. Or Ruth. And what if Fox had been using her as Simus proclaimed? Such things were said to happen on the plantations, where wealth had stolen the Holy Spirit from certain owners and turned their hearts to wretchedness, but out here in the woods of southwest Virginia, where they were all struggling to civilize the very ground where they walked, where they were required to live as Christians together or descend into chaos . . . out here, it was unthinkable that a man on his own home place with a young and helpless servant and a nearby wife in his bed . . . and children . . . The walk seemed to take forever. It was the Lord protecting him, giving him time to meditate. What if Simus had told an untruth to besmirch the girl's owner and clear himself? On and on, this walking. *If thy brother shall trespass against thee, go and tell him his fault between thee and him alone . . .* It was a mile or so between houses, going by road. *If he shall hear thee, thou hast gained thy brother . . .* What if Simus had visited Bett by crossing the creek? The road dipped and swayed. Jester Fox had accused Daniel of taking the girl himself. Those coarse words were beyond comprehension. Unless his neighbour was familiar with such a crime. The moon rose higher and peered all the way down to the place, somewhere behind him, where there must still be a pool of shining blood as if the earth had received a wound. *No cede malis*, he whispered. What if events were shaped by conditions rather than faith?

Finally the Fox place could be viewed from the stony road as he scuffed along it. The small house stood stark and creamy against the night, lit by the sky as everything was but reflecting that light like another white moon. Daniel felt the strain in his thighs as he pushed them harder and faster uphill. Awake is what he wanted Jester Fox to be. And asleep, all the rest of them. Four that he knew of: Jester Fox and two almost-grown sons and a wife. But there might be smaller children so he must not frighten them. And where did the housegirl sleep? He thought of the threat Jester Fox had made. A beating. And the girl was with child. Still, he must not plead overmuch for her rights but instead make a case for the innocence of the two child-slaves. He would point out that a girl of such tender years could no more know what she was about than one of their own daughters. No, he would liken her to a young horse, as the comparison to a daughter might ignite things further. He would say that Simus had been injured and that her heart had surely gone out to him and that the two of them had been lonely for company of their own kind. He would remind Jester Fox that such children as they were knew nothing of consequence to their acts.

As he came to the slope of land that held up the house, Daniel measured the distance from road to door and back to road again, as if he might have to find his way out quickly, remembering thickets and holes and making no false steps. He walked across the open ground without any sign of hesitation, although he felt now a great desire to stand and think out his argument. The reason the girl must not be punished or the boy either . . . neither of them. And what of recompense? A hound barked fitfully and howled with malice or longing. It made the hair rise up on the back of Daniel's neck. The moon made a fool of him, standing so stark on the yellowed grass.

Inside the house, a lamp was put out and the front door opened a crack. "Who's out here?"

"I am here to inquire after the girl," Daniel replied unsteadily.

"And why should you bother when all her trouble be the fault of yourn?"

"Come now," said Daniel, "let us help each other in this matter and seek the best outcome for everyone." In the dew-covered yard, the moon lit up trees and slender stalks of wild grass as if there must be something in all of it worth seeing while Fox stood in a narrow opening that emitted no light. "I would speak to her," said Daniel, coming fully up the porch steps. But as he reached for the door, he felt a shove at his shoulder and stumbled backward, then lay flat on the ground that had slammed into him, trying to catch his breath. The door shut loudly. The sky was written with stars. The moon had taken itself to some corner above or lowered itself into a patch of branches, but the stars kept poking at the dark, making breathless spotted light.

He pushed himself up, brushed off his shirt, and found his way around to the back of the house. There, behind the washtubs, was a shack and he stood for a minute, looking, then walked over to the thin wall of boards and knocked. A moment passed. Hearing nothing, he pushed at the door but there was only a heap of matting on the floor, nothing else. He thought of the place where Simus slept, realizing it bore a resemblance to this, and wondered if he and his neighbour were similar in a way he hadn't noticed. He smelled the close air of the shack and quickly dismissed this thought because he was seeking to protect a girl without anything to be gained by doing so while Jester Fox was surely lost to all decency.

Stepping outside and glancing toward the house, which, without the moon, still reflected the light as if it bore witness, he moved into the bushes at the edge of the yard and felt his way back to the road, sore inside and out.

He could not remember what it was he had planned to do.

Wishing he had told Simus to bring the wagon and then remembering the injured hand, he thought what a bother the owning of someone could be. A hired man would be sent home during illness. A hired man would have his own lodgings and family, whereas Simus was a dangerous, wilful child. Not an animal, after all, Daniel thought now, for an animal can be tamed. He came to the patch of blood on the road, still glistening. Then he heard a wolf howl in the distance and almost managed to laugh at himself. He was surrounded by the forces of nature. Even though the sons of Virginia had forged a great democratic union, the light of Christ had not been brought into these woods. He was walking on a path of blood. Jealousy and lust and pride and despair he had met in the last several hours and it was the woods and the fields and shadowy hills that provided the backdrop. He could not imagine that any wicked act could take place under a roof built by human hands.

Again, his prayers were wordless, but they addressed a heavenly parent who cared for the universe. He made this address less through thought than through the five senses. Or were there more than that? He stopped, gave himself over to inner and outer light. In the middle of the road, in the middle of the night, on his long walk home, he was magnified, taking in substance through every pore. Eyes closed, he took it in as a plant will absorb light. He smelled those plants, which imbued the air with their musk. He sensed the peace of animals in nests and holes. He tasted the coming of morning and heard the wind in the leaves. He felt in the soles of his feet the resistance of ground. In his back and hips he felt the weight of his bones while his skin was an instrument being thrummed. Then at last he opened his eyes. Nature must not be blamed. Only man betrayed his place in it. He took in the reappeared moon as a reminder of Christ.

I'll go again tomorrow, he told himself. To make things right.

Reaching home, Daniel only glanced at the house, although inside it was everything he valued, or so it seemed to him. He walked quickly past the shelter he had built for his family and into the low-lying meadow, which had lost its flowers but which was seeded with flowers to come. The slapping of a hat across a face – it was the first violence directed against him in his life and it had been followed by worse: that terrible accusation. The threat to Simus! The shove off the porch! Love thy neighbour, he told himself as an owl cried out from a thicket. Then all was quiet. The wind had stalled. The trees held their peace. The moon hung on thick, silent branches. He had found his direction and moved softly into the timber lot, where he could hear the four pigs rustling and snoring and a sadder sound rising in waves. When he pulled the canvas away from the hut's opening, he saw Simus kneeling over a girl whose cries grew louder when Daniel hunched himself in to stare at her in amazement. His Quaker hat brushed against the canvas and fell off. "What is . . . ?" The girl was huddled against a grumbling sow.

"She hurt bad, Masta."

"Don't call me that word." Daniel saw that the boy's right hand was wrapped in a piece of the girl's torn skirt. He felt sweat on the back of his neck. "She must go back, Simus. Jester Fox will be out looking for her. This is a great danger to all of us!"

"She don."

Daniel picked up his hat. "Simus, she must go home now before Jester Fox comes back here to do more damage."

"She don go there."

Daniel shivered. "But she belongs to Jester Fox," he said meekly, for the idea of ownership revolted him and he had no wish to support it. Masta. "Do you see?" It was something between ordering and pleading. "It is breaking the law to keep her here." He was law-abiding, after all, and harbouring a runaway was perhaps a capital offence. He thought of his father: firm abolitionist. All of his people. And himself. He knelt beside the girl, who was curled against the pig. He studied her face, which was unusual, with deep-set eyes and a flaring nose and angular jaw. It was a strong face, neither ugly nor beautiful to him, but impressive. On her head, the girl wore no kerchief in the way of a slave but her dress was torn from the making of the bandage and her skin, wherever it was visible, was swelling into welts. Daniel felt ashamed and found himself relenting somewhat. "No one knows of this hut for now," he allowed quietly, letting his eyes rest on the injured girl. Relenting by a narrow margin is all it was. "But she *must* leave by dawn."

On his knees, he backed out of the sorry shelter and found his way home, opening his door very quietly and climbing the ladder very slowly as he took off his worn black coat and hat, sign and symbol of his beliefs. His sons were spread across the mattress and he pushed them together to make space for himself, pulled off his shirt, then found his nightshirt under a pillow and pulled it on over his head. Cold was blowing into the house through the great gap in one wall. He must somehow build a chimney now without his neighbour's help.

Now Daniel told Mary to keep the children close to the house. He said it with emphasis in order that there be no misunderstanding. "Stay away from the timber lot, all of you. There is to be a butchering tomorrow and I don't want the animals excited. I shall take Mama Ruth to her Prayer Meeting this morning and, Mary, you will keep the children away from the pigs."

Isaac began to protest but Daniel narrowed his eyes and firmly shook his head. There might, after all, be some evidence of the runaway's visit to the timber lot.

Mary faced her father. "Simus is skinning a rabbit for us. I must go fetch it as I said I would. For our First Day supper."

"What you must do is watch the little ones very closely. I shall fetch our supper when I return." Daniel would not say more, and after he and Ruth left, Mary sat on the steps with Jemima on her lap with thoughts running fast through her head. "A pig is a pig," she said to her little sister. A pig is a pig. And Simus was her only friend in all of Virginia and her father was always and forever thinking about Ruth and forgetting about her. Her life! Everyone always needing something – help with this, help with that, listening ears, clever hands – but Simus was different. He was helping *her*. He was training her to do what she had never done before. They had started by using stones in the creek, leaning out over the water's surface and skimming a flat stone across it to make it skip. When she could skip nine stones out of ten, he had taken her up to the meadow, where he showed her how to aim the stone and when she could hit a target, he had taught her to use the stone to kill a rabbit in a snare. Hit hard and fast, he had told her, showing her the place to make the quickest kill. In her other life – her old life – Mary had loved going to school. But here in Virginia she could stand with her bare feet right in the creek. She could run! That had not been allowed in Brandywine. She thought of the nursery, where she had slept with her brothers and Jemima, where there had been curtains at the window and a rocking chair and a rug. She thought of the picture of a tree that her mother had made with her needle and thread. Mary had started a sampler, but it had never been finished. She had it somewhere, rolled up in her clothes, but it made her feel peculiar to look at it now, with its tiny blood stains and crooked letters and as she sat on the steps and held Jemima, thinking of the nursery and thinking also that Simus must be missing her, she remembered a nursery game. "One two three four," she said quickly, counting Jemima's toes before she pulled on the child's stockings. "Where is Jemima's littlest pig?"

Jemima loved it when Mary covered her tiny toe and then suddenly revealed it. "Stay here with your brothers," Mary told her. "I'll be back in a few long minutes."

Inside, she took her new dress off the clothing shelf, looked at the sleeping baby, and told the boys not to move an inch. "It is your job to watch baby. I will go see to your pigs." She told Jemima to sit on the bed until she got back. She took off her old dress and left it lying on the floor and pulled the new dress over her head. The swing of cloth around her ankles gave her confidence and she gave a small skip and then strode away fast, leaving the door ajar and thinking of how the meadow had been a bog and had made her friend's leg break and how good things can come out of bad like flowers out of mud or nice dresses out of slave-made indigo. There were a few straggly cornflowers left in the grass and she made a little wreath for her hair while she walked. And all the while she was picking and weaving, she was moving toward the timber lot.

uth learned about the runaway slave at the Prayer Meeting,
where the sermon was about property. "What we own, it
is our earthly duty to tend," the pastor told his little flock.
"What we own, we tend, for the Lord has given us everything that
is ours." At one time, Methodists had been fiercely abolitionist.
They had broken away from the Episcopal Church with Francis
Asbury as their first bishop and in those early years evangelists
rode across Virginia, North Carolina, Tennessee, and Kentucky
preaching against the evil of slave owning. But the Southerners
had considered the churchmen wrong in this preaching, feeling
that to emancipate their slaves would lead to social chaos, and
now some churchmen had surrendered to the doctrine of necessity and Pastor Dougherty was among them. "The fowler's snare
is knotted with secrecy," he told the listening Christians.

Daniel and Ruth were sitting on a bench they had brought in
the wagon, Ruth with her feet crossed at the ankles and tucked
back so as to hide her split-open boots. The pastor was saying,
"And in spite of the words of Paul to the Ephesians – that each
slave must obey his master – I am informed by our brother,
Jester Fox, that one of his own dark children has rebelled and
is living without protection in contradiction of God's law. This
child is in error and must be returned to Mister Fox because
we form a community here in Jonesville based on Christian

laws." He looked around solemnly, searching each face, as was his weekly habit, and several of his parishioners answered back in the affirmative. Satisfied, the pastor raised his voice to address the Almighty: "Lord! We ask Thee now from our humble church and humble hearts . . . we ask Thee to admonish the one who is fled and teach her the example of Jesus Christ, who gave His life to redeem *her* in spite of her selfishness and grievous ignorance. Let that her selfishness not lead to an outbreak of the same among other workers," the pastor continued, striking at the one fear his congregants held in common and launching then into the parable of the prodigal, proving the nature of repentance and the Lord's readiness to welcome all those who return to His guidance. "It is a sin," he announced, "to look upon God's gifts as a debt due to us. I say this with regard to the sinner who harbours another sinner, to that one who is tempted by secrecy, dashing into the fowler's net when destruction stares him in the face. He will commit a sin that is condemned by the law of the land." Here, the pastor's eyes stopped for a moment to regard the closed and wary countenance of Daniel before moving on restlessly to other faces.

Ruth also looked at Daniel, who looked down at his feet. She wondered where he had gone when he'd ridden away under the light of the moon only a few thin hours after Jester Fox had accosted him. She remembered the vehemence on both sides of the argument. She had never seen Daniel truly angry until that moment when the terrible words fell on him just as she came to the window to hear what was being said. But the anger had taken a cowardly form as he spoke through his gritted teeth, trying to be reasonable.

When she and Daniel filed out of the church, people were shaking their heads over the ingratitude of a girl who had been allowed to work in a house among white people.

"She can read and write, what I hear."

"Won't help her out hiding in the woods."

"Should know better."

"Might as well cut her own throat as hide out there."

On the trip home, the road stretched and lengthened. It grew cumbersome, bumpy, and tedious and Ruth felt she was discovering new corners right and left. The wind beating through the trees blew at her straw hat so that she had to tie it under her chin with the purple ribbon and put a hand on the top of her head. Mulberry kept slowing and shying at swirling branches. Leaves blew past, a few drops of rain. Ruth listened to Daniel urge the horse, but they seemed to be moving toward a place they did not want to visit. When a gust of rain came at them, they avoided speaking of it, as they had so far avoided speaking of everything else. "Lord," Ruth prayed, "let us be no part of this." The road had narrowed. Out loud she said, "Only a criminal would hide a runaway."

Daniel muttered, "So it would seem." It began to rain harder. He flicked his whip. They came to a clearing in the trees and the rain came down on them.

"There was no sign of rain this mornin," Ruth heard herself say while she counted up Daniel's mistakes. Onesimus was not the first of them, although he had brought trouble since the day he first came, using up Daniel's savings and losing them their best horse, breaking his leg, then creating rage in their neighbour. Slaves had no creed, no laws, no families, and should not mix with civilized people. Ruth looked at the man beside her, whose face was wet in spite of his hat and who had used words instead of fists to defend himself. What if Mister Fox killed him and she was left with his five ungrown children? She stared at the side of the road, imagining a grave and Daniel lying in it with his hands across his chest. She would have to send the children off to the poorhouse, just as she had been sent, and she felt a rare tug of compassion for her forgotten mother as she pulled her cape across her face so as not to get wet. "Next slave better be smarter," she said.

"No more slaves, Ruth Boyd."

At home, they counted the children and Daniel asked where Mary was. The boys were playing with a wooden ball. The baby was wet and whimpering. Jemima was sitting very still on the bed. "Has she . . . left . . . thee . . . all . . . alone . . . ?" Daniel's voice was tighter with every word. Ruth pointed at the dress on the floor and he rushed out into the rain, slipping on the steps and catching himself. There was no sign of Mary in the meadow, so he ran on without stopping, as if he had it in his power to change anything, trees snapping, bare branches whipping at his flesh. He stopped to catch his breath. He ran again. He fell down on jutting stones and stood up, calling out his daughter's name. Then "Oh my child" because, on the bank of the creek, she was kneeling over the body of Jester Fox, who lay face down, washed by rain. Beside him lay a stone and on his head there was a gash. "Child?"

Mary looked up and shook her head. On her indigo dress was a dark wet stain.

Daniel stood frozen under trees that tattled down to the creek. He saw that Bett was there too, holding Mary's hand, and wondered where she had come from. What had they done? Whatever it was must be undone because it made no sense, and when Simus appeared and took Jester Fox by the arms and began to pull him away through the mud and leaves, Daniel struggled in his heart and mind. He felt all the love he could make himself feel for his neighbour, as if that would bring him back to his feet. He worked at that love, crouching down. Let him rise, he prayed, and he saw the two girls still huddled together and that, above all, was strange and the dead man was now on his back, blue eyes open, face meaningless, even the small mouth and the curling red beard, sodden, framing it. In that face and body there was nothing left to heal, no inch over which to negotiate, and the forest moved around them when the two girls stood. They walked sleepily, leaning together, and when they reached the body in the leaves, they stepped over it and went on.

A lready that day the horse and wagon had been on the road three times, although each trip seemed to have been years apart. The ride to Prayer Meeting, the long ride back home along the lengthening road and through the expanding forest and slanting rain, and now a journey in harder rain with Jester Fox in the back of the wagon sliding aimlessly back and forth. At the frame house the two sons came out at a run while Daniel sat dripping and the rain kept falling. The boys rushed at the wagon as if they knew what it contained and their mother ran out of the house with an apron thrown up around her face. "Dear Jesus, dear Jesus." She threw herself down and beat at the wet ground with her fists, muddying herself. She yanked at her hair while the sons shouted at a small group of workers. "Get away," one son yelled, shooing his hand in the air. The other shouted, "Damn you niggers, get over here!" The younger looked to be sixteen or seventeen, and both had their father's red hair.

Daniel said formally, "I have brought your father, who fell on a rock of our creek." He sat hunched on the seat of the wagon to forestall any show of nervousness. While the boys opened the back and grabbed at the body, making noises of anger and bitterness, Daniel did not turn. His stomach was clenched, his hands shaking. He believed that Jester Fox looked dishevelled but wet and clean. His red hair, once matted with blood, would be rain-plastered to his head, on the back of which was a deep cut and a shallow concavity.

While Julia Fox beat at the grass, which was wet and plastered like her husband's hair, Daniel began to climb slowly down as if he should not rock the now empty wagon. He told the widow he was sorry that her husband had fallen. He told her it had happened while he and Ruth were at Prayer Meeting and that there was no reason he knew for his neighbour to be wandering where he didn't belong when the weather was inclement and the rocks slippery.

Julia shouted, "He come down for water, as is in our rights."

Daniel said, "Though I saw no bucket," his voice as kind as he could make it be.

Two little girls came tumbling out of the house and Julia Fox began hurling whatever came to hand, a hammer, a stick. There was the rain with its smell and feel and the flat sound of it striking softened ground. The sons had managed to get the body into the house, where it must be soaking the floors. Daniel climbed back onto the wet seat of the wagon, glancing back at the frame house with a new sense of shame. Often he had wondered whether it was pride or envy that was the worst of his sins, and now, as he looked at those straight boards and windows of glass, he knew it was envy that most assailed him.

"You'll pay for this!" the widow yelled, shaking her fist at Daniel's retreat, and he felt a great pity for her.

It came as a surprise, nevertheless, when three boys rode onto his land later that afternoon. Daniel kept his eyes on the rifle one of them was holding. They wore scarves on their faces, but he recognized the red, unruly hair of the two Fox boys and held up his hand. "Now, boys, you are fired up by justified grief," he said, managing a tone of authority although he was made nervous by the rearing horses and the gun.

The third boy, who was no Fox, called out, "Give over your murderer!" and aimed his rifle at Daniel's face.

Daniel merely stood.

One of the redheads shouted, "Let him learn what happens when a nigger kills a white man!"

The door opened and Mary came out to stand by her father. She looked at the rifle before she looked at the boy who held it and then took her father's hand, which was hot and damp. She opened her mouth but she could not put it to language.

Benjamin crawled out from under the porch. "Simus down there," he said, pointing, and the three angry boys rode off, breaking low branches and pounding the meadow grass flat while the family stood bolted to the porch that was a thin collar on their newmade house.

When the riders came back, Simus was tied behind one of the horses, running, then falling, then sliding face down, dragged by a rope that bound his wrists, dragged and scraped across ground roughened and ridged by horses' hooves. Daniel rushed down the steps to grab at him, but Simus cried, "You don hep me."

And Daniel stopped.

Because this was the day for one of the pigs to be killed and hung on a hoist, it stood to reason that the younger children would later confuse the two events. All the anticipation had led to this: by nightfall, Simus was hanging where nobody knew how to find him.

How long is the life of a tree and how long is the life of a slave? Here, in the soil just around and covering the roots of the locust, there are drops of blood and a tree does not bleed. Above the ground, a boy is hanging – not by his neck but by his hands, one of which has been torn by a knife – and there is no one around to see him kick or to find him in time to cut him down. The sky is hovering over the thorny branches, as if it would drop around the boy and become his shroud. The sun blinks shut for a minute, but no one notices the tiny night. Simus feels his arms pulled up hard like things unplanted. He thinks that if they stretch an inch or two more, his feet will touch the ground and he will somehow root himself again. He thinks about this new meaning of being free – only to touch the ground. He thinks it might be enough but it will never be guaranteed and he next feels the skin of his back and sides pulled tight by the sag of his weight. Then his bare feet jerk down and up and he feels his whole body jump and spin and he knows that someone is sitting above him up in this tree. "Set me down now! Please!"

"This'll teach you to bash a white man's head!"

Simus is thinking about Jesus and those thieves dying by His side. There was three altogether, he says to himself, without making a sound. Then he remembers how Bett told him the story of Osanyin the healer, a god with only one arm, one leg, and one eye after his house fell down on him and how, because he was so injured, he needed the help of humans. She told him about Osanyin while she was mending his leg. And later, she told him again when he had injured his hand . . . *Osanyin is African*, she said, *as we are*. For time uncounted, this story is there in his head. Then he considers Hiram the pig, set to be killed with the sharp end of a pole axe so that all there is left to do is to open the neck and lay it over a trough. A pig, after being killed, is scalded and scraped and hoisted up high enough to be gutted, but a boy is hung first, still alive. A boy is hung by his hands and left to rot. A boy is owned, like the pig, and has no right to decide his own circumstance. His past is unrecorded and his future is nobody's guess. This is therefore not a murder because it is done to someone who cannot be deprived of what he does not own. Indeed, the boy will hang until his arms are pulled out of their sockets, and still his feet will never know the ground as a plant would define being free. He will hang until animals come to feed on him. He will not be found for three days and nights of looking and by then all of Bett's herbs and unguents and potions will be useless except those concerned with the laying out of what corpse is left. There will be part of a leg, both shoulders, half a face.

But while he dissolves, he will also retrace.

He knows the ground he walked as a child in every molecule of his two feet, and while they dangle, they keep hold of their sensitivities and send messages up his legs to his brain. While they dangle, they roam the slave encampment by the Tennessee border with its ruts and ridges so heartfelt. They touch the prickly stubble behind old auntie's cabin, where the ground grows something that opens and shuts, something that prickles and burns, and where the cook pot swings over its arid blur of smoke. He stumbles on acorns and crawls into leaves that are almost clean what with smelling so dry and sharp. He hears old auntie's shout and he goes on down to the riverbank, which is slick from the washtubs and white-bottomed feet. He lies on his chest and hears his heart pound soft against that ridge where tufts of waxy green emerge in the summer and the water's taste is thick like meat. He holds his face up over that taste and puts his tongue down to it, thinking of the wild animal he had once seen doing this.

For a while, long or short depending, he spins and then hangs solitary, tongue and feet tasting, first watching the land and trees revolve and finally seeing only a slice of it out of a slice of one eye. The main image, recurring, has been the trunk of the locust tree, which is thicker than one man or even two men and possibly thicker than three. Each time he sees it in his revolution, it seems thinner, two boys, then none and the gorse bushes all along the edge of the field and the fallen-down trees covered by errant, roaming weeds. Spinning, he's frightened to the point of terror at not knowing what will be next; but hanging, he becomes philosophical. He has been sacrificed. To save Mary.

He dangles and thinks more and more of the tree, the span of its trunk contrasting with the branches that are meagre like his arms. The trunk is strong, but the life of the tree is shallow in the skin, as is the life of a slave. The tree will not read or write and neither will the slave. The tree will feel its past in its roots, which are stuck hard in the ground, but the present is there too, in the dangling feet of a boy, like ants in the blood. When he runs out of water, his insides will shrivel and his brain will shrink, but the ants will keep marching all the way to the gloss of the creek. The boy will not think clearly then, so he must think now of all the times he has been through and of what he can still know. There was the long ride he endured inside his ma's tight belly, and later a moment when she called out, Son! and he felt swelled up on that. Son! He thinks now of that word and remembers being with his brother in the stiff corn stalks by the well and how they built something of the stalks without cutting them, how they bent and wove those stalks like strong fellows and rested underneath, and he thinks next of a baby inside Bett and her touching the bare skin on her own bruised self and then his. And the baby is the same as he was inside the dark of his mother and maybe it is the thing he calls the dickens, for we are made in His image, and yet he longs now to understand His purpose. Soon I will know, he thinks, and his next thought is for Mary, who instructed him and befriended him and was pleasant in his company, even baring her clean feet and learning from him and that had been the best part of his life.

Dear Taylor Corbett I would come back home if I could for my heart is to sore to bear. I would come if my dear father would allow and leave Virginia where my one friend here was killt crueally. I am so sad. We are taught to forgive but this murder is beyond that rule. How I wish to speak to Caroline as I used to do, but she will never write to me. She also cannot forgive.

Mary Dickinson   21 Novbr 1799

The house Ruth had helped her husband and the dead slave build was more or less finished but for the chimney, and now Daniel was doing his best to follow the measurements for a drawing flue in his worn manual while Ruth handed him one stone after another. Small Ruth, not but sixteen and never the mistress of anything but a butter churn and a china dish. Small Ruth, for whom there were such obstacles as a husband in name only and five unhelpful stepchildren. For Ruth, nothing had changed. But Mary had withdrawn from all of them. She kept company only with the fugitive slave girl, Bett. While she ignored her family and her household duties, Ruth milked the cow, carried the milk to the creek, skimmed it, and later carried it back to the house. She churned, she packaged, she delivered. She harvested what she had earlier planted. She fed Benjamin his choice of edibles and kept the other children alive enough to live another day. When Bett left a tonic at the door for Joseph's cough, Ruth threw it away because what slave knew a thing about medicine? At the almshouse, she had known someone dead of a fit brought on by a hoodoo remedy, and she knew that Bett had been doctoring Missus Fox when her fourth child was born with a squinty eye. When Bett moved herself up to the lean-to for warmer shelter, Ruth begged Daniel to send her back to the Fox place for good, saying, "She'll bring trouble on us."

As if they hadn't had enough.

∽

Daniel thought of nothing but the dead man lying at the edge of the creek and the boy dragged off later that day. In his mind, Jester Fox lay face down in the mud and Simus hung from the locust tree; it was one picture, always with him. He knew the details of the tree as if he had stood at its foot when Simus was lifted into it, instead of riding and walking and searching. He remembered the deep indentation on the back of his neighbour's head as if he had put it there. One body on the ground and another in a tree. The image would not be erased. And those words: *You don hep me.* What did Simus mean? That he was incapable of helping? That he had caused all the hurt the boy was suffering. Or . . . was it a warning. You. Don't help me. Because Simus was *letting* himself be taken? And again the picture of Mary kneeling over Jester Fox with Bett. And again the terrible thorny tree. He was worn down by a lack of sleep, but how could he sleep when he brooded over Joseph's cough and his unredeemed mare and the unsold land and his corn that might be flattened any minute by rain. How could he sleep when he must try not to think about Jester Fox and the locust tree? At night, he carried Joseph across the planks from one corner of the cabin to another, patting his little back to help him breathe and humming whatever lullaby he could find part of to remember. *Oh won't you come along . . .*

He had caught sight of Miss Patch pulling heavy loads to Elkenah Wynn's new mill, her ribs showing between the straps of the harness, and he had felt such regret at the sight of her shivering frame that his own chest ached. It seemed to Daniel that everything had come from the trade of this horse for an innocent boy. All of it had come from that. He must go to the auctioneer and find a way to take her back.

But there was a runaway girl in his lean-to who could bring them all to ruin. "One of these days," Ruth kept saying, "the widow Fox will come up this road to take back what belongs to her and you best be ready for trouble as she'll put the law to her side."

The law. What good could come of hiding a girl who was sooner or later to be found anyway? He must speak to his neighbour and argue convincingly on Bett's behalf. So young, in such a delicate condition, he would say, reminding the widow of God's example of mercy. He could not keep the girl. Ruth was partly right. There was Mary to consider, who was growing too attached. Ruth had seen the two girls walking hand in hand. "Like friends!" she'd exclaimed. And Mary did not go to the meadow or into the timber lot or down to the creek. The creek and the timber lot and the meadow – all of them – were avoided. At night, when Daniel climbed up the ladder and lay down beside his boys, Mary got up and crossed to the door and ever so quietly lifted the latch. Sometimes Daniel climbed down the ladder then and stood at the window and watched the dim glow of Mary's lantern pass through the milk gap and into the night. He stood on the cold floor he had built by placing one board next to another across the beams like a bridge.

M ary stayed close to Bett. She walked back and forth under the trees or stayed in the lean-to as the weather cooled, making herself count backwards. This before this before this, as if any of it could end differently.

At night, Bett went out collecting plants as if there might be a use for them. She hung them on the walls of the lean-to. She pressed oils from certain seeds and stored those oils in hollow gourds. When Mary asked questions about the plants, Bett told her about her grandmother and the Cherokee woman who had cared for the slaves at the Tidewater plantation where she had lived as a child. "The two of them, they used to wander all the way to the hills and nobody ever stopped them because they were known to be healers." Bett was showing signs of the baby she carried inside, and she now and then put a hand on her belly and studied her friend who lay on the big bed for hours at a time.

"Did your grandmother teach you all this? I would like to learn."

"I learn from the plants," is all Bett would say, knowing her only value to this place. Her secrets must be kept. "There is the spirit of the plant and there is where it lives, whether in the root or the stem or the flower. Such knowledge cannot be taught in any usual way." She had been accused of making magic once or twice in the past. Witchcraft, a Tidewater neighbour had called it, because there is also knowing when a plant should be picked and whether it is to be crushed or boiled and such knowledge is rare.

The days grew colder, and Jemima and Benjamin began to bang on the lean-to door begging for admittance. Even Isaac now and then wanted to come in. The little shack felt crowded when they were all there and Mary wondered how the family had ever lived in it, but she did not turn the children away because their childish antics eased her grief and she sometimes agreed to tell them a story. Most of the space in the lean-to was taken up by that first bed Daniel had made large enough for several sleeping people. The rest was covered by heaps of drying roots so that the children had to step around them carefully. On the walls, there were plants and gourds and bits of softened bark, but the little fire Bett kept burning on the ground was comforting as there was still no fire in the cold log house.

Mary positioned the three children on the bed, backs to the wall, reminding them that once they had lived in a house with furniture and a German stove and a spinning wheel. She told them that Isaac had gone off every day to school and she began to tell them the story of Aeneas, thinking it would keep her mind occupied. "In this story," she told the children, showing them a picture pasted in the front, "the hero has a perilous journey." She liked the word and said it again. "Perilous. Because he is running away from his enemies." She looked at Bett.

"A hero does not run away," Isaac announced.

"Troy has been conquered by the Greeks and some of the Trojans are going off with Aeneas in ships to find a place where they can be free and Juno is making trouble for them because of a prophecy."

"In Africa," Bett murmured.

"What is prophecy?" asked Benjamin.

"Very like a promise," Mary said, but she remembered asking her mother why the prophecy had been false and suddenly her eyes filled with hot tears. If only her mother could come back and explain everything.

"More forecast than promise," said Bett, waving her spoon, and Mary thought of the bedtime ritual when her mother waved her brush and let Mary braid her long hair. "When Juno made a storm, all but seven ships sank and the Trojans sailed for seven years looking for a new homeland," she said.

"Who is Juno?" Benjamin asked.

"Remember? *For what offence the Queen of Heaven began to persecute so brave so just a man . . .*" But she stopped then, for there were such pictures jumping in her head that she put her hands over her eyes. *So brave, so just a man.* Simus had not said a word in his own defence when they dragged him away. Now she and Bett were locked together in a secret and the thought of her mother brought only pain and she turned her thoughts to Luveen, who had raised her as gently as any mother but who had sometimes let Mary bring Caroline Corbett into the kitchen to fashion tiny cakes for a family of fairies who lived under the stairs and hung upside down when they slept. It was Luveen she needed.

Bett was telling the boys that her own people had wandered in search of a homeland too. "There was a war between the forest people and a band of invaders from the savanna, but it all happened such a long time ago that there is no reckoning when." Isaac and Benjamin had never heard Bett say more than a few words and they listened with different reactions. Benjamin thought she was nice to his sister, who was always sad now, and Isaac thought she had married Simus because they were matching in colour. He wondered how she had come all the way from Africa to Virginia, but Bett was still telling her story. "Those mixed people," she was saying, "were so changed by being together that they had to leave the first homeland and they wandered *far* to build a new city that would hold them and they called that place Ife and time folds and unfolds around it still." She smiled, remembering her grandmother telling about Oduduwa, who had led the people on that journey, and who had seven grandchildren who founded seven states, but she could not name the grandchildren or the states so she asked Mary if she would open her father's book and read to them, "Please."

Mary borrowed the book from her father then and opened it. *Arms and the man I sing* . . . remembering the night she had asked her mother why Achilles had been a hero to the Greeks when he had hidden in his tent and let them fight without him. It was a fair question, but her mother had given her that steely look that followed most of Mary's questions. "There is always an argument in thee, Mary," she had said, taking Isaac into her arms and kissing his shaggy head. "Achilles is my hero *because* he refused to fight. He came out of his tent only when his best friend was killed by Hector." Mary had once mentioned this moment with her mother to Simus.

"Why Achil drag Hector behind his war chariot if he so fine a hero then?" he had asked. "Hector so brave he never even cry out."

"Ah, kil, eeze," Mary had corrected in her teacherlike voice. But now she had the terrible thought that Simus had let himself be taken without a cry of protest because of Hector's silence. She had never bothered to explain that Hector was already dead when Achilles dragged him around the battlefield. Horrified, she threw down the book and jumped to her feet. "I will read no more of heroes," she told her brothers bluntly, and their pleas did not change her mind. She had given Simus false ideas of bravery. Worse than that was the knowledge that she had stood by her father and watched Simus be dragged away, an act of such cowardice that she could not even bear to think of it. Sending the children back to the house, she lay on the lean-to bed and stared at the wall. *Are not two sparrows sold for a farthing? And one of them shall not fall on the ground without your Father.* "Why did Simus die," she asked Bett, "if God decides?"

Bett came to sit by her. The pieces of Onesimus she had been given by Daniel were buried along with a white bird she had caught and bled. She had buried his bowl and spoon under that hut where he lived as they were the last things he had touched, and also the shingle knife, although she would not speak of this. "Onesimus is with us. I have seen to it."

"What of the other one?" Mary hid her face.

"Him we don't want lingering. Put him away from you."

"I cannot."

"Then come out with me tonight and I will show you what to do."

Mary closed her eyes and dreamed that her mother was holding Simus, running her hands through his wiry hair. When she woke, she lay in the dark, counting backwards all over again. Two sparrows. And one of them shall not fall.

It was bitter that night, but Bett led Mary shivering in her mother's shawl out to the forest, where she told her to find an animal small enough to kill. It might take much time. She must not snare it or trap it. She must call it to herself even if it took many hours. Mary had gone back to the log house after the small sleep and the hard dream. She had taken supper and gone to bed and then gone out quietly after dark when everyone in the house was asleep. Now she walked through dead leaves and hoarfrost, kicking at bushes and sometimes even crawling on hands and knees to inspect the ground for something to kill. What she found was nothing but a mole, blind and easy to catch, and Bett gave her a needle and told her to let its blood run out of its tiny neck and say, "You will not come back." All that time, during the walking and crawling and waiting for the mole, Bett had stayed by Mary, and when the killing was done, she pulled her up like an old woman wobbly on her legs and walked her back to her father's house for what was left of the night.

The next morning, while Daniel was crouched over the wagon hitch, Mary came toward him moving with the slow, automatic gait that was usual to her now so that she seemed to be sleepwalking. "I must speak . . . of Bett."

Daniel did not look up. He had just then been talking to himself with some severity, reminding himself that the girl must be returned to the widow Fox, for two months had gone swiftly by and the girl was no longer a runaway but a fugitive. He would take her back in the wagon, for she was heavy with child, and convince the widow to be lenient, reminding her of the mercy shown to the prodigal son.

"Papa? Are you listening?"

"Not now, child. I am busy with my own thoughts." He found it hard to look at Mary and moved farther under the wagon with his face averted, running his long fingers over the hitch, which needed attention from the blacksmith although every dollar Ruth earned was being saved for Miss Patch. Repairs could wait; he had traded his horse for a boy and the thought of what had occurred through that purchase so horrified him that he fought against it day and night. Horse for a boy. It was ludicrous and obscene. I must take the girl home, he told himself, and after that speak to the auctioneer, who will hear me and grant a reprieve. He raised his head then and met his daughter's eyes. "I am going to speak to Julia Fox and appeal to her sense of Christian mercy."

Mary howled, "Bett can never go back there! She is . . . she has . . . will soon have a baby and is so frightened of those murdering boys that she is afraid to set foot outside in the sunlight! If we send her back I could never be happy again. If anything should happen to her, oh, what then?" Mary was winding her skirt in her hands. "But . . . I had the idea," she went on modestly, "that we might ask the widow to make an exchange."

"An exchange?" Daniel noticed that Mary was wrapped in a warm shawl of her mother's and it pained him to see it so ragged. "An exchange of what?"

"For Simus. Because they killed him."

Daniel crawled out from under the wagon and pushed himself up to a sitting position with his legs spread on the ground. "You think Julia Fox owes us a *slave*?" He bit down on the word.

"Bett would be so grateful to us."

"I do not want the girl, Mary Amelia. Nor her gratitude."

"You do not want the girl *to die*, do you, Papa? And yet you alone can save her." Mary's lips trembled. She wiped her eyes with a fist. "I could sell her medicines." Mary looked sideways at her father. "We could pay the widow that way. Now and then. To keep Bett here with us."

Daniel stared at the sycamore trees that stood like sentinels behind her. "We saw the result of my last purchase, Mary," he muttered, fiddling with the hitch again, shoving it away and then pulling it against his chest. "Thee has a life ahead that must have no such regret."

"When we have paid the full price, we will free her. We will not own her for more than an hour." With the toe of her boot, Mary made a slow circle on the ground.

"Bett could not make enough potions in two lifetimes," Daniel stammered.

"They are not potions, Papa." Mary reached for his hand. "And widow Fox doesn't seem to care much for her. Perhaps the cost will not be so great."

When he dismounted in front of the widow's white house, Daniel touched his hat, for Julia Fox had come out with her floured hands on her hips and he had forgotten his practised words. Speechless, he stood and looked at a woman who had been left with four children to feed in the wilderness of Jonesville. The door to the house was open enough that he could see the disarray within and hear the sounds of children squabbling and a dog whining as if unfed. "I do not see you at Prayer Meeting," he finally managed, and she yelped, "What good is praying after what the Lord done me?"

Daniel considered this. The Lord is no agent, he wanted to say, but instead he announced that he had come about the missing girl.

"Missing!" the widow snapped. Her cap was askew and she straightened it and glared. "We know'd all along where she is." She stared at him. "And if you intend to keepin her, you count me out ninety dollar right here or I am decided on selling her south to teach her a lesson better'n ta run away."

Daniel repeated, "Ninety," without a note of dignity because he had hoped for something feasible, something he could manage. Such as a simple exchange of milk and butter for the widow's children. He looked down helplessly. "I have no wish to own the girl," he said, "only to keep her safe. There has been far too much teaching of lessons already."

This seemed to infuriate the widow. "Ninety, and you to give over her spawn when it's growd enough to work." She pointed a finger at her barn. "And a sow bred and bigged in this upcoming spring, which still ain't enough to cover my loss."

Daniel saw that she had thought all this out long before his arrival and he stood with his arms at his sides, bested by her logic. A long, hard year it had been, a breaking year, and he possessed at that moment only fifteen dollars. But if Ruth had been the making of the three silver coins he held . . . well, she belonged to him as did the cow, Tick, and the milk and the creek and the money was therefore his. But he felt uneasy, for there was Miss Patch to consider. Twice more he had seen his mare pulling heavy loads to the mill at Swift Current. Once he had spoken softly and once he had not, since at that sighting he saw sores along her flank and spent the minutes as she passed wiping his eyes to clear them.

When a little girl rounded the corner wrapped in a blanket to ward off the cold, he touched his hat superstitiously. The child had an eye that was crossed and she sucked on her thumb for nourishment. There were brown weeds between the boards of the porch where he stood and where, a few months before, he had received the blow that had sent him reeling. "I will make no promise about an unborn child," he said. "But I will pay for the girl as I can over time. She will belong to you until I can guarantee her freedom with a final payment." He took a step closer and levelled his gaze. "In return, you will keep your sons off my land or I will report the murder."

Daniel put his three coins into the widow's hand and she put them to her nose and sniffed before turning to go into her house, leaving the child regarding Daniel with that crooked eye.

Riding Mulberry up to this house, he had been surprised that the hill was not steeper, but riding back down, he stroked the mare's dark neck and thought only of the widow's bitterness against the Lord. *What good is praying after what the Lord done me?* Prayer was a matter of listening, not asking. Prayer was an opening of the heart in order to find right wisdom and action. When his wife died, he'd blamed the doctor, not the Lord. Disowned by his community in Brandywine, he'd decided to pack up his children and go where he might find tolerance. He had driven past the wealthy plantations crowning the hilltops of Tidewater Virginia, moving west to the rugged hand-hewn cabins of the valleys, sure that his character would adapt to the new landscape. He thought now that he should never have wished for such a thing.

Mary told Bett that she was safe now but that she must stay hidden on the Dickinson land. "The widow will look the other way as long as you stay out of her path and don't tempt her sons to mischief."

After that, she began to bring the boys out to the lean-to every morning, calling it The Schoolroom, so that they would attend to her with all seriousness. She found that teaching her brothers excused her from working with Ruth and gave her reason to stay close to Bett.

At first she tried to teach the Catechism. *Does he who has found grace have reason to fear?* The questions and responses were taught to all Quaker children at an early age. But Isaac and Benjamin became restless, and, after all, what use were such questions in Lee County, Virginia, where people were hung in trees? Better to go back to the *Aeneid*, which catalogued a darker, truer world. Mary again asked her father for this, his most precious possession, as she desired to read rather than recite its contents, and he put down the bowl of mortar he was mixing and told her to take the words in their scrolled leather cover back to the lean-to as if it were his heart she carried.

I sing of arms and the man. She ran her eyes down the page. Her mind chattered. *Why could I not have fallen at your hand. . . .* Her head ached and she took the book back to her father and brought out her old *Manual of Geography Combined with History and Astronomy*, saying to the boys, "Papa will not let you stay in Virginia if you do not do your sums and learn geography." In what direction from Asia is Europe? From Europe is Africa? In what direction from Hindoostan are the Japan Islands? How would you go by water from Nova Zembla to Cape of Good Hope? Here was comfort. She made the boys draw maps on the slate with wet fingers: circles and squares. How many sides to a circle? She had only paper enough for her letters home. A circle is infinite. Dear Grandmother Grube . . . Dear Taylor Corbett . . . What people did Columbus find in America? Answer: Savages, who obtained their food by hunting and fishing. What people from Europe came to America? Answer: The Spaniards, the English, and, after them, the French. Where did the Blacks or Negroes come from? Answer: They were brought from Africa as slaves to the Whites. Mary glanced at Bett, who was quietly humming, pouring something into a hollowed-out gourd.

✒

The new century arrived, as if the world might really change and the dead reappear. 1800. The chimney was at last complete. The sky cleared. The creek began its trickle over thinning ice. Bears woke and wandered hungrily. Birds flew from one place to another, searching for places to nest. Ruth went down to the creek with the cream she had brought from her customers, passing the lean-to where Bett now lived. She no longer asked when Bett would be leaving. She had given that up the day Daniel went to the widow with her dearly saved cash, spending it for a girl who was only another mouth to feed. Bett did not milk the cow or wrap butter in packets or work the earth.

She thought she was someone special, and now Mary kept her company, passing by Ruth as if she did not exist. Once Ruth had seen the girls holding hands and yelled out, "Which one of you is blind?"

꩜

One day in late April, Bett led Mary to the door of the lean-to and said, "This is my time."

Time?

At the sound of the latch being set – a scraping of metal on wood – Mary thought of the stone at the door of Christ's tomb. She put her ear to the splintery wood and heard Bett at her vegetal work in the dark, lighting a fire and pouring water into her iron pot, and she remembered her mother screaming behind a different door in Brandywine, after which nothing was ever the same: no more reading in front of the fireplace with its big cooking pot, no more skipping to the Academy, where Taylor Corbett sat on a bench with Isaac and she sat with his sister, Caroline. Could she have guessed that her mother would never again brush her straight hair, remarking that it must have come from her father's side of the family? She heard Bett whimper and thought of the tomb and of Jesus, and of Simus, who had died for her, and it was all bound together, for this was his child.

꩜

It was a morning of hush, of no singing birds, of no children's cries. Bett thought of the Fox place, where there was always the thundering of boots and slamming of doors and the two little girls laughing and shouting. Perhaps they had thought it fitting that she move out of the nursery to a hut when her grandmother died. Perhaps what happened to Bett was of no interest to those little girls as long as she could tend to their every need. Bett could, after all, take herself out a pitcher of water to clean her hands. She could do her business behind a bush, as she would not notice such inconvenience any more than a dog would notice it. While Bett thought of these things and the first deep contractions hit, a new anger bloomed in her. It was directed at Missus Fox, who had not wanted to see that Bett was visited in that hut, a fact she would never admit. She did not blame the workers who were kept down by the field in their quarters. They had no way of protecting her. Once they crawled into their cabins at night, they ate their mush and went to sleep, as was their right. Their lives were harder than hers, or so they must have thought, but she had once lived in a house at that Tidewater place, had once spoken with trust to her mistress there, had once taken Saturday baths in the kitchen and the next morning listened to her grandmother speak of the African gods while the white family went to church. Now Bett spread her red cloth on the dirt floor and walked round and round it to measure the circumference of pain that was to come. What had Onesimus suffered on the locust tree? What would she suffer compared to it? She remembered her grandmother's husky voice calling on Nana Buruku, who managed birth and death. She remembered that at the rising and setting of the sun, the living and the dead exchange day and night, so she squatted and crossed her arms to call her grandmother back, but the light, slanting between logs, the warm air, and the smell of the ground brought back instead the way she had previously lived behind her master's house. She remembered the times Rafe Fox had come to her hut and pissed against it while she lay under his father. She remembered the weight of that man and the smell of the piss and the jabbing pain and how Eb also cornered her and grabbed her although not while her grandmother lived. She sipped very slowly at the concoction she'd brewed – lobelia, squaw vine – and felt better until it was worse and then it became unbearable. Had not her mother and her grandmother endured this? Had not every woman before her endured it including the first mother, who was some colour or no colour, some hue, some belonger to some race, who was the mother of all those mothers who came after? And what crime had those mothers committed except by relationship? She pulled her medicine bag close, took out the chalk she kept hidden there, and crawled onto her knees to draw a white cross on the red cloth, dividing the world of the dead from the living. Between the astonishing vise-squeeze of contractions, she squatted low and made herself drink, made herself breathe, made herself think of the creature inside her, troubled in its ground, turning and bursting, tearing her flesh. She talked to herself, *Ancient Father, Sovereign one, Dark stone coming down*, but remembered Mary's raised hand and again, not hearing herself, begged the seed to assume its form, drinking more of the tea her grandmother had taught her to make.

That old woman had been brought over in a ship, curled up, nearly starved, surely raped. That old woman had landed in Cuba before coming to Charleston on another ship and, having come to an enlightened Virginia house, taught herself the words in the cookery book so she could sleep indoors, civilized. That old woman was known as Molasses and what was her name in fact? Bett didn't know; Bett was never told. Bett knew only her grandmother's hands and arms, voice and face. Healer. Known far and wide. Who am I, then? Only the grandspawn of a woman called Molasses. She thought of the other one she had loved, Onesimus, who had been more alone than even she had been and who would, from this day, be her child's father since she willed it that way.

When there was no response to her fist pounding on the door, Mary broke through the feeble lock and found Bett lying on the bloodied cloth, still and most surely dead. Out of her body something like a fleshy string connected her to an infant who lay quiet between her legs. Mary ran fast, yelling for Ruth, who was in the garden, picking early peas. "Bett's got a baby and she's not moving a bit!"

"Well, nothing is born without suffering," Ruth said coldly.

"What would *you* know about suffering?" Mary's indignation was hot as flame as she tugged at the girl who was her stepmother, at least in name.

Ruth put down her hoe and entered the lean-to fearfully. The newborn was down on the floor, smudged with blood, and the sight made her almost faint. There was blood leaking out of the girl and it made a dark, sticky smell and Ruth closed her eyes and held her breath. She had never touched a person in such a place, but she pushed at Bett's stomach flesh, for she had listened in the kitchen during the long hours of Joseph's birth and knew this birthing was unfinished. Bett's eyelids fluttered and after some minutes a mass slipped out of her and still there was more to be done. "Find a knife."

"Ruth, no!"

"For the cord."

When the afterbirth hung from her hands, Ruth pushed it at Mary with a noise of disgust. "Take that filth outside and bury it deep, less you want a wolf to eat it and make the man-baby grow up wild."

The birth of Bett's son caused no stir in the log house, for she did not visit and the rare cries the family heard from the lean-to were quickly hushed. The child was given the name Bry, and Mary was nurse to both mother and child.

One evening in July, as his children were preparing for sleep, Daniel saw that Mary was sitting with Jemima, sewing a little dress for the baby and telling her sister how he was learning to smile and would soon turn over. Ruth was frowning down at her own handwork and neither girl was speaking to her. Daniel got up from his bench, pulled a coil of hemp cording from his trunk, and fastened it to the corner posts of the bed where Mary and Ruth and Jemima slept. While he worked at this, Mary stared at him and when Daniel went to the corner, to the pile of blankets and quilts, and began to hang them one by one on the line, she said, "But where am *I* to sleep?" She had stopped her work.

There was the grey blanket being hung. It had been carded and spun and woven in one piece by Grandmother Grube. There was the brown blanket woven by Grandmother Dickinson and the Tree of Life quilt that her mother had made, second best to the one her father had given to the naked Cherokee at the Mennonites' creek. There was a worsted quilt brought from England on the ship with her grandparents in the year 1725.

Each of these was a precious part of Mary and now they made a wall meant to warn her away from her bed! It was all too clear what her father was doing. She shot a hard look at him, willing him to change his mind, but he had lined up the blankets and quilts without cracks between them and was sitting again by the fire, looking down at his hands, as if even he was surprised by what they had accomplished. "What bed am I to occupy?" Mary asked again too loudly. When her father pointed at the ladder, she stood up fast, making a noise of it, and rushed to the line he had hung with the fabric of her life and pulled down her mother's second best quilt and ran out the door with it.

At the sound of its slam, Ruth's skin reddened as if she'd been struck. There had been a year or more, early in her sterile marriage, when she had imagined the thing that was about to take place. What would her husband say to her? She had imagined tender kisses and wondered what they would be like. No one had ever kissed her except maybe her mam when she was a child and now she glanced around the room noting the order she had brought to it, as if for reassurance. This place. Where she lived. When the others read in the evenings, she found work to do with her hands, never mentioning her inability to decipher written words, but using the time to make patterns that helped her remember her customers' orders. When someone ordered more than the usual amount of butter, she had no way to remember except by changing the location of an object. The wooden spoon, which belonged on a shelf by the fireplace, put her in mind of Missus Craig and it was relocated if that lady desired an extra square or two. The silver spoon was for Missus Dougherty, and the saltcellar was for Missus Jones, who changed her mind so frequently that Ruth could not remember where the saltcellar originally belonged. She let her eyes rest on these things in order to restore her confidence, bunching the shirt she had been mending into a mess of cloth and looking down at her worn brown linsey, which was damp from her heat. The door was shut against mosquitoes and the fire was warm from the cooking and Ruth fanned herself and tried to still the rocketing in her heart.

Then Daniel sent Jemima to sleep with the boys in the loft and sat holding Joseph, staring at Ruth, who stared at the floor. Did she not understand? He began to feel angry. Had he not waited? Had it not been two years and more since she had come to them and in that time hadn't they grown used to each other as tenders of children and animals and fields? The misery of dear Rebecca's death. The awful journey, the long, homeless weeks. Building the house with Simus. And dear Joseph, who barely walked and wouldn't speak and now Daniel brushed at the child's sandy hair and wondered why he loved him more than all the rest. He gathered the child to him and thought of Ruth's strange lack of curiosity. He thought of Jester Fox lying in the mud, with Mary kneeling over him, although he tried not to stay with that thought for long. Tonight his daughter had run into the dark and yet here was another girl in his house, eating, sleeping, breathing her essence in and out so that it surrounded him. And was she not grown? Did his eyes deceive him? She was surely comfortable in her womanly hips and rounded bosom, even under the corset she had ordered from Silas Murray, although what did she know of marriage? Daniel made himself consider Ruth's innocence. If he wondered about her feelings for him, she made them clear when she stood up and went to the ladder and climbed it, putting her arms around Jemima and carrying her back down to the bed. "Did you know that Satan," she was telling the child, "was the best singer in heaven?" Quickly, she stretched out next to Jemima, taking her boots off, but leaving her dress buttoned and her hair up in pins.

Daniel sighed and carried Joseph up the ladder to the loft and told the older boys to lie quiet and say their prayers so that only the Lord could hear. "I shall sleep below with Mama Ruth."

The boys looked surprised, knowing little or nothing about the ways of husbands. "What if he makes wee on our bedding, Pap?"

"He has been to the privy. Do not jostle him. Now, goodnight." Daniel lifted the burning candle and carried it backward down the ladder, blowing it out when he touched the floor. There was another candle on a nightstand next to Ruth, who was lying with an arm around Jemima. The candle's flame cast its eerie flickering over his wife's young face and he saw that her eyes were shut, that her forehead was creased, and he knelt down beside her, his pulse beating fast in his throat. Leaning close, he sniffed at his wife's armpit. Then he began to pull the pins out of her hair where they were available to his long fingers, placing them one by one in a small dish that sat empty on the stand next to the burning candle. It was painted with a picture of a ship on blue water and it was precious to Ruth, a thing she had from her lost family or the almshouse, for there had been nothing in between. He had put the painted dish on the nightstand as a sign of his regard and now he moved Ruth's head to one side and pulled more pins from her hair and when there were loosened braids on the pillow, he arranged them around her head and stared down at her, inserting a finger between her collar and throat, feeling her tremble like the candle flame.

"What doin there, Pappy?" Jemima opened her eyes.

Daniel got off his knees, feeling the stiffness in them, and sat beside Ruth on the bed. "Sleep, child. Listen to the owl in the woods." He removed his boots, his pants. He had forgotten to bring down his nightshirt, so he stretched himself out carefully. "*By night the light stubbles*," he whispered, putting his mouth close to Ruth's ear. "*By night the wife runs her ringing comb through the web. . . .*" He could think of nothing else to say to her.

Only once had Daniel gone back to visit the locust tree after he had found what was left of Simus and carried the pieces to Bett for burial. He had gone back on a warm spring day after Bett's child was born, hoping the sight of dripping flowers would erase the sight that haunted him and bring back the elation he'd felt on first encountering the expanse of land he had bought with his last two warrants. He remembered the smell of the unplowed meadowland and the pond he had found by accident and the way he had jumped off his horse and walked out of his clothes and entered water that was hard on his naked skin. He remembered opening his eyes under the water's surface to see what living things might be bathing with him and he had seen nothing in the murkiness, but something large and fleshy brushed against his thigh and he had yelped, lifting his feet high with each step until he was back on shore again. He remembered that he had first seen the huge locust tree on that happy day.

Now he braced himself. When he could see the great tree in the distance, he dismounted and put his right hand on the neck of his horse and walked along like that, drawing some comfort from the animal's warmth while remembering the sight of Simus hanging among the dark, dangling pods that John the Baptist had fed on during his long ago stay in the wilderness. Simus had had no shelter of leaves, for the locust drops them in late summer and stays bare of them for half the year. His death was therefore more terrible, given no shroud of green, and mocked by the rattling pods that were said to be sweet. And those long thorns growing out of the furrowed trunk must have pierced the boy's flesh as he hung and twirled. Daniel stood with his hand on his horse and took many deep breaths.

What grieved him was not the white perfumed flowers hanging on bare branches as if they'd been casually tossed but the small, innocent articles of faith so lovingly placed around the base of the tree. He crept a little closer, focusing on a thimble that lay rusting and upended. Who might have placed it there like a tiny urn? And the length of ribbon, which had once held colours in its grain, and the wooden button? Had they been left by other men's slaves? Each offering had been chosen and sacrificed, like the boy himself. He thought of John, the locust eater, who had said, *Unless a grain of wheat falls into the ground and dies, it remains alone; but if it dies it bears much fruit*, and he did not understand the words anymore now than he ever had but he drew out his handkerchief and bent to put it by the rusty thimble.

After such a death, what hope was there for his neighbours, who had ignored it, or for the ones who had enacted it, or for the man who had bought a boy and brought him to this end?

PART 2

Ruth called her child John, for the Baptist, and fed him a mixture of blood and cream until she could no longer lift him. Had anyone seen a child smile in its second month or laugh in its third? Had any baby such muscled legs, such a firm grip, such unswerving eyes? How was anyone to dispute her claims? Little John was swaddled so tightly that, according to Missus Dougherty, he looked more papoose than Christian. "It be the way to raise them straight," Ruth asserted, for she had seen it at the almshouse, where they hung the orphans on hooks in their swaddling clothes to straighten their spines.

Daniel's relations with Ruth had hardly changed. He was quiet with her, even taciturn except in the dark of night, when he was undone by her heat next to him. Together they had made a child who did not resemble his others in the least. John was dark-haired, robust, and pink-skinned from the Virginia air he breathed, although that breathing seemed to steal the air from Joseph. "This one, especially," Rebecca had said on her death-bed, instructing Daniel to care for her fragile newborn above all the rest. But Joseph's smile was vanishing; his laugh was a disappearing note. He lay on his cot by the fire, watching people come and go without joy or complaint, as if he had given up the last tiny shred of will. Seeing the pale face, the large eyes, Daniel remembered a moment at the slave auction when he had thought of this child for no reason. He had looked up at a boy on the auctioneer's stage and thought of small Joseph, even then wondering why his own child's face had appeared to him. Had it been a warning?

Bett was not welcome in Ruth's one-room house, but Mary brought tonics to the door for Joseph, and Ruth called them slave hoodoo and threw them away, saying she would not have such potions near her own baby boy, saying Joseph only needed blood and cream and an extra bit of rabbit stew, if he would but eat. Ruth was absorbed in the antics of her own child and in negotiations with her customers and in feeding the family and making butter.

Daniel was preparing for the spring planting. That March of 1802, Frederick Jones had bought a team of oxen and in April he loaned them to Daniel so he could break up the virgin soil on ten acres of the land bought from Michael Shoffert. Since the murder of Simus, the whole acreage had been neglected. Daniel could not look again at the locust tree, but he kept to a corner of the acreage and did not explore farther. Frederick Jones said that, with oxen, a plow could cut furrows five inches deep, throwing a ribbon of grassy sod on the side and laying another ribbon of soil on top when seed corn had been dropped. He said Benjamin was old enough now, at seven, to walk behind the plow dropping seeds. Then for the next three months it would be a contest between weeds and moles and Daniel as to which would win.

It was the custom to plow a corn field three or four times and Daniel recited Virgil as he fought the unturned ground. *Before Jupiter's time no farmers worked the land . . .*

By June there was a worthy crop of hay for the livestock and the evil spell that had hung over the Shoffert land seemed almost to be lifted as if, after wind and storm, the weather had finally cleared. But long before Daniel had purchased his first six acres, Cherokee had built villages on the riverbanks of southwestern Virginia and Kentucky and farmed the low-lying fields. They had fought the Shawnee, who built their own villages until Napoleon bought their territory. And now a Shawnee from the north named Tecumseh was trying to stir up the tribes. The British were said to be arming his followers, and the people of Jonesville crowded into Silas Murray's store to read the *Weekly Bulletin* that came from Petersburg. Rumours were exchanged, and tension began to build.

The two sycamores grew taller. The children grew taller and found shelter in the one sycamore with a hole at its heart. The corn ripened according to its ancient, internal clock, and by late June, when the high stalks cut off the breeze, Daniel was wet with his own heat when he came in for his noon meal. Little John had pushed out of his carapace of linen and spread his wings, doing his best to follow Jemima wherever she went. And as Ruth's child grew and strengthened, Rebecca's lastborn withered. It seemed that one thing caused the other, and Daniel could not love little John. He hovered over Joseph, more and more attached. *This one especially*, Rebecca had said, and Daniel remembered the eyes grown large in her frightened face and he did love Joseph especially and yet he could not make him well.

In the lengthening evenings of fall, when the family and animals had been fed, Daniel sat with the children in front of his fireplace, cracking and eating the meat of walnuts and hickories. This was the hour for reading, when Joseph leaned against him, taking short, laboured breaths. *Father Aeneas now was mulling mighty cares this way and that within his breast: whether to settle in the fields of Sicily, forgetful of the fates, or else to try for the Italian coast.* . . . But the firelight was dim, and Daniel, exhausted by his work in the field, sometimes dropped the book and put his head back and closed his eyes, only to think of things he did not want to think of or to see unwanted pictures behind his eyelids. Then he would pinch himself and sit up to read again.

Once, on a cold night, he opened his eyes with a terrible groan and slouched to the door as if he'd been ordered outside. He stayed out in the night for a long time while Ruth worried and the children wondered and when he came back he was rolling a great log of hickory. He told the children that he had walked over the tracks of a bear on his way to the woodpile and had then gone down to the timber lot to check on the pigs. The log was green and so large that Isaac had to help Daniel get it into the fireplace, where it quickly burst into flame. As Benjamin and Jemima came close to watch, a sweet sap began to ooze out of the log and Ruth brought a spoon and the children took turns coating it with the sticky treat. Isaac and Benjamin had been busy that day husking corn and cribbing it and now they made a game out of shaping the sap into balls that could be rubbed into each other's hair while Jemima fed sap to the doll Simus had made for her, that innocent creature of the blind oak race.

Then real winter descended. The cold was harder that year than anyone in Lee County could remember. "North wind," muttered Ruth when Joseph developed a cough. Bett made a willow tonic that Mary brought into the house, but Ruth sniffed at the unstoppered gourd and poured its contents into the snow.

"I have given this same tonic to the pastor for his cough." Mary's usual quiet voice was hard and sour.

"And you told him you were the maker of it or he would never have swallowed it down." Ruth loomed in the doorway, blocking it. "You give our neighbours false hope along with falsehoods! Go find Joseph a sourwood tree and bore a hole just over his head. Now then, just listen. If you but put a piece of his hair in that hole he'll be cured the day he grows past it."

Mary reported Ruth's prescription to Daniel. "My little brother is sick and she wants to put his hair in a tree!"

But Daniel only smiled weakly. He had smiled at Ruth too, when he heard her idea. Perhaps there was no connection between nature and reason. It might be that every human success simply required faith. He had begun to believe that Joseph was suffering from the sins of a father who had lost his way. But which sins? He looked at his precious four-year-old in the narrow fireside cot. Rebecca had given her life for this child. He remembered the tiny head in its white linen cap and her pale hand resting so lightly on it. He made himself think of Rebecca as he sat staring at the pattern of the flames in the stone fireplace and he wondered then whether God was a fiction, an understandable human wish. He remembered the words of the widow Fox: *What good is praying after what the Lord done me?* He had thought her words heresy, but what if the widow was right?

The Catechism asked whether he who has received grace might have ground to fear, and Daniel knew the answer well enough. *I must keep under my body and bring it into subjection.* But how to do that with a young, ardent wife? Was doctrine more important than experience? He had tossed and turned in the darkness of the loft where he slept with his sons and finally descended the ladder. Now he could not climb that ladder again. He had bedded Ruth Boyd and created a child, convincing himself that there was love in the act. But what if his sin consisted of submitting to lust? Did he love Ruth Boyd?

Unless his sin consisted of something else. He had traded a horse to acquire a human being. From that trade had come two deaths. Daniel sat with his feverish child and thought there wasn't enough air in the world when he listened to him cough. Only two days before, he had counted the eighty-six dollars he'd managed to save. Most of it came from Ruth's butter. A little came from the sale of seed corn and fodder. Forty-six dollars. Ten would soon go to the widow for Bett. How could he ever take back his horse?

"Wiley Jones once went to a doctor in Rosehill," Mary announced the next day, even as she blushed at the mention of this name. She had come to the door with rendered lard from a possum she'd managed to snare and kill.

Daniel replied that doctors were dangerous enough in Pennsylvania, where some of them had actually studied medicine. "Not one of them could save your mother," he noted, half to himself. "We must pray for guidance, Mary Amelia. In this, I could use your help."

"Rosehill is not far," Mary said, although she had never been there. She saw that her father was as much Quaker as he had ever been.

Daniel next said that it was too far to take a sick child in such inclement weather. He said doctors were costly and rarely did anything but put cups and leeches on helpless patients. "Warm weather will clear up his cough," he insisted. And, indeed, there was a respite in early March just as some of the birds gone for the cold season began to come back. For a week or two, Joseph seemed better. Things were returning to normal with Daniel walking his fields and planning his crops while Ruth spent five dollars to buy a second cow and two mallard ducks.

Then suddenly Joseph worsened and Mary again made her plea. "He is too pale," she said. "His eyes fill up his entire face."

Joseph lay on his cot without taking much notice of them and Daniel decided the time had perhaps come to reconsider.

"The doctor's name is Mister Howard," Mary said as they stood looking down at the sickly boy.

Daniel listened to Joseph cough. He heard his daughter's advice and the sound of his own guilty heart, which beat on and on without his volition. At last, he told Isaac to bring the wagon round to the door of the house, so that Joseph could be carried out, wrapped in Mary's quilt.

Daniel had in his pocket the money he'd saved. Next to him, Mary was holding Joseph as if he might break. The child was coughing and Daniel took up the reins and the sun came out from behind a cloud and the landscape brightened. Birds chattered. The coins jingled in Daniel's pocket and Mulberry's hooves marked out a rhythm on the road to Rosehill. Clump clump . . . clump clump . . . *horse for . . . a boy*. Daniel listened. He leaned forward and shivered and then sat up straight. The truth of it drummed in his head. He dropped the reins and put his hands over his ears, but the racket persisted . . . *Horse for . . . a boy . . .* as Mulberry plodded dutifully along a road surrounded by trees and more trees, their branches squeezing. Mary held Joseph, nuzzling him with her cheek against his. He remembered the long ride with Simus taken behind this horse in this wagon on a day like this. The trees were the same and the sky and the scent of the roadside grass. Here, by this outcrop of rock, he had said, *Do you want to ride up here with me?* and Mulberry had been plodding . . . *Do you build? Do you want to ride up here? Won't you come along with me?*

At a crossroads ahead, he could see a large rock that resembled a bird of prey. He could hear the words of the auctioneer: *The road to my place is marked out by old Eagle Rock when you come ta redeem.* Daniel grabbed at the reins, tugging hard to stop Mulberry's plodding pace.

Joseph opened his eyes.

Mary said, "Why are we stopped?"

Daniel stepped out of the wagon and stood looking up the road that met theirs. Lord, if I make this right . . . He could not kneel in front of his daughter to bargain with God, so he stood with both hands pressed against his chest. Mulberry blew out her breath, then a great silence fell upon horse and birds and small creatures while they all waited. A red-tailed hawk slowly circled overhead.

When he climbed back in the wagon, he looked at his son in Mary's arms and turned the horse up the road to his left. "This should not take long."

The road meandered along, making twists and turns until it petered out to a trace that led into a scabrous valley, bleak and apparently uninhabited. But there behind trees, as if called from a dream, sat the auctioneer's house, shades drawn down, unwelcoming. A three-legged cat skittered under the porch. As they rocked to a halt, Mary grabbed Daniel's arm.

Mulberry lifted her muzzle and whinnied.

In the nearby field, there was aggrieved horse response.

Mulberry lurched forward then, yanking the wagon across barren ground until she was stopped by a snaking fence. Beyond it stood Miss Patch, weathered and wound down. Daniel said, "A moment here, please, Mary."

Mary clung to her brother as her father ran toward the desolate pasture. He did not feel himself climb the fence and he was sure he could not be looking at his much altered, much offended mare. Even so, he crossed the field making sounds in his throat as if answering some injury. "Good lady," he said to her then, as he always had in the past.

From the other side of the fence came a shrill cry, and Daniel turned as Mary began her useless pilgrimage, carrying Joseph to the auctioneer's crooked porch. There was the sound of her hand banging on the door and her shouted request for water, for mercy, for help. Then the door opened and she pointed her chin in the direction of the pasture, as if the horse and not the child might explain her need. But the auctioneer looked down at the boy and shook his head, taking off his glasses and wiping them on his sleeve.

Afterward, Daniel watched Miss Patch plod alongside the wagon, lifting her head to smell her release. All around was nature in its exuberance without meaning. He brought his child home and laid him out on the puncheon table he himself had made. He washed him with water and soap – a soft cloth between fingers and toes, behind the ears, inside the nose, around the fragile testicles, as if warmth and cleanliness could ever comfort him again.

Daniel's bargain with God. He had been four years in Virginia and now there was nothing left to argue against or resist. By evening, he was pushing a spade into its dirt. When the spade hit a stone, the hollow sound seemed to come from his heart. Why enliven the souls of children, only to watch them perish? "I will make no more daughters, or sons," he said to the Lord. "I curse Thy enterprise, which may not be senseless but the sense of which now eludes me."

In later years he would wander out to his shed, a building to harbour his two horses – one of them given back freely by the auctioneer – Ruth's three cows, and a fine group of pigs. And there he would sometimes find Ruth's little John with his half-brother, Isaac. "Go back to your studies," he would say to the child whose very existence wounded him. And he would then chide himself for his steel closed heart and wish that Ruth had not come to his house in Brandywine and that she had never stayed. "I planted an apple seed there," she had told him, pointing at Joseph's unmarked grave. She had also said, "To bring forth fruit," but Daniel had told her that his sin lay not in the purchase of a boy for the trade of a horse but in the unholy lust he had once felt for her.

Mary kept to herself, avoiding everyone but Bett. Without daily lessons to attend, Benjamin got up to mischief of one sort or another while Isaac went off to the woods with Frederick's son, Wiley Jones. Older than Isaac by five years, Wiley was teaching him how to hunt squirrel. The two of them sometimes surprised Ruth with an offering for the iron pot and Isaac, forbidden by Daniel to touch Wiley's gun, had learned how to skin the animals and preserve the pelts.

Jemima, old enough now to help Ruth in the house, wandered out to the lean-to, where she could be close to Bett's child, teaching him nursery rhymes and counting games and ignoring Joseph's cot that sat empty by the fireplace.

Mary spent her time stretched out on the lean-to bed counting again. First Jester Fox came upon us, she told herself. After me walking down to see Simus in my indigo dress. After dropping my old dress on the floor that Simus made. After being told to watch the children because a pig was to be killed. *And one of them shall not fall without your Father.* . . . Fathers could not be counted on.

It was Bett's child who kept Mary breathing as she counted back. She counted as she rocked him in her arms. She counted as she fed him his first corn cake. She counted as she taught him to spell his own name: B-R-Y. She counted as she lay by his side trying to sleep.

One night Bett woke her from a nightmare. "Come out and walk with me," she said, pulling Mary's arm. "I'll show you where the seng roots hide so that when you're an old woman, you can be out in the woods leaning on your cane, all bent over collecting them, getting wealthy and fat."

Mary rolled over and smiled in half sleep. "We will be picking them together," she said, smoothing her hair back and rubbing at her face. For two years and more they had lived as sisters, raising Bett's child, and she had been comforted by the feel of Bett's hand on her arm and the sound of her soft, low voice. She no longer walked in the woods and she did not want to leave the lean-to now, in the middle of the night. The crack of a branch, the cry of an animal . . . But she got off the bed dutifully and reached for her cape as Bett took her hard by the arm and did not let her pull away even as they went past the meadow and down to the dreaded timber lot. It was long past midnight and the mosquitoes were thick and Bry had to be covered with a blanket as Bett carried him on her back. Swatting at mosquitoes, stepping through the underbrush, Mary unbraided her hair. "The nippers are going after me." She slapped at her face.

"You should forgive your father, Mary."

"Will the nippers stop biting me then?"

"Perhaps they will. Your father is grieving, as you are. And just look over there." Bett was pointing at a dark mess of growth. "This is where they hide. Do you see? It's easiest in the moonlight, finding the seng roots under their shiny leaves. Remember that when I am no longer with you."

"Whatever does that mean?"

Bett was digging at a root, using a small knife she carried in her bag. "You can come with me if you don't marry."

"Who would I marry in this sorry place? Come *where* with you?"

"I saw you staring at Wiley Jones."

"I do not stare. It's impolite. And you can't leave me." Mary felt small and cold.

"And Wiley Jones was staring back at you. He is not what you think." Bett continued to dig. "When Bry is old enough, I will take him north."

"You must never try to escape or they will catch you and do what they did to Simus!" How could she live without Bett?

Bett shouldered her bag, saying nothing.

The two girls, ghostly in the dark, climbed up the slope that rose behind the lean-to, a furry hill dense with thickets and a hooting owl.

When Mary tried again to teach her brothers geography or history, Isaac soon lost interest and ran off to be with Wiley Jones while Benjamin became distracted, idly shredding the leaves of Bett's collected plants. It was Bry who listened attentively. *What great bay lies in the northern part of North America? What large river from the east flows into the Mississippi?* Isaac and Benjamin didn't care, but Bry studied Mary's book as if he could already read them, causing Bett to laugh and say it was against the law to teach a slave. *Mountains, where are they? Rivers, where do they rise? Lakes, what are their outlets?* Bry listened while Mary protested that it was none of her doing, that Bry was a word thief, and for a few minutes or an hour the air would clear and there would be light enough to lift their spirits, for they were only two girls sharing a tiny space with a child to hold and feed and keep happy and clean and during the nighttime wandering of Bett, Mary lay next to that child, running her fingers over the bones of his dear, sleeping face.

"Mister Craig is suffering a complaint," Missus Dougherty whispered to Ruth after Prayer Meeting one Sunday, "and asks would you bring along Mary when you come for their cream. I gave him a bit of her tonic and he seemed to benefit . . ." Missus Dougherty had taken Mary's tonic for an irritation of the bladder. She had given Mary a small coin in return, along with her thanks. "The Quaker folk have something special about them," she said, half to herself, adding that the efficacy of Mary's tonic might have had something to do with the holy water of the creek, which Mary said was an ingredient.

"Mary is no doctor," Ruth retorted, feeling diminished in her role with the butter churn, "and these days she does not go out."

Missus Dougherty said Mary was of course grieving for her brother, which was understandable, but it had gone on long enough and would be mended by usefulness.

But Mary's grieving looked more like blaming to Ruth. Blaming Daniel for Joseph's death, although Joseph had seemed ready to die from the very day Ruth had come to the house in Brandywine, where he barely took the breast his mother offered and then spit up what he swallowed. Ruth thought once more of the weaklings at the almshouse. It was Mary who had begged her father to take the sick child out on a cold March morning to see a medical man when poor Joseph should have been left in his cot. What good in the world are cups and leeches to a sickly child? Now it was Daniel who grieved and Daniel who wept when he thought no one could hear. Ruth had little John balanced on her hip and when she pinched his leg, he let out a healthy wail. Well, then. Her boy was strong and fit. Ruth tugged at her hat and put a protective arm around little John as she nodded to Missus Dougherty and decided that one Dickinson in the healing business was certainly enough.

As the wagon drew up, she pushed John up over the wheel, which was warm to the touch from an hour in the sun – an hour of listening to the pastor preach about land stolen from the Red Indian, only he said it wasn't stolen because they had never made any claim to it. The Jonesville men should be arming themselves, the pastor had warned.

The sky was noisy with cranes and geese. Their squawking and honking made a racket overhead, and the roadside trees tossed as if all those wings above had raised a wind. It was going to be a hard winter according to Mister Jones, who made his forecast based on the thickness of his sheep's grey wool. Ruth looked at the brittle landscape and tried to forget about Mary and her potions, but Daniel was clearing his throat, readying himself for an announcement. "Ida Dougherty wants to see our Mary out doctoring," he announced and scratched at the beard he was growing. "I wonder if she hopes to heal Mary or Hiram Craig."

"So Missus Dougherty would have Mary sitting by a man's bed?" To show her disapproval, Ruth narrowed her mouth and gave her full attention to a prairie chicken that had fluttered up from the field, its feathers the same muted colour as the grass. "But the pastor says times are dangerous and girls should stay home."

"Mary is eighteen. She needs occupation." Daniel snapped the reins, finding Ruth's admiration for the pastor more irritating than usual today, when the tedious sermon had been used to frighten his neighbours into taking up arms. The president had quietly paid some millions of dollars to Bonaparte, thereby purchasing half of North America and aiding the French in their war against the British. Americans would be caught in the middle. It was no time for a minister of the cloth to be pugilant. Daniel had spent the hour of that unreasoning sermon thinking about Isaac, who, at fourteen, was spending far too much time with Wiley Jones. With such a one as inspiration, Isaac might want to join any available fight. Occupation. It was the only answer for his children. Now, during a long, meditative ride home, a vision came to him – the vision of a paddlewheel turning in Sawmill Creek.

At home, he unhitched the horses and went straight to the lean-to, where Mary kept her sister and brothers every First Day until noon. It was an arrangement that suited Daniel well, connecting the children to the faith of their ancestors, since Mary led them in the practice of meditation, and allowing Daniel to sit beside his wife at the Methodist Prayer Meeting. He tapped on the door and she opened it without greeting, for she had been cold to him since the day of Joseph's death. Months ago, that had been, and he refused to broach the subject. "Tomorrow, you are to take up the service of healing, Mary Amelia," he said gravely after sending the other children home and bringing her outside, away from the ears of Bett. Even to himself he sounded like a Quaker Elder. "It is time to take up your cross. Hiram Craig suffers a bladder complaint," he explained, standing under the midday sun in his Quaker hat and adjusting his shoulders, which were stiff. Then, although his hand went to his heart, he walked away to eat his Sunday dinner without further comment.

Mary felt the slight temptation of pride. And ambition. In the lean-to, Bett was making mush to be soaked in milk and it would be eaten by Mary on the edge of the bed with Bett at a squat before her son, who sat on the ground with his legs out in front of him. In the lean-to, there were no plates, no towels for the wiping of hands or drying of lips. Every spoonful of mush would be eaten and any leftover milk would be put to curdle for another day. In the log house, they would eat venison shot by Wiley Jones. They would eat with knives and plates. Mary looked around at her surroundings. "I need a tonic for Mister Craig's bladder," she said casually. And when Bett handed her a bowl and she put it between her knees to feel its heat through the layers of fabric, she added, "I must know the recipe. He may ask."

Bett looked at Mary in an odd way. "It is not possible to tell recipes," she said. "I learn from the plants and each one has its provenance. Such knowledge is my bridge."

"Bridge?" Mary decided to watch Bett prepare the tonic, noting the place on the wall where the plant was hung and counting the black walnut husks that Bett ground and whatever else she added to the iron pot. "Bridge to what?" She was eighteen years old and living in a shack without her own bed, and tomorrow when her father returned from his morning ride around the fields, she would take Mulberry into town and cure Mister Craig with Bett's tonic. She would be glad to do it. She even looked forward to it, although she could not admit it to Bett, who knew cures for sore throats and sore stomachs and sore muscles and loose bowels and loose teeth and everything else that could happen to a body in this world. Bett had made tonics for slaves and now she went on making them and if Mary sometimes gave them to people in Jonesville and they sometimes gave her a coin in payment, what was the harm in that?

Bett said, "My future. In the north. Bridge to that." She glanced at the wall where the hanging plants were too inconclusive to be deciphered by Mary's unknowing eyes. The tickweed she needed for Mister Craig had been picked in July and dried in the shade. Its oil was highly poisonous, but the plant had benevolent uses. Hanging next to it was a rhubarb root to be mixed with green hellebore but first to be soaked or ground or singed depending on the need of the patient. In the daytime, enough light filtered into the lean-to that Bett could see to poke stalks through stems and hang her plants up to dry. By nightfall she could go outside and collect more plants to boil or dry, safe from the fear of the Fox boys. She could straighten her back and look up through branches that had lost their leaves. She could smell the cures that lived in the dirt, emitting more of themselves in the dark. She knew which vine corrected slow childbirth and which root relieved asthma. She saw that Mary was watching . . . "Ragwort, which is taken for rheumatic pains, is also used for eye inflammation, although of course these uses require different parts of the plant," she said coyly and smiled to herself. "Where sarsaparilla is concerned, it combines well with yellow dock and dandelion and red clover, but for certain conditions it must only be mixed with burdock . . . oh, and it is the dark roots that are best. Then there is slippery elm, whose roots are used for births while the leaves are used on gunshot wounds . . ." Bett peered at her hands, as if they held mysteries she could not name. "Tomorrow I will take a tonic to Mister Craig."

Mary said, "No one takes medicine from a slave, Bett. And there are the Fox boys to consider. I will manage Mister Craig."

Daniel, who spoke Latin and loved his Virgil, had asked Frederick Jones about finding a teacher for the children of Jonesville – but the neighbour saw no merit in such a plan. He depended on his son's prowess in bringing home game and had not wasted time on his schooling. "If your boys need occupation, better to build the mill you have mentioned before," Frederick Jones advised, and Daniel remembered the vision he had entertained on his ride home from Prayer Meeting. Perhaps occupation would have to take the place of Virgil for the time being.

When he passed Michael Shoffert driving a mule cart heaped with hay later that week, he yelled out to him, "Say there, neighbour, I need a man to build a mill. Do you know of one such?" Surprised by his own outburst, he even doffed his hat.

Shoffert pulled his mule to a halt and studied the man who had bought his hundred acres and never put it to any use but to plant some hay in one corner. He said, "I have me a nigger I was thinking to sell. Or I could hire him out at two bits a week. He built Mister Wynn a good mill as a matter of fact and he could plow up your unused fields." He rubbed his chin. "I had it in mind to sell his woman too, but they would surely be grateful to stay together, having two little ones to raise. Although they do not attach themselves as we do," he admitted.

Daniel agreed to hire the couple for the time it would take to build the mill and see it into operation, and the next day Shoffert sent over a man wearing deerskin pants, a leather vest, and a bright scarf around a neck that was surely as thick as another man's thigh. The man called himself Floyd, and Daniel took him to the rapids, which Floyd said had good rise but no access by road. It was therefore no place for a mill, he said glumly, and Daniel let himself study the big man's face, taking note of the depths of Floyd's eyes and the light reflected there. Daniel had grown up around millers, some of them said to be thieves for taking a portion of the product, and he had never wanted to join the trade. A miller was meant to provide a service and make no profit. Now he suggested to Floyd that they build a mill downstream, closer to the road, and he wrote to his father that night, requesting a bed stone and a runner stone, glad to give his father proof that he was prospering. Floyd built a shed first, for the animals, and brought his woman and sons to sleep there with him and to help Ruth with the churning and gardening.

Then, for many days following, Daniel and his sons watched Shoffert's slave fell an oak tree to use as the foundation of a dam, then pack brush and leaves and dirt against it so the land was harried and drowned, one thing consuming another. The boys helped by dragging a bushy limb to the site and leaving it to be lifted by Floyd, who seemed stronger than anyone in the world. They watched him fell a great white oak for the wheel, laughing at them for their fear of the axe, even brandishing it over their heads as if it weighed nothing. But Isaac became restless even then. The process of making a wheel seemed tedious to him and he thought of Wiley Jones, who had begun to visit the town, going to the door of Silas Murray's store, where people gathered to gossip, or the blacksmith's shop, where the bellows could be heard from the street and where boys and men stopped to lean against a wall and discuss the idea of a war. Wiley said the blacksmith would beat at a piece of iron, stopping every few minutes to examine his handiwork. "Plowshares into swords," he had commented once, holding up a bayonet.

Wiley was a stout boy of medium height with a shock of yellow hair. He had grown up in the fields around his parents' house, coming back to their heavily accented English at the table and escaping again when meals were done. He was proud of his father but embarrassed by him, and he often made his escapes with the willing Isaac, who was greatly impressed when a squirrel was killed by one shot and even more so when Wiley brought down a bird in flight. Isaac was always thinking about one thing or another, and chattering on about the strangeness of the universe. Sometimes Wiley let him hold the rifle. It had been made by a gunsmith in Philadelphia and purchased by his father when he got off the ship from Hamburg. Wiley said the rifle's aim was perfect, although Isaac found the gun heavy and daunting when he lifted it, and once when Wiley said he could pull the brass trigger, which was soft to the touch, Isaac forgot his father's ruling and closed one eye and peered out of the other at a tree that was ready enough to receive injury. He aimed and fired, but the report threw him back and Wiley said his future wife and children were sure to die by starvation.

While Isaac was secretly learning the skills of manhood from Wiley Jones, Benjamin stood alone near the rushing creek watching Floyd construct the mill. He had found a knife on the side of the road with a handle of inlaid ivory, and as the slave dug a pit and put a gate at each end, Benjamin whittled at sticks, making them pointed like the bayonet Wiley Jones had seen at the blacksmith's forge.

———

Then winter came and snow lay over the wheel and work was suspended for three long months. Ice formed on the cogs of the tailrace and Benjamin retired to the log house to help Ruth keep track of orders while Isaac went with Wiley to set traps and collect pelts. By now, only Daniel had a coat, and it was threadbare. The children had outgrown or outworn their Pennsylvania clothes and Ruth had come to Virginia with only a thin cape. At milking time, she went to the cow shed wrapped in a blanket, pleased when little John clung to her as she tried to leave. She always bent down and kissed him then, for no one had ever needed her but Benjamin.

There was talk that winter of a wolf pack, hungry and on the move. Frederick Jones had lost three sheep and Daniel worried about his pigs. "They suck out the blood," Isaac reported excitedly, "and leave the flesh. Wiley is going to shoot me one for a coat."

Jemima reported that Bry had found a possum frozen to a tree.

"Not likely," said Isaac, who liked to show off the education he had acquired. "It was only pretending to sleep."

Benjamin laughed at the innocence of a sister who would believe such a thing as a possum stuck to a tree. The two brothers were huddled together at the smokey fireplace with their feet in worn boots extended toward the heat, with Joseph's cot sitting empty nearby. If they thought about their brother, who had coughed and wheezed on such nights as this, it was with a guilty sense of unbrotherly relief. Tonight he would have required constant attention as it was bitterly cold and the fire was bigger and smokier than usual. Daniel cast a long look at the cot and remarked that the lean-to must be even colder than the log house and that Mary should be invited to join them in the house.

Ruth made no comment when he rose from his bench and opened the door. As a blast of cold blew over them, she hunched over little John, who was on her lap, thinking Mary would be too proud to come. Too proud and too full of blame. She had set herself against her father for too long now to forgive him. But a few minutes later, Daniel returned, leading Mary by the hand. He pulled one of the blankets off the line and wrapped it around her, then put his arms around the blanket, pressing her close. Jemima jumped up to hug Mary's cold legs. And then Bett and Bry came stumbling in, having come through a wall of snow without wraps although Ruth had never invited the runaway or her boy into the house. After all, Missus Fox had a crooked-eyed girl born under Bett's care and there was that unlikely birth, with Bett lying on the ground and her blood leaking out . . . Ruth remembered the feel of the flesh she had touched. And now the little boy birthed that day was making his way to Jemima's side, wearing boots that had once belonged to Benjamin. Jemima had even found a place for him by the fire, putting her doll of the oak race into his small, dark hands.

In the days that followed, Bett made her many remedies, and when the weather allowed, Mary brought them to the settlers who were taken sick in the cold, claiming them as her own. She collected modest fees from her customers and put the money aside with the thought of helping her father with his annual ten-dollar payment to the widow. She visited Mister Craig and Missus Emory and a boy named Rob, who was apprenticed to the blacksmith and was suffering a flux. She visited Silas Murray, who put the remedies into vials and set them on his counter – one for Cough and Sore Throat, another for any Itch or Eruption of the Skin, one for Fever of the Joints, and one for Digestive Complaints and Unruly Bowels. People were glad to find remedies that did not require them to visit Doctor Howard, who was costly, and as Mary began to have followers who wanted consultations, she began to think she would be a midwife. She would learn Bett's recipes. She would learn to fix a broken limb.

Daniel decided that in the spring, when the mill had walls and a roof, Ruth's butter and Mary's medicines would be sold there. He might sell cider, as well, and other supplies for travellers who stopped to grind grain. Grind once, sift once, he told Isaac, who was soon to find occupation at the mill. But Isaac's thoughts wandered to the woods, where there were things to hunt, and to the blacksmith's, where there were things to hear. He wanted to hunt not as his sister did with her snares and traps but with a gun. He wanted to hear from other boys and men about politics. He was fifteen that winter and while he cribbed the corn and cut firewood and mucked out the shed, he dreamed of grooves and bores and the buck he would shoot, as Wiley had done the winter before, with a single bullet.

By May, when the millstones arrived by oxcart, only Benjamin was there to watch the paddlewheel pull the river up and around and down again and in its turning make the millstones grind. Isaac had gone into town with Wiley Jones but Benjamin, with his mother's fair hair and pale skin, with her patience and her practical mind, watched every move of Shoffert's slave as he piled stone upon stone, building a room that would serve as a stopping place for travellers. He watched Floyd build the walls of this millhouse and then build a second floor so that when he carried the ground meal up a ladder he could spread it out with a rake to cool. Benjamin did not converse with Floyd but stood off to one side under a newly greened oak and one day he looked up to see Bry dressed out in feathers balanced on a branch. The boy, who had never seen a black man before, was studying the slave the way a crow will study a raven.

As the dam began to hold and a little reservoir of water collected behind it, Bry came back every day. Wearing a torn cambric shirt decorated with feathers and bits of cloth, he resembled an exotic bird in a forest of leaves as he climbed up to study the man with his similar skin. His understanding of the world came from his two mothers and from seven-year-old Jemima. He had spent no time around men. Now he watched the slave's movements and listened to his patterns of speech. When the big man laughed, Bry practised making the sound in his own small throat. When Floyd chopped, Bry watched his arms and hands. Floyd could stand in the rushing water as it rose around him until it reached the red scarf tied at his throat. Then, without blinking, he lifted his feet and lay on his back on top of the water like a dead fish, laughing, looking up, pointing a finger straight at the clouds.

When Bett and Mary came to the mill to grind corn, Bry saw that they were unequal in the eyes of the man he admired. He saw a difference between the two mothers and he saw that it widened or narrowed depending on who was speaking to them. He saw that Mary was more tolerant when he stole vegetables from Ruth's garden. When Bett caught him at it, she stamped her foot and clapped her hands in his face. By the time the seedling on Joseph's grave had grown from the seed Ruth had planted into a little tree, he had used the first fruits for his target practice, smiling when questioned by Mary and declaring that apples were like fingernails and would quickly grow back. She had laughed and patted him approvingly and in such ways as this, he found a confidence that was unusual in the son of a slave.

Raising her child, Bett thought of the steadiness she had known in that kitchen where her grandmother had cooked and lived, sleeping behind the chimney with the grandchild left to her when her daughter was sold. She thought of her grandmother's habits, her stories and instructions. Collect bur-duck seeds in late summer and store them dry. Take the roots in the fall of the first growing year. Plant when the moon is full. Dry pennyroyal in the shade; it promotes birthing early or late. Look for squaw vine near evergreen stumps. Pick a stem, never cut.

As her boy got older, she told him about this great-grand-mother, taking him into the woods at night so he would learn to move quietly in the dark. She taught him to walk without making footprints and to read the direction from the moss on certain trees. She told him that one day they would walk away from this place and that knowledge would then be required of him. "There will come a time when you will have to think for yourself or for both of us." Bett was a slave, but her child had no concept of any such thing and she was glad of that par-ticular ignorance in him. Sometimes she told him stories of the mpemba, the land of the dead, where a sun rises and sets just as it does in the land of the living, and sometimes she spoke of a city that sits on the crest of a mountain, a city where each clan has its own street and where his ancestors, called mbuki, healed the sick.

Her son passed these stories on to Jemima, for they were similar to the Bible stories she liked to hear from Mary whenever she could escape the watchful eyes of Ruth. Jemima was slow to read, but Bry invented a language made of simple shapes. He showed her where spirits nestle in the bark of trees and the sticky substance they leave. He showed her the carapace of a locust where a spirit had once been trapped for three days and said he could feel sound on his skin and he could close his eyes and step into a pool of water being lapped at by a wolf and then disappear down the wolf's dark throat. Bry lived on the other side of things and she went wherever he went. He was five and she was eight. Then he was six and she was nine.

From Jemima, Bry learned to climb trees and swing from one to another on vines, for she was no more reserved than Isaac when it came to play. Jemima ran barefoot, climbed sticky pines in her long dress, and waded into the creek to catch trout and catfish on a sharpened stick. She packed corn cakes and the two of them set off with a make-believe map. When they found a cave on that furry hillside behind the lean-to, Jemima made rocks and stumps into furniture and cushioned them nicely with leaves.

One late summer day, with the field corn shucked, Ruth had boiled the toughest kernels in water and lye to get the husks off, and she took the iron pot outside, calling Jemima to drain off the water and skins. It was a warm day and Jemima was in the cave, where Bry was telling her an elaborate story about a place where everyone spoke a different language. In the distance, she heard Ruth call and she looked out at the sky to judge what was left of the light, hoping Ruth would not try to find her. Mama Ruth was hard to satisfy. Nothing Jemima did was ever quite right, and now the stepmother appeared at the cave's entrance and grabbed Jemima by the arm and brought her to the hominy pot that sat balanced on a rock and Jemima knocked it over with her foot.

"Well, that's the Devil's work," said Ruth. "You know, Miss Jemima, the first time I kicked at this ground I started a garden and we been eatin of it ever since. Now you go on down to the crik and fill up that pot again."

"I can't carry that pot full a water, Mama Ruth. You know that."

"I know the Devil is stronger than Jesus, is all I know."

"Bry can help me."

"You leave him be. You're too big to be with such as he."

"But my sister told me to look after him."

"Well I am your mama, and I say nix to that."

"You are not my mama!" Jemima shouted, leaving the overturned pot and the hominy on the grass and running fast back to the cave. She could hear Ruth's protests and became somewhat afraid, but in the dark of the cave, she found a message written in the secret language scratched in the dirt: □×□+, *Find Me*. Turning fast, she saw that there were clues strung out from the door of the cave, across the meadow, and on to the creek. First, a picture drawn in the dirt. Stick figures – a boy in pants and a girl in a ruffled skirt. Next, a leaf wrapped around a stone because Bry always left that sign. It was his signature. It might mean that he had climbed up a tree to watch her hunt for him. He claimed he could walk a mile without ever touching ground. Or it might mean only that she was on the right trail. Trees swallowed her. A stick broken into a cross. She could hear Ruth yelling, but she would not turn back and went deeper into the forest. Ruth had told her that the real cross was made of pine and that's why a pine tree always bled. "You come on out, Bry, right now this minute!" Jemima commanded, stamping her foot. She did not like this game. It made her feel all alone and she made a mark on a fat pine to see if it would bleed. Then she sat on the ground and built a village of twigs by snapping them into pieces. She thought of the cross Bry had made and knew she wouldn't be able to find it again. She was lost. She made nightshirts for the stick people out of leaves and stretched out next to them. Bry would find her and make up a story. There would be a hero. There would be a queen. Jemima rolled over to look at the sky and tried not to be afraid.

When Bry found the spot where she had stopped to examine his stick figures, he knew how long she had stood there by the mark of bare feet in the grass. When he got to the timber lot, he called her name because he knew that she wasn't close to finding him. When she didn't answer, he climbed into a hickory tree and looked down to see her lying asleep. Her head was on the tiniest of houses and she had an arm flung out with a stick person in her grasp. She lay like that with her face to the sky and he came down from the tree and lay beside her, touching her face and tracing his name on her skin.

One day Bry followed Isaac into the shed, holding to the dark edges and staying out of sight while Isaac put feed in a trough and laughed as one of the sows pushed a piglet away. "If you ever want to help, you'd be welcome," Isaac said quietly to the hiding boy. He stroked the piglet's bristly back. "Two of these pigs were raised up by your pa before he died."

Bry looked at him, wide-eyed.

"You ever see where he was killed?"

"My pa? Sure I did." It wasn't true. Bry knew nothing of this.

"It's only a tree," Isaac said. "But maybe you should see it."

"A tree," Bry repeated.

"It's special. There are offerings put there." Isaac had found it for himself when Wiley refused to take him. Isaac said the tree had a collection of little things – a wooden whistle, a handkerchief, a penny from the island of Jamaica, a rolled-up tobacco leaf.

Bry did not know what an offering was, but the next day he agreed to be taken from the only place he had ever been to a huge tree that stood a good hour's walk away. Isaac took him by way of the creek and then north to the Shoffert boundary, and Bry followed nervously in Isaac's wake, for he admired the older boy. "It's a ways still," Isaac called back when Bry seemed to lag, "but I know these woods all right."

Isaac was always kind, even when Bry had refused to share the toy wagon Wiley had made. It was blue and had turning wheels and Benjamin had hidden it once, but Isaac had taken Bry to the cowshed and given it back and now he was going to show Bry where his father had died.

At the tree, when they came to it, Bry looked straight up for some time. When he looked down, he did not touch the small glass bottle or the coloured stone or the dirty ribbon at the base of the trunk because Isaac said they were never meant for living flesh. "How did he die?" Bry asked with his smallest voice.

"A man named Mister Fox beat your mama," Isaac told him. "Then your pa pounced on Mister Fox and his boys killed your pa. For the pouncing." The day was warm and Isaac looked at Bry, whose eyes were sad, and told him there was a pond nearby and maybe they should now proceed to look for it.

Pounced on him, Bry thought. He said, "My pa would never be killed by just boys," and felt the proud claim of that.

"Well, they hung him on this tree," Isaac said, wondering if he might be going too far. Bry was only six and looked to be tired and somewhat upset. "And he never made any sound that I heard when they dragged him away and then they rode off and just left him here and he couldn't get down." He added, "Your pa wasn't full grown either and there were three of them."

Bry stood under the thorny tree, his hands on his narrow hips, forced to believe what Isaac said because the older boy had been there and seen all of it with his eyes. He said he had seen the boys come into the yard on their horses and he had seen one of them shoot off a gun. "And it was Benjamin who told them where to look for your pa," Isaac said. "Just like Judas."

Bry swallowed and kept still.

"Did you know him?" Isaac asked because he couldn't remember clearly the order of events. And Bry said he talked to his pa at night, although it wasn't true. No one had told him about this father. With Isaac, he kicked the dirt and doubled up his fists, but later, lying in the lean-to bed and looking out on the very same moon that had shone down on the black tree through that dark night, he wondered how long it took . . . no water, he thought, and he cried into the pillow Mary had made for him. No one to sponge his lips like Jesus. He thought he would kill the two sons of Mister Fox when he was old enough and he wondered who the third boy had been because he would kill him too when he found out.

For many nights after that, the thought of his father burdened him, but the hours he spent awake in his bed were not wasted, for he used them to move his understanding forward bit by bit. Three boys had come into the yard on their horses. They had shot off a gun. They had made the horses prance around the yard on their iron feet and Benjamin had told them how to find the hut. Over and over he ran the words and images through his mind. Someday, he thought, I will do unto them as they did to my pa. He did not speak to Mary or Bett of this. It was his secret to hold hard to.

When Bry turned seven, Bett took her son to the site of the fallen hut where Simus had lived and where she had buried the spoon and bowl and the shingle knife. No one had cleared the pile of thin logs away and she told him to take them up one by one and lay them out in a circle end to end. "Stars sometimes fall to earth," she said. "And they must have a map." She knelt in the centre of the circle and spread a red cloth on the ground, saying it was the cloth on which she had given him birth once before and this was to be the second time.

Bry looked at the cloth and backed away. He did not want to go into the mysterious place he had come from, wherever that was. He did not want to be born again on a cloth where Mama Bett was even now drawing a cross with the chalk she kept in her medicine bag. It was the kind of cross she drew on the ground in the woods, with circles at the end of each point, and at times like that she always acted strange.

Touching the sides of her son's face with both hands, Bett told him to stand in the centre of the cross and call out to his father in a loud, clear voice. "By what name?" Bry asked, and she said, "Only call out 'Father!'"

"But what is his name?" Bry would not take a step. He kept his eyes closed and she gave him a push so that he stood for a minute at the centre of the cross and then she pulled him to her and gave him a red cloth bag that held five stones of various co-lours. She said his father had come for an instant while his eyes were closed, and now he had gone back to his death like great Oduduwa, the ancient father.

At the lean-to, Bry told Mary that he had called his father back to earth. Thinking he had done well to inform her, he spread his arms and hopped about, but Mary narrowed her eyes to slits and said it was wicked to say such a thing and even raised her hand before he ran outside and climbed a sticky pine and was gone for the rest of the day.

That evening, Mary entered her father's house during the family meal to ask for help. "It is Bry's seventh birthday," she explained. "And I want him to know about Simus. That he was a Christian. Before he gets wrong ideas."

"I want to come," Jemima said, and Mary answered that Jemima would always want what she couldn't have.

At that, Daniel stood up, pushed back his bench, and said that he and Jemima would forgo their peaches in order to visit the lean-to. Still chewing the last of his bread, he led his two daughters outside and along the narrow path through the milk gap, sure that Mary must be reproaching herself for speaking so coldly to Jemima since she was one to judge herself as harshly as she judged others. Supposing that she was suffering regret, he waited to hear an apology. But there was none forthcoming. Mary had become as unknown to him as the little lean-to he had built eight years ago, and he ducked his head and came through the narrow doorway to be assailed by a bitter smell, as if his memories clung to the splintered walls along with Bett's plants: memories of his children cold and hungry and full of their separate fears; of freezing nights, with all of them stacked like kindling on the bed while he slept alone in the wagon alongside a boy who lay on the ground in a pile of leaves. Bett was lighting a pinenut candle and its smoke brought tears to his eyes. "Why have you given Bry his name?" he had asked her once, and she had answered that it was for black bryony. "Which is poisonous," he had said, and she had answered, "It also heals."

Now his eyes moved to the wall, hung with its herbs, some of them no doubt poisonous and others perhaps healing. Wondering why he'd been asked to come, he noticed that Bry was sitting in a shadowed corner, fingering a small red bag.

Mary had put herself at the farthest wall and she stood quietly, with her hands clasped. "This being the anniversary of Bry's birth," she said, "I wish to tell him of his father and for that I ask my own father's help."

Daniel saw that she had grown to womanhood without his noticing and he suddenly missed the girl she had been.

"Now then," she said, opening her old Barclay's *Catechism*, "seeing it is by the spirit that Christ reveals knowledge of God, is it by the Spirit that we must be led?" She paused. "Bry, put aside that heathen bag."

The child opened his mouth, but Daniel said quickly, "Ye are not in the Flesh, but in the Spirit, if so be that the Spirit of God dwells in thee." It seemed an unusual way to introduce Bry to his father.

"Papa, it is for Bry to answer me," Mary stated. "His father was a Christian and he must learn the responses."

Daniel saw that Bett's lips were moving and that Mary seemed not to notice.

"And as touching brotherly love?" Mary asked, peering at the open page.

"We are taught to love one another," Bett said softly.

Mary glanced at her, frowning. In the dark, the lean-to was more pleasant than it ever was during the day, when all the cracks showed and the dirt floor was often covered with baskets and gourds, but Bett must understand that this world of theirs had grown too small. It was all about to change. "Bry, is it necessary for our salvation to keep the commandments?" she asked, staring now at the boy as if she would lay claim to him. This morning Wiley had said that Bry would have to stay in the lean-to with Bett. He thought that Bry was too wild to live in a house, but she would prove him wrong. He had said this after coming upon her lugging a pail of water from the creek. "I am building a house for you," he had said, gazing at her upturned face.

Now Mary looked at her father, who remembered his Barclay's after all these years. In the dim light, she could see grey strands in the hair at his temples and in the beard he had grown since Joseph's death and she wondered how she had failed to notice these things when she had given such attention to another man's face. She looked at Bett, who was sitting on the dirt floor in her faded dress staring at walls badly chinked, soiled with rain and mud and tears, and at Bry, who was still clutching the red cloth bag. She could not leave them behind. They must be always close.

The night was very still, without breeze. Mary was trying to create a mood, to inspire a seven-year-old child, but why? Daniel stared at Bett, whose hands lay on her tired dress. He had seen her make clothes for herself and her child out of remnants. He had seen her put Bry in the cast-off shirts of Benjamin or Isaac. But Mary was cleanly dressed in good grey linsey. The wool in its weft had come as a gift from Wiley Jones, who raised sheep with his father. His mother had spun it and woven the fabric as a gift. Daniel wondered then if he had been invited out to the lean-to so that Mary could make an announcement. Perhaps this performance had nothing to do with Simus or Bry. Perhaps Mary wanted to fortify her position, to warn her parent, to ready him for a proposal by showing her maturity? Wiley Jones had been making weekly visits to the Dickinsons, bearing gifts. But Daniel did not like Wiley Jones, and wanting no confession of new faith from his daughter, he got to his feet and announced that he and Jemima should be off to their beds.

Mary stepped forward to take him by the arm. "Tell Bry there are no spirits in the woods, Papa. He must learn so that he can live in the world. I am going to teach him our Catechism. I will also teach little John."

Daniel lifted the latch. "John will be Methodist." He ducked under the lintel, and as he did so Bry ran streaming past.

"Blessed are they that do His commandments that they may have right to the tree of life," Mary called after him.

"Your acolyte has escaped," Daniel said dryly, letting the door slam.

∽

The space between house and lean-to was so dark that he put out a hand to feel his way. "I wish you success in your efforts," he called back, remembering his mother, who had trained him in the Catechism with a willow stick.

"Pappy," said Jemima, stepping along beside him. "I see no stars in my sky."

Daniel looked up through the trees that lined the path. Blank dark. Emptiness. As if the hand of God had taken everything away. He looked at his house, through the window of which he could see the flickering of firelight as if the house meant to encourage the sky. And whereas the stars were cold and life-less, the black air around him was tangy with woodsmoke and he could hear Bett calling her wild boy. He sniffed at the air and moved toward the place he had built with the help of that child's father, although he knew in some part of his mind that Bry was more likely the offspring of Jester Fox. There was his dust-coloured skin to consider and the attitude of his mother, who had named him so strangely. Still, here was the log house he and Simus had built. Daniel walked on through the dark, knowing his wife would be waiting for him to lie down beside her. And something stirred in him at the thought of it, although he could not allow himself the pleasure of such lust.

While Daniel watched the shadows of firelight behind the curtain of blankets that still made a wall around his bed, Mary and Bett lay in the lean-to with Bry asleep between them. Their bed had been large enough for a family, and the two grown girls and the small boy had space enough for comfort. "I am going to marry Wiley Jones," Mary said quietly. "He is building a house for me. We will have to make Bry better civilized."

Bett said, "I can never live with Wiley Jones."

"Of course you can."

"Wiley was often at the Fox house, Mary. Did you not know that?"

"They were only boys."

"And now he is a man who will decide your life. But he will not decide mine."

"Decide my life?"

"It is what husbands do." Bett was surprised by the great difference in their understanding . . . it was a dichotomy, a word that suited her since she knew herself to be both stupid and wise. She was stupid because of her bondage – for who would credit a slave? – but was wise because she knew what men could be. Leaving Bry on the bed asleep, she got up to stand on the bare ground of the lean-to, swept clean that day.

She had pounded it so the dirt wouldn't rise with their foot-steps. She had cooked for Mary and for herself and her son and she had made a remedy for Pastor Dougherty, a man she had never met.

Mary was considering Bett's words. "My father does not keep Ruth from her butter or church."

Bett said, "He uses her money as he pleases."

Mary considered this. Ruth had three cows. She had bought another hog and two sows. She sent piglets to market every spring and fall. Every morning and evening Floyd's woman, Cherry, milked the cows and every week she and Ruth made butter from the cream. Never did Ruth have a penny for herself. But Ruth's needs were few, after all. "I am twenty-two," Mary said. "I cannot live in this shack forever. We will have a better life with Wiley."

"You do not know him as I do." Bett felt the old dark of the slave hut where she had lived with its stink of man piss. "I will stay here with my son."

"But we have our patients." Mary felt a rush of irritation. It was she who had saved Bett from the widow and her dangerous sons, she who had moved into the lean-to to keep Bett company . . . She thought of the timber lot and the fallen man lying in the mud and told herself she had always done everything for the good of Bett. And now, when she offered her a true home . . . She rearranged Bry's sprawling limbs and turned her back on mother and son. Bett may have loved Simus more than I did, she thought. And losing him to death may have been even more terrible for her, but losing Taylor Corbett to the distance between time and place, to the space between mountains and valleys is also terrible; it might even be worse. All these years she had written her letters of hope and with the last one she had sent a pillow stuffed with rosemary.

*Dear Taylor Corbett. I hope to come back soon. I await
the wellcome that matters more to me than any other.*

He had not replied. She could hardly remember his face. She got
up and opened the door, looking up at the sky, while the night
pressed down, leaking its dark into their lives.

It took Wiley Jones a year to build a house on the edge of his father's property and Mary waited patiently, although more and more she visited patients with Bett's tonics. They were composed of ingredients Bett refused to name combined in amounts and ways she kept to herself. "Mister Lyle's hands are swelled up," Mary might say. Or "Missus Cornet's stomach has been cramping" and Bett would send her back to her patients with something specific for each complaint and most of them were relieved of their various irritations and comforted by Mary's attentions. She had that something about her, they said, that came from her Quaker background. Or they said that, like her stepmother, she was gifted, that the creek and the ground it ran through were blessed. For Mister Craig's bowel complaint there was something unnamed simmered in milk. For Mister Sharpe's asthma, there were ground anise seeds steeped in aqua vitae and something unnamed.

Wiley worked alone building his house and making weekly visits to the Dickinsons bearing gifts. Knowing Daniel's aversion to weapons, he never brought his gun onto the property but came with venison or quail, asking to see Isaac and hoping to see Mary. "Your house is ready," he told her one day on the path between the lean-to and the house, noticing the way she had knotted her hair at her neck and the strong hands that were tucking it under her cap.

"My house." Mary had walked past it many times, but now it was real. She was going to marry Wiley Jones and be someone entirely new.

"I am going away, to be back in ten days. Will you meet me at the pastor's then, just after midday?"

Mary had agreed to this. She had met Wiley's eyes and said she would meet him anywhere, and ten days later, in the shade of the sycamores, she told her father she wanted the wagon. "Wiley Jones has asked for me."

Daniel's heart beat against his jacket.

"He is a friend to me, Papa."

"Taylor Corbett is a *Friend*." Daniel gave the word emphasis.

Mary tugged at her apron and said she had heard nothing from Taylor Corbett. Not for a very long time.

"Letters go astray. Perhaps he's found no one to carry it. Have some patience for once, child. This alliance with our neighbour is too quick." The son of Frederick Jones liked only to hunt and trap and fish and travel as far afield as possible in search of risk, and these were entertainments Daniel did not admire. In truth, he had more doubts about Wiley Jones than he could easily explain.

"He has called here many times."

"But there should be. . . . With thy mother, it was . . ."

"I know, Papa. And I shall do my best."

"And shall Wiley Jones do his?" Was it no longer usual for a young man to speak to a girl's father? Had he moved his family into such an uncivilized place that all custom was abandoned?

Mary said, "He has built me a house," meaning to prove something to her father. Daniel turned, needing a minute to think, but she followed him into the house, insisting that she must have the wagon as Ruth slammed her mallet into a piece of venison Wiley had brought and told Isaac he must go get hot ashes from Missus Jones because he had let the fire go cold during the night.

"I shall walk," said Isaac, seeing Mary's look of panic.

But Ruth said there was also the wheat to be threshed and the wagon was needed for that and what did Mary want with it?

Mary decided that, if her father did not grant her the use of the wagon, she would *never* marry Wiley Jones or anyone else. Without the wagon this very morning, she would live in the shabby lean-to forever. So it would be decided. She kept her eyes on her father and her hands clenched at her sides while she thought of Wiley's straw-coloured hair and serious eyes. He had kept her family fed over the winter just passed. He had taken Isaac under his wing like an older brother. This morning she had gone to the creek to bathe in privacy and think of the words she would to say to him in the pastor's house. She had soaked in the water and silence and prayed, and when the bathing was finished, she had collected her clothes and put them on again. But for the trip into town, she would wear the grey dress Wiley's mother had made for her. It was even now hanging in the lean-to, waiting for her to become what she might become. She had waited a year. She would rebraid her hair and reknot the braid at the back of her neck and go off in the wagon. If only her father would grant it to her. Nothing else would she ask of him – not land or dowry. And once she was married, she would be someone else, a different person, unhaunted.

❦

Daniel had spent the first part of the morning trying to decide whether to sow his winter wheat in the corn stubble or in regular rows. With the first method, the stubble would have to be cut with a hoe during a freeze, but he would avoid the plowing.

He looked at his daughter's upturned face and told Benjamin to hitch Mulberry to the wagon and told Ruth she would have her fire and that the wheat would get flayed in good time. He said a smooth piece of ground near the stacks had been cleaned of weeds and the boys would spend the day removing the straw and taking the grain to the mill. At the moment, he could not remember why any of this mattered. He must hand his daughter into the wagon and give her the reins. "As to Bett, your husband may assume payments to the widow," he said somewhat bitterly.

Outside, he stroked Mulberry's ears and tried to speak in his accustomed way but something caught in his throat. "Go on with thee," he muttered as he watched Mary climb up and speak the horse into a trot, skirting the apple tree, which was once again bearing its fruit. In front of them, Ruth's chickens scattered, taking short flights into the bushes while John ran ahead to move something out of the way. An auger. Who had dropped it? Daniel felt a flash of temper like a separate being as he watched his daughter slip away.

That night, Bry left the lean-to because one mother had gone out into the woods with her collecting bag and the other was gone for good. He was eight years old and alone in the dark for the first time and he heard sounds and thought of wolves and wondered if he should go back to the safety of the lean-to. He wandered on, wondering why Mama Bett had refused to go to the house Mister Wiley had built. Mister Wiley had once made him a wagon and painted it blue and said that Isaac and Benjamin should not touch it. Mother Mary had told him that in the new house he would have a room of his own and the thought of that made him feel strange but he picked up a stick and slashed at a tree, hearing the whack of it with satisfaction.

As he walked, being careful to make no sound and leave no mark, as he had been taught, he thought that Mary must surely be missing him and would be glad to have him suddenly appear if he could find his way to her. It meant a crossing of the creek, which was rushing along in front of him and which was dangerous, and the moon was small, without much light, and he heard the sound of metal rattling and crouched down, frightened, unable to see. Squinting, he made out the vague shape of a man on the other side of the water. He was dark, like Floyd, and squatting as he drank from a metal flask. There were chains tying his wrists to his ankles so that he stumbled when he tried to move and the two of them, man and boy, peered at each other across the noisy water and the boy stepped into it carefully so as not to unbalance anything. A cloud floated over them and the poor light of the moon was further diminished. "Why is that chain on you?" Bry asked as he climbed up the farther bank, noticing the rise and fall of the old man's body as he took in and gave out breath. When he got close enough, he put his hands around one of the arms ringed by its iron cuff and eased the man gently down the embankment, and slowly, slowly they crossed the stones of the rushing creek and he kept hold of the arm as they passed through the pinewoods and over dry needles underfoot, Bry thinking of Bett, who was somewhere collecting and would know how to help a man like this, and of Mary, who was asleep in a house he had never seen. They went on, man and boy, without even the sounds that might connect two animals, and after a long, shuffling, trembling journey, they came to the mill, which was inhabited by Floyd and his wife and two sons on its second floor. At the tiny entrance, Bry called out, "Hey?" in his boyishness because he had spoken only once to Floyd and was afraid of angering him or, worse, of making him laugh. Floyd opened a shutter and came down and let them in and there was a file that cut through the chain on the old man's wrists and tea made of yarrow and Bry remembered Floyd's kindness the time he had brought him a broken wheel from the toy wagon Mister Wiley had made.

After that, it was a matter of when to leave, and once outside again, the old man looked up at the stars, pointing and talking tunelessly about a country in the north and a river to be crossed that was called the Ohio.

Upstairs in the new house, there was a bed where the married couple slept in a state of pleasant tension, Mary sometimes waking with a quick intake of breath to touch her new husband and run her hand down the length of him, still unbelieving. She was a married woman. At the wedding, there had been no one but Missus Dougherty to act as witness. Even so, Mary had felt emboldened and triumphant. Her husband was different. He smelled of leather, gunmetal, and oil, and she moved against his difference, putting her past away. The past was what lived on her father's land and she would convince Bett to leave it behind by promising to set aside space for an infirmary.

"As I predicted," Bett said one day some months later when she finally arrived with her plants and gourds and bags and Wiley had sent her to live below the house in two cellar rooms with Bry. It was true then. Wiley determined everything – when meals would be taken and what would be eaten and who would sit at the table with him. Never Bett, never Bry, for they were cast as servants, with their own door at the back.

"It isn't what she is accustomed to," Mary said to her husband. But it was a meek reproach. She was glad he had relented and allowed Bett to live with them.

"Bett knows her place," he answered. "It is you who misleads her, not I."

"What she *knows* is every symptom of every illness," Mary told him, explaining her need of a place to keep her patients close. In such a place, she could offer Bett's medicines along with cleanliness and rest. She would earn a livelihood. She and Wiley were conversing that spring day in their upstairs room, with its pine bed and cupboard, which he called a chiffonier. They were keeping their voices low, so as not to be overheard. "I have so many patients," she whispered. "I am too much on the road." Some of the farmers were buying workers now, and there was a sickness in some of the slave quarters so severe that Mary had reported two deaths. Doctor Howard called it Nigger Consumption and treated it with his homemade pills. He had once or twice asked for Mary's help.

Wiley was buttoning his shirt. His father had given a piece of land to the Methodists for a campground and it was going to be dedicated in the next hour. "You should come with me today. It will be important to my father. And, Mary, if you must have Bett's help, take her along when you see your people. I don't want sickness in my house."

Mary knew she could never explain Bett's presence at her side when she visited a sickbed. How could she admit her dependence? She said, "Bett would not like to be a public slave."

He picked up his boots and followed his wife down the narrow stairs in his stockings. "It isn't a question of what Bett would like. It is a question of what you want from her."

"Friendship. That is all I want."

"A slave has no room for friendship." Wiley pulled his boots on and stepped down hard on each foot. "Nor has a slave's mistress. You have only to free her if you want her love, but you seem intent on having her thank you daily as her saviour."

"It is her pride I am saving."

"Or is it yours? Mary, Bett knows herself a slave. The trouble is she is bewildered as to who her mistress is. How much does your father still owe the widow?" Wiley's eyes brightened. "Let me pay it and it will be clear to Bett where she belongs."

"No!" Mary gripped his sleeve. "Bett would then ask for her freedom. And once free she would have to leave Virginia. It is the law now." She paused. "She has no way to fend for herself."

Moving to the door, Wiley lifted his gun from its rack above the lintel and ran his hand along the barrel. It was called "sweet," this gun, because of the position of the lock and pan against the barrel, the strength of the springs, the speed of the hammer fall and the aim. He had oiled it only the night before and now he cocked it, lifting a knee. Mary had once seemed sensible. Her cool exterior, her quiet, watching face. Her uncanny ability when hunting – an unwomanly skill he admired. He had been attracted to that. He had courted her through every sign of her indifference, surprised when the wagon he made for Bry meant more to her than meat or quail. But Mary was tied to Bett by some knot no one could see. He had said so time and again. Now he said, "Bett will survive. She always has," and turned from his wife. "The boy is old enough to be put to work," he added, lifting his leather jacket off a peg by the door. "He cannot live here for free."

Mary clutched at him again. "Wiley, dear, let him be. He gathers heaps of plants for us. He is learning so much now – history, geography, even my Catechism. He's an intelligent, clever boy and has . . ."

". . . no friends. He lives in the trees like a monkey."

"Jemima is his friend!" Mary looked at her husband's weather-hard face. He who paid attention to wind and rain and frost because these things altered the location of game and who knew the cardinal points of the compass by the thick bark and moss on the north side of a tree. When he found a deer, he stood still, out in the open, until it grew accustomed to his presence. But with Bry he lurched and loomed and ordered. "You frighten him so. Can you not remember yourself at that age? And think of Jemima. She was lonely when our mother died. And then we left Luveen and she was even lonelier. But when Bry was a baby she adopted him."

"*You* adopted him." Wiley thought of the child his wife had not conceived. "Jemima treats Bry like the servant he was born to be."

Mary began to pace. Perhaps it was somewhat true that Jemima was whimsical and spoiled. She often came to see Bry. They spent hours together. She had seen Jemima point at things she wanted and tell him to bring them to her – sewing scissors, a softer pillow – and he would rush to obey. A dead bird must be buried. A needle must be threaded. She made him read to her, saying her eyes hurt when she looked at letters. She'd put her hand to her temple and squint and hand him her father's favourite book. She'd been forbidden to take it outdoors, but she often put it in the pocket of her apron before she took Bry out to the woods. Mary said, "Bry enjoys the attention and it does no harm."

"Jemima is too old to be amusing a slave boy. She is what now, eleven, twelve?" He opened the door and lifted the gun and took aim, as if what he saw in the undergrowth was Bett's son wearing his usual necklace of feathers. The sunlight caught the filigree that was imbedded in the wooden stock and the brass glimmered. Mary saw this and suddenly shuddered, clapping a hand over her mouth. "Oh," she said. "Oh Wiley, no." But that was all she said, for anything more would have shattered their lives.

Wiley had not noticed Mary's shocked surprise when she recognized the gun. The thought of pretty Jemima, with her curls, out in the woods with Bett's boy nagged at him as he mounted his bay. Pushing his boot heels into dark flanks, he rode through the thickets that surrounded a house that seemed no longer to be his, filled as it was by Bett and the boy. And now there was something else to consider – the new campground only a few miles down the road from Daniel's house. His hunting dog always seemed to know what was ahead; he could smell it coming, even taking a scent from the grass, but humans were at a disadvantage when it came to foretelling circumstance. Humans loved to gather in crowds to pray and be healed, to sing and to celebrate the Lord, but what if his father was right and the camp-ground was going to bring more business to Jonesville, more travellers, more settlers? Sooner or later there would be too many people and they would overkill or scare the game and hunting would be finished in these parts and he would need to find an-other livelihood. Right now skin and fur paid for powder and lead and sugar and salt. Skin and fur were currency in Jonesville. But all that could change and then where would he be?

The donated ground was uncovered of grass and full of mud raised by horses and wagon wheels. A few people sat on benches, but most were standing and mingling, waiting for the pastor to bring a stirring to their blood. Soon enough, it began. "Bless these pines and oaks above us," Pastor Dougherty called out over the human voices and the soft whinnying of horses and lowing of an ox standing beside a cart. Wiley could see him at the front of the little crowd, waving his arms and already covered in God-given sweat. "Bless every limb, for each will provide us with timber for the tabernacle we are going to build here!" Wiley saw his father standing close enough to feel the heat of the pastor's skin and smell its stench. He dismounted and tied his horse to a post as the pastor began his sermon with Nehemiah 2:20: "*The God of heaven, he will prosper us; therefore we his servants will arise and build.*"

Wiley saw Daniel under his old Quaker hat with Ruth and little John. All men are equal, Daniel might have said, to explain why he did not remove the hat, and his neighbours were too polite to point out that it was God being honoured by the doffing of hats in this instance. Daniel liked to tell the story of King James, who, when receiving Quaker founder George Fox, had taken off his crown, saying, "One of us should surely be unhatted." Well, Daniel's coat had been patched beyond remedy, but his name was carved into the wooden plaque at the entrance to the campground along with the names of other men honoured by the community. "They are Quakers," Wiley's father had explained years before. "And most queer in their ways and the daughter you admire being the queerest of them for her tonics and laying on of hands." For richer for poorer, the pastor had intoned on their wedding day, and now Wiley wondered which it would be. He caught the eye of Rafe Fox and looked quickly away. They had once been friends but that had ended with an argument at the base of a locust tree. He had shouted. He had stayed on his horse and then turned it abruptly and ridden away. Now Rafe put his hand out. "New house . . . new wife. Or so I hear. Congratulations would seem to be in order." There was a hint of doubt in the spoken words.

Wiley took the hand briefly and let it drop. "That's about right. I built me a house and it's already full." His smile held no warmth. "But I've got a strong growing boy ready for work at the mill when I take it on." Pleased with this inspired boast, he watched Rafe's reaction.

Rafe was studying Wiley's boots, which were easier to look at than his eyes. The boots were better made than any around Jonesville and the fact that Wiley had made them himself, as he made his breeches and hats, his jackets and gloves, was something Rafe quietly envied. This was a man with no need of a slave.

They had been friends in the past, but now the two of them sniffed at each other like dogs.

When Old Missus Fox died in her bed one night the following spring, word travelled fast in Jonesville. What next? But the neighbours had not long to wait, for when Rafe rubbed his hands in the loam of his fields and tasted it on his fingers, it had the flavour of iron and sweat. When he looked at the sky, it had been there forever, glaring. Everything hinges on me and the dirt under my feet, he thought to himself. And he thought he would combine iron and sweat to bring forth the Lord's unwoven raiment. Cotton. It was said to be a wonder in this southwestern part of Virginia that such a thing could ever grow, but he had ordered two workers from the east and nearly convinced his neighbours about the benefits of the new upland seed. What of the British blockade? they had asked. And he had answered, "They will never blockade what they need."

The Fox boys buried their mother behind the house and drove a wagon up the road a few hours later. They wore sombre faces as the horse pulled the wagon under branches that showed the first hints of spring: twigs so pink they might have been full of blood, small birds jumping and singing. "Say there!" Rafe shouted as he steered horse and wagon onto the ground in front of Wiley's house, where a sweet smell leaked out of the chimney. He poked at his sleepy brother with an elbow. They were about to acquire a strong growing boy for hard field work. He closed his eyes and counted the spots inside his eyelids, waiting for Wiley to emerge, but when he opened them, there was only a boy standing on the porch. "Our ma's passed," Rafe said as if the child might expect some explanation for what was about to take place. Bry was winding a piece of string around his fingers and Rafe figured him to be nine or ten, remembering the girl whose hut he had pissed against, sometimes with Wiley for company. He had watched his father visit the hut every night. He had watched and counted the minutes because he was curious. Then he had stopped counting and the girl had run away and his father had been killed and here he was as Wiley came out of his new-built house while Eb sat on the wagon seat half asleep, full of drink.

Rubbing his leg with the butt of his whip, he said, "We come for the boy, Wiley," and lifted his shoulders in a shrug.

Wiley looked at Bry. "You go on inside."

But Bry stood stock still.

"See here," Rafe blurted. "You have no rights and we've got a cotton crop to get in the ground." He had his eyes on Wiley's boots again.

"Could be you do." Wiley rubbed his forehead with a finger, as if he had found a source of pain. "But you won't grow enough cotton in these parts to pay for so much as one little boy."

"We wasn't talking of payin." Eb sucked on his cheek, now somewhat awake. "You best hand him over to us now less you got funds at your disposal to buy what your wife gets for free." He laughed in the gutter of his throat. "Our ma's passed and we want him back."

Wiley stretched his fingers, flexing them. "You can't take him *back* to a place he has never been."

There was a moment of nothing. Then Eb said, "Wiley, you start to aggravate me. But let's us each and all remember what we once shared in." He cleared his throat noisily. When he spat, his aim was legendary and he spat often, even between sentences, but just now he held back. He was a year older than Rafe and Wiley with a mouth full of yellow teeth.

Wiley lifted his voice. "Mary! Will you come on out here!"

There were footsteps, the fast click of her boots, then Mary stood at the open door. She raised her eyes to search her husband's face.

"They want Bry," Wiley told her.

She reached out fast and pulled Bry against her racing heart. "You cannot take him. He is mine."

Eb unfurled his fingers, as if counting regrets. "That is not the true case, ma'am, though we never did come to collect until our ma passed as she had no fondness of him."

Mary let go of Bry's shoulders and reached up, feeling for the rifle that hung over the door. Long ago she had seen it held by a boy with straw-coloured hair and a scarf on his face. The boy had pointed this gun at her father and then dragged Simus away. Boy turned to man, she thought, and she stared at her husband as the old picture came to her, that third rider on his fire-breathing horse. She dropped her arms and bolted past the men without looking back. She might have run to her father, but what could she say to him? Blame and more blame. Instead she ran to find Bett, who had told her that men determine everything. She ran past her father's house and on a half-mile to the mill, losing her breath, remembering the first time she had run for Bett – how young and strong she had been, how strong and quick.

∽

From a distance, Bett heard a cry of such anguish that she put down the bowl she was holding, now meaningless, and looked out through the trees toward the distant house where she lived in two cellar rooms with her boy. For herself, at that moment, she cared nothing, not a whit, and she ran to Mary, wiping her face on her apron and untying its strings.

The creatures Bry found huddled around a fire in the drafty slave quarters barely looked up. One of them moved a stick in a pot that sat on rocks and another lay sleeping or dead. From a corner, two boys glanced at Bry with indifference until the female, still stirring, curled a finger at him. The dirt floor was wet and Bry lifted his boots as if they had never touched mud. He had lost his childhood, although he could feel it on his skin. Why was he being punished? What had he done? He took note of the faces, the clothes, the sleeping planks. Savages stirring and eating mush. There was wind and rain and he lay on damp straw in astonished confusion. Why was he there? If I run, they will come after me, he told himself, pressing his fingernails into his palms. He remembered the story of his father hanging on a tree. He thought of the old man he had found in the forest. He had walked for a while with that man; he had drunk from his bent canteen. He had led him between friendly trees and taken him all the way to the mill, where Floyd had cut the chains from his wrists. With that thought, Bry knew an hour or two of wet, cold sleep before a horn blew in the dark and he followed two boys, six men, and a woman out to a muddy field, the boys describing the tendencies of the man who managed them. Driver, they called him. Man without name. "Cotton harder than corn or wheat," the boys said, as if he would understand the comparison. "Don grow good and hard to get da weight." It was April cold. Wearing his woollen shirt, Bry stumbled along, shivering beside the boys in thin linsey, his stomach in turmoil as well as his mind. What was this place? How long would he have to stay? He rubbed at his eyes. The sun came up and lit the gunmetal ground and he saw that his skeletal companions were covered with grime. "You a sof nigga," said Wimpie, the oldest of the three.

"Leave he," said Miver.

"My pap died on a tree," Bry told them proudly.

"Tink he son of Jesus." Wimpie stopped long enough to put both hands on his thighs and laugh, showing buckteeth.

Benjamin had sometimes ridiculed Bry, but never about his father. No one had ever questioned that claim. Now Bry dragged along beside Miver and Wimpie and wondered when Bett or Mary or Wiley would come for him. What was he doing in this terrible place?

Cotton. First there was plowing, the ground prepared by throwing up ridges. Bry was considered old enough to struggle through soggy fields with a mule-drawn plow creating ridges six feet wide for the seed. Later there were furrows plowed between the ridges to hold water. Ridges and furrows. The other workers had been born to this, but Bry ached for a past that had been taken away from him in the course of an hour. At night, when Miver pushed his plank up close, they exchanged no words but listened to each other's shaggy coughs while Bry lay on his side and searched through moments from that other life: Mary putting food on the table and calling Wiley to eat. Bett coming up from the underground rooms to cook and serve. "How is he faring?" she might ask about someone in town who was sick. It was a mystery to Bry, the two mothers healing patients in their different ways, one alone in the dark, one in the light. He could hear, even now, the small clink of Wiley's cup, since the table made a sounding board for knives and cups and plates. "Fetch us water, boy," Wiley would say. And now he lay cold awake and wondered why no one came to take him home. It was all a mistake. Of course it was.

Because of the rains, the cotton was slow to sprout and Bry was put to chopping wood, always wet. His boots were ruined, his shirt and breeches torn. There was never a minute when he was not worse than hungry. He was famished. Starving. How did the others bear it? Sore in his muscles and feverish, he was expected to grind his own corn and plant any vegetables he meant to consume. *Consume*, that was the driver's word. Something like stealing, it sounded like. He was made to haul his own water to drink in spite of his blistered hands. There was no water in which to wash. All of them reeked. A corn patty and slice of cold bacon was breakfast before dawn in the dark while the driver's horn was blowing, and for dinner a bowl of mush in the darker dark. He went to the field hungry and his stomach, all day, seemed to tumble and sink. The only solace was the deep, low voice of Jimbo. It was a cavern Bry crawled into night after night as it spoke of Moses and a river of blood and a plague of locusts and a rain of hail and fire and the longing, wearying escape of slaves.

When the cotton sprouted in late May, the constant hoeing was more drudgery. By midday, Bry was faint. His shoulders ached. The driver sat on his horse while Bry and the others were put to scraping the dirt into little hills around each group of plants. Jimbo was in the lead with his hoe, working fast, smooth, even singing, and Bry tried to keep pace in order to hear that harmony. Once, in the cabin, Jimbo had made Bry laugh, playing an invisible fiddle and pulling his own legs up and down with invisible string. But that was in the cabin. In the field there was no fiddle, no smile – only the mournful song – and one afternoon, Jimbo stumbled and twisted his foot and the driver came charging up to him on his horse and lashed out with his whip. Before he raised his eyes to see, Bry heard the sound of the leather in the air, the sound of the strap on flesh. He had never seen anyone beaten. The hot sun. Green cotton spinning. Bry put his head down, everything going scabs in the dust, and Miver whispered, "Don neva look."

When Bry opened his eyes, he saw the flesh of Jimbo's back turned into meat and fell over, crashing into the tender plants.

At the next hoeing, he kept his eyes on the ground. The strongest stalk in each hill was now allowed to stand, the rest to be hoed away. "Ain nobody come to save ya yet," the driver shouted at him. "Yo mama have to suck on me firs she want you back."

Bry's hands shook. Sweat made the hoe handle slippery and he cut through the wrong stalk. The driver's legs dangled down the sides of his horse. He liked to chew on an unlit cigar or a twig and his teeth were brown. Bry had seen him spit on the kerchief that hung around his neck and use it to clean his face.

That summer of 1810, Jemima began to visit the Millhouse to ease her heart. She was thirteen, with lightly freckled skin, curly hair, and her mother's delicate blue-eyed face. She did not tell her father where she was going, but on those quiet walks to the edge of his first six acres, she pretended she was about to board a travelling coach and disappear through the great Cumberland Gap up ahead. What lay beyond that sheer wall of mountains, that curtain between her small world and the great western plains? Once, Mister Daniel Boone himself had stopped at their farm to refill his water flasks at the creek. He had spoken to her father and she had stood close by and listened. How long ago? I was only a child . . . The two men had much in common, since Mister Boone was born to Pennsylvania Quakers who had been disowned when his brother had married a non-Quaker girl. The family had moved to Tennessee and later Mister Boone had moved his own family into Kentucky. But first he had opened up the gap and widened the trail that went right by their door. Jemima remembered him as tall and friendly. He had made her father seem small and pale. Her father had talked about the weather and his fields and his disapproval of the trade in cotton, which "necessitated the keeping of slaves." But Mister Boone referred to them as servants, saying they were to be thanked for their part in the American experiment. He had lost two sons and a brother in a terrible attack by Indians, but he was oddly forgiving. "They murder our wives and children out of mistaken vengeance, when they should be glad of us since we bring innovation."

Mister Boone had stopped to visit with her father on two or three other occasions and each of those visits had surprised her, for what did her father have of interest to say to such an explorationist? He had never been anyplace. He had not travelled even the last fourteen miles to the gap in order to look beyond at what Mister Boone described as a rumpled carpet of hills as far as the eye could see, telling stories that were already legends about those first forays along what was then called Hunter's Trail. First the eastern Virginians had formed a company and obtained the Ohio land grant from King George and then the colonial government had refused to build forts and defend the new territory, which was claimed by both England and France as well as some Indian tribes. Jemima remembered hearing about this from Wiley, who loved to tell history at the table in his own house, although he was silent at Daniel's table. "The governor sent President Washington out to confront the French, only he wasn't president then and we weren't even a country," Wiley had told them one night. "And when Washington and the Virginians tried to capture a French fort . . ." He had paused dramatically and Isaac had shouted excitedly, "The French and Indian War!" Now Isaac was excited about Tecumseh, who was trying to start another war, pulling tribes together to fight the government.

While Jemima made secret visits to the millhouse, Mary and Bett kept close to each other in the new house. It was a time to console each other for Bry's absence, his terrible suffering for which they had no cure. Wiley went off hunting on foot and left them together in a scratchy, tearful peace. When he was not there for long days at a time, Bett moved up to the main part of the house, staying with Mary for comfort at night. But Mary had dreams she could not bear. A boy on a horse, a glowing gun, another boy hanging in a tree. She saw Jester Fox lying in the mud but she did not see herself. She was never a part of her dreams.

Bett suffered the torment of helplessness. She longed to go to Bry, to feed him and protect him. She muttered threats in her sleep. Once, she woke to tell Mary a story. "My grandmother told me that when she was a child someone was brought up for kidnapping a boy. In our old country, which is called Guinea," she said, sitting up in the bed and hugging her knees. "And how did that child get returned, do you think?"

Mary said, "I promise we will find a way to –"

Bett shook her head. "That boy was returned when they offered another slave in exchange."

"You can't be thinking of going back there?" Mary put her arm around Bett.

She told her to be patient. She would speak to her husband when he returned. "Besides," she said, "they would never take you in exchange for a young field worker."

Circling Joseph's small, sunken grave and its giving tree, Daniel often spoke to his dead son out loud. "Bry has been taken into servitude," he said, avoiding the word *slavery*. He did not like to report such news, but it brought some relief to the heaviness in his breast. He told his child that he had made no contract for Bry with the widow and now what argument could he reasonably make? Mary was pacing and crying, Bett was in despair, and Jemima begged to visit the boy four or five times a day until Daniel forbade her to leave the property. Worst of all, Isaac had found a Shenandoah musket through some secret negotiation with the blacksmith. He had equipped himself with powder and pouch and kept all of it in the shed as if Daniel would not find it there. Now the presence of a firearm on his property kept him awake at night as if it might ignite a war without Tecumseh's help. He could not bring himself to confront his eldest son, who might then become even more subversive.

Ruth had her butter business. She had Prayer Meeting on Sunday. She had the garden to supervise and the family to feed. Ruth had occupation. She did not need to change the flat plane of her world. All this he said to Joseph, with never a mention of John, whose life was somehow connected to Joseph's death.

By September, the first bolls were as white as clouds and covered the fields so that, on his horse, the driver might have been flying. Bry thought of Pegasus and made himself remember stories as he worked. Each slave was given a sack that hung over the front of his body, but Bry's hung down past his feet so that he tripped on it and it swung in front of his working hands and hindered him. There was a basket at the start of his row and it must be filled at the end of the day with two hundred pounds of cotton, nothing less. The plants were taller than the boys and their branches shot out, breakable and not to be broken, hanging over the water furrows like clouds over glass. Beneath the bursting bolls the water trembled and the cotton was reflected and magnified. They were to pick down one side of a row and up the other, leaving only unopened bolls, nothing wasted, nothing dropped. The filled sack was to be emptied into the basket and if a branch should be broken during his toil, he would taste the whip. Miver and Wimpie used both hands to pull the cotton and drop it in the sack, but Bry had no skill and could only grab with one hand and pull back with the other, staggering under the weight of the swinging sack, dropping tufts and stooping down to get them. Hungry and burning with sweat, he stopped to take off his shirt and felt an icy bite from behind. It was a pain he had never imagined. Tears flooded his eyes and spilled down his face. "Move on," shouted the name-less one as sweat stung the open cut.

That night he was not allowed to go back with the others but was kept in the field to pick up the tailings. Darkness had fallen. He was starving, his back stung, he was cold and asleep on his feet but he had to scurry between the plants, bundling up what was left on the ground. Nameless was waiting at the other end of the field. As he dragged the basket of cotton toward the gin shack, the sky got blacker and it started to rain. He tried to hurry, but the basket was heavy. If the cotton got wet, he would be hit again by the stinging whip. Someone at the gin shack lit a lantern. He saw it blinking, let go of the basket, and ran for the trees at the edge of the field.

Two hours later, at Mary's house, he went around to the back and pressed his weight against the door to the cellar. "Mama Bett, it is Bry out here," he whimpered. "I got a whipped back," and let himself sob. He had crossed fields at a run. He had climbed in and out of trees and struggled to find his footing. His face was streaked with tears and when Bett threw the door open, she pulled him inside. "Oh, son!" She sounded frightened. "What have you done?" She led him to a chair and took his chin in her hand to examine his face – so longed for, so missed. She kissed his wet eyelids and yanked at his shirt, already torn, bedraggled. Cleaning the wound with water and soap, she said, "You might have washed this."

Bry hung his head. "I coundna reach."

"Could not," Bett corrected. "No slave talk here."

"I am a slave," Bry whispered.

"No one may own your mouth." Bett crossed the small room, plunged her hands into a pot, and brought them out slick with the oil of wild tobacco leaves. She kissed the child's thin, bare shoulder, cursing the wound, although she had certainly seen worse, and gentled the poultice into his flesh, kneeling before him. "There now. You will heal."

"Never. I will not!" Bry took a breath. "You never came for me!"

Bett got to her feet, gripping the chair as if she had suddenly aged. She went slowly to another pot, taking it down from a flimsy shelf she herself had built, and applied a second poultice on top of the first, this one of pine resin and hog's grease.

"I'm not going back, Mama. You don know." He began to cry again.

"One stroke! You are the one who doesn't know. I lived there for years. Years! And I've shed enough tears for us both, so dry your eyes." How could he be expected to understand when she had never told him. "Go on now, child. You don't want to be found. Hurry on up before it gets light and get back to the quarters. I'll find a way to bring you home. It is a promise I am free enough to make." She rubbed his short hair with a softened hand.

"You'll see me when they come for you to bury me!" he shouted, rushing back into the night and through the thick trees to find Floyd, who slept at the mill with his slave children and slave wife. The devil's fingers snapped at him but he ran with the bandages damp on his back. Floyd was like him. They were the same. Bry felt sacrificed. Floyd had cut off the chains of that old slave man.

At the mill, Floyd opened the shutters and growled, "You bring em down on us, boy. Go on back where you belong. Ain't you a nigger too?"

∽

It was on the following Sunday that Bett walked to the Fox place for the first time since she had run away years before, going through the forest in order to stay out of sight. The old farm had burst its boundaries and covered itself with white bolls of cotton – rather, the hands of nine slaves had covered those acres with cotton, and among them was her child. She worked her way to one side of the quarters, peering into the nearest cornfield where a boy was running in a crooked line, waving his hands. She whistled. Would he hear? The whistle brought him to the fence and she asked after Bry. Would he fetch him, please?

For a long while, as the sun moved across the sky, she tried to enjoy her anticipation, but the waiting was cruel and went on for hours. She told herself that he had spent six days gathering bolls with swollen fingers and dragging gunnysacks full of the stuff to the selfsame wagon that had captured him. She persuaded herself that he was too tired to visit the mother who wanted to touch his face, his arms, his reedy neck because he knew that if he went to her, if she touched his skin, if she made him feel hungry and sad and sick for home, he would cry and beg again. She told herself it was only this that held him fast to the wretched cabin while the others plucked at their weeds and washed their bodies and clothes and cooked up a Sunday meal or tried to stand up and dance. Unless he had given up on her.

One night in March a young woman appeared at Mary's door somewhat out of breath. The face was pale under her netted hat as she explained her errand. "I am Elizabeth Ransome from Richmond," she said. "I accompanied my father, who has business at the home of Rafe and Ebenezer Fox, where he has taken sick." Her way of speaking was from someplace else – a Tidewater drawl. "I am told you have the means to help him as the nearest doctor is quite far away."

Mary drew in her breath and hesitated, but how could she refuse? She climbed into the Ransome wagon. Perhaps she would catch a glimpse of Bry at the Fox house. Did he wander around the property, climbing in and out of trees? She got into the Ransome wagon and took another look at her visitor, who appeared to be younger than Mary by some years. So nicely dressed, Mary thought, struggling with a sense of envy she had never felt before. At her father's house, they found Daniel on his bench and Benjamin hunched over the table mending a broken harness. Mary introduced the visitor, who took in the humility of the house while Daniel rose politely and Benjamin sprang up as if he had never seen a pretty girl before. He found himself staring at a face so articulate it might have been carved and he suddenly felt impoverished. Mary asked if he would please follow them in his wagon so that he could bring her home after she had seen the girl's father. She clutched a black bag that her father had given her for her doctoring trips. It had belonged to her mother and now held a vial of laudanum, wads of cotton, a knife, and a small container of salts.

The two wagons rolled out to the road in utter darkness and the horses trotted past outlying fields of corn and black stretches of forest. The stars were only pricks of light and the smell of damp earth was sweet. There were settlers in the clearings now – a bachelor who travelled with a pair of bulldogs, playing the fiddle wherever he went; a young couple who were going to farm, and the blacksmith, who would stay in Jonesville as long as it provided customers. Between those dwellings the crowns of trees met overhead, and under the trees, there were rustlings of large and small creatures.

At the Fox house, in the narrow hallway, Mary could hardly breathe. The house had the feel of a place abandoned by women years before. Nor was there sign of the male inhabitants. She heard the baying of hounds somewhere outside and thought of Bry again, out in the quarters, unreachable.

Miss Ransome's father lay on an iron bed in a small back room that overlooked a rear porch. Mary put her palm on the old man's wrist. "You must both come back with me to my house," she told the daughter nervously, for she was anxious to quit this place. "My husband is away for the present and you can rest comfortably there."

Angel of mercy, the daughter called her, clasping Mary's hand in her own.

Mary thought Miss Ransome must be glad to escape this dismal house, and while Benjamin gathered the Ransomes' trunks and helped the sick man into the wagon, she took a look at the dusty parlour out of rude curiosity, wondering how the boys who had murdered Simus managed to sit in the chairs or pick up the Bible or look at their faces in the hanging mirror.

At her house, she settled her patient in her own marriage bed. It was the chance she had wanted to be able to tend to a patient properly, with Bett at her side, and she would find something to say if her husband suddenly returned. She left father and daughter together and went downstairs and then outside and around to the back of the house. Opening the door without announcement, she found Bett standing by a window at which the curtains were always drawn. Tonight the curtains were open.

"Please put out the light," Bett said, pointing at Mary's lantern. Seeing Bett's tears, Mary asked what was wrong, but Bett kept her eyes on the starry sky.

Mary held out her hand. "We have a patient upstairs. He needs a tonic."

"What are his symptoms?"

"Heart, I believe."

"What age?"

"Perhaps forty."

Now the healer began to cry soundlessly. How, she wondered, could anyone live so long as that? She reached for the hanging gourd with the hawthorn tonic.

"How is it that you have your girl mixing my father's medicine?" Elizabeth Ransome asked one morning as Mary put a plate of biscuits on the table next to a bowl of butter.

Mary winced. "Are you concerned for her?"

The younger woman widened her eyes. "My concern is for *you*, Missus Jones. And of course for my dear papa. I expect you know we must keep an eye on them."

"Bett mixes things strictly to my orders."

"The Negroes have practices." Elizabeth reached for a biscuit. She wiped her hands on a cotton napkin and looked over at a pile of grey pelts in the corner. "Are you expecting your husband back soon?"

Mary wondered why the question had been asked. Perhaps Miss Ransome was worried about losing her rights to the upstairs room, where she slept beside her father at night and read to him when he was awake. The old man did not speak but the daughter sat beside him, applying a cloth to his head and directing Mary as to his needs. Now Mary said she did not know when her husband might return. "It is the season to bring in provisions," she said as a warm streak of sun came through the open window and slid across biscuits and butter and the small painted table. For just a moment she longed to confide in her guest, to say that her husband's trips were longer than ever, that she rarely saw him for more than a day or two at a time. But Mary could think of no way to explain this – not to her guest, not to herself. There was no way to speak of her confusion without revealing what she could never say to anyone.

"And he is a woodsman," mused the guest, staring again at the stack of pelts. "With the Indians fed weapons and promises by the Redcoats, you must live in a constant state of worry and dread." Touching the napkin to her lips, she added that the Redcoats were blockading the mouth of Chesapeake Bay, making trade impossible.

Mary did not care about the Redcoats. She was watching that streak of sun melt the butter and wondering what to do about her marriage. Why was there no child to prove their love? Were her caresses inadequate? Was that it? She had no mother to ask. Did Wiley know that she had discovered his crime? Was she loyal to him only because she blamed herself? If she had protested that Simus was innocent when they dragged him away, her husband would not be a murderer. But how could they ever speak of it without unravelling their lives? Each of them had a burden that could not be shared.

"I do wonder that your husband and brothers have not joined a militia," Miss Ransome commented.

Had Mary missed some part of the conversation? She looked at her guest and blinked to show that she had not been following.

"Those purple shirts on the Kentucky boys look very nice, I think." Miss Ransome got up then, leaving her plate and cup on the table to be collected and washed.

And does she know what labour each cup and napkin cost me? wondered Mary, who was proud of the home she had made out of wood and cloth and wilderness. "My brothers are pacifists," she said. To change the subject, she said, "May I ask what business you have with the Fox brothers?"

Elizabeth Ransome fluttered her hand. "We bring them two field workers."

"Slaves."

"And very much needed in these parts, from what I hear. Will you have yours bring my father's breakfast up to our room?" Elizabeth made a tiny curtsy, then turned and went to the stairs.

Yours. Bett had come in and was standing with her feet planted firmly apart, remembering a thousand encounters from an earlier time in her life. Once, when she had run crying to her grandmother about a small verbal injury, the old woman had told her that she came from a kingdom where white men had no importance. "Your great-grandfather was nganga mbuki. Yes, he wore a mark on his skin because he worked with the spirits of plants. Your grandfather was the same. Those are your ancestors." While Bett watched the white woman ascend the stairs, she took a deep breath and held it for some time.

The Ransomes went home the night Mary was called to a house in the hills. A boy had knocked on her door. Would Mary come with him? He was stamping his feet for some reason and it was very late. Mary mounted the bay, packing her black bag in a pannier with a loaf of bread. The boy rode beside her on a lame donkey and found the path up the mountain in darkness while Mary listened to the howl of wolves. "Will we meet up with them?"

"Donno, ma'am."

After climbing for a while, thick fog settled in and the air was moist and chill. Mary thought of Wiley walking alone somewhere in the dark. Had he gone north or west? She tucked her cape around her legs and kicked at the bay, who picked at the path with its loose stones. "No moon tonight."

"No, ma'am."

A growling wind had joined the growling wolves. Time passed and they climbed into fog. The horse shied at the sound of an owl. *May he who has received true grace have ground to fear?* Mary wished she had memorized poems instead of the Catechism. "Do you know any rhymes?"

The boy took up a chant about hunters and Mary hitched up her skirt and lifted her right leg, which was sore in the stirrup. "Why is the donkey lame?" If Wiley had met with an accident, she would never know. They rode on. At times Mary could make out the rear end of the donkey but more often it was lost in milky vapour. "Are you up there ahead?"

"I am."

At last the shape of a small cabin made itself felt in the mist. Mary dismounted, tied the bay to a fence, and felt her way along a narrow path. In the dark cabin, a woman lay on a log bed with an infant tucked into her arm. The stench of the place was overwhelming so that Mary held her apron over her nose and breathed through her mouth as she moved toward the bed. "Is there a candle?" As her eyes adjusted she saw four children sitting at a table as if carved from the same piece of wood. "Where is your papa?"

"Gone off."

"No one else here?" Mary was stunned. She ventured close enough that the woman took hold of her hand, moving her lips.

"Is there pain?" Mary asked.

The rough hand gripped hers.

Mary felt her way to the cold fireplace to see what the children might eat. "We must light the fire," she said to the boy. "Go to your nearest neighbour and ask for a cinder pot."

The boy said, "Ain't nobody near."

Mary pondered her situation, wishing for Bett. With proper care, the mother might surely be saved. She told the boy to go back down the mountain to her house and to bring Bett and a cinder pot and some food. The boy did not flinch as Mary used a small piece of coal to write out a pass on a found scrap of paper. *This alows Bett to* . . . She suddenly stopped her hand. Bett had not been on a road in twelve years. How would she react to the huge nothingness of the hills? She would likely be afraid with only a boy to guide her. Mary finished writing. . . .

move as she well . . . and gave up the paper. "Tell her to bring her medicine bag. Use the word *emergency.*"

When he left, taking her bay, the boy tucked the slave pass into his sleeve and Mary sat down by the mother, cutting slices of her bread and murmuring to the children that more food was on the way. None of them responded. In the middle of this fouled night they were sleepless. Checking the cupboard, Mary found two turnips, three cabbages, and six potatoes. There was a bowl of ground corn. The four children ranged in age from seven or eight to three. "Have you a cow?" None of them answered. Mary picked the children up one by one and carried them to a cot in the corner of the cabin. While they leaned against one another, some of them dozing and some of them watching, she sat down again by the woman and put the new child to suckle after uncovering a leaking breast. How many births had she attended? None. Mary opened the door and stepped outside where the air was fresh. She remembered her mother and wondered if there had been this smell of putrefying flesh. The fog had cleared. Millions of stars were studding the sky and she thought of the boy alone on the mountainside travelling by their light. The donkey was grazing and she could make out the shape of a cow behind a spindly gate. Someone had brought a wife and children to this high, hidden place, built a cabin, and put up a fence. She opened the gate and the cow lumbered to her feet and lowered her head. "Pail," said Mary, too late, as she saw the swollen udder, but she turned then and the cow moved fast and rammed her hard against the fence. Collecting herself, she found the pail hanging on a hook at the side of the cabin, and when the cow saw the pail she mooed and stood to be milked. Mary thought of Ruth and the thousands of hours her stepmother had spent on her milking stool. All for us, she thought guiltily, and so that Papa could have back

Miss Patch. She had been unchristian to her stepmother and this wicked cow was giving good milk. When Mary looked up she saw the four children standing outside the fence holding hands against the night. A wind had come up again. She took the pail to them and let them drink.

When Bett and the boy arrived at dawn, riding the horse together and carrying a small pot of fire, Mary was sitting by a dead woman and her baby. She woke slowly, finding her way into the present as if she had followed the dead woman's spirit into the thick laurel brambles that covered the mountainside. As if she had been there beside her, both of them looking for their lost husbands. She shook herself and went to the cot where the four children were nestled. Who will care for them? she lamented as the boy lifted the baby from the cradle and gentled it, cooing in a universal language. The sun had begun its slow crawl through the glassine windowpane and into a corner of the cabin. It brought no warmth but the thought of warmth, and Bett lit the fire and began to cut up the turnip and a wilted cabbage. She looked at the boy. "Is your papa coming back?"

The boy looked at his mother, who could no longer help him guess.

"We are going to wake the little ones and you must take them outside while I make breakfast. Do you know how to milk?"

"My ma does it. She –"

"Not anymore she does not," Mary snapped.

The boy looked surprised. He had not yet taken his jacket off and now he went to his mother, sidling up, and laid a hand on her. Mary saw that he did not understand, being a child of this wild place. "She will not wake. Has thee seen nothing die?" It was an intolerant question but it had been asked. "It is time to take your brother and sisters to wash." The boy was given instructions. He was to take them to the latrine first and then the

254

rain barrel. When they had filed out, Mary shut and bolted the door and looked at Bett. "Thank you for coming."

Bett had stirred water and milk into cornmeal; she crossed the floor and uncovered the woman and removed her sour dress. "She put herself to bed," Bett said and felt sudden tears sting her tired eyes. She judged the white woman to be not much older than she was.

Mary filled a pan with water and soap and a little camphor from her bag. Now they dragged a wet cloth from hairline downwards over the face and then over the neck and around the shoulders and armpits and breasts. "Her milk is still leaking," said Mary in horror. "Shall I save it?" Beside them, the infant was unaccountably calm. "Shall I?" She squeezed tenderly at the right breast, but at that, the baby began to squall. Bett lifted it and put it on the hardening flesh, but the baby squalled harder at the smell of camphor and death and Bett took it quickly away and warmed up some milk. Mary continued the washing, finding all the quiet places and dark places and known and unknown places on her patient's body. She found a black dress in the chest and Bett still held the baby as Mary got its dead mother into a sitting position and held the open neck of the dress over the drooping head. Mary wondered about a chemise but pulled the dress down while lifting an arm. Had this poor woman delivered herself of her child? Had her husband gone for help and met with an accident? She lifted the other arm and inserted it into a sleeve. "Silk," she said in some disbelief. She found bloomers, and when Bett put the baby back in its cradle, the two living women pulled the bloomers up over the dead woman's hips. They rolled her over and stripped her bed and lay her out on the straw mattress and looked next at her hair. "We could make plaits." Now the woman was turned face down while they found her brush and began to work. The hair was oily and tangled, but they brushed it until it shone and then Bett began to braid it, slowly and carefully as if she had been braiding hair all her life. Mary studied the woman's hands, one of which had been burned and neither of which was adorned. The hands were large and calloused as they had needed to be. "What do we do with her feet?"

"She needs no shoes in her grave."

Mary was watching Bett move her hands over the woman's body, then turning it over to lay a cloth soaked in camphor across the unseeing face. Coins. They must be silver. Mary searched through the chest and through the cupboard, where she found four shillings. "We can put them back when she is in her grave."

They stood for a minute and stared. The woman looked refreshed, as if she might rise up and put the coins in her pocket and hold her baby to her breast. The morning arrived and the full tilt of sun hit the lonely room as Bett lit two tallow candles, one for the head and one for the two bare feet.

They did not leave but waited in the dead woman's house for many days, Mary tending the motherless children while Bett roamed the hills, gathering curled ferns and wild fruit. She made a drink for all of them, naming it heartbreak tea. She taught the children where to find berries while Mary used a snare for birds. It was a time that brought back the years they had lived so closely together in the lean-to, sharing the care of Bry, sharing meals, sharing what could be shared. To the children, they told stories. To each other, they remarked on the variousness of the orphans – this one shy, that one demanding. Perhaps they would take them all home in the wagon and keep them for good. "From now on you must travel with me," Mary said, pleased at this notion. "We will charge by the patient, as Doctor Howard does. There is need for us."

"You sell my medicines as your own," Bett said, acknowl- . edging this for the first time.

Mary flushed. "We will share everything."

The two women worked in harmony then, even digging the grave together, which took three full days. When they had it dug, they lifted the dead woman with the help of a sheet held at both ends and laid her out on a bed of leaves. Mary looked at Bett and was grateful.

In the late afternoon of the third day, four children stood above the hole in the ground that cradled their mother while Mary cradled the dead woman's baby in her arms. The children had complained about the cabin's smell, and they were relieved when it followed their mother's stiffened body out into the hole, although they peered down at her wistfully. The boy, whose name was Ephraim, was angry. He wanted his mother left above ground until his father came home. How was he going to explain his mother's disappearance, otherwise? But Mary promised to stay until an explanation could be offered to someone, whoever came. "Have you relations?"

The boy did not answer.

It was customary to ring a bell when a person was buried – one toll for each year of life – but there was no bell in the house and no one to hear it so the children threw a heap of fresh dirt into the grave and covered it with leaves. They stood in clean clothes and Mary told them to walk around the little mound they had made three full times in order to create a ceremony. Afterwards, the children brought sticks and stones and leaves and created a picture on top of the grave. The picture showed a sky with rock clouds and four stick figures sitting by a grave with a baby. *Mama*, Ephraim scratched in the dirt. Mary told them to make a story about themselves. "When my mother died, I told her all my secrets. She is someone you can talk to now about anything." It wasn't true, but the lie might help.

"I, Julia," said the seven-year-old, standing by the grave, "am your next to oldest and very careful in my needlework and very good to my brothers, Mama."

"I am Matlock," said the five-year-old. "See?" He held up five fingers.

They circled the grave while Ephraim sang the chant of the hunter and wolves that had brought Mary to their rescue. Later they went about their small tasks – foraging, cooking, washing, milking – until on the twelfth day they heard the neighing of a horse and the children rushed into the forest to greet their father, who had a sack of flour hanging by his stirrups and a box of provisions tied behind his saddle pack. He had not gone for a doctor. He had helped his wife deliver their fifth child and then ridden his horse away in order to feed his family. Bett showed him how to feed the infant using a small vessel with a spout. He did not require much instruction, but noted that the companionship and help of an adult would be missed. As Mary walked with him to the pasture to show him the donkey's wrapped leg, he touched her hand and thanked her and asked if she had a husband where she lived or if she would like to stay on with him.

When the two women made the journey down from the mountain on Wiley's Bay, Mary's arms were wrapped around Bett in order to hold well to the reins. Passing Daniel's house, they saw him standing on the plank steps as if waiting. "Papa? We are restored to civilization!"

"To what end, dear one? We have both lost everything." Daniel stared at a spot of nothing over Mary's head. "Your husband came home to find his house empty but for a note you had left in the middle of the night. Now he has followed your brother, who has gone off to fight the British." Daniel's fingers fussed at his sides.

Mary slid off the horse. "Which brother?" she asked, though she was thinking only of Wiley. "How – When did this happen?"

"He wanted to take Isaac's place at the mill. I told him to go find your brother and bring him back and then we might talk about partnership." Daniel paused. "Imagine him, thinking he could take Isaac's place. . . ."

Mary did not remount the horse but took hold of the reins and led him past her father while Bett sat above her, clinging to the shaggy mane. Mary's mind was flooded with words but she did not voice them. Instead, a sound strange to her came out of her throat, a pent-up keening, while she held the reins and walked beside the horse her husband had not had for his journey.

They called it a war, but it was a thing any boy would be longing to join, and a few days later Benjamin brought out a musket he had acquired and began to polish it in the presence of his father. It had become a tradition in the family to eat the Sunday midday meal outside when the weather allowed because Daniel had bought an iron stove for the kitchen he was still planning to build. It sat with its chimney poked into the trees and Daniel talked to himself as he cooked while Ruth and little John went to Pastor Dougherty's Sunday Prayer Meeting.

It was the proximity of Joseph's grave that inspired Daniel's talk, usually of the weather and the animals and always of Isaac and Benjamin and Jemima. This morning Ruth had killed one of her chickens and Daniel now tossed it in a bag with flour and salt. He was heating a skillet when Benjamin appeared with the musket and, shocked beyond anger, Daniel dropped the floured chicken on the bare ground. "Here now. Whoa. Benjamin, there are plenty of trigger-happy boys to stand with your brother in this fight." He pointed to the outside table, and Benjamin sat down. "Listen now, son. War is no place for those of us who do not espouse violence even in a noble cause, which this is not." Daniel had bent over to retrieve the chicken and was dusting it off with his hand. Then he came to Benjamin and touched his sleeve, leaving a floury mark. "Surely you must agree," he said. "Or have I wasted my life on two unworthy sons?"

Benjamin inhaled slowly, as if measuring something finite.

"There will be more travel on our road now," Daniel went on, plucking miserably at the sleeve. "The mill will serve your country's needs better than your death will do."

Benjamin put his head back and looked into the trees he knew were his father's to cut or let stand, to give to his children or burn to the ground. "All right, Father," he said, using the title the children never used. "Give me a deed to it and the two front acres."

Daniel gaped at his son, plainly mortified by Benjamin's willingness to take what had not been offered. Had Benjamin never noticed the example he'd set, treading the narrow path of virtue through unmarked woods? Forest? Jungle! "A deed? But then I must have your promise –"

Benjamin laughed. "Pap! A Quaker does not make a vow."

Heartsick, bullied, Daniel rode into Jonesville the following day and drew up a deed to the mill. He could never manage his farm without one son at the very least, and John was too young and never a worker. John's nose was always in a book. Constrained, put upon, bargained out of his land, he put Floyd's oldest boy in charge of the pigs Isaac had abandoned, although two of the sows wandered off within hours and were not seen again. Floyd's younger son was given the job of the small milk herd. "Five cows," Daniel teased the boy. "You must count to four and add on one. Or three and add on two. But never subtract, as your brother did with the pigs." The boy, who was six, had to drive the cows to pasture, return to the house, hitch Miss Patch to a cart, and haul water up from the spring. There was now a tank near the kitchen door that must be filled. Once that was done, he took food to his father and brother, knowing that he was a boy of some consequence.

To supply the millhouse, Benjamin pressed cider from Joseph's apples. Ruth, eager to do for him anything she could, supplied butter and cornbread while Jemima offered to provide a daily stew. How else, she argued, would the millhouse become a stopping-off place for soldiers and emigrants? It was a plan that might have provided harmony and kept what was left of the family intact, but Daniel would not have Jemima in the company of travelling men. Strangers! He left it to Benjamin to ready the millhouse for commerce and Benjamin drove Floyd hard, insisting that he accomplish more than was possible seven full days a week. "We will appreciate the Sabbath when we are finished creating the world," he quipped out of hearing of his father, who did not bother to check on his son or ask what Benjamin was requiring of Floyd but set aside a piece of Shoffert land for the growing of future apples. From apples, cider. From apples, vinegars, medicines, and applejack. From apples, pies and cakes and butter and sauce. Wood for machinery, cogs, wheels, and shuttles. Why had he never thought of it? Benjamin had found enthusiasm.

Floyd built shelves to hold sugar and flour and molasses and bacon, and Benjamin wanted a long narrow table with benches on either side. He wanted pewter cups but settled for wooden bowls into which he could pour soup or cider, and then Jemima took matters into her own hands. At fourteen, she had no idea of the outside world but now she walked each morning from her father's house to her brother's newly built place of business. Her heart-shaped face with its clear blue eyes served her well enough. In the little town of Jonesville, people's heads turned to gaze at her. Curly blond hair and a small, upturned mouth – she was a rarity among the hardworking countrywomen. Only Ruth was unmoved. "Your beauty don't earn no points with the Lord," she would say.

"I know all about girls from my time in the place where I lived."

Jemima was curious about this and found she had two impressions of herself. In public places, she felt admiration directed at her. But at home, she felt undeserving of favour, as if something was wrong with her, something she had been born with and could not erase. As she grew into an early womanhood, she sometimes caught Ruth staring at her and felt ashamed.

Daniel had built his mill and given it to Benjamin, and now there were customers who stood in line, waiting for wheat to be ground and building up thirst. Benjamin had found a press for the apples growing on Joseph's tree, for Bry had been right and the fruit had reasserted itself. And little John, being more outgoing than his brothers, was sometimes permitted to travel with Benjamin for provisions. He was often lyrical, and if anyone approached the wagon, he would explain the benefits of fermented apples in his tremulous voice. "Remember the bite that caused Adam's fall? Try just a swallow and see . . ." as Benjamin doled out a cup of cider in exchange for fabric or twine or tools or sugar or seeds.

Daniel had finally relented and allowed Jemima to help, although she must of course come home before the rise of the moon. Each afternoon, when she went to the millhouse, she wiped down the table and put a stack of wooden bowls at one end. There were only three spoons, so her stew must be runny. Three spoons and seven bowls and nothing to be done but bring in a deep pan of water from the creek and keep it stove-hot for the washing up. Most important was the cider, which was admired for its flavour and severity so that one winter day, when a customer opened the door and let himself in, he asked for a sample before he removed his hat.

"First close the door," Jemima instructed. "Shall you want it warmed to do the most good to your bowels?"

The customer spoke softly, his words all and each polite. "If *thee* would warm it for me."

Jemima's face felt hot. It was a form of tease she did not like.

"Your stew. Is it saucy?"

"So I am told, Mister Fox." Benjamin had gone to the barn a good while before to find a chisel, but he'd left his knife and she used it to cut off a chunk of corn bread to sop up the stew. Then she took up a bowl and walked to the stove.

"So you know me."

"Umm. By reputation." Jemima poured cider into the bowl and plunged a hot poker into it.

"As I know your cider. Will you take a swallow of my drink to lessen my fear of poisoning."

"I never would do that."

"Which? Kill or swallow?" He drew closer.

Jemima touched the knife that lay on the table. She angled herself and dropped it into her apron pocket.

Rafe said, "Just one swallow."

Hearing Benjamin's boots in the brittle snow outside, Jemima reached for the bowl and let herself swallow deeply as the door swung open and Benjamin came in stomping, dropping a satchel of tools. His breath hung in the air. "You find no welcome here, Rafe Fox."

Jemima looked at Rafe's face, which was sun-browned even in winter. She watched the Adam's apple in his neck move up and down while his eyes darted from one thing to another, and she had no word for how she felt.

"I have found welcome enough," Rafe said.

———

A month later, when he came upon Jemima walking on the icy road, he told her that his chariot was at her disposal.

"That horse looks too weary to carry another cruel burden," she said, stamping her boots.

"A pretty lady is never cruel. Or will your brother perhaps object?"

Jemima looked behind her, then allowed herself to be pulled up to the seat of the cart. "It is not just my brother," she said.

"My reputation precedes me, as you said."

"Your past."

"My past precedes me? That is unscientific." Rafe's cheeks crinkled into a smile. "And my history has been wildly misre-membered, miss."

Jemima bit her lip, trying to stay calm.

"I wager you've listened to some exaggeration of a tragic event, Miss Dickinson. And it would be swimming upstream against the current of your family's unlikely beliefs to try to ex-plain. But do you know what I have discovered? I've discovered that what happens in the past is best left there."

Jemima's hands were in her lap. She rubbed them together. "Not so. My mama died a long time ago, but I think of her all the time," she said. "And a wager is a wicked thing, Mister Fox."

"Just where might you be if your mama had survived?"

"Pennsylvania. Brandywine."

"Being a good Quaker girl? Or would you be out riding in a chariot with your champion?"

Jemima frowned. "Good Quaker girls don't have champions. And if we did . . . how could you ever be mine when you stole my dear nephew?"

"You should be careful about that claim. It does not flatter your sister."

"My sister adopted Bry. When he was little . . . just born . . . she –"

"She did not bother to purchase him. Don't you think she knew we would take him back? You will find that property is not a matter of sentiment."

Jemima said, "Will I? When will I find that?" as Rafe put his hand on the back of her neck, and his mouth against hers, and she felt his moustache, his lips, his teeth. Her hat slipped to one side and she pulled away to straighten it, then put her lips back on his.

Only once did Mary enter the millhouse and that was on a day in early June to assist a wounded boy. Mary remembered him fondly. He said he'd been wounded by an arrow on his way to Upper Canada and he'd talked on and on, holding a flute and sometimes blowing on it unmusically. He was the second patient she had treated in her house – young Dooley Jenkins, lying on a pallet in the kitchen, talking about Tecumseh, who was fighting for the British. War had been declared. Poor young Dooley. They had not saved his leg, but she had watched the operation when Doctor Howard came to amputate.

Doctor Howard had been rushed that day, explaining that with the new gin coming to Lee County, there were frequent injuries, more and more cotton pickers to be doctored, more sickness in the crowded slave quarters. "Who would believe that the new short cotton would make us all rich!" he said with satisfaction, adding that he could use Mary's help at birthings. Most farmers in Lee County still had no more than four or five slaves and if one of them was sick, it caused serious work delays. And so it happened that, on occcasion, Mary was called to assist Doctor Howard, taking up her black bag and travelling farther and farther afield. But Mary did not like to go alone.

"Do you know what he does for birthings?" she said to Bett. "He uses chloroform to make things easier for the women. He prescribes bloodletting to relax the womb and ergot to speed contractions. All because he is paid by the patient and does not want a labour to take more than an hour. He has so much work that I am asked to take on the Clarke plantation in his stead. But I must have your help." Mary was proud of her new status.

Then at last they began to travel together, bouncing in Wiley's horsedrawn cart over rocky trails and across unplowed fields. In the slave quarters, they found a tubercular patient living with several other coughing workers on a damp and pestilential earthen floor. There were children with worms and diarrhea. Men with scabies. Pregnant women without enough food to nourish themselves. Bett's presence lessened Mary's fear, for she did not like the quarters and was hardly welcomed there. It also seemed to alleviate her patients' suffering.

On their second visit to the Clarke plantation, with its fifteen workers, they found a labouring woman squatting in a corner and Bett went to her directly. When she knelt beside this woman, five others formed a circle around them while Mary sat on a distant chair, hearing them speak in a language she did not recognize. Bett's tea was boiled up and taken and in good time the baby's head emerged. After that it was Bett who was called, Bett who was asked for her tonics, and Bett who looked after the sick if they were slaves. "Bring the nigro," a messenger would tell Mary, "as them workers like the aid of their own kind." Mary collected payment of a dollar for each case and offered advice to anyone ailing in the big house where the Clarke family lived. In the cart, going home, she and Bett divided the coins.

For Bett, it was a large discovery, this new sense of belonging she felt. Field workers, house workers – all of them, her people. Because it was not a matter of skill or education that defined them, but only the colour of their skin. In the quarters, she was welcomed with touches and smiles while Mary sat on the chair that had been brought for her and bandaged an infected arm or blistered back. "They are fed lies and false cures by Doctor Howard," Bett told Mary during a long ride home. Her voice was bitter, as if it was Mary who had invented the plot against her people by being white. "Remember the boy with the wounded leg?"

"Doctor Howard had to amputate. I couldn't make it right."

"And I had to cure the infection he caused." Rheumatism. Consumption. Scrofula. Doctor Howard's Nigger Pills. Bett pocketed the two dollars Mary gave her and held her tongue. She was making a mash from the cotton root now that stopped conception and caused miscarriage. She had decided on this course when she'd found two women at one plantation labouring on the same day.

A month later, when she was called to tend to a fourth miscarriage on the Clarke plantation, Mary began to wonder about Bett's medicine. So many mothers were losing their babies. "Are you giving them something?" she finally asked, afraid of the answer she could read on Bett's face. The two of them were homeward bound after a harrowing day. They were unduly tired and Mary was cross. "You must tell me that you could never do such a *terrible* thing. You must. I could not abide it."

"There are too many babies," Bett answered. "The women are bred like sows."

Sickened, Mary closed her eyes, letting the bay have his rein. "It is wrong. Wrong." She would speak to Doctor Howard. He would intervene. "You are imagining this. What an idea."

"I do not imagine this. Men are brought in for the purpose. Why don't you inquire if the women have husbands?"

"Husbands? Those people do not marry. Why ask?"

Those people. "I ask because I have a mouth and a brain. And after I buy my son's freedom, I will buy the freedom of other children before they get sold away."

Mary's voice was brittle. "And since each and every freed-up slave has to leave Virginia, you'll be sending those children into homelessness. What will they do for shelter and food? And whatever would you do with more children? Wiley will not allow you so much as a dog."

"Yet I feed his hunting dog, do I not?" Bett snapped. "And that dog sleeps at my feet." She leaned her shoulders against the rough back of the seat and looked up at the shapely clouds while Mary used her handkerchief to dab at her face, then wrapped it around her hand so the reins wouldn't toughen her skin.

When the wagon came for Bett, it held two men and a warrant. Daniel had seen it pass his house and recognized the driver and the passenger. He came fast down the narrow path that had been worn between the two houses with Floyd's two young sons in his wake along with little John. "Shoo," he hissed at them. "Back with you, back." The children disregarded him because there were two men standing at Mary's steps speaking with loud voices. Mary was standing above them, and Daniel was reminded of the child who had stood at the bedside of her dying mother in the same attitude of fury. She had taken the same position then in her clean gingham frock with its starched white collar. It must have been the last time in her life that her clothes were starched, he thought now, wondering how it was possible that he had brought her to live among people so brutal. One of the two men was Rafe Fox and the other was the sheriff, over from Rosehill. Years ago, Daniel had snatched Mary away from meetings of silence that went on for hours, from the careful scrutiny of every motive and deed, from a community of justice, and now she was scowling down at whatever news Rafe Fox had brought while Rafe bowed to Daniel like a gentlemen. "I'm afraid there have been complaints about the girl you have use of from us," he said wearily, as if he did not like to impart such gossip. "And I can't undertake the risk of that, sir. The poisoning of unborn infants, sir. No, I cannot! Especially now that Doctor Howard has sent this man to me with a warrant for her arrest. The only solution, other than letting him take her to jail, is that she stay under my supervision." He scraped at something with the toe of his boot and took off his hat to spin it.

Daniel remembered the gesture. It was what Jester Fox had done long ago, before their lives were ruined. He said, "I will buy her here and now."

Rafe pointed to his companion. "It is a case of breaking the law against slaves practising medicine and administering poison substances. She is not for sale."

"Your mother and I had a binding agreement," Daniel said through his teeth, feeling unaccountably old. "*I* look after Bett."

"There is no paper to that effect, sir, and in any case your debt remains unpaid." Rafe drew himself up to full height. "There's legality involved here." He put a foot on the bottom step of Mary's porch. "I'm forced to take her back."

Daniel cast a look at his daughter, wondering why the debt had never been settled, as Bett pulled the door open and stepped out, dressed in black. "I see that you have grown," she said to Rafe, and no other word was spoken between them. She walked past Mary and got into the wagon without aid.

When they pulled away, Mary went to the bedroom and tried to calm herself enough to pray. Dear Father . . . but the thought of her earthly father came to her and she ran outside, where only John still stood by her steps. "Where is Papa? Why am I alone?" She wondered then, Do other fathers give up so easily? Do other husbands depart without a word? And thought, May you, oh may you, little brother, grow up to be a different kind of man.

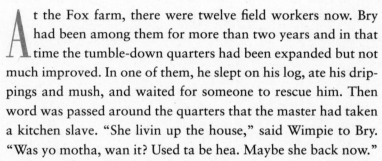

At the Fox farm, there were twelve field workers now. Bry had been among them for more than two years and in that time the tumble-down quarters had been expanded but not much improved. In one of them, he slept on his log, ate his drippings and mush, and waited for someone to rescue him. Then word was passed around the quarters that the master had taken a kitchen slave. "She livin up the house," said Wimpie to Bry. "Was yo motha, wan it? Used ta be hea. Maybe she back now."

Sick with apprehension, Bry had no way to ascertain the truth of the matter until Sunday, when the slaves were given the day off to wash their rags and do whatever praying they could do. If she is there in the house, she will want to see me, he thought, although she had sent him back to this place without even a piece of cornbread or a drop of milk, and he had been angry and hurt by that. Now he felt only a quaking fear. For three nights, then, he could not sleep. He dragged himself through his toil and lay awake in a new kind of terror. "The men use 'em," Wimpie had said. "The house gals."

On Sunday, he sat with the others, trying to listen to Jimbo and longing for his mother with his full heart. Just to see her come through the wobbly door would make his brain cloud up and then a storm would surely hit him and he would be broken by it. Those were his thoughts while Jimbo connected a long exhortation to a parable. He tried hard to attend, but he noticed a few specks of cornmeal in the dirt and put a finger down to bring them to his lips, still fidgeting. Then the door squeaked open and all of the listeners stood up fast and surrounded Bett, leaving a little room for Bry to squeeze in close to her clean-smelling flesh. He was taller than his mother now and she looked up at him with sorrowful eyes pulling his arms around her shoulders and nestling in. Who was there to inhibit them? For the first time in their lives they found themselves together in the midst of their own people, and all of them, every person in the flimsy shack, was moaning, in tears. "Oh Lord," shouted Wimpie, "Bry Mama here!" And two or three people shouted amen to that.

When Bett looked around she recognized only one of the slaves in the cabin, a man named Julius, who was old now and missing his teeth. He had been there when she was a girl. He remembered her grandmother and the fine mutton roast she always cooked for the slaves on Christmas Day. "How you been, Julius?" Bett put her hand on his arm. "Oh my goodness, how you all been?" Bry looked at her in surprise.

"I's good as ever, little gal," Julius said, giving her chin a pinch. "We sorrow to have you back wid us. We glad to see you and sorrow."

"You been takin care my boy?"

"Such as we kin do it we did."

Bry kept an arm around his mother, but his mood had changed. He had realized, in the last few minutes, that his mother was no different than the others. Cleaner, but not much luckier, she even spoke like a slave in these surroundings. Bry examined the flesh on his inner arm, feeling peculiar, as if his insides were made of nothing. Who was he?

——

In the Fox kitchen, the pots still hung where Bett's grandmother had once put them over the iron stove. There was the bin for potatoes and the hanging basket for onions. The kettle still made its sound and the stove must still be blacked and the fire set every evening to hold through the night. When Bett came into the kitchen, even the smells brought back her grandmother's presence, but there was no solace in the memories.

One day, Mary came to the fence. She sent a message and Bett came to the corner of the property to meet her in the black dress. The two women stared at each other.

"What have they done to you?"

"I shaved off my hair."

Mary saw nicks, cuts. She was at a loss.

"To make myself unappealing."

Mary asked about Bry then, and Bett stiffened and said, dreamlike, "They work him like a man," and wiped at her head with the back of her hand.

Bett said they made her visit the quarters on any occasion of illness. Apparently her doctoring was fine as long as it freed the Fox brothers from the expense of Doctor Howard, who had brought the accusation against her. She was doctor and housekeeper both. She looked tired. "I aid the sick because all the purging and calomel and salt has made them weak. They talk of Black Vomit and name it a disease." There was Rafe's pawing and provoking that made everything worse, but she did not mention that. Once, he had managed to push her down. "Any of my girls," he'd told her, "should make me ten or eleven babies before she's done."

"I did this to you," Mary said suddenly. "I told Doctor Howard to put a stop to what you were doing to those unborn babies."

Bett's face was closed.

Mary stood at the fencepost in the road. They were separate, she and Bett, never to be joined again. Each of them would return to a life she could not share with the other. Mary climbed onto her horse. "It was Wiley holding the gun when they took Simus," she said over her shoulder, because she owed Bett this last truth.

Then she rode back to the house where she must now continue her life without husband or child or friend, thinking not of Bett, for that was too painful, but of Wiley, who had left and not come back. *Dearst, I have to go to find yor brother Isaac I will return. Ther is meat dryng on the rack. Yor Wiley.* He had left with his usual satchel and enough food to keep him alive for perhaps a week.

Mary often thought of this satchel in the despair of night. In her mind she filled it with two pairs of stockings, a flask of water, a pound of dried corn, and another of smoked meat. She knew her practical husband had taken an extra shirt and a mending kit. Wiley was sufficient to any wilderness, but would he find Isaac? Husband, where are you now as I make my way home? Will you ever come back or did I betray my thoughts that day of the campground dedication when I saw you holding your gun? But if I had confessed what happened that day Simus was taken, he would still be alive. Oh Wiley, Jester Fox was grabbing at Bett, red in the face, hands on her neck, calling her harlot, and Simus made a leap at him, but I got there first, trying to stop him. I didn't want Simus hurt. And maybe then it was an accident. Maybe I only fell with the rock in my hand. Bett doesn't say, except that I looked as blue as a cornflower in that dress when I came down to the timber lot.

———

All the way home, Mary spoke in this way to her husband, sometimes weeping, sometimes chastising him for his diligence. Isaac does not need you now, she would say. Isaac does not need you, but I need you.

One season passed to the next. "We hear a new missus up the house," Julius said to Bett one Sunday and she looked straight at her son with such pity in her expression that he felt a chill run through him to his fingertips. She put a hand on his head as if to direct his thoughts away from what she had to say. "It is Jemima," she told him quietly.

Bry pushed hard away from her, hurling himself out of the cabin, the door gaping as he disappeared into the fast-growing corn. He ran for a long time, cutting his feet on the ruts and stalks. This was the field used by the slaves for their portions, but he lay down in a furrow, covered his head with his arms, and beat at the ground with his feet and legs, caring nothing for the plants. Back in the cabin there was sad singing and he heard pieces of it and knew he would have to kill Mister Rafe and wondered how to do it. He thought long on this while he lay there listening to the crows and the rustling cornstalks. Panting. Furious. How? When? The thought of it made the cornfield spin. He must find a weapon. Must go into the house. The house where Jemima now lives. Then came a thought: she will get me free. She's come here for that and nothing else. She's given herself for me. He thought this without shame. He sucked in his suffering breath and imagined the day. He would take Jemima and go north, as the old man with the chain on his wrists and legs had done. Stars. One always in the same place. The old man waiting to welcome them. We will get hungry in the wild, he thought. We will have to crawl through the woods all night without sleep. The woods will be full of wolves and bears and snakes. How will I know the right way? And how will we ask when catchers and their hunting dogs will be after us? What places bear names where land is measured between springs and trees?

A few days later Jemima walked hurriedly down the rutted road past the cotton fields and turned into the cornfield. She cut through the cornrows, which were erect and tasselled and whispering old grass words. The conversation between one stalk and another was intense and private, but the whispering made a rustling company and Jemima parted the stalks so that she could move between them without being seen. She was sixteen years old and an outcast, just as her father had been in Brandywine. For making my choice, is what she said to herself. Just as he did.

It took a time to cross the field, moving the stalks away from her face with her hands. These plants had been here as small things when Rafe first brought her out to the shade hut where he had hidden a jug of brandy and a handful of flowers. Now she slipped under the hut's thatched roof and brushed off the wooden bench where she had first sat with Rafe. Months ago that had been and she had seen no sign of Bry then or after, although she had looked for him. She had supposed that she could not ask after him for fear of another lecture or worse. What would Rafe think? But now she had sent him a message through Bett, telling him where she would be. She waited, the bench growing hard under her, and looked through the cornrows until she saw someone coming in a tall black hat. "That hat makes you stick out a mile," she hissed as he got within hearing distance. Then joy, it was, to hold on to him after years apart.

"Who did that to you?" He levelled a look at the scratches on her arm and frowned to hide his great pleasure at being with her.

She lifted her arm to look at it. "Just Charlie, my old cat," she said absently. "I brought him along to keep me company in that house." She pointed, as if Bry might not know where she lived.

"You're wearing his boots."

"Whose, Charlie's?" She tried a small laugh, lonely for everything gone, her family, her childhood.

"He should buy you new ones." Bry spun around and kicked at the bench.

"Who cares about boots? Look at yourself. I come all this way through the cotton and corn after all this time and what do I find but bare feet to greet me." She used a rude word in their secret language.

Bry drew her to the bench she had cleaned of leaves. Then his hands were on her, feeling each bone for change.

"I brought you Papa's book."

"Did he give it to you for me?"

Jemima wondered at his innocence. "He won't come after it, that I know, as he won't even come to see me. Nobody will. But please . . . I want you to read it to me the way you used to do. Will you do that for me?" She searched his face for its known expressions – anything, even the way he used to cross his eyes to frighten her or poke out his tongue, the way he crinkled his face when she made him laugh, but he was serious now, and thinner and taller. She handed him the book wrapped in a cloth. "I can find a way to come here. It is not so hard to leave when he goes away every evening." She sat staring at the friend she had loved best in her life and a misery came over her as she remembered him combing her hair with her boar-bristle brush in the warmth of their private cave. It was a feeling of hunger, an emptiness that made no sense, for here he was, big as life although older and worn to a hardness she did not recognize. She put her head on his shoulder and let herself breathe, something taken, something given back. She put her hand in her dress and pulled out her brother Benjamin's knife with its handle of ivory. The book had been heavy. The knife was undeniable, and time blew in through the slats of the hut from the hot, dry fields.

"Go get my sister." These were the first words Isaac had spoken in days. He had walked from the state of New York and down through Pennsylvania. He had worked his way from one farm to another over a period of months. He was carrying his rolled-up blanket and a dry canteen. He was foot-sore and half delirious and he threw himself at the pig trough and drank thirstily before he said those first words to Floyd's oldest boy, who was tending the animals. Twisting one forefinger around the other as if he'd invented a game, he repeated, "Go get my sister, do you hear?" Was he making no sound with his lips? Floyd's boy looked scared or deaf, holding his head at a slant. "How old are you now?" If this was home, he had come back to it after a lifetime away. What language did they speak? "What month is it?" he asked. What year?

"She gone." The boy stood with his mouth open, staring hard at someone who had once been straight-backed and clean.

"Gone? My sister?"

"Yesar. To Mista Rafe."

"Why? Is he ill?"

"Nosar." The boy thumped at his chest. "To be the wife of he. It Jemima, I sayin about."

Jemima married to Rafe? Isaac felt limp. He sat down hard on a bale of hay. "It's Mary I want. Please get her for me. I need

283

food and something for my feet. Say nothing to my father, do you hear? Don't you tell him I am down here or I'll cut off your damned tongue."

"Nosar." Floyd's oldest boy saluted and Isaac frowned and lay back and let his thoughts drift. What in hell was his little sister doing getting married to Rafe Fox? His thoughts tumbled in disarray until he slept, and when Mary arrived, breathless from running, Isaac crawled slowly to his feet, bent over like an old man, and she came into his arms and held him, even weeping, although she said, "Brother, if anything happened to my husband, you know I'll blame you."

"It was our father who made him go. But listen." He was patting her back, which felt bony and small under his hand. "You have a brother who has come a long way."

She saw Wiley's fine rifle braced up against the wall of the shed. "Where is he, Isaac? You must tell me."

Isaac said, "Maybe he ran off as I did. After the explosion. Maybe in that case, he could be . . . anywhere."

"Anywhere." Mary was clutching at him.

"There were a few of us running together . . ." Isaac hung his head and patted her roughly again, as if that would give her courage to face what might be ahead. ". . . and some were killed when we took to the streets." His knees wobbled. He wanted badly to lie down, even at her feet. "How is Papa?"

"Unforgiving."

"And Jemima is married to that devil Rafe?"

"Not married. Just left. Months ago. Almost a year now. Papa pretends she has gone back to Brandywine. It's his feeble excuse for her disappearance since no one has seen her at all. She never goes anywhere."

"Our father has never told a lie in his life. What happens when she decides to take a walk into town?"

Mary said nothing to that. There were different forms of falsehood. Isaac was peeling off layers of fabric, and she told him she would find some of Wiley's clothes for him and bring him a plate of food. There was rabbit stew simmering, even then, in her fireplace. "Do you want to come now to my house? I have room for you."

But Isaac lay down on the dry straw of a stall at the back of the shed, too tired to take another step, and Mary went back to her house, then brought food and clean water to wash the infected blisters on his feet. She knelt beside him. She bathed and bandaged his feet. She retired the terrible boots he had worn over hills and through valleys thick with water and snakes and festering mud. Isaac sat up briefly to eat. Then at last, unvisited by family or even dreams, he slept for three days while Floyd's wife Cherry came into the shed and milked the cows and Floyd's sons tended the pigs and news went up to the house that the prodigal son was back.

On the third night, when he woke to find Floyd's oldest boy at his side with another plate of food from Mary, he tried to remember how he had come there. Already he had forgotten specific places where he had worked scything hay or picking fruit. He seemed not to have spoken except to barter for a meal in exchange for labour. What he remembered was in pieces.

He told Floyd's son, "You know what? They've got a slave regiment up there. Can you imagine? In Upper Canada."

The boy shook his head.

"Slaves, British soldiers, all of them escaped from down here. They took me prisoner. Imagine that!" Chewing on a bone, Isaac laughed quietly. So many words it would take to ever tell how the Virginians had marched on foot, new boys and men untried, and boarded a ship and sailed across water as wide as the sky. He had forgotten how to string that many syllables together, so he stared at Floyd's boy, who was hammering at the trough where it had sprung a leak and asking how they'd ever captured him, those soldier slaves.

"Oh, that was easy enough. First, we got to a place by the name of Queenston Heights. Because up there every name is a king or queen."

Isaac took a breath and sighed at the memory. "I didn't even fire. Not so much as a bullet. Though I loaded a cannon. I did that."

Floyd's son leaned against the pig trough, gaping.

"They treated me fine. For some time I was with Wiley and we sat up and talked all night. Just about everything got discussed by the two of us in that stockade. You should get yourself up there, boy. It's just like here, only better. You and your brother . . . and Bry. You ever see him? You should run off and join up with that regiment."

"He over the same place like Jemima."

"But have you seen him, is what I meant."

"Nosar, I don't care to."

"Well, that's a fine friend you are. Will the Fox brothers eat you up?"

"They got a driver chase around niggers with a whip."

Isaac put out a hand to rub the neck of the sow that lay at his feet.

He had missed his pigs. He had missed everyone. And now he was back and even his brothers did not come to the shed to welcome him home. "Where is Mary? I'm hungry again." He began a long conversation with himself and decided he could not take Mary up on her invitation as it would only make trouble for her.

He smiled at Floyd's boy. "We had General Pike to command us," he said. "Ever hear of him?" He looked at the plate he had cleaned of food a few hours before and told Floyd's boy that even when Pike was killed, they had come on into York like a horde. "That was after we were traded out of the stockade. Then the explosion when the Britains blew themselves up. Rampaging is what we did. Right down one street and up another is how we went and we broke into stores and took whatever we could."

The boy stared. "Why you do it?"

But Isaac thought he owed no explanation to someone who would never understand such a circumstance. The sound of guns and screaming and horses and mules and cannons rocketing. Men with blood coming out of their mouths grabbing at nothing, calling for mamas and left-behind sweethearts. He studied the boy, who had grown so much taller. "Slaves. Wearing uniforms," he mused.

∞

That very day, Daniel was cooking sausages on the outside stove that sat with its surface rusting a little more with each rain. Ruth and little John had returned from rejoicing in the Lord and Daniel would feed them, as was his weekly habit. First Day, the Quakers called this respite of worship and rest, and yet he did not think of Quakers or of his past. He cared nothing for his father's approval now, for his father had never made the journey to Lee County that might have afforded him some consolation in the loss of Daniel and the grandchildren. No consolation, no forgiveness – Daniel thought, and now his eldest son had come back in such unmanly fashion as to be hiding in the cowshed like a fugitive. And why should he not, Daniel wondered, when he expressly disobeyed my rules and beliefs? Is this not still my land? Am I not his father? Do I not decide how we are to live? He added a chopped onion to the sausages and thought a little more on this, feeling some secret relief that Isaac was safe. Then he moved his thoughts to Benjamin, who had taken the wagon on a buying trip for the millhouse. Two weeks he'd been gone, and the millhouse would have closed except for his own ministrations with the grinding stones. How had his children come to such irresponsibility? He could not dwell for a single minute on Jemima, who tore at his heart with her vagrancy. His children were grown or growing, although the best one of them lay underground very near to the outside stove where he was so busy with sausages. To that buried one alone he spoke and he did this every week, reporting on the stray dog that had adopted them and other subjects suitable to a four-year-old. "His tail is long with a white spot at the end, which he endeavours to catch." Only good news for Joseph, who had no way to intervene in human events, although sometimes Daniel mused about the one hundred and ten acres he considered his own and the two he had given to Benjamin. The Shoffert land was still largely unplanted, he admitted, but fallow ground made the ideal seedbed and in the coming July father and sons would stride across it, scythes moving in unison. Of course it would not be Daniel and his sons doing that. It would be Floyd and his sons who would broadcast the seeds and later rake and bind and lay out the sheaves to be flayed.

As usual, Daniel mentioned Rebecca. He looked down at the grave and then up at the apple tree that had grown so sturdily from Joseph's flesh and spoke of Rebecca's exemplary life, but such talk made him tearful and he soon changed the subject. "Did I mention I once saw a panther at the top of a tree in Lancaster?" he said to lighten the mood. "Someone shot at it – that I remember – and it jumped out of the tree and broke its legs." Here he stopped, wiped his face with his handkerchief, and looked up to see Benjamin.

"You all right, Pap?" Benjamin had been away for two weeks and now he pointed back to the family wagon in which he had just unexpectedly arrived. It had a new canvas top. "Look there! What do you see?"

Daniel saw the new top and under it a seated girl, fanning herself. He recognized her. It was Elizabeth Ransome. And here was old Daniel, cooking sausages on an outside stove and talking out loud to his buried child.

"We married each other," Benjamin said.

Behind the wagon, Daniel saw two men, who were apparently tied to its shaft. "Who are they?" he asked suspiciously.

"Come greet your new daughter and I will explain."

The two men were stretching and moaning and wondering if there might be water to drink.

Benjamin yelled, "Mama Ruth, come say hello to Missus Benjamin Dickinson."

Ruth came out of the house and stood. "Married," she said coldly, nodding at Elizabeth, who had stolen her dear Benjamin. John was called outside and Benjamin helped Elizabeth out of the wagon as if she had never put shoe to ground. When Daniel came across to her, he brushed her cheek with his beard, muttering his welcome as if it should not be overheard. Then he asked again, "Who are these men?"

Benjamin said, "Wedding gifts" as he untied them.

Daniel told John to bring water. The two exhausted men had walked behind the wagon all the way across Virginia and now they sat down hard in its shade.

With so many people to be fed, the family elected to sit outside with plates on their laps. Sausages with onions, cornbread with cream. Elizabeth fanned herself and gazed at the house as if she had forgotten how humble it was. She looked at the sycamore trees. "We forgot to call Mary," Daniel said, tapping his forehead with a finger. "In all the excitement, we forgot to send for her."

John seized this opportunity to absent himself. And what about Isaac? he thought, pushing away from the table angrily. He had been down to the shed to see his brother for himself, finding him thinner and dustier. Isaac smelled like the animals now and made sorry jokes about his adventures, but he was the eldest and ought to be here.

Once John had gone off to get Mary, Daniel found his voice. "I'll have no slave on my land. You know that," he told Benjamin.

"And does this holy edict include Floyd and Cherry and their sons, who plow and plant that land for you?"

Daniel examined Benjamin as if to find a visible flaw, reminding himself that there were words not to be said. He had taken ownership of the slave family only months before when Michael Shoffert had needed to sell them. It was an act of decency meant to keep the little family together, but Benjamin would not understand.

Then John was returning with Mary, driving her in her own cart. As they alighted, Mary ran to Elizabeth to greet her and then turned to her father, speaking in her quiet voice, pleading with him to welcome Isaac to the meal.

Daniel remembered that she, too, was his child still. "Thy food is there to be eaten," he said.

Benjamin was pulling his half-brother by the arm. "John, I know you are a boy yet," he said, "and too young to be taken seriously, but come over here to the shade. I have an offer to make." He took John's plate away, leading him into the clearing.

Mary wanted to ask her father about Wiley. Isaac was back but not Wiley. How could she learn about Wiley's whereabouts? If he had been taken prisoner, what could they know of it? She watched Elizabeth watching Benjamin under the trees talking to John and remembered the happiness of new marriage. "You are Isaac's father," she said. "This is his home and you must forgive him." She did not mention Wiley.

Daniel rose. He turned and went into his house, closing the door on her pleas.

⟨∾⟩

In the shade of the twin sycamores, Benjamin was laughing. "Remember our fort?"

"I do." John remembered the time Benjamin had tied him to a stake and thrown arrows at him.

"Good. Your memory is what I require. For our new enterprise." Benjamin did not want to sound proud, but how could it be helped.

"Thank you, but Pap says I am to study. It is his plan, that I should use –"

"You should use your fine ability at figures," Benjamin said.

"But I must wait for employment until I am older. Pap says that –"

"Do you remember Mister Franklin? What *he* said?"

"That time is money?" John knew it was Benjamin's favourite quote.

"The point is that the more you give of yourself, the more you receive. Pap would agree with that."

John thought Daniel would have said that the more one receives, the more one must give. He said, "Let Isaac help you. Give him welcome. Our father will still not speak to him."

"Brother, this is a great chance for you. I need a bookkeeper. Those two men over there know everything about the cotton plant."

"Which none of *us* knows in the least." John's voice was small.

"We have always and so far known nothing of anything," Benjamin conceded, putting an arm around John. "And just look. I have a wife and two acres and a mill and two workers. I have property, brother, and I'm going to have more, and you will be my partner."

"Isaac is the oldest," John murmured, shaking his head.

"It is not age I need but faith. Lend me your faith, little brother, and I will make us wealthy as kings."

Isaac had gathered a bunch of cornflowers, tied them together with a piece of string, dusted his hat, and walked away from his father's land after three weeks in that shed. Soon he found himself on the porch of the Fox house, where he stood for an instant, then knocked. It was a hot day and Wiley's leather breeches were sticking to his legs. He tugged at them and waited, over-warm, uncomfortable. But his little sister was here somewhere and even if the sun beat down straight on his head and the skinny poplar tree in the yard gave not an ounce of shade he would stand here and wait for her.

"I heard tell you were back," cried Jemima gladly as she opened the door wide. She had come into the worn light of the hall from someplace else. She was dishevelled, her hair uncombed as if she had been asleep at midday. He handed her the flowers and put his arms around her, thinking of Rafe, wondering if she was safe with him.

Jemima said, "This is where I live now. Papa won't come. Nobody will. I am in disgrace."

"I came."

She sniffed at the flowers, which had no smell.

"And look at you . . . mistress of this big house!" Isaac looked down the hall, at the far end of which was an open door leading to a back porch.

"Mistress of nothing," she said and took a step in the direction of the front door. "We can talk outside."

"Can you not talk in your own house?"

"Oh, it's not mine." Jemima cradled the cornflowers and stepped out and along a path that led through high grass toward a kennel full of barking hounds. Isaac paused once to look back, knowing that his father had once come here with the body of Jester Fox. Jemima would not remember that time, she had been so small, but he remembered everything – even the smell of his father's wet woollen coat after he came back with the wagon saying Jester Fox was killed, which was a strange word to use for an accident. Now Jemima led him on past the hounds, who had set up a howling. "Shall we let them come along with us?"

"Lord no! They're no company for a human being." Jemima pressed at her skirt, which was torn at the hem. A few brittle leaves blew across the grass.

Looking at her, Isaac had an idea. "I wonder if there might be . . . I've been thinking. You know I'm good with livestock. Can you find a place for me here? I could build a small hut on the far side of some field."

"I told you, I am mistress of nothing."

"You have a husband. A house. Fields. Servants. Your childhood friend is one of them."

Jemima held the blue flowers up to her face. "I have no husband," she said.

"I think I could help Bry. I know a place where he could be free."

"You want him to run off and get savaged by those hounds?"

Isaac took her hand and pulled her down in the grass beside him. He let his legs sprawl in Wiley's hot leather pants. He put his head back and set it down on Jemima's lap. "Pap won't speak to me either. We are both outcasts. Find me something to do here, will you? Please. I have no place to go." He began to tell her a little of his journey.

A few months later, Missus Dougherty was serving coffee and biscuits with butter and jam to her usual guests. She was saying that she had been the first to visit Benjamin Dickinson's rented house those months ago when they had settled into married life. She was explaining that it was furnished with various pieces from her, along with a horsehair divan and a set of china from the Ransome family. "Silver candlesticks too," she announced. "All very pretty, although I wonder if the father will mind his son growing cotton in order to keep such a wife."

"It's a backbreaking crop," Missus Craig agreed.

Missus Dougherty rolled her eyes heavenward. "I was referring to the keeping of slaves such a crop requires."

"Isn't the mill adequate for Benjamin's income?" asked Missus Sharpe. "He is sole owner."

"Not exactly. I am told that he has taken young John as a partner," Missus Dougherty said disapprovingly. "Although he is called to be a preacher."

"And the older brother home from the war," said Missus Jones, studying her cup, to keep her eyes unreadable. She was thinking, But not my son.

"*Partnership* is a loose term," mused Missus Craig, who was longing to ask about Mary but was sensitive to the feelings of Missus Jones.

"I believe Isaac, the oldest boy, is working for Rafe Fox," Missus Sharpe noted, "who, as you may know, is also keeping the young daughter."

There was general assent. Heads nodding, shaking. But what could be said about a situation so catastrophic? Rafe Fox, son of the widow, taking an unmarried girl into his house. A young Quaker girl, sister of Mary and stepchild of Ruth. It was best to leave the details to the imagination, for speaking of them would only make them worse.

"Is this Missus Dickinson's butter?" Missus Sharpe then asked. "It seems –"

"Not today," said Missus Dougherty, with a lift of her chin.

✑

At that very moment, Elizabeth was sitting with John in her small rented house. It was owned by the blacksmith and sat at the edge of Jonesville near his place of business. Benjamin had given his half-brother certain duties, and now Elizabeth was sipping coffee with him as if they were contemporaries exchanging family news. It was thrilling to John, this new adulthood.

He practised particular postures while sitting across from Elizabeth and then berated himself for vanity. His father was of course displeased with him, but he was trying to keep up with his studies while also helping Benjamin. He was helping at the mill, keeping the books, and running errands between his brother's seeded bottom land and the small rented house, where Benjamin lived with Elizabeth, who always made him welcome and was happy to entertain him with stories of her former life in Richmond. She told him about her sisters, her friends, her cousins, and the social events they had attended while he listened as if she were reading to him from a richly descriptive book.

Today, while she talked, he focused on her hands, which held a bag of silk threads and an embroidery hoop, although she rarely put needle to cloth. Once she had unfolded a scene of flowers and birds and fruits, an entire mythology. "Of course they are not real in the least," she had laughed, "for I am quite without training in natural science." She had been taught to read, to play the piano, and to speak a little French. "You yourself are reading Virgil," she said now. "Or so your brother has told me. And I believe he is just the tiniest bit provoked by that." The afternoon was hot and her right hand went for a moment to the back of her neck and lifted her hair. In the bottomland, the wedding workers would be hoeing and separating delicate plants. Elizabeth watched a blush crawl up John's neck.

"Our *Aeneid* is lost." John looked at his feet, which were awkwardly crossed in front of him. "It seems that Jemima may have taken it with her and there is no way now to get it back. But there are the Georgics, which I study for the poetry."

"I wonder that you do not find it in your heart to visit your sister."

"It is my father's decree."

"Perhaps Jemima would not have run away with Mister Fox if your father had fewer decrees. And now your brother Isaac is living there too. Mister Fox is stealing your family."

John winced.

"I think Isaac heroic," Elizabeth proclaimed. "This is a terrible war to have fought. They've set fire to our capital, for heaven's sake. Benjamin would join up but for the mill and the promise he made to your father." Elizabeth turned her face to the window. "Another decree. He is not to be a patriot."

John congratulated himself for having the strength of mind to disobey his father in at least one thing. His partnership with Benjamin proved that he had an eye on his future. Virgil was no guarantee of employment, after all, and he liked the making of cider and the keeping of accounts. Also, perhaps, orcharding. He had a pamphlet that said that scratching the bark of an apple tree will hasten its bloom, that beating it will bruise the layer just beneath the bark and check the descent of sap, forcing an early bearing. Benjamin had a small orchard that had come from the seeds of Joseph's tree, and John thought that, with care, it could begin producing fruit in summer and finish long after the cold season had arrived. He would make sure that Floyd and his boys used all care in picking – never snapping off the stems, which causes the onset of rot in the fruit, and never jiggling the apples in moving them, which causes bruises. His father would come to see that his work had only broadened his outlook. John sat back in the overstuffed chair, feeling very adult, now that he was thirteen, and asked Elizabeth if she had many visitors.

"Oh but no one comes here," she said with a pout in her voice. "Missus Dougherty has pronounced me too grand, which is only the fault of my candlesticks, and now no one will tap at my door. But do not, for a single minute, concern yourself," said the young bride. "Missus Biblethumper may think me worldly, but I am humble enough to do without her."

"I'm sure she does not think any such thing. She has always been helpful to our family," John said loyally.

"In what respect, I wonder? She seems to have severed relations with your mama."

Elizabeth was wearing a lavender frock, linen, with grey silk trim. The skirt seemed fuller to John than other skirts and the waist above it child slim. He rearranged his feet. "She started my mother in business. And she now encourages me in my calling." He gave the words utmost dignity.

Elizabeth's laugh was bell-like. "Oh, I know. Benjamin once introduced himself to my cousin as a Quaker and then told an acquaintance of mine that he has not a jot of faith. It is your age and the result of your father's confused beliefs that leads you to spiritualism."

John was sure that his father had never been confused. As for himself, at this moment he longed to fall to his knees. He felt the surge of faith in his throat that presaged another vision and he touched his face to be sure it was still part of him, looking at Elizabeth, whose skin just above her bodice was the colour of clotted cream. It is the coffee makes me shaky, he thought, but he could hear, as if that old man were standing behind him, the voice of Reverend Ansley, who had spoken at the campground two Sundays back.

The reverend's tones had expanded and contracted, and John had felt a vaporous leap of something at his back. Perhaps his mother's angel was finally returned. Even now, he could come under that spell in a matter of minutes and yet his loins ached, his hands trembled. A bead of perspiration ran down his face as he looked at Elizabeth. His brother's wife. He watched her hair catch the afternoon light, and it was like opening his eyes under water. He pushed up from his chair and felt his way to the hall, where he took hold of his hat. If taking coffee with Elizabeth could so unhinge him, how could he understand God's will or serve Him? His trembling hand reached for the door, but Elizabeth was laughing again, having followed him into the hall. "I know such a scrumptious story about one young man who was called to preach. Just listen and tell me if you sympathize, for he was out walking on a dark road one evening when he heard a voice overhead telling him to *go-o-o preach go-o-o preach.*" Elizabeth waved her bare arms in the air. "There are truly mad people who hear voices, you know."

Swallows rushed in and out of the barn with tiny grubs for their nestlings. I should be like them, Jemima thought as she entered the dark, assailed by the smell of dung and hay. Why am I not? "Rafe?" She squeezed her eyes shut and opened them wide to adjust to the lack of light. She grabbed up her skirt and moved through the clutter that surrounded her – a broken scythe, a winnower, Eb's plow, various tools she could not name. "Ra-aafe?"

He stood in a stall with his hands in a pail. Water glistened on the withers of his horse and pooled in the straw at his feet.

"I need my sister," Jemima said, coming close to him. "I truly need her. She doesn't even know about . . . this." She put her hand on her round belly. "She'll know what to do when my time comes."

"Jemima, listen to me. Horses, pigs, even people have babies." "

She was running her hands up and down her arms. "Just help me make peace with my people, Rafe. Let Bry go home and they will forgive you. I know they will. It is not much to ask." She touched his unshaved face. "They think you stole him."

"They think I stole you."

Jemima sank to her knees. She was tired. The baby was weighing on body and mind. All day, she had been walking and thinking.

Rafe said, "If they want Bry, they can make an offer. He has more value now than he did when he came here."

"It's his freedom I want. Can you not make me a gift of it? I promise I will never ask for another thing in all my life."

Rafe stroked her hair. "If I give him up, I have to replace him. Don't you understand simple economics? What the devil has come over you, lately? Let your pa make me an offer. Or your brother. He's been playing cards, making wagers. He's rich. Bry is fourteen years old, iron strong. He's going to be somebody's slave. Let him be Benjamin's if you like. For the right price."

Jemima's eyes were suddenly dark, which made her face seem pale, almost gaunt. Pressing against Rafe, she pulled his hand up to her face and took one of his fingers into her mouth. It was something he liked. It had once been a signal between them. "Please let him go." She looked off to the house, to the porch with its chairs, where she had sometimes rocked herself into an afternoon sleep during the last long year. She looked at the field between the house and barn, at the corn, which was soon to be cut, when even her meeting place with Bry would be exposed. She looked into herself, where her child lay in a curl, opening eyes that were as big as they would ever be, naked, hairless, unloved. Was it Rafe's? If not, Bry would soon hang from a tree.

She could not go to her father, but she could visit the millhouse. This she did on horseback later that day, taking the ride at a gallop, and finding her brother with Floyd, fixing a shaft on the paddlewheel. Calling his name, she slid off the horse and steadied herself. "I need your help."

Benjamin turned. Two years it had been since he'd seen his runaway sister. "The Fox family is growing," he remarked, looking hard at her. "Should you be riding?"

"I have no choice. I need your help, brother. Please, whatever I have done, put it aside for the time it takes to get Bry away from Rafe. I beg you. Please, brother. He is not meant for that life."

"But you are?"

"How can he be expected to sleep on the ground and eat scraps and feel the lash every time he brushes against a damned plant?"

Benjamin studied his sister. Her hair was lank, her skin pale, her fingers weaving patterns while she spoke of Bry's wretchedness with unseemly language, lips stretched across her pretty teeth. "When is the Fox cub due?"

"Too soon." Then she said, "You are my one hope in the world."

Benjamin, who was not tall, had to bend a little to look in Jemima's red-rimmed eyes. "That unholy child in your belly is where your hope lies. Not with me."

That evening, she watched Bry move through the cornrows.

"That damned hat," she said as he came into the coolness of the shelter and ran a hand through her wet, tangled hair. On her way to meet him, she had pulled off her dress and walked into the pond with her body all bare. "How do you like that?" she had said to the child, giving her belly a slap. Then she had come to the hut dripping and cool in order to put her skin against Bry's.

"Did they put leeches on you? You're too pale." He wrapped his arms around her and took the coolness into himself. A bird landed on the thatch overhead and they heard it scratching.

"What if my sister won't come when it's my time?" Jemima sat down, feeling lightheaded.

"Only because she remembers what Rafe did and hates him very rightly."

"She was a child. How can she remember? It was all a mistake."

"Is that what he tells you? Do not forget who I am." Bry dropped his arms and leaned away.

"Bry, I've been thinking and thinking. I've been listening to Isaac since he came back because he tells me about Upper Canada, where he was living with a regiment of escaped slaves."

"I know. He talks to me too."

"He says there are whole towns up there of such people. There are lakes and forests and houses just as there are here, but slavery is against the law. I want you to go there and wait for me."

"I am staying with you."

"Not if this –" She put her hand on her belly again. "Have you ever considered what this baby might be?" She looked at the field of growing corn beyond which was the growing cotton and in the far distance the white house. "I can't birth a slave. I would have to smother such a thing as that."

Bry got to his feet and ran into the field of corn, leaving Jemima and his tall hat behind.

∽

When Rafe appeared at the millhouse later, he was looking for Benjamin. The place was crowded. Five or six men stood around the long table, which had been cleared of spoons and bowls with only cups and tankards remaining. Benjamin was just then unfolding his faro cloth and looked up at Rafe without surprise. "You lay down your wager to enter this game," he said evenly, without showing his interest.

The men assembled around his table were on their way to Kentucky. Some would go as far as Ohio. A few would go as

far as Missouri. They were family men, honest men in unfamiliar territory. They had settled their wagons on the last escarp-
ment, eaten a camp meal, and seen wives and children into
their wagons for the night. It was customary then for a young
father to enjoy a cup of cider at the millhouse. By ten o'clock,
Benjamin had watched them drink, had learned their gestures
and abilities, and bidden farewell to the faint of heart.

"I am not here to wager. I am here to sell," Rafe said.

"Who? My sister? Are you so tired of her?"

"The boy. I find that he doesn't suit me. What would you pay
for him?"

Benjamin pushed the bench back and stretched his legs as
if considering. "Is he so useless? Why would I want such a
boy or wish to enrich a man who keeps my sister unmarried
in his house?" He stood up, thrust his hand into a pocket of
his jacket, and put several coins, both silver and gold, on the
table. For his house site, Benjamin had chosen a fine spot in
front of Daniel's cabin at the edge of his two gifted acres. In
this way, when Daniel stood on his plank steps, he could watch
Benjamin's bricks being shaped and fired; he could watch a
house being constructed from the ground itself. But the making
of bricks was heavy work. Benjamin stood at the table where,
already that night, he had made enough money to buy wood for
brick moulds. "I run a clean table," he said to the man who had
ruined his sister's life. He was housing his workers in the cellar
of his unbuilt house. It was large enough to accommodate the
boy. And when his cotton was ready to be picked, his workers
would lay down their building tools and move to the cotton
fields, which Bry knew how to work, while the soil they'd freed
up from the cellar hole would lie there composing itself, later
to be mixed with sand and clay for the making of bricks, a
thousand of them put into moulds every day and carried to the

drying racks. Heavy work. Was Bry strong enough for that? Under the long table, there was a box in which Benjamin kept the faro cards. He knew which were rough, torn, smooth, or bent while the travellers, rubbing their hands on their breeches and putting their cups on the floor, called bets and waited for the cards to be drawn. The first one was discarded. The second one was the dealer's. The third card made someone a winner, if anyone had chosen it. "I will wager two hundred dollars against the boy," he said, shuffling the cards. "If I win, you produce him here by tomorrow morning or pay that amount."

Rafe called out a card and Benjamin's eyes travelled over his scuffed boots and ill-made breeches. He drew a first card and then a second. There were other calls around the table, but when Benjamin pulled the third card from the hidden deck it entitled him to take possession of a boy who had been born on the Dickinsons' property. Now he would be returned. He put his head back and laughed at the ease of it. "There's some justice in this world," he said, "after all."

W hen he got home from the millhouse, Rafe found Jemima in labour, begging for her sister. Frightened, he got back on his horse, attached the cart, and rode to Mary's house. "Your sister is labouring," he yelled when Mary opened her door. He tilted toward her, still on horseback. "Her baby is coming. She is begging for you."

His tone of voice made Mary grab her cape and drop it and grab it again. She stumbled into Rafe Fox's cart as if every suffering she had known had not been caused by him. Jemima was having a baby! She tried to compose her face but wanted to scream out. Hurry, she coached Rafe in her mind. Hurry and I will forgive you everything.

Night had fallen long ago and the house was dark. In the back bedroom where Elizabeth's father had once lain, Jemima was wrestling with her sheet and chewing on her hand like a trapped animal in the iron bed. "There now, darling, Mary is here. Take heart, little sister. You are only giving birth to your baby."

Jemima started up. She pointed at the window, beyond which was the covered porch. "It's here on me," she screamed. "It's crawling up my leg!" The evening was somewhat chill, but she was wet with perspiration.

Mary went to the window and looked out. When she came back to the bed, she said, "Here now. Let me come wash your hot face."

"No! Don't you see his long nail?"

"Who has given you laudanum? What's in this cup?"

Jemima began to shriek, describing the shape of the thing that was biting her leg, eating her from the feet up, she said, swallowing and spitting her out. "Here, on my arm," she said, howling. "I am going to hell for it . . ."

"I have taught you the falseness of hell," Mary said sternly. "Now, look here at me."

Jemima flung her arms up and beat the headboard and clenched her jaw and began to retch as Mary touched her face with a cloth she had dampened in the water bowl. She touched her sister's abdomen, which was small for a ready baby. A few minutes later she found Rafe at the table with his head on his outstretched arms and a bottle of brandy on the floor by his feet. "Go, please, and bring Bett to me." She could not make herself say his name. "Please. I need her."

Rafe swung his head left and right. "Better have Doc Howard, if it's serious."

"But he makes terrible mistakes. Truly, I've seen it. And Jemima will feel easier with a woman's hands."

Rafe ignored her and shouted for his brother, telling him to ride hard for the doctor.

It was a wait.

Then Doctor Howard came at dawn, with the sun scratching at the sky. He joined Mary in the bedroom, shutting the door behind him and examining the thrashing girl on the bed with large, unwashed hands. He pushed and prodded and inserted something. Then he straightened, wiping his hands on a cloth he extracted from his bag. "Missus Jones," he said gravely, "you go out there and call your brother-in-law to the parlour, where we can speak in private."

Mary had not thought of Rafe as a relation. She had not

thought of his house as having a parlour. He sat at the table with his head still resting on his arms and the bottle still at his feet and she shook him violently, calling Doctor Howard into the room rather than try to move Rafe. While the doctor talked, breathing hard and using unfamiliar words, Mary looked at the watch chain that moved rhythmically on his vest. His eyebrows were thick and he drew them up whenever he wanted to make a point. "One of two things got ta happen damn quick, excuse me, madam." The high, reedy voice was no match for what he had to say. "I believe," he began ominously, drawing out the word, "that you will most likely have to choose between mother and child."

Rafe put his head down again. He knew nothing of birth except among horses and dogs, but Doctor Howard explained that a craniotomy, so-called, would save Jemima. "That is, of course, if it goes well, while a caesarean will endanger her but save the child although there is never what we might call a guarantee." The doctor leaned down and peered at Rafe. "I mean to say, it is your decision to make as the husband." He added, "And father. You might need a few moments in which to think or pray."

Rafe looked at the doctor as if trying to decide why he was there in the room.

Mary, hovering with exhaustion and fright, insisted now that Rafe bring Bett to the house.

Doctor Howard said, "You'll lose them both at that rate."

Mary said, "If you don't bring her, my father . . ." But what would Daniel do? He had refused to see Jemima even when Isaac went to plead with him. Isaac, the outcast, who was living in a tiny cabin at the edge of Rafe's land.

Rafe said, "What was that first choice, doc?"

The doctor said, "A means of extracting the child to save the mother's life."

"Cranium means head," Rafe said, blinking.

"That's what it means."

"The baby's head."

"Your baby will not be born of himself. The only way it will survive is to cut the mother open." He looked at his watch, apparently tired of explanations.

Mary fell into a chair and held her own hands. "I will go find Bett myself, do you *hear*?"

"Is that what you wish for your sister?" Doctor Howard sneered. "Your kind is built another way, you know. Or you ought to know, since you have seen them at their birthings. And don't forget that slave medicine is against the law." He lifted his bag and shook it. "I can get up another warrant, Missus Jones."

Mary had not seen Bett since the day she'd confessed. *It was I who told Doctor Howard. . . .* She turned to Rafe. "We must let her try."

He pushed his chair back and got slowly to his feet, going out of the room, down the hall, and out the back door, where he stood for a moment, then jumped off the edge of his porch. It was a short enough ride to the hut, and when Bett came outside at his call, he reached down and lifted her onto his horse.

Out there behind the house the ground was barren and dust rose around them so that for long minutes Bett covered her nose with one hand and held on with the other. When they stopped at the house and she heard Jemima screaming, she said calmly, "Free my son first. Or I will not save yours."

Rafe clamped his elbows into her sides. "I'm afraid Mister Benjamin Dickinson won Bry last night in a card game and I am obliged to deliver him today." He dismounted and pulled her down, then slapped the horse and let it drift to the stable as he pushed Bett ahead of him to the porch. They could see

Doctor Howard through the open door, pacing in the hallway.

"You wagered my son?" Bett's voice was venomous.

It was now late in the morning and the bedroom curtains were drawn but she could hear Mary pleading and Jemima moaning and calling out. Mary came to the bedroom window, drew back a curtain, and looked out at Bett. She pulled up the window sash as Doctor Howard entered the bedroom, and Bett stepped over the low sill, went to the washstand, and cleaned her hands. Her eyes were half closed as she walked to the foot of the bed, pushed the doctor aside, and put her hand on Jemima's body. "Oh child." She looked up at Mary. "What has she taken? I hope there is time. Her pulse is very faint . . ." she glanced at a cup by the bed, picked it up and sniffed.

Doctor Howard was rustling in his bag, grumbling.

Bett used both hands, first putting her ear close to Jemima. For Mary, the room had begun to spin. "Too high," Bett said. "Must be turned," she muttered. "Can you help me, Mary? I need you over here."

At this, there was a loud slam of the door and Mary turned to see Doctor Howard leave, his indignation like a cloud that settled over the room. Jemima had stopped struggling. She lay panting and moaning, only now and then turning her head. Bett was applying gentle pressure with her hands, feeling for the baby, trying to move it little by little from whatever position it was in. "Breech," she told Mary. Then, to the unborn infant, "Your mama didn't mean to harm you when she took the tansy, so you must turn now and come out to your life. We are right here waiting." She managed a quick backward look at Mary. "We are losing her," she whispered and began then to search with her hand until she found a tiny foot. "There's no time to turn this child. It's the only way." Mary began to sob, although the sound of it in her ears seemed small. The baby was folded inside Jemima, all buttock and leg. Jemima no longer struggled or panted. Bett tugged very gently, very carefully, until she beheld her granddaughter in her hands.

Bry was waiting behind the bushes dressed in the yellow shoes Jemima had given him, shoes meant not for planting or picking but for standing on a porch, drinking something chilled. Shoes that had once belonged to Rafe. He had been waiting for hours. Now he climbed the steps of the back porch and looked through the open bedroom window with its curtains blowing. It was easy to enter and when he did he saw Jemima's baby swaddled. He went closer. "Where's your mama?" he asked the newborn. "You should be by her." He picked up the infant as tenderly as he could manage and felt something for which he had no name.

There was confusion in the house. Someone was howling. He heard running feet and looked into the hall to see his mother coming toward him, swatting at the air. "Child, look what you did. Poor Jemima took the tansy. Give me that baby girl and run fast to save yourself!" Moaning, she took the baby from her son. "Go now, child! He's seen the baby and he'll kill you sure. Stay away from the Dickinsons' place. It is Benjamin now who owns you. Take yourself north to that regiment Isaac speaks of."

Then he was moving. Where was his knife? He felt for it in his pocket and thought of the baby, who had made little creaks like a fresh-caught mouse. Peering around the side of the house, he saw Mister Rafe holding Jemima tight, laying her down in the wagon, shouting at anyone who was there to watch. Mother Mary was bent down on the wagon seat and Bry wanted them to take the baby too. But where were they going? Was Jemima hurt? Mister Rafe had a fine horse from Kentucky and it was something strange that he was taking the mule.

In order to study this fact, Bry climbed into a cottonwood, still in his slippery shoes. For no reason at all he thought of a time in the past when Jemima was spreading washing on a bush and he'd taken hold of a piece of it. "Now you have to do whatever I tell you to," she'd said, "because that is my real mama's handmade cloth and she might come out of the ground to bite you." Bry had said his own pappy died on a tree and Jemima said to never mind about that, and all of it had happened when they were too young to know better.

What is the cause of an eclipse? When Mother Mary taught Isaac and Benjamin, he used to listen from above, perched in a tree. Angel on high, she had called him until he could recite the lessons back and draw the letters in the dust, and she then began to teach him to read and write.

Mama Bett laying Mister Wiley's table, placing the fork and knife. "Look at these fingers writing words and nobody knows you're here."

The wagon was moving so slowly it was easy to follow and stay out of sight. When he rode his horse, Rafe carried no whip because a horse has feelings – that's what he said – a horse ruminates. But a mule is half-donkey, half-horse and can't even reproduce. He'd said that to Jemima. Like a half-breed, he'd said. Now she was lying in a wagon behind a mule, Mister Rafe was shouting, and Mother Mary was small with her head in her lap.

Bry had not been off the Fox place for years but he had no interest in his surroundings. He was following Jemima. Tansy, his mother had said. What did that mean? Ahead, he heard the wagon wheels make the sound of turning. They were going to Mister Wiley's house, taking Jemima there. *I am staying with you*, he had promised. But she was vanishing and he could not follow her.

Somewhere in the dark there must still be a log house built by my father, is what he thought as he climbed another tree and watched the wagon rumble up the road. He would go to the cave and leave a message. Stay clear of Benjamin. All of them. It made no sense, but nothing did. And there was the house, still the same with its door that has never opened for him but once when the night was too cold for breath. Then the grass, where Jemima used to invent their games. He went through it making soft sounds with the yellow shoes. They had made blisters, but Jemima did not like to see him with bare feet.

The sycamores were taller, but the cave was the same, even holding the logs they had used for furniture and an old plate of acorns and sticks. He took one of them in his hand and wrote on the ground in their secret language. Come find me, □×□+, adding the word *Queenston* in perfectly formed letters.

Then he was passing places he had never been, moving north, sore-footed, cold now, his breath making shapes that he tried to read. He smelled the sap in the trees and sometimes his two hands gripped; his feet swung out and held. At the top of a sticky pine he took a jubilant breath, his stomach still strong enough to pull. So it took injury to heal. He scanned the world with its commotion of branches, checking the moss side of the trunks for north. The night was a wrap around him, but he climbed, practising his old way of ambulation, dogs maybe coming and men with guns and yelling voices, men who were happiest hunting a human being. When he felt hungry, he remembered how Mother

Mary sat with Mister Wiley at the table and how it was Mama
Bett who washed the clothes and swept the floors and cleaned the
dishes, which was altogether different than it had been before.
Which mother do you love most? Jemima had one time asked.

They are the same to me.

No, Bry. Two things are never the same.

They are equal.

Different things are never equal.

One and one are equal.

People are not numbers, silly. One is always stronger. One is
always kinder or older or more beautiful or more afraid.

Bry loved Mama Bett because she was strong and warm
and she allowed him to live in the trees. Perhaps she was more
beautiful, though he had not thought of that. Leave him grow
wild, it will serve his interests better than civility, she had said.
But Mother Mary wanted to make him civilized. On full-moon
nights she read books to him. She taught him adding and dividing. The Catechism. She taught him to read the stars. *What river
between Virginia and Ohio?* The echo of her teaching voice.
Which direction and how far? Tree by tree, foot by foot. He
had not been more than two miles from the Dickinson place or
the Fox farm in his life. *For what is Kentucky noted?* He had
the very slight idea that there were caves in the vicinity because
there were caves everywhere.

Kentucky is noted for caves. The stars were speckling. Soon
it would be light. He did not hear dogs. He was too tired to
hear. Why was he hungry for meat after years of eating mush?
He pulled a fistful of leaves off a stalk and stuffed them in his
mouth. He should decipher the plant before eating it, but he was
too hungry and he told himself there were animals who connive
with the dark. Possum is what he'd get. Out of a hollow. The
devil is temptation. When he killed it, he would build a fire.

R uth's voice. "Who?" There was no light on this porch where visitors were rare.

"It is Bett out here. I must speak to you."

Ruth gave the door an inch of distance from its frame.

"Please, may I come in? I have brought you Jemima's baby. She will need milk any minute now. Have you some at hand?"

Ruth opened the door and reached for a lump of infant so small as to be less than a jar of cream. In the light of the fire, she studied the tiny face. "Lord, have mercy."

"It is Jemima's. With Bry."

"But where is Jemima?"

"I could not save her. This baby is hungry, Ruth. Do you have something to feed her with, something with a spout?"

Daniel was snoring behind the hanging wall of quilts.

Ruth said, "What should I do?" Then, "Jemima is . . ." taking it in.

"Rafe is bringing her to Mary's house for laying out. Bry is gone north to the black regiment. Keep the baby away from Rafe. I can't take her north with me. I may be caught."

Ruth had gone down to the creek day after day, year after year, although blood had frightened her angel away. And in all that time she had never spoken her longing as the angel had told her to do. With the children to raise, the butter to churn, the garden to hoe, the meals to cook, she had never been sure what it was she wanted. Now she gave Bett a warm wrap and all the cornbread left in the iron skillet. She gave her the boots from her own feet and a woollen jacket. She wished Bett well and sat down by the fire to think. *Speak out*, is what the angel had said, and in all these years she'd had no idea what to say. There was a hill out behind the house that she had never yet climbed. There it sat, round and inviting, shimmering in the sunlight while she did not even know its grasses. There was the cave where the children had played games of pretend. She had never once gone inside, afraid of the darkness and cold drafts and spiders. Ruth sat on the bench by the fire with a newborn infant on her lap and remembered that Missus Dougherty had been her friend until Jemima went away with Rafe. She had been with her when John was born. Ruth had said things to Missus Dougherty that day after taking a sip or two of laudanum before John's birthing. She had said that Daniel had waited for two years before he bedded her. She had told her about the feeling of Daniel's long fingers in her hair. They had been close. Now Missus Dougherty barely spoke to her and no longer needed her butter.

Ruth's eyes wandered over the room. In one corner was the prized bureau, purchased in Baltimore by Benjamin, just for her. By Benjamin, who was her favourite, even including her blood kin son, even in spite of his upcoming red brick house that would block her view of the world. The bureau had four drawers and a marble top and she kept her hairbrush and mirror there on a tray with a linen napkin, all of which looked very nice. I would like to be buried in that bureau, she had told Missus Dougherty one day, and the pastor's wife had laughed, saying that they would have to remove her arms and legs and put them in different drawers parcelled out. Ruth could re-member the room at its different stages in its different lights with its several babies like the one now asleep on her lap. Little John lying in the corner in a trundle bed. Benjamin patting her, curled up next to her, Joseph in his cot beside the fireplace. The room was a series of pictures, with the dish and the linen napkin always there, although sometimes on the bureau of a different year. Same drawers and pulls, but full of baby things and seeds, unmended shirts. A shopping list, which could not be written or read, was memorized as salt for the top drawer, along with sugar and soda. Coffee in the second drawer, with ground corn and flour. Cloth in the third drawer for piecing a quilt.

She looked at the window, remembering the boy who had fitted it into the wall. He had carried the churn and believed when the angel spoke, but she had never looked at him. "In the matter of keeping slaves and such," Missus Dougherty always said, "it is an institution to foster grief." Who can eat cotton? A man must grow corn, wheat, oats, and timothy grass. She some-times looked at the brick walls rising up in front of her house and wondered how it was possible to consume such quantities of earth and ash?

Ruth shifted her legs where the new baby lay. She took Daniel's grandchild up in her arms and walked to the wall of quilts. That first night, Daniel had picked her up from the bed as he would little Joseph or Jemima and lifted her dress off her shoulders and arms and set her down again, bare. So long ago that had been. And now, for years, he hadn't touched her. "Husband," she said softly. "Open your eyes."

On the road, an oncoming mule and wagon swerved reck-
lessly and Daniel reined in Miss Patch so suddenly that she
threw him. The driver jumped down and Daniel held up his
uninjured arm, then lowered it. His head had a gash.

"Father of a whore! You are damned lucky not to be dead,"
Rafe shouted.

Daniel got to his feet and leaned over to pick up his hat as if
it should be treated more tenderly than a man. He remounted
his mare, holding his arm at an angle. The pain in his shoulder
was intense and there was a trickle of blood in his eye, but a
sense of grace had come over him. "Should we not be consoling
each other?"

Rafe went back to his empty wagon.

Daniel rode on. At Mary's door, he entered without knocking, as he had done since Wiley's departure. He had sometimes
come to his daughter's to eat a meal or pray with her, but what
he saw now was Mary sitting quietly by her sister's body, which
lay on a cot, covered by a quilt. She looked up at her father.
"You are hurt, Papa."

"Never mind."

She gestured at the room, which was in disarray, with broken
crockery on the floor. "Rafe could not be restrained. He is looking for Bry. And Bett."

"I do not want to think what they'll do to Bry when they bring him back. I am sure he has gone north, is what Bett says. She follows him."

Mary put her hands over her face. "No one will show any pity."

Daniel knelt beside Jemima. His chest felt noosed, the cut on his head throbbed, his shoulder ached; he reached out and plucked at the quilt. He had not seen this child for almost two years, and gazed now at a face yellowed and aged. Her long hair was rubbed into tangles. Her arms were covered with scratches, her nails bloody.

Mary, too, stared at her sister, trying to imagine a girl so hungry for love that she would run away with a man, unmarried. Or was it the other way? Had Jemima loved Bry and found her way to him through Rafe? She wondered how she had lived without her sister's company and how she would live on alone for the rest of her life. In truth, she had taken too much for granted, believing that anything lost could be found again. Jester Fox was only the first of her sins. She had kept Bett from freedom out of her own selfish need. On a shelf of the corner cupboard there was a plate with two doves painted on it, heads under wings. Mary thought of two runaways, crossing mountains and rivers, hunted. Bett had saved Jemima's baby through all the knowledge she had gained in a hopeless life. Now she was forced to flee. It would be cold in the mountains. Soon enough the rivers would turn to ice. Mary looked at the room, which contained the meaningless trifles of her meaningless life. A bowl of apples sat on the sideboard as if someone might still wish to eat them. The clock still said its weariness out loud. There was a pillow on the chair, embroidered. *Hold Me Too Dear.* She thought of the Day of Revelation, when all things will be decided. *Is he going to find you with your lamps trimmed and waiting?* If the dead could not return, what did she now owe the living? She stood up, feeling almost serene, and found a cloth to soak in camomile for the cut on her father's head. "Stay here with Jemima," she told him calmly, with a sudden understanding of what she must do. "I will find a dress for the grave and send Ruth to do the laying out."

Daniel searched her eyes.

"I must find Bett. She carries no pass."

"Take the baby with you. She will not be safe here."

Mary leaned over and kissed the top of his head.

"You were only a child, Mary," he said softly. "When Jester Fox fell."

She packed the medicines she might find useful in the black leather bag. It smelled of a thousand drops of relief and a thousand of forgetfulness. Another thousand drops had been spilled in the name of hurry or sorrow or waste. The bag was the gift from her father that had meant most to her. Perhaps it was even the only gift from him, since he did not offer humour or sentiment. Thee is thy mother's child, he had always said. Tick tick tick. Would her grave be abandoned the day it was dug? Childless, who would remember her? Mary took her cloak from its hook. It had been the attire of her doctoring trips and smelled of something like yeast in its seams. Who will trim the wicks and clean the stove? "Wait here for Ruth," she said again.

She took a last look at her sister, who lay with her face uncovered, eyes forever closed, then crossed the room and went out of her house and harnessed the bay to her cart. In it, she placed the medical bag, a pillow sleeve full of rags and bits of cloth, and a blanket in which to wrap the baby. Overhead, clouds were swimming fitfully. Birds were beginning to sing. It would soon be dawn.

———

And Abraham rose early in the morning and took bread and a skin of water and gave it to Hagar. . . . And sent her away. Daniel glanced at the table. Two cups, two spoons. Two geese flying north on two plates. Who was it set for? There was crockery on the floor in large and small pieces as if walking was to be, from now on, a penance.

On the campground so generously given by Frederick Jones, small huts had been built inside a fenced enclosure. The huts contained crude beds for the use of campers who came with food and bedrolls to the summer revival meetings, but the group that was waiting under the tabernacle roof was there only for brief prayers and a eulogy. The Craigs sat on a bench, elbows on knees, as if afraid to be noticed. The Sharpes were there, looking dolefully at the floorboards. Frederick and Julia Jones stood at the back, watching the road as if Wiley might come home from the war in time for this funeral. There were others waiting to give their condolences to Daniel and Ruth. Among them were three of the children they had raised: Isaac, Benjamin, John.

When Daniel pulled into the campground, a group sheltering under the tabernacle roof came out to help with the coffin he could not lift. His shoulder was tightly wrapped but it hurt almost unbearably. And there was Isaac, his prodigal. Then all three sons came forward and took up the coffin along with Hiram Craig. They carried it under the roof and balanced it carefully on a bench at the front near the altar. He led Ruth to a seat. Then, for those gathered, a long hour of sitting and shifting and checking the road commenced, after which it was clear to those gathered that the pastor was not going to appear. Nor was Mary, which the neighbours thought was odd. Benjamin's wife,

Elizabeth, was sitting with her husband and his two brothers. Her eyes were covered with a hand and her dress was sombre. Mister Sharpe cleared his throat in a meaningful way. Still, no one spoke. More minutes. Waiting. More shifting. A baby was taken out to be fed. Below the simple cross that adorned the altar, Jemima lay shut away in her coffin wearing the dress Mary had chosen. Ruth had laid cornflowers over its stain.

And it was Ruth who finally stood up, smoothing the back of her skirt and moving toward the coffin uneasily. She turned to her neighbours, nervously smoothing her skirt again, and looked at each one in turn. Each of them had known Jemima. Each of them had bought butter and medicines from the family. "Eighteen of you are here," she said softly, counting, nodding at Daniel, who was slumped over in his old Quaker hat. "Eighteen of you left your labours in your houses and fields." She dipped her head. "And we thank you for that."

Among the neighbours, the women sat in dark dresses and hats with brims. They were farmwomen now, even those who had been raised in far-off towns. *Speak out*, the angel had said. And Ruth had neglected to do it. Among the eighteen, there were women with knowing smiles, women who spoke behind their hands, and men who judged others more strictly than they judged themselves. Her palms were damp. "One of our children . . ." She said it so quietly that only three or four nearby listeners could hear. "One of our children," she said with a little more force, "was lost to us. Didn't Matthew say in the Bible, *See that you do not despise these little ones. For I tell you that their angels will always see the face of my Father in heaven.*" Ruth opened her hands as if to show that they were empty. "Once I was told to speak out, but I never knew what to say. All those words in the good book, you know, sounded so right and wise that I could never find my own."

At this, Hiram Craig stood up and pushed past shoulders and legs to come forward. He took Ruth's right hand and put his Bible in it, open to Matthew.

Ruth said, "Well, I thank you, Mister Craig, but I can't read." Her face was set and stern. "In that Brandywine poorhouse I never got schooling up to the day I was brought to the Dickinsons as a servant. Then there were five children to raise. They lost their mama, though I didn't care so much about that or their feelings. Jemima was not but two years old and I was a child myself and I did not love her. When she climbed onto her papa's knee, I was even bitter. It was myself who wanted to be loved. I had neither mama nor papa, you see. And some time after that, we came here to Jonesville before it had a name or anything to it. There were no houses yet except for Mister and Missus Jones, who had already built." Ruth nodded at the coffin. "Her father being then in search for a place where his children could be raised with neighbourly love, the wagon was stopped just three miles up this road. And soon there were neighbours enough." She paused, then said, "and maybe none of us can be blamed for one lost sheep in our pasture, being so busy as we must have been. But I think God must have a mean streak, though, if He made us in His image, since we showed Jemima no pity." Seeing shocked expressions all around, Ruth took the lid of the coffin off and dropped it on the floor. "Unless *we* invented meanness just in order to entertain our own selves. What does it say in here?" she waved Hiram Craig's heavy Bible but paid no mind to the page. "It says, *He looked for some to have pity on Him, but there was no man, neither found He any to comfort. They gave Him gall to eat. And when he was thirsty they gave Him vinegar to drink.* And so it was with us." She looked over at Isaac. She took a deep breath and looked into the coffin. "Jemima, I know your angel will see the face of our Father."

Under the tabernacle roof there was utter quiet.

Ruth handed the Bible to Missus Sharpe, who handed it down the line of seated neighbours to Mister Craig. Then she went back to her bench.

Daniel was staring at his wife in astonishment. Then he got up and began his slow advance. By the coffin there was a small hammer and a pile of wooden pegs on the bench. He took up the hammer and leaned down for the lid, but the pain in his shoulder stopped him and he stood perplexed. Then he looked to Isaac, his eldest son, and held out the hammer with a small shrug of apology for what he was unable to do for himself.

Louisville Intelligencer

Fifty dollars Reward. RAN AWAY from the
subscriber, a Boy, about 15 years in age, straight
up about five feet nine wearing yellow shoes
bound and lined, trowsers, sometimes a top
hat, green on the underside any person who will
secure him so that I may lay hold of him shall
be reimbursed every expence, and a generous
reward from R Fox. Jonesville, Virginia, Lee
County, Sep 20. 1815 This one is required for
payment of a wager.

L ike those who had gone before and those who would come after, Bett walked. Travel by night. Beware of dogs. Beware of fast water and sucking sand. In the best situations, where a traveller could read, there were no written signs. There might be a tree drawn over waves on a card in a window. A quilt hanging by one peg on a laundry line. In the absence of such signals, the North Star was the only guide. Her head wrapped in a scarf as she set out, Bett wore Ruth's given boots and woollen jacket.

As always, she carried her cloth medicine bag as well as the soft woven bag in which to collect mushrooms and plants. She had packed hickory nuts and sunflower seeds and there was a dented flask. Years before, she had concocted a strap for the bags that fit across her shoulders so that each lay more or less flat on her back, leaving her hands free to forage. She had no books, only the stories of a lifetime. When she woke in the afternoon, after a long morning sleep, she would search ground and trees and bushes for edibles and give herself one pleasant memory each day, since regret would slow her pace. She would pull up a clump of yarrow, to make her see what she must see. Mandrake. Poppy. Comfrey. Chamomile. Even the tansy is useful, if given with knowledge. She thought of Mary. Their need of each other for years. It felt as strange to her as the clothes on her back.

This was a country not of kills, or even creeks, but of runs; and she came down the valley between steep ridges. She went past a field where a man was standing in his wagon, driving a team of horses, and she hid behind a bush and waited until he had gone. Home for supper, as it was night. The valley was green and ancient. Up ahead was a tiny cabin with a stone chimney, smoke on the rise. Wondering if Bry might have passed, she wanted to stop. The porch railings were topped with unflowered plants in pots that gave off the scent of geraniums, and she thought of picking some leaves for her bag, but it has been said often enough that stolen herbs make a patient sicken. She passed two narrow houses and on the porch of one was a rocking chair. Perhaps this was the edge of Rosehill. She turned away from the road then, looking for shelter cut out of the forest. In the north, we will have sheep and a spinning wheel, she said to herself. Washing our lambs will make for an occasion, after which Bry will shear them and I will twist and wind the clean wool as I learned from my first mistress. I will make Bry a coat to keep him winter warm. I will dye it whatever colour he chooses. We will have corn planted out in rows and we will top it while it is green, cutting the stalk above the ear to make winter feed for our flock of sheep. She quickened her pace.

In the woods, she met a man and boy. The boy had walked from North Carolina. The man from a near plantation. They were expecting a wagon to come along, an abolitionist, and soon the three vagabonds were crossing a field together. It was a cool night and Bett put her hand on the boy's warm shoulder, as if she needed aid. She leaned against him and he allowed this and she told him that her son had set his face toward the north and she was going after him.

The man, who was old, chanted, "*And they utterly destroyed*

all that was in the city, both man and woman, young and old,
and ox, and sheep, and ass, with the edge of the sword."

The boy said, "What that about?"

The old man whistled. "How the children of Israel were delivered out of bondage. Ain't you know it?"

In the dimness of moonlight, the boy looked sullen, as if a secret had been kept from him.

"What people rised you up?" the old man asked.

The boy kicked at the ground, but Bett pressed against his shoulder with her weight, remembering the feel and smell of her own lean son. The boy said excitedly, "I know what happened. It was your boy who climbed up in the masta's house and chop him up. That was your boy with the axe."

"Not so," Bett answered. "He has no guilt, only a broken heart to carry where he goes." She thought back on the visits Isaac had made to the quarters, telling Bry and the others about the escaped slaves who had formed a regiment in Canada. "To fight us," he had said with a laugh. "And who can blame them?" She might mention this to the boy, who was offering his support but would he believe her? Then something else came to her mind and it was terrible: not wanting to dishearten him, she had not told Bry that Jemima was dead. What if he had waited nearby, hoping to see her? He'd be found in a matter of hours by the dogs. She put more weight on the boy's firm shoulder.

The three made little noise as they continued across small holdings in the dark. Before dawn they were met by a wagon. The driver was wrapped in cloth the colour of night and wearing a broad-brimmed hat. He gave a birdcall. "This be him," said the old man, but the boy was not sure. "This the one we was told to espec," the old man insisted.

The boy stood behind a tree as if that way he would not be seen, although the tree was small. The old man reached out for

Bett and she was convinced, since she had no real belief in the dangers she faced, but the boy was untrusting and the old man stayed behind with him, electing to walk on to the next station, some kind of mill. From her whispered conversations in the quarters of various farms, Bett knew there were people who aided runaway slaves, but how were they found? Who had summoned this wagon with its Quaker driver? The wagon had a shallow space under its floor and she squeezed herself into it, lying face down with five bags of freshly ground wheat flour on the wagon bed above her. Freight to be delivered in due time. She could not turn or shift. Perhaps such people as the driver, she thought, need to make the task seem more dangerous than it is. She had not been much in the world. But were there ears listening? Surely there was no sheriff waiting for her at the next crossroads. There were men who suffered boredom, who desired conspiracy and importance, that much she knew after living with Eb and Rafe Fox. There were men who lived on the bounties paid for runaway slaves.

Down at the bend in the bottom of the road, a woman was hanging clothes on a line. Bett could see her through a hole in the wagon's side. She had travelled among just such people, healing them. Later, at another place, a man swung a scythe. When they passed a white woman casting seeds from a pail, the image of Ruth came to her – Ruth had sown seeds with a waxing moon, had put hair in the trench when she planted her beans, and moved a healthy chamomile into any area of plants that were not thriving. Ruth had known that cabbages profited by being near sage or mint, that garlic repelled pests and aided the growth of tomatoes and asparagus. How, Bett had asked once in passing, did Ruth know these things? From my fine upbringing, Ruth had said, telling Bett that she had been leased out to the Dickinsons like a farm animal. Then she added, "Though I was sure never lowly as a slave."

Mary hurried the horse in what was becoming darkness and remembered the colour or no colour of her skin, which would make her journey easier than Bett's. The roads were full of men who made it their business to check on the movements of anyone who wasn't white. Anyone else must have a pass clearly written and signed. She clucked at her horse. Twelve miles north of Jonesville she saw a small store. In its dark window was propped a card with a drawing of trees on water.

Feeling large and ungainly, Mary rang the bell, peering through a tiny circle of glass in the door, clutching the dark baby close and pulling at her hat, wanting to look respectable. An elderly man in a dressing gown stepped out of a room at the back and came to the door.

"My baby," Mary gestured at the bundle pressed against her. "I wonder if you could spare a cup of milk." She stepped inside.

While the storekeeper went to his root cellar, she glanced around in the dark, seeing that she had come to a place with provisions. On a back shelf there were three loaves, one brown and two white. When he returned, she asked the storekeeper the price of a loaf, scanning the place for something more to take with her. Pickles. Onions. Pig's feet. "I see you have cheese," she said gratefully and moved to a chest in the corner as if through deep water. She had eaten nothing since the day before, nothing since Rafe had come to collect her with his cart. *Your sister is labouring.* It seemed years ago that she had been so informed. Passing a counter, she heard the sound of ripping fabric. A nail.

The old storekeeper watched her examine her skirt. Was he taking note of her features, studying her through his small spectacles? "I am looking for a runaway," she said boldly. "Also her son. To take them to safety." The storekeeper nodded. Then, as if he could not communicate in words, he wrote a number on a loose piece of paper.

Mary saw that it was only a bill and paid what he asked. "What does it mean? The picture of trees on water."

"It indicates a mill, missus."

"I saw no logging in these parts."

"Flour mill, missus, just up the road. You could try for your runaways there."

Mary went back to her horse and cart and went the way he had indicated. The horse moved along the black road through black trees and Mary tore off a piece of bread and a wedge of cheese, letting go of the reins and leaning back to pick up the baby, who had begun to fuss against her dress. She had poured the milk into a clean gourd and now put some into the tiny clay vessel with a spout that had been used to feed Joseph. It was part of the bundle Ruth had given her for the baby's care. She fed the baby and chewed on her own cold meal, remembering the time she and Bett had driven through a snowstorm and been stranded late at night. They had been coming home from the Clarke plantation and finally curled as one under a blanket so that they collected the biting frost in one set of lungs and released it into the other. They had no wick for the lamp they had brought but Bett drew Mary's hands into her own and then wept until the tears froze on her face, describing her longing for Bry. Mary had wondered if her own longing was different. How did it feel to be a mother in that bodily way?

When she made out a sign for the Ressler Mill and a small light behind one of two windows, she reined in the horse and stepped out of the cart again. Through the lit window, she saw the miller wipe his hands on an apron before he came to the door. "I am seeking a boy and his mother. They might not be travelling together."

He shook his head. "I'll see to your horse," he said, leading the way through the mill without comment, as if strange women often came to his door. "I'll bring supper," he said, and Mary meant to say that she had eaten in her cart, but the thought of warm food made her hungry again.

In the moonlight that poured silvery through the window of the back room, she made out the shapes of a chair and table. Bed. She could not discern the colours of the quilt, but she felt its rough texture when she put the baby down on it. Well fed, the little one lifted her fists and blew bubbles out of her thumb-wide mouth. Mary unbuttoned her boots and stepped out of them. One of her stockings had ripped, but that could be mended along with the skirt that had been torn by the nail. She must keep up the appearance of self-regard, although she had none left to draw upon. A chamber pot, a pitcher of water, a washbowl. Mary supposed this was as fine a room as a runaway slave would encounter, though certainly there were places that were finer, hotels that served the tobacco merchants and slave merchants and cotton buyers. There were places with pretty settees and carpets and chandeliers, although Bett would never see them.

When the miller tapped at her door and she opened it, she saw that the light had been put out in the granary. She received the bowl of warm milk and a piece of bread from his hands and remembered to say, "I thank you." She noticed a cold sore at the corner of his lip. "A concoction of sage, alum, and sugar will heal that sore," she said.

Her benefactor answered that he was much obliged.

By afternoon they had not stopped, not even slowed, and the road was dry and dusty so that Bett choked on it. "Mister!" she called up, but the road went mildly on and the driver did not seem to hear. Were there patrols? Everything would be wild in Kentucky but a certain lawlessness might make travelling easier. One day, when there was a time for it, she must think over how all of this had come about, how Bry had run for one reason and she for another, and how the newborn child was in the in-between place of a lost soul.

The wagon bumped along and Bett tried for a little comfort but could not find it, mashed in as she was and remembering a game she had played as a child. A girl – what was her name – hiding in a closet. Always so easily found. Was Bry like that? Would he betray himself with noise or sudden movement? Would he build a fire when he shouldn't? Bett thought of the night that little girl had disappeared and how for some time uncounted she had sat in her grandmother's kitchen, making herself learn not to care. And when she was sent to Jester Fox, never a dint was made in that shield of uncaring until Mary took her in. Then it was all as it might once have been, having a friend until that, too, came to an end. Betrayal after betrayal. And now she would never see Mary again.

———

"Whatcha got there in them bags?" Sudden men, shouting.

The wagon slowed and Bett clung to the boards. There was a commotion of wheeling, circling horses, neighing, clattering hooves on the stones of the road. Through the small hole in the wagon's side she could see the horses' legs and then the legs of the men dismounting, boots to the ground. She heard them threaten her driver, and knew he would give in to cowardice and turn her over because of the shouting and yelling. He was on his knees. She could see his head bent down in its hat, until he was swallowed up by the horses and she was a stick trying not to break.

"Two runaways reported." A deep voice was making words to explain.

"A witch doctor and her savage son." This voice was quieter, almost apologetic. But they were rough with the old driver now, pushing him so that he fell against his wagon right close to her face.

"You wouldna be one a them abolishioners, wouldye?"

"Bleedin hearts?" Someone was climbing on the wagon, rocking it hard. "Let's us take a look."

"This un's mine if he's in a flour bag."

"Pokem first. Makem bleed."

The driver made no resistance as they began their search and Bett did not let herself breathe. Time by time she took her thoughts somewhere else to calm herself. She tried to think of her grandmother young and of herself as nothing and she heard her grandmother's voice and smelled drying plants. She felt better for it, but her arms were bent hard under her as all of this went through her mind and one of them was prickling with the needles of sleep and she wondered if an arm could die before the rest of her. Then two or three men got on to the bed of the wagon and it nearly collapsed on her. They were cutting holes in the flour bags, the contents spilling over her through the cracks in the wagon's floor. There was a knife pushed down through those cracks and she screamed, but the sound was so dry that it couldn't be heard and it was then, with the floorboards pressing against her back, that she saw the features of her mother's forgotten face. And what do you think of your daughter now? she asked without sounding the words. Wherever did they take you that day you went away? You have a great-grandbaby now, born of my woes, but what difference do we make in this world unless we find our true shape?

At last, the men got down off the wagon and the horses made noisy commotion again with their mouths and hooves. Bett took the sleeping arm out of its bent-up place and loosened her grip on the underneath boards. It began to rain as they rode away and she tried not to shiver but remembered that it is a help against cold and that some of the flour would be washed away although she was coated and sticky and lay in discomfort, frightened, longing to get back on her feet. She wiggled her fingers to keep them awake and moved her legs that were wet with the urine she had passed when the men rode away. Her bowels complained and she bit her lip enough to make it bleed.

By evening they had come to a river that would have to be crossed, and when the wagon stopped, Bett climbed down barely able to walk and stumbled into a thicket to relieve herself.

"They are waiting to help just up the path," the driver called out to her.

From behind the shield of a hackberry bush, she heard the wheels turn against underbrush and clatter over a wooden bridge. It was a strange form of goodness, she thought, this great charity that was anonymous.

Up the path – a gristmill. Resslers. Bett's nerves were a surprise to her. Wasn't she used to addressing closed doors behind

338

which some form of suffering always waited? Wasn't she holding her medicine bag as usual, although her legs were shaking and she was covered with pastry flour? The rain had let up, but it was still part of the air and she went through the wet grass, picking her way around puddles standing like mirrors.

At a small, ramshackle farmhouse with a bird painted on its window, Mary spoke the three words she had been told by the miller were required of her: "I have freight." She showed the baby.

"The barn is there open." It might have been her Grandmother Dickinson's voice with its Old World accents.

When she reached it, Mary was brought up short by the scent of dried timothy grass. It reminded her of the barn at the Clarke plantation where she had watched a slave sale in March. A mother had been sold to a man from out of town while her daughter went to someone up from Tennessee. "She never would learn," Mister Clarke had complained, as if saddened by willful ignorance. Mary had edged up to the weeping mother. "Oh the poor child," she had blurted out. "If only you had run away before this could happen."

The woman had only glanced at Mary. "I oughta not take a little chile with me if I run, missus, could I?" That mother had thought of her child first. Perhaps Jemima had done so too, in her way. She remembered Bett saying she would go north the very minute Bry was old enough and Mary had argued the danger of that and convinced her father to take Bett in, although it had cost him more than he could afford. He had thought Bett would be free when the debt to the widow was paid. That's what she had told herself, as well, even when she did not say to her husband that the payments were now his to make. What is it about the smell of a barn, or a garden or an opened trunk that can remind us of past mistakes? she wondered, pacing the floor with Jemima's squalling baby. The farmer's wife had said she knew a woman who could suckle her, but Mary was afraid of calling attention to the stolen child. Instead there would be cow's milk warmed at a stove. She spread a cloth and put the baby on a hay bale. Skin the perfect colour of an autumn leaf. The fingers fit tightly around Mary's thumb. And the eyes were large and expressionless, dark brown shot with amber lights as if waiting to see what life would bring. Mary remembered Bry as a newborn, a little noisier, darker of skin and mood, being the child of tragedy, not love. "You are so like your father," she had told him. But she had wondered about that.

Mary put her face on the baby. Nothing so sweet as this, she thought, and her own skin itched, so she rubbed the baby with her hands and a bit of Bett's witch hazel, then wiped her with a cloth, thinking of Bett's great knowledge – the way she had gone out in all seasons but especially in early spring, when the sap began its rise, to strip the bark off certain trees and boil it down. There were those who thought the tonics were trickery and hoax, like Doctor Howard with his threats or Ruth, who had tricks of her own. Mary remembered the dress her father had bought her because he thought Ruth could not sew.

When the farmer's wife came in with the milk, the two women sat together enjoying the sound of the newborn's noisy satisfaction. A baby's hunger was as uncomplicated as fright but easier to cure, Mary thought, as Luveen's lullaby came into her head: *There's a new world a'coming, won't you come along with me. . . .* all of it there to be sung, and how good it would be to bring this little one to the wondering eyes of Luveen. Then

Mary wondered if the old woman might not be dismayed. It was not going to be an easy life for this little girl. *In what river are the falls between Lake Erie and Lake Ontario? How high is the precipice over which the water falls?*

"So much to learn," she whispered to the baby, who was feeding efficiently. She then asked the farmwoman about other travellers. Had she helped anyone get as far as the Ohio? Where was the best place to cross? What was the route? Had she seen a woman with shorn hair? Or a boy of about fifteen years of age?

The response was a vague description of the next stopping place. Apparently no one could be trusted, not even a white woman travelling with such a baby as this.

Cleveland Morning News

ONE HUNDRED DOLLAR REWARD.
Ran away from the subscriber, calling himself
Bry, about fifteen years, 5 feet 9 inches, and of a
copper color. He can read and write and may have
forged a pass. I will give the above reward to any
one who will secure him in any way so as to make
good on my debt to another. R. Fox. Jonesville, VA

A place that was mellow with light slanting past each dusty house and yard and barn and beyond it an old church lost in a grove of papaws. Then an overgrown lot. A young girl had brought Mary here, making a deal of conversation when all that awaited them was the lot with its weeds and trees and a dismal shed. The girl pulled a piece of canvas away from its front. "Go in," she said, "where that newborned chile can repose."

"My horse must have . . ." Mary instantly wished she had not made her words sound like an order. She carried the baby to a pile of hay that sat in a shine of reflected light and laid her down softly. Beautiful baby, tenderest of smiles. She looked for water and moved to a corner to uncover a dish that might contain food. It held a soupy gruel made of tapioca and yams that she tipped into her mouth. A table. A stool. She put her head on the table as exhaustion overtook her. When she closed her eyes, she felt the great loss of Wiley that always came to her when she was close to sleep. If only he could help her now in this search. If only she could tell him that it didn't matter anymore that he had been with Rafe and Eb that day. She raised her head when she heard a sound.

"It's some goat milk." The girl asked if she could do the feeding and Mary smiled and wondered how many arms this child would know before she was grown. Never the arms of a mother.

The girl said her father was sold but her mother was free and they had a deed to three acres through the charity of a samaritan.

Mary listened to the story while the girl fed Jemima's baby. "You are very good at that."

"I had my own one, but he passed to God."

When the baby had eaten her fill, the young girl placed her carefully back on the hay. Then Mary lay down on it too, thinking how foolish she had been to believe she would ever find Bett or Bry in this patchwork of mountains and valleys and hills. Perhaps they had crossed through the Gap and gone more directly into Kentucky, although the way would be treacherous. Who could say what a fleeing boy or a searching mother might do? With her cart, Mary might be well ahead of them, even if they were on the same track. And if they never allowed themselves a road? How would they ever cross paths? Her search was hopeless and she fell hard asleep.

At some hour of darkness a wind came up and sharp needles of rain began to strike at the bare tin roof. What was the smell in the air? Lightning. She lifted her head and picked herself up, moving at a crawl, seeing that the baby was asleep, and shoving through the canvas flap. Out in the rain, the stars had fled. All around were the trees dripping tears and the dark sky was weeping between them. Mary unbuttoned her dress and pulled it over her head, standing now in her corset and bloomers, stockings and boots. A few hours earlier she had passed a slave cemetery where a painted sign read:

> The small and great are there; and the ser-
> vant is free from his master. Job 3:19.

In her bag there was a bar of hard soap and this she retrieved, taking off her underclothes and boots so that she stood only in her skin to rub soap and cloth against each other, and even the taken-off dress that had buttons made of ivory and was cut from hard flax. It would never be the same after this foaming rigour of suds. She put her head back and drank in cold rain. All the babies she and Bett had brought down together, one and the same. All the mothers. And the croups and the fevers, the bones set, pleasures and fears. *And the servant is free from his master.* As Mary scrubbed the soft bloomers and the rough stockings with soap made of bacon grease, she wondered what it would take to make her clean. Should she take off this layer of skin and the next? Should she rub to the bone and then try to sing? What good would she be without skin? She laughed at herself then and dragged the hard soap through her hair, first untying her braid, so that the soap could bring the blood up to her scalp and the rain would act as rinse. Oh the preciousness of tears; what would our flesh be without them?

Before sunrise she donned her damp clothing and set out after a meal of bread and cheese. Her cape would cover the dress until the sun emerged to dry it. Someone had left a small packet of food in her cart, nicely wrapped, and the thought of the girl coming out before dawn gave her new heart to go on. Or should she go back? She lay the baby in a nest of cloth and remembered the time she had sat with her father on the banks of the Powell, begging him not to cross. It was too wide. Too fast.

It was cold on this hilltop and there were colder mountains ahead. Bett couldn't have come so far. How could she manage such distance? For Bry it might be easier, but Mary would never find him in all the thickness of forest. She climbed up into the cart, which was wet. The road she had taken to come here was full of deep ruts, muddy from the storm, but she turned the horse and set off toward home. The baby began to cry, and she could feel the ache of it in her breast. Mothers let down milk and yet she had none to give, only a wooden cask wrapped in wet cloth given by a childless girl. For a time she went on, but the cry was meaningful and she stopped the cart, getting down in some haste, pulling the hood of her cape up against cold and fog. It made no sense to be out here on this hilltop alone with a baby to be fed and her own dry breasts. It made no sense to seek two runaways who were trying not to be found. In the distance she could make out the shape of a woman, moving as if sore of foot or slightly lame. It seemed to Mary that such a one should be taking more care, for who knew what might come along in the dawn to trouble her? Mary poured the goat milk little by little into Joseph's feeder. She picked up the howling child and gentled her, whispering, bringing that lullaby back to her mind that had once belonged to Luveen.

All night Bett had been climbing steadily and her legs were cramped and her feet were ragged and as dawn lit the edge of the forest, the landscape rolled itself into steeper hills, into colder valleys, and these were rent with the sounds of owls and wolves as if one thing must always be hunting another. Bett had walked through a night of hard rain. She had gathered handfuls of wild mulberries and savoured them.

How good it would be to lend her body to the purpose of finding a warm place to rest as the sun came up on the side of this endless mountain while the birds awoke and took flight, going south. She stopped in her tracks and looked up at the heavens, full as they were of noisy, awakening life. She thought that if Bry had wings, he would be lifted and carried over the hard miles to come. Her legs. Her feet. How heavy she felt. How earthbound she was with so many mountains and valleys and rivers to cross. And now she had come to a hollow in the side of this mountain still dark, not having been found by the sun. But there was no sign of shelter, only a narrow twist of road and a wind that cut through her wet clothes and the crying of something sounding almost human, like a child. Ahead was a mountain higher than any she had seen and darkly forbidding in this cold predawn, but she moved on past a grove of sugar maples fired with the colours of death and into a mass of hemlock. Would she find Bry before the snow came? The North Star was always there, out-shining the moon, but there were no mulberries in this hollow and the maple trees were untapped and she looked at the road, which would make travel easier, and saw that someone was up there, leaning against a cart, a woman in a long, dark cape. Fog clung to the trees that grew beside the road and she crept a bit closer, smelling the hemlock pitch and the musk of the deer who had slept between the trunks, her senses sharp. The cry was sweet and piercing, a baby's cry, and Bett listened, moving forward, careful not to be seen. On the ridge, the woman was walking, going back and forth on the road, up and down, doing her best to soothe the child in her arms. Her song was carried on the wind, and Bett came out of the trees and began to run toward her, hiking her skirt up for speed.

D aniel put his spade in the dirt under the apple tree, thinking of the grave he had dug years before. He watched as
his sons came across the yard carrying the coffin. It was
a simple box and they moved easily, as if treading an expanse
of quiet water, Benjamin talking, John's head bowed, Isaac, as
eldest, bearing the weight of one end alone. Ruth came out of
the house looking at the ground as if she could not meet the
eyes of the living. I have disappointed her, Daniel thought as she
came to stand by him in her worn dress, her apron, her boots
and cap, and he was glad to have her there nevertheless.

They lowered Jemima into the darkest dark and Daniel prayed
in his silent way but there was no absolution for the father.
Ruth took a carved wooden doll – the one Jemima had loved in
her childhood – out of an apron pocket and set it on the ground
amid fallen apples while Daniel thought of the night she had
climbed the ladder to the loft and carried Jemima down. *Thee
must find a proper mother for thy orphans*, his father had said,
and Daniel ached for Ruth Boyd, although he turned from her
now and went alone to the shed. There was the harness on its
peg, the saddle on its shelf, and Miss Patch moving her ears at
the sound of resolve in his step.

To reach the land he had bought from Michael Shoffert,
he went briefly onto the road and when he looked back he

saw the house he had built and beyond it the future house of Benjamin. It was made of red brick and had four chimneys, two at either end. In his mind, as if drawn there, he saw the white pillars of the front porch arrayed like sentinels. On the road, there were puddles in which he saw his reflection, and that of his horse, whose dark hooves glittered while she blew out her cheeks and shook her long head, jingling the bits of metal on her harness.

He thought then of Mary, his dearest and wisest child. Stubborn and certain, she had gone to do right, pulling the hood of her cape up and tying it firmly against the wind. She will find her way, Daniel thought, and he gave thanks for that.

He came to a rippling brook that fed all the acres he had bought, keeping them fertile and promising. Like children, Daniel thought, and he rode through the water into high grass that swept at his legs. There, ahead of him, leaning against the dusk, was the tree he had left so long unvisited. He slid off his horse and reached for the axe he had brought in his saddle pack. *For if a tree bears not fruit, it must be hewn down.* He could hear his father's voice, far away and indistinct, and looked at his hardened hands.

Then he stood in autumnal shade, listening to the sharp click of pods, feeling the worn handle of his ready axe. But when he lifted it, there was a rustling sound that flooded the chanted air. It came out of bark that was ravined and cavernous and from the golden leaves, exhaling. It matched his own breath, and he stood listening, hearing fallen pods rub against roots, beginnings against source, tree out of tree.

He thought of how he had built his house out of numbers of trees and that what he had taken had not been given, and he thought then about Simus and said, "Thee did not choose me, but I chose thee." It was a confession of living flesh.

He dropped the axe, letting his eyes travel time and length and span, and he went on breathing in, in, seeing, at the base of the trunk near the ground, a glint of thimble, embedded. Enough to hold all of them, everything. And when he raised his eyes to the darkest branches overhead, a trace of pale moon was waiting to take back the sky.

ACKNOWLEDGEMENTS

Thanks first and always with love to Michael. For every grace during this journey. For support, counsel, and fond interest. I am hugely grateful. And yours.

Ellen Seligman, extraordinary editor beyond any reckoning, I thank you in every language. This book was waiting for you.

Blessings on Kendra Ward for her thoughtful help and on Heather Sangster for her patience and insightful copy editing.

Ellen Levine, dear friend and agent, thank you for constant support and encouragement throughout.

Ann Close, thank you for your careful reading of early drafts of the manuscript and for your belief in the book.

Sara Dickinson, eldest daughter of my brother Skip, thank you for coming with me to Jonesville, Virginia, along the same route Daniel took in 1798. Inspired by a trip Ruth and Martin Dickinson made many years ago in search of family history, we became sleuths, raiding the Jonesville courthouse for census records and property deeds and discovering Benjamin Dickinson's slave-built house, thanks to the Masons, who are its present inhabitants and who gave us a tour that included the cellar where Benjamin's slaves were shamefully kept. We saw what is left of Daniel's cabin (a pile of logs and most of the stones from the fireplace) and three fallen gravestones under a gnarly tree.

My beloved friend Connie Rooke did not live to see the book

finished, but her comments during the early stages of writing came with a sure understanding of what I was trying to convey long before I had any idea of that myself. Her love and enthusiasm are lost treasures. I particularly appreciate her recommendation of John Ehle's remarkable novels.

Michael Redhill, Dionne Brand, Molly Rothenberg, and Martha Sharpe read early versions of this story and provided insights into character and structure that were invaluable. I thank each of them for care and patience and wisdom. My daughters, Kristin Sanders and Esta Spalding, are both sensitive readers who know my weak spots and help me see past them. Daughters, my appreciation for your skill and truth-seeking is boundless, along with my love.

Susie Schlesinger, thank you for creating a workspace for me at your ranch, making it possible for me to meander with horses and commune with Annie, the oldest sheep in the world. And thank you, Eve Jones, for saving Miss Patch.

Dr. Janet Yorsten, true healer, thank you for essential medical advice.

A few books were indispensable. I found *Pioneer Life in Southwestern Missouri* by Wiley Britton, published in 1929, in my mother's library. What a feast of information. "The children all went barefooted in the spring and summer time, and often contracted stone bruises on the bottoms of their feet which made it difficult for them to walk and those having stone bruises were excused from helping to hunt and bring in the cows or other stock." Thomas Jefferson's *Notes on the State of Virginia* is an exhaustive account that includes every bird or bush native to the state as well as a study of population, laws, rivers, mountains, and public revenues. *A Reverence for Wood* by Erick Sloan was a lucky discovery with lovely renderings of mauls and augers and yokes and such. There are a number of vivid slave narratives in print. Among the best and most beautifully articulate is *Incidents in the Life of a Slave Girl*

Written by Herself by Harriet A. Jacobs. *A Midwife's Tale: The Life of Martha Ballard Based on Her Diary, 1785-1812*, by Laurel Thatcher Ulrich proved the rigours of healing in an age before birth was much attended by doctors. *Birthing a Slave* by Marie Jenkins Schwartz brought graphic reality to the practice of breeding that was fairly common on plantations. Suzanne Lebsock's *The Free Women of Petersburg: Status and Culture in a Southern Town, 1784–1860* describes the complex relationships of free and enslaved African Americans with white neighbours and masters. Perhaps most useful of all were copies of *The Foxfire Book*, which contain chapters on butter churns, snake lore, moonshining, "and other affairs of plain living."

Immeasurable is my debt to my brother, who brought me to my first Quaker Meeting when I was sixteen and thereby changed my life. Skip was a questioner. His provoking curiosity is another lost treasure. This book would not exist without it.